On the back cover of this volume, Phileas Fogg (note the initials!) says that it is a wise father who knows his own son, and that P.J. Farmer does indeed know Father Carmody. Mr. Fogg goes on to assure us that the Good Father (Carmody) will have the egg excised from his chest at *his* father's earliest literary opportunity. Yet even the most casual reader will have observed that by the middle of Part III *the egg is gone*.

What is the meaning of this curious lapse? Surely a man who so notoriously lives his life "by the clock" is incapable of a simple chronological error of this kind. Just so. Therefore it was no error. What, then?

A message? Perhaps even—a warning?

Who *is* this man called Fogg? And who is Farmer that Fogg is mindful of him?

And Father   re is revealed i

FATHE

It is no secret that I am an admirer of Philip Jose Farmer's writings. I consider him one of the great innovators in the area, the author of a number of classics and pivotal works. From "The Lovers" to the Riverworld books, from the exceedingly clever "Sail On! Sail On!" to pocket universes to Tarzan, Doc Savage and King Kong nostalgia pieces, I have followed him, delighting in his invention and the scope of his imagination. And I never know what he is going to do next, which is a piece of the fun as well as tribute to his originality. He has influenced an entire generation of writers, myself among them, and he is still going as strong as ever. Stronger, probably.

And so . . . I had enjoyed his *Night of Light* back when it came out, which is where I first encountered Father Carmody. I knew that there were other stories about him, but I'd come across only one of them. When Jim Baen mentioned recently that they were to be collected and published in the new line of books he was editing, I began immediately to look forward to the occasion when I would become acquainted with all of the rest. When Jim asked me more recently whether I would care to say a few words to go before, I was glad for the opportunity to endorse again the works of a writer to whom I have long felt indebted.

It is good finally to see all of Father Carmody together in one place. He is an interesting person, leading a colorful life.

Ite, missa est. **Enjoy.**

— Roger Zelazny

FATHER TO
THE STARS

by

Philip Jose Farmer

**A TOM DOHERTY
ASSOCIATES BOOK**

TOR
science
fiction

**PINNACLE BOOKS
NEW YORK**

FATHER TO THE STARS

A TOR Book.

Acknowledgements:
"The Night of Light" was originally published in *The Magazine of Fantasy and Science Fiction*, (c) 1957 by Fantasy House, Inc.
"A Few Miles" was originally published in *The Magazine of Fantasy and Science Fiction*, 1960 by Mercury Press, Inc.
"Prometheus" was originally published in *The Magazine of Fantasy and Science Fiction*, (c) 1961 by Mercury Press, Inc.
"Father" was originally published in *The Magazine of Fantasy and Science Fiction*, (c) 1955 by Fantasy House, Inc.
"Attitudes" was originally published in *The Magazine of Fantasy and Science Fiction*, (c) 1953 by Fantasy House, Inc.

Cover art by Janny Wurtz
First printing: July 1981
ISBN: 0-523-48504-2
Printed in the United States of America

PINNACLE BOOKS, INC.
1430 Broadway
New York, NY 10018

**COMING SOON
FROM TOR!**

*The Other Log of
Phileas Fogg*

by

Philip Jose Farmer

FATHER
TO THE
STARS

TABLE OF CONTENTS

THE NIGHT OF LIGHT

On Earth it would be a fearful thing to see a man chasing down the street after the skin from a human face, a thin layer of tissue blown about like a piece of paper by the wind.

On the planet of Dante's Joy the sight aroused only a mild wonder in the few passersby. And they were interested because the chaser was an Earthman and therefore, a curiosity in himself.

John Carmody ran down the long straight street, past the clifflike fronts of towers built of huge blocks of quartz-shot granite, with gargoyles and nightmare shapes grinning from the darkened interiors of many niches and with benedictions of god and goddess leaning from the many balconies.

A little man, dwarfed even more by the soaring walls and flying buttresses, he ran down the street in frantic pursuit of the fluttering transparent skin that turned over and over as it sailed upon the strong wind, over and over, showing the eyeholes, the earholes, the sagging empty gaping mouthhole, and trailing a few long and blond hairs from the line of the forehead, the scalp itself being absent.

9

The wind howled behind him, seeming to add its fury to his. Suddenly the skin, which had fluttered just within his reach, shot upwards on a strong draft coming around a building.

Carmody cursed and leaped, and his fingers touched the thing. But it flew up and landed on a balcony at least ten feet above him, lodged against the feet of the diorite image of the god Yess.

Panting, holding his aching sides, John Carmody leaned against the base of a buttress. Though he had once been in superb condition, as befitted the ex-welterweight amateur boxing champion of the Federation, his belly was swelling to make room for his increasing appetite, and fat was building up beneath his chin, like a noose.

It made little difference to him or to anybody else. He was not much to look at, anyway. He had a shock of blue-black hair, stiff and straight, irresistibly reminding one of a porcupine's quills. His head was melon-shaped, his forehead too high, his left eyelid drooped just enough to give his face a lopsided look, his nose was too long and sharp, his mouth too thin, his teeth too widely spaced.

He looked up at the balcony, cocking his head to one side like a bird, and saw he couldn't climb up the rough but slick wall. The windows were closed with heavy iron shutters, and the massive iron door was locked. A sign hung from its handle. On it was a single word in the alphabet of the people of the northern continent of Kareen. SLEEPING.

Carmody shrugged, smiled indifferently, in contrast to his former wildness to get at the skin, and walked away. Abruptly the wind, which had died down, sprang into life again and struck him like a blow from a huge fist.

He rolled with it as he would have rolled with a punch in the ring, kept his footing, and leaned into it, head down but bright blue eyes looking upwards. Nobody ever caught him with his eyes shut.

There was a phone booth on the corner, a massive marble box that could hold twenty people easily. Carmody hesitated outside it but, impelled by the screaming fury of the wind, he entered. He went to one of the six phones and lifted its receiver. But he did not sit down on the broad stone bench, preferring to dance around, to shift nervously from side to side and to keep his head cocked as one eye looked for intruders.

He dialed his number, Mrs. Kri's boarding house. When she answered the phone, he said, "Beautiful, this is John Carmody. I want to speak to Father Skelder or Father Ralloux."

Mrs. Kri giggled, as he knew she would, and said, "Father Skelder is right here. Just a second."

There was a pause, then a man's deep voice. "Carmody? What is it?"

"Nothing to get alarmed about," said Carmody. "I think . . ."

He waited for a comment from the other end of the line. He smiled, thinking of Skelder standing there, wondering what was going on, unable to say too much because of Mrs. Kri's presence. He could see the monk's long face with its many wrinkles and high cheekbones and hollow cheeks and shiny bald pate, the lips like a crab's pincers tightening until they squeezed themselves out of sight.

"Listen, Skelder, I've something to tell you. It may or may not be important, but it is rather strange." He stopped again and waited, knowing that the monk was foaming underneath that seemingly impassive exterior, that he would not care to display it at all and would hate himself for breaking down and asking Carmody what he had to tell. But he would break; he would ask. There was too much at stake.

"Well, well, what is it?" he finally snapped. "Can't you say over the phone?"

"Sure, but I wasn't going to bother if you weren't interested. Listen, about five minutes ago did anything strange happen to you or to anybody around you?"

There was another long pause, then Skelder said in a strained voice, "Yes. The sun seemed to flicker, to change color. I became dizzy and feverish. So did Mrs. Kri, and Father Ralloux."

Carmody waited until he was sure that the monk was not going to comment any further. "Was that all? Did nothing else happen to you or the others?"

"No. Why?"

Carmody told him about the skin of the unfinished face that had seemed to appear from the empty air before him. "I thought perhaps you might have had a similar experience."

"No; aside from the sick feeling, nothing happened."

Carmody thought he detected a huskiness in Skelder's voice. Well, he would find out later if the monk were concealing something. Meanwhile . . .

Suddenly, Skelder said, "Mrs. Kri has left the room. What is it you really wanted, Carmody?"

"I really wanted to compare notes about that flickering of the sun," he replied, crisply. "But I thought I'd tell you something of what I found out in the temple of Boonta."

"You ought to have found out just about everything," interrupted Skelder. "You were gone long enough. When you didn't show up last night, I thought that perhaps something had happened to you."

"You didn't call the police?"

"No, of course not," the monk's voice crackled. "Do you think that because I'm a priest I'm stupid? Besides, I hardly think you're worth worrying about."

Carmody chuckled. "Love thy fellow man as a brother. Well, I never cared much for my brother—or anybody else. Anyway, the reason I'm late, though only twenty hours or so behind time, is that I decided to take part in the big parade and the ceremonies that followed." He laughed again. "These Kareenians really enjoy their religion."

Skelder's voice was cold. "You took part in a temple orgy?"

Carmody hawhawed. "Sure. When in Rome, you know. However, it wasn't pure sensuality. Part of it was a very boring ritual, like all ritual; it wasn't until nightfall that the high priestess gave the signal for the big melee."

"You took part?"

"Sure. With the high priestess herself. It's all right; these people don't have your attitude towards sex, Skelder; they don't think it's dirty or a sin; they regard it as a sacrament, a great gift from the goddess; what would seem to you infinitely disgusting, wallowing in a mire of screaming sexfiends, is to them pure and chaste and goddess-blessed worship. Of course, I think your attitude and theirs are both wrong: sex is just a force that one ought to take advantage of in other people; but I will admit that the Kareenians' ideas are more fun than yours."

Skelder's voice was that of a slightly impatient and bored teacher lecturing a not-too-bright pupil. If he was angry, he managed to conceal it.

"You don't understand our doctrine. Sex is not in itself a dirty or sinful force. After all, it is the medium designed by God whereby the higher forms of life may be perpetuated. Sex in animals is as innocent as the drinking of water. And in the holy circle of matrimony a man and a woman may use this Godgiven force, may, through its sacred and tender rapture, become one, may approach that ecstasy, which is the understanding and perhaps even glimpse of—"

"Jesus Christ!" said Carmody. "Spare me, spare me! What must your parishioners mutter under their breaths, what groans, every time you climb into the pulpit? God, or Whatever-it-is, help them!

"Anyway, I don't give a damn what the doctrine of the Church is. It's very evident that you yourself think that sex is dirty, even if it takes place within the permissible bonds of matrimony. It's disgusting, and the sooner the necessary evil is over and done with and one can take a shower, the better.

"However, I've gotten way off the track, which is that to the Kareenians these outbreaks of religio-sexual frenzy are manifestations of their gratitude to the Creator—I mean Creatrix—for being given life and the joys of life. Normally, they behave quite stuffily—"

"Look, Carmody, I don't need a lecture from you; after all, I am an anthropologist, I know perfectly well what the perverted outlook of these natives is, and—"

"Then why weren't you down here, studying them?" said Carmody, still chuckling. "It's your anthropological duty. Why send me down? Were you afraid you'd get contaminated just watching? Or were you scared to death that you might get religion, too?"

"Let's drop the subject," said Skelder, emotionlessly. "I don't care to hear the depraved details; I just want to know if you found out anything pertinent to our mission."

Carmody had to smile at that word *mission*.

"Sure thing, Dad. The priestess said that the Goddess herself never appears except as a force in the bodies of her worshipers. But she maintains, as did a lot of the laymen I talked to, that the goddess's son, Yess, exists in the flesh, that they have seen and even talked to him. He will be in this city during the Sleep. The story is that he comes here because it was here that he was born and died and raised again."

"I know that," said the monk, exasperatedly. "Well, we shall see when we confront this impostor what he has to say. Ralloux is working on our recording equipment now so it'll be ready."

"OK," replied Carmody indifferently. "I'll be home within half an hour, provided I don't run across any interesting females. I doubt it; this city is dead—almost literally so."

He hung up the phone, smiling again at the look of intense disgust he could imagine on Skelder's face. The monk would be standing there for perhaps a minute in his black robes, his eyes closed, his lips working in silent prayer for the lost soul of John Carmody, then he would whirl and stalk upstairs to find Ralloux and tell him what had happened. Ralloux, clad in the maroon robe of the Order of St. Jairus, puffing on his pipe as he worked upon the recorders, would listen without much comment, would express neither disgust nor amusement over Carmody's behavior, would then say that it was too bad that they had to work with Carmody but that perhaps something good for Carmody, and for them, too, might come out of it. In the meantime, as there was nothing they could do to alter conditions on Dante's Joy or change Carmody's character, they might as well work with what they had.

As a matter of fact, thought Carmody, Skelder detested his fellow-scientist and co-religionist almost as much as he did Carmody. Ralloux belonged to an order that was very much suspect

in the eyes of Skelder's older and far more conservative organization. Moreover, Ralloux had
declared himself to be in favor of the adoption of
the Statement of Historical Flexibility, or
Evolution of Doctrine, the theory then being
offered by certain parties within the Church, and
advocated by them as worthy of being made
dogma. So strong had the controversy become
that the Church was held to be in danger of
another Great Schism, and some authorities held
that the next twenty-five years would see pro-
found changes and perhaps a crucial break-up in
the Church itself.

Though both monks made an effort to keep their
intercourse on a polite level, Skelder had lost his
temper once, when they were discussing the
possibility of allowing priests to marry—a mere
evolution of discipline, rather than doctrine.
Thinking of Skelder's red face and roaring
jeremiads, Carmody had to laugh. He himself had
contributed to the monk's wrath by pointed
comments now and then, hugely enjoying himself,
contemptuous at the same time of a man who
could get so concerned over such a thing. Couldn't
the stupid ass see that life was just a big joke and
that the only way to get through it was to share it
with the Joker?

It was funny that the two monks, who hated
each other's guts, and he, who was disliked by
both of them and who was contemptuous of them,
should be together in this project. "Crime makes
strange bedfellows," he had once said to Skelder
in an effort to touch off the rage that always
smoldered in the man's bony breast. His comment
had failed of its purpose, for Skelder had icily
replied that in this world the Church had to work
with the tools at hand and Carmody, however foul,
was the only one available. Nor did he think it a

crime to expose the fraudulency of a false religion.

"Look, Skelder," Carmody had said, "you know that you and Ralloux were jointly commissioned by the Federation's Anthropological Society and by your Church to make a study of the so-called Night of Light on Dante's Joy and also, if possible, to interview Yess—providing he exists. But you've taken it on yourself to go further than that. You want to capture a god, inject him with chalarocheil and make him confess the whole hoax. Do you think that you won't get into trouble when you return to Earth?"

To which Skelder had replied that he was pre-pared to face any amount of trouble for this chance to kill the religion at its roots. The cult of Yess had spread from Dante's Joy to many a planet; its parody on the Church's ritual and Sacraments, plus the orgies to which it gave religious sanction had caused many defections from the Church's fold; there was the fantastic but true story of the diocese of the planet of Comeonin. The bishop and every member of his flock, forty thousand, had become apostates and . . .

Remembering this, Carmody smiled again. He wondered what Skelder would say if he knew how literal his words were about "killing the religion at its root." John Carmody had his own interpreta-tion of that. In his coat pocket he carried a True Blue Needlenose, diminutive assassin, .03 caliber, capable of firing one hundred explosive bullets one after the other before needing a new clip. If Yess was flesh and blood and bone, then flesh could flower, blood could geyser, bone could splinter, and Yess would have another chance to rise again from the dead.

He'd like to see that. If he saw that, then he could believe anything.

Or could he? What if he did believe it? Then

what? What difference would it make? So miracles were wrought? So what? What did that have to do with John Carmody, who existed outside miracles, who would never rise again from the dead, who was determined, therefore, to make the most of what little this universe had to offer?

A little of good food, steaks and onions, a little of good scotch, a little drunkenness so you could get a little closer but never close enough to the truth that you knew existed just on the other side of the walls of this hard universe, a little pleasure out of watching the pains and anxieties of other people and the stupid concerns they had over them when they could so easily be avoided, a little mockery, your greatest joy, actually, because it was only by laughing that you could tell the universe that you didn't care—not a false mockery, because he did not care, cared nothing for what others seemed to value so desperately—a little laughter, and then the big sleep. The last laugh would be had by the universe, but John Carmody wouldn't hear it, and so, you might say that he in reality had the last laugh, and . . .

At that moment he heard his name called by someone passing along the street. "Come on in, Tand!" Carmody shouted back in Kareenian. "I thought you'd gone to Sleep. You're not going to take the Chance, are you?"

Tand offered him a native-made cigarette, lit one of his own, blew smoke through narrow nostrils, and replied, "I've a very important deal to finish. It may take some time to complete it. So—I'll have to put off Sleeping as long as possible."

"That's strange," said Carmody, mentally noting that Tand had answered him in terms as vague as possible. "I've heard that you Kareenians think only about ethics and the nature of the

universe and improving your shining souls, not at
all about dirty old money."

Tand smiled. "We are no different than most
peoples. We have our saints, our sinners, and our
in-betweens. But we do seem to have a Galaxy-
wide reputation, though quite a contradictory one.
One depicts us as a race of ascetic and holy men;
the other, as the most sensual and vile of so-called
civilized people. And, of course, strange stories are
told about us, largely because of the Night of
Light. Whenever we travel to another planet, we
find ourselves treated as something quite unique.
Which I suppose we are, just as all peoples are."

Carmody did not ask the nature of the important
deal that was keeping Tand from going to Sleep at
once. It would have been bad Kareenian form to
do so. Over the glowing tip of his cigarette he
studied him. The fellow was about six feet tall,
handsome according to his own race's standards.
Like most intelligent beings of the Galaxy, he
could pass for a member of Homo Sapiens at a
distance, his ancestors having evolved along lines
parallel to those of Terrestrials. Only when he got
closer could you see that his face, though manlike,
was not quite human. And the feathery-looking
hair and blue-tinged nails and teeth gave you a
start when you first met a native of Dante's Joy.

Tand wore a gray brimless conical headpiece
like a fool's cap, stuck jauntily onto one side; his
hair was clipped quite close except just above the
wolflike ears, where it fell straight down to cover
them; his neck was encircled in a high lacy collar
but his thigh-length bright violet shirt was severe
enough. A broad gray velvet belt gathered it in at
the waist. His legs were bare, and his four-toed
feet wore sandals.

Carmody had long suspected that the fellow was
a member of the police force of this city of Rak. He

always seemed to be around, and he had moved into the place that lodged Carmody the day after the Earthman had signed housepeace there.

Not that it mattered, thought Carmody. Even the police would be Sleeping in a day or so.

"What about yourself?" asked Tand. "Are you still insistent on taking the Chance?"

Carmody nodded and shot Tand a confident smile.

"What were you chasing?" added Tand.

Suddenly, Carmody's hands trembled, and he had to dig them in his pockets to hide them. His lips writhed in silent talk to himself.

Now, now, Carmody, none of this. You know nothing ever bothers you. But if that is so, why this shaking, this cold sickness in the dead center of your belly?

It was Tand's turn to smile, exposing his humanly shaped but blue-tinged teeth.

"I caught a glimpse of that thing you were chasing so desperately. It was the beginnings of a face, whether Kareenian or Terrestrial, I couldn't say. But since you doubtless conceived it, it must have been human."

"Wh-what d'ya mean, *conceived?* I, Conceived . . .?"

"Oh, yes. You saw it form in the air in front of you, didn't you?"

"Impossible!"

"No, nor fantastic. The phenomenon, though not common, does occur now and then. Usually, a change takes place *in* the body of the conceiver, not outside. Your problem must be extraordinarily strong, if this thing takes place outside you."

"I have no problems I can't whip," growled Carmody out of one corner of his mouth, his cigarette bobbing from the other corner like a challenging rapier.

Tand shrugged. "Have it your own way. My only advice for you is to take a spaceship while there is still time. The last one leaves within four hours. After that, none will arrive or depart until the time for the Sleep is past. By then, who knows . . . ?"

Carmody wondered if Tand was being ironic, if he knew that he could not leave Dante's Joy, that he'd be arrested the moment he touched a Federation port.

He also wondered if Tand could have the slightest idea what he was planning as a means to leave Dante's Joy in full safety. Now, having regained full control of his hands, he took them from his pockets and removed the cigarette from his mouth. *Damn it,* he said, silently mouthing the words, *why are you hesitant, Carmody, old buddy? Lost your guts? No, not you. It's you against the universe, as it has always been, and you've never been afraid. You either attack a problem, and destroy it, or else ignore it. But this is so strange you can't seem to grapple with it. Well, so what? Wait until the strangeness wears off, then . . . BLAM! you've got it in your hands and you'll rip it apart, choke the life out of it, just as you did with—*

His hands clenched in memory of what they had done, and his lips stiffened into the beginning of a silent snarl. That face blowing through the air. Wasn't there a resemblance . . . could it have been . . . *No!*

"You are asking me to believe the impossible," he said. "I know that many strange things happen here on this planet, but what I saw, well, I just can't think that—"

"I have seen you Earthmen before when confronted by this," interrupted Tand. "To you it seems like something from one of your fairy tales or myths. Or, perhaps, from that incredible phenomenon you call a nightmare, which we Kareenians do not experience."

"No," said Carmody. "Your nightmares occur outside you, every seven years. And even then most of you escape them by Sleeping, while we human beings can't encounter them except by means of sleeping."

He paused, smiled his rapid, cold smile, and added, "But I am different from most Earthmen. I do not dream; I have no nightmares."

"I understand," replied Tand evenly and apparently without malice, "that that is because you differ from most of them—and us—in that you have no conscience. Most Earthmen, unless I have been misinformed about them, would suffer troublings of the mind if they had killed their wives in cold blood."

The narrow walls of the booth thundered with Carmody's laughter. Tand looked emotionlessly at him until he had subsided into chuckling, then said, "You laugh loud enough but not nearly so loud as that."

He waved his hand to indicate the wind howling down the street.

Carmody did not understand what he meant. He was disappointed; he'd expected the usual violent reaction to his amusement at the subject of his "crime." Perhaps the fellow *was* a policeman. Otherwise, in the face of Carmody's laughter, how explain the stiff self-control? But it might be that he was untouched because the murder had happened on Earth and to a Terrestrial. An individual of one species found it difficult to get excited about the murder of a person belonging to another, especially if it was 10,000 light-years away.

However, there was the universally admitted deep empathy of the natives of Dante's Joy; they were acknowledged to be the most ethical beings in the world, the most sensitive.

Abruptly bored, Carmody said, "I'm going back to Mother Kri's. You coming along?"

"Why not? Tonight's the last supper she'll be serving for some time. She's going to Sleep immediately afterwards."

They walked down the street, silent for awhile though the wind, erratic as ever, had died down and made conversation possible. Around them towered the massive gargoyle-and-god-decorated buildings, built to last forever, to withstand any treatment from the wind, fire, or cataclysm while their inmates slept. Here and there strode a lonely, silent native, intent on some business or other before he took the Sleep. The crowds of the day before were gone, and with them the noise, bustle and sense of life.

Carmody was watching a young female cross the street and was thinking that if you put a sack on her head you wouldn't be able to distinguish her from a Terrestrial. There were the same long legs, the wide pelvis, seductive swaying of hips, narrow waist, and flowering of breasts... suddenly the light had changed color, had flickered. He looked up at the noonday sun. Blindingly white before, it was now an enormous disc of pale violet ringed by a dark red. He felt dizzy and hot, feverish, and the sun blurred and seemed to him to melt like a big ball of taffy, dripping slowly down the sky.

Then just as quickly as they had come, the dizziness and faintness were gone, the sun once again was an eye-searing white fire, and he had to look away from it.

"What the hell was *that*?" he said to no one in particular, forgetting that Tand was with him. He found out he was shivering with cold and was drained of his strength as if he'd been upended and decanted of half his blood.

"What in God's name?" he said again, hoarsely. Now he remembered that something like this had happened less than an hour ago, that the sun had changed to another color—violet? blue?—and that he'd been hot as if a fire had sprung up in his bowels and that everything had blurred. But the feeling had been much quicker, just a flash. And the air about three feet before him had seemed to harden, to become shiny, almost as if a mirror were forming from the molecules of air. Then, out of the seemingly much denser air, that face had appeared, that half-face, the first layer of skin, tissue-thin, whisked away at once by the wind.

He shivered. The wind's springing up again did not help his coolness. Then he yelled. About ten feet away from him, drifting along the ground, blown down the street and rolled into a ball by now, was another piece of skin. He took a step forward, preparatory to running after it, then stopped. He shook his head, rubbed his long nose in seeming bewilderment, and unexpectedly grinned.

"This could get you down after a while," he said aloud. "But they're not getting their hooks into John Carmody. That skin or whatever it is can go floating on down into the sewer, where it belongs, for all I care."

He took out another cigarette, lit it, then looked for Tand. The native was in the middle of the street, bending over the girl. She was on her back, her legs and arms rigid but shaking, her eyes wide open and glazed, her mouth working as she chewed her lips and drooled blood and foam.

Carmody ran over, took one look, and said, "Convulsions. You're doing the right thing. Keep her from biting her tongue. Did you have medical training, too?"

He could have bit his own tongue then. Now the fellow would know a little more of his past. Not that it would help Tand much in gathering evidence about him, but he didn't like to reveal anything at all. Not without getting paid for it in one form or another. Never give anything away! It's against the laws of the universe; to keep living you have to take in as much or more than you put out.

"No, I didn't," replied Tand, not looking up but intent on seeing that the wadded handkerchief thrust into her mouth didn't choke her. "But my profession requires I learn a certain amount of first aid. Poor girl, she should have gone to Sleep a day earlier. But I suppose she didn't know she was liable to be affected this way. Or, perhaps, she did know and was taking the Chance so she might cure herself."

"What do you mean?"

Tand pointed at the sun. "When it discolors like that it seems to raise a tempest among one's brain-waves. Any epileptoid tendencies are revealed then. Provided the person is awake. Actually, though, you don't see this very often. Hereditary tendencies to such behavior have been nearly wiped out; those who gamble on the Chance usually are struck down, though not always. If one does come through, he is cured forever."

Carmody looked unbelievingly at the skies. "A flareup on the sun, eightly million miles away, can cause that?"

Tand shrugged and stood up. The girl had quit writhing and seemed to be peacefully asleep. "Why not? On your own planet, so I've been told, you are much influenced by solar storms and other fluctuations in the sun's radiations. Your people—like ours—have even charted the climatic, psychological, physical, business, political, sociological, and other cycles that are directly dependent upon changes on the surfaces of the sun, that can be predicted a century or more in advance. So why be surprised because our own sun does the same, though to a much more intense degree?"

Carmody began to make a gesture of bewilderment and helplessness, then halted his hand because he did not want anybody to think that he could for a moment be uncertain about anything.

"What is the explanation for all this—this hibernating, these incredible physiological transformations, this . . . this physical projection of mental images?"

"I wish I knew," said Tand. "Our astronomers have studied the phenomenon for thousands of years, and your own people have established a base upon an asteroid to examine it. However, after their first experience with the time of the Chance, the Terrestrials now abandon their base when the time for Sleep comes. Which makes it practically impossible to make a close examination. We have the same trouble. Our own scientists are too busy fighting their own psychical stress at this period to be able to make a study."

"Yes, but instruments aren't affected during these times."

Tand smiled his blue smile. "Aren't they? They register a wild hodgepodge of waves as if the machines themselves were epileptic. Perhaps these recordings may be very significant. But who can translate them? No one, so far."

He paused, then said, "That is wrong. There are three who could explain. But they won't."

Carmody followed the direction of his pointing finger and saw the bronze statuary group at the

end of the street: the goddess Boonta protecting
her son Yess from the attack of Algul, the dark
god, his twin brother, in the metamorphosis of a
dragon.

"Them . . . ?"

"Yes, them."

Carmody grinned mockingly and said, "I'm
surprised to find an intelligent man like yourself
subscribing to such a primitive belief."

"Intelligence has nothing at all to do with
religious belief," replied Tand. He bent down over
the girl, opened her eyelid, felt her pulse, then
rose. He removed his hat with one hand and with
the other made a circular sign.

"She's dead."

There was a delay of about fifteen minutes.
Tand phoned into the hospital, and soon the long
red oil-burning steam-driven ambulance rolled up.
The driver jumped off the high seat over the front
of the vehicle, which was built much like a landau,
and said, "You're lucky. This will be our last call.
We're taking the Sleep in the next hour."

Tand had gone through the girl's pockets and
produced her papers of identification. Carmody
noticed that he'd done so with a suspiciously
policemanlike efficiency. Tand gave them to the
ambulance men and told them that it would be
best probably to wait until after the Sleep before
notifying her parents.

Afterwards, as they walked down the street,
Carmody said, "Who takes care of the fire department, the police work, the hospitals, the supplying
of food?"

"Our fires don't amount to anything because of
the construction of our buildings. Stocking food
for seven days is no real problem; so few are up
and out. As for the police, well, there is no law
during this time. No human law, anyway."

"What about a cop who takes the Chance?"

"I said that the law is suspended then."

By then they'd walked out of the business district into the residential. Here the buildings did not stand shoulder to shoulder but were set in the middle of large yards. Plenty of breathing space. But the sense of massiveness, of overpowering-ness, of eternity frozen in stone still hovered in the air, as these houses were every one at least three stories high and built of massive blocks and had heavy burglarproof iron doors and windows. Even the doghouses were built to withstand a siege.

It was seeing several of these that reminded Carmody of the sudden cessation of animal life. The birds that had filled the air with their cries the day before were gone; the lyan and kin, doglike and catlike pets, which were usually seen in large numbers even on the downtown streets, were gone. And the squirrels seemed to have retreated into the holes in their trees.

Tand, in reply to Carmody's remark about this, said, "Yes, animals instinctively sleep during the Night, have been doing it, from all evidences, since the birth of life here. Only man has lost the instinctive ability, only man has a choice or the knowledge of using drugs to put him in a state close to suspended animation. Apparently, even prehistoric man knew of the plant which gives the drug that will induce this sleep; there are cave paintings depicting the Sleep."

They stopped before the house belonging to the female whom Carmody called Mother Kri. It was here that visiting Earthmen, willy-nilly, were quartered by the Kareenian government. It was a four-storied circular house built of limestone and mortar, capped by a thick shale roof, and set in a yard at least two hundred feet square.

A long winding tree-lined walk led up to the

great porch, which itself ran completely around the house. Halfway up the walk, Tand paused beside a tree.

"See anything peculiar in this?" he asked the Earthman.

As was his habit when thinking, Carmody spoke aloud, not looking at his audience but staring off to one side as if he were talking to an invisible person. "It looks like a mature tree, yet it's rather short, about seven feet high. Something like a dwarf cottonwood. But it has a double trunk that joins about a third of the way up. And two main branches, instead of many. Almost as if it had arms and legs. If I were to come upon it on a dark night, I might think it was a tree getting ready to take a walk."

"You're close," said Tand. "Feel the bark. Real bark, eh? It looks like it to the naked eye. But under the microscope, the cellular structure is rather peculiar. Neither like a man's nor a tree's. Yet like both. And why not?"

He paused, smiled enigmatically at Carmody, and said, "It is Mrs. Kri's husband."

Carmody replied coolly, "It is?" He laughed and said, "He's a rather sedentary character, isn't he?"

Tand raised his featherish eyebrows.

"Exactly. During his life as a man he preferred to sit around, to watch the birds, to read books of philosophy. Taciturn, he avoided most people. As a result he never got very far in his job, which he hated.

"Mrs. Kri had to earn money for them by starting this lodging house; she retaliated by making his life miserable with nagging him, but she could never fill him with her own enthusiasms and ambitions. Finally, partly in an endeavor to get away from her, I think, he took the Chance.

And this is what happened. Most people said he failed. Well, I don't know. He got what he really wanted, his deepest wish."

He laughed softly. "Dante's Joy is the planet where you get what you really want. That is why it is off-limits to most of the Federation's people. It is dangerous to have your unconscious prayers answered in full and literal detail."

Carmody didn't understand everything he was being told, but he jauntily said, "Has anybody taken X-rays? Does he—it—have a brain?"

"Yes, of a sort, but what woody thoughts it thinks I wouldn't know."

Carmody laughed again. "Vegetable and/or man, eh? Look, Tand, what are you trying to do, scare me into getting off the planet or into taking the Sleep? Well, it won't work. Nothing frightens me, nothing at all."

Abruptly, his laughter ended in a choking sound, and he became rigid, staring straight ahead. His strength poured from him, and his body grew hot from his belly on out. About three feet before him there was a flickering like a heat wave, then, as if the air was solidifying into a mirror, the vibrations condensed into matter. Slowly, like a balloon collapsing as air poured out of holes torn in it, the bag of skin that had appeared folded in on itself.

But not before Carmody had recognized the face.

"Mary!"

It was some time before he could bring himself to touch the thing that lay on the sidewalk. For one thing, he didn't have the strength. Something had sucked it out of him.

Only his reluctance to display fear before somebody else moved him to pick it up.

"Real skin?" said Tand.

From someplace in the hollowness within him Carmody managed to conjure a laugh.

"Feels just like hers did, as soft, as unblemished. She had the most beautiful complexion in the world."

He frowned. "When it began to go bad . . ."

His fist opened out, and the skin dropped to the ground. "Empty as she was essentially empty. Nothing in the head. No guts."

"You're a cool one," said Tand. "Or shallow. Well, we shall see."

He picked up the bag and held it in both hands so it streamed out like a flag in the breeze. Carmody saw that there was now not only the face itself, but the scalp was complete and the front of the neck and part of the shoulders were there. Moreover, many long blond hairs floated like spider webs from the scalp, and the first layer of the eyeball itself had formed beneath the eyelids.

"You are beginning to get the hang of it," said Tand.

"I? I'm not doing that; I don't even know what's going on."

Tand touched his head and heart. "These know." He wadded the tissue in his fist and dropped it in a trashbasket on the porch.

"Ashes to ashes," said Carmody.

"We shall see," replied Tand again.

By this time scattered clouds had appeared, one of which masked the sun. The light that filtered through made everything gray, ghostly. Inside the house the effect was even worse. It was a group of phantoms that greeted them as they entered the dining room. Mother Kri, a Vegan named Aps, and two Earthmen, all sitting at a round table in a great darkened room flickeringly lit with seven candles set in a candelabrum. Behind the hostess was an altar and a stone carving of the Mother Goddess holding in her arms Yess and Algul as twin babies, Yess placidly sucking down upon the left and scratching the breast with unbabylike claws, the Mother Boonta regarding both impartially with a beatific smile. On the table itself, dominating the candelabrum and the plates and goblets, were the symbols of Boonta; the cornucopia, the flaming sword, the wheel.

Mother Kri, short, fat, large-bosomed, smiled at them. Her blue teeth looked black in the duskiness.

"Welcome, gentlemen. You are just in time for the Last Supper."

"The Last Supper," Carmody called on his way to the washroom. "Hah? I'll be my namesake, good old John. But who plays Judas?"

He heard Father Skelder snort with indignation and Father Ralloux's booming, "There's a little Judas in all of us."

Carmody could not resist stopping and saying, "Are you pregnant, too, dearie?" and then he walked away, laughing uproariously to himself. When he came back and sat down at the table, Carmody submitted with a smile to Skelder's saying grace and Mother Kri's asking for a blessing. It was easier to sit silent for a moment than to make trouble by insisting on the food being passed at once.

"When in Rome . . ." he said to Skelder and smiled to himself at the monk's puzzlement. "Pass the salt, please," he continued, "but don't spill it."

Then he burst into a roar of laughter as Skelder did exactly that. "Judas come back to life!"

The monk's face flushed, and he scowled. "With your attitude, Mr. Carmody, I doubt very much if you'll get through the Chance."

"Worry about yourself," said Carmody. "As for me, I intend to find some goodlooking and likely female and concentrate so much on her I'll not notice until long after that the seven days are up. You ought to try it, Prior."

Skelder tightened his lips. His long thin face was built for showing disapproval; the many deep lines in forehead and cheeks, the bony angles of cheek and jaw, the downward slant of the long meaty nose, the pattern of straight lines and whorls, these made up the blueprint of the stern judge, showed the fingerprints of a Maker who had squeezed out of his putty flesh an image of the righteous, then set the putty in a freezing blast to harden into stone.

The stone just now showed signs of being human, for it was distended and crimsoned with hot blood flooding beneath the skin. The pale blue-gray eyes glared from beneath pale gold eyebrows.

Father Ralloux's gentle voice fell like a benediction upon the room.

"Anger is not exactly one of the virtues."

He was a strange-looking man, this priest with his face made up of such contradictory features, the big pitcher-handle ears, red hair, pug nose, and broad smiling lips of the cartoon Irishman, all repudiated by the large dark eyes with their long feminine lashes. His shoulders were broad and his neck was thickly muscled, but his powerful arms ended in delicate and beautiful woman's hands. The soft liquid eyes looked gravely and honestly at you, yet you got the impression that there was something troubled in them.

Carmody had wondered why the fellow was Skelder's partner, for he was not at all well known, as the older man was. But he had learned that Ralloux had a fine reputation in anthropological circles. In fact, he was placed on a higher plane than his superior, but Skelder was in charge of the expedition because of his prominence in other fields. The lean monk was head of the conservative faction in the Church that was trying to reform the current morality of the laity; his taped image and voice had appeared upon every Federation planet that owned a caster; he had thundered forth a denunciation of nudity in the private home and on the public beach, of brief-contract marital relations, of polymorphous-perverse sexual attitudes, of all that had once been forbidden by Western Terrestrial society and especially by the Church but was now tolerated, if not condoned, among the laymen because it was socially accept-able. He wanted to use the Church's strongest weapons in enforcing a return to former standards; when the liberals and moderates in the Church accused him of being Victorian, he gladly adopted the title, declaring that that age was the one to which he desired they turn back. It was this background that was responsible now for the furious look he was giving Father Ralloux.

"Our Lord became angry when the occasion demanded! Remember the money-changers and the fig tree!" He pointed a long finger at his companion. "It is a misconception to think of Him as the gentle Jesus! One merely has to take the trouble to read the Gospels to perceive at once that He was a hard man in many respects, that—"

"My God, I'm hungry," said Carmody loudly, interjecting not only to stop the tirade but because he was famished. It seemed to him he'd never been so empty.

Tand said, "You'll find you'll have to eat enormous quantities of food during the next seven days. Your energy will be drained out as fast as it's put in."

Mother Kri went out of the room and quickly

returned carrying a plate full of cakes. "There are seven pieces, gentlemen, each baked in the likeness of one of the Seven Fathers of Yess. These are always baked for certain religious feasts, one of which is the Last Supper before the Sleep. I hope you gentlemen do not mind partaking. A bit from each cake and a sip of wine with each is customary. This communion symbolizes not only that you are partaking of the flesh and blood of Yess but that you are given the power to create your own god, as the Seven did."

"Ralloux and I cannot do that," replied Skelder. "We would be committing a sacrilege."

Mrs. Kri looked disappointed but brightened when Carmody and Aps, the Vegan, said they would participate. Carmody thought it would be politic in case he wished to use Mrs. Kri later on.

"I do not think," said the woman, "that you would mind, Father Skelder, if you knew the story of the Seven."

"I do know," he said. "I made a study of your religion before I came here. I do not allow myself to remain ignorant on any subject if I can help it. As I understand it, the myth goes that in the beginning of time the goddess Boonta had two sons, self-conceived. Upon reaching manhood, one of the sons, the evil one, slew the other, cut him into seven pieces and buried them in widely separated places, so that his mother would not be able to gather them together and bring him back to life. The evil son, or Algul as you call him, ruled the world, restrained only by his mother from destroying humanity altogether. Wickedness was everywhere; men were thoroughly rotten, as in the time of our Noah. Those few good people who did pray to the Mother to restore her good son, Yess, were told that if seven good men could be found in one place and at one time, her son would be resurrected. Volunteers came forth and tried to raise Yess, but never were enough qualified so that seven good men existed on this world at one time. Seven centuries went by and the world became more evil.

"Then, one day, seven men gathered together, seven *good* men, and Algul, the wicked son, in an effort to frustrate them, put everybody to sleep except seven of his most wicked worshippers. But the good seven fought off the Sleep, had a mystical union, a sort of psychical intercourse with the Mother"—Skelder's face twisted with distaste—"each of them becoming her lover, and the seven pieces of the son Yess were pulled together, reunited, and became alive. The evil seven turned into all sorts of monsters and the seven good became minor gods, consorts of the Mother. Yess restored the world to its former state. His twin brother was torn into seven pieces, and these were buried at different places over the earth. Since then, good has dominated evil, but there is still much evil left in the world, and the legend goes that if seven absolutely wicked men can gather together during the time of the Sleep, they will be able to resurrect Algul."

He paused, smiled as if in quiet mockery of this myth, then said, "There are other aspects, but that is the essence. Obviously, a symbolical story of the conflict between good and evil in this universe: many of its features are universal; they may be found in almost every religion of the Galaxy."

"Symbolism or not, universal or not," said Mrs. Kri, "the fact remains that seven men *did* create their god Yess. I know because I have seen him walking the streets of Kareen, have touched him, have seen him perform his miracles, though he does not like to do them. And I know that during the Sleep there are evil men who gather to create

Algul. For they know that if he comes to life, then
they, according to ancient promise, will rule this
world and have all they desire."

"Oh, come now, Mrs. Kri. I do not want to decry
your religion, but how do you *know* this man who
claims to be Yess is he?" said Skelder. "And how
could mere men fashion a god out of thin air?"

"I know because I know," she said, giving the
age-old and unarguable answer of the believer.
She touched her huge bosom. "Something in here
tells me it is so."

Carmody gave his long high-pitched irritating
laughter.

"She's got you there, Skelder. Hoist by your own
petard. Isn't that the ultimate defense of your own
Church when every other has crumbled?"

"No," replied Skelder coldly, "it is not. For one
thing, not one of our so-called defenses crumbles.
All remain rockfast, impervious to the jeerings of
petty atheists or the hammerblows of organized
governments. The Church is imperishable, and so
are its teachings; its logic is irrefutable; the Truth
is its possession."

Carmody smirked but refused to talk any more
about it. After all, what difference did it make
what Skelder or anybody else thought? The thing
he wanted now was action; he was tired of fruit-
less words.

Mrs. Kri had risen from the table and was
clearing up the dishes. Carmody, wishing to get
more information out of her, and also wanting the
others unable to hear him, said that he would help
her clean up. Mrs. Kri was charmed; she liked
Carmody very much because he was always doing
little things for her and giving her little compli-
ments now and then. Astute enough to see that he
had a purpose behind this, she still liked what he
did.

In the kitchen, he said, "Come on, Mother Kri, tell me the truth. Have you actually *seen* Yess? Just as you've seen me?"

She handed him a wet dish to dry.

"I've seen him more times than I have you. I had him in for dinner once."

Carmody had difficulty swallowing this prosaic contact with divinity. "Oh, really?"

"Really."

"And did he go to the bathroom afterwards?" he asked, thinking that this was the ultimate test, the basic distinction between man and god. You could think of a deity eating, perhaps to render his presence easier to his worshippers, perhaps also to enjoy the good things of life, but excretion seemed so unnecessary, so un-divine that, well . . .

"Of course," said Mrs. Kri. "Does Yess not have blood and bowels just as you and I?"

Skelder walked in at that moment, ostensibly for a drink of water but actually, thought Carmody, to overhear them.

"Of course he does," the monk said. "Do not all men? Tell me, Mrs. Kri, how long have you known Yess?"

"Since I was a child. I am fifty now."

"And he has not aged a bit, has always remained youthful, untouched by time?" said Skelder, his voice tinged with sarcasm.

"Oh, no. He is an old man now. He may die at any time."

The Earthmen raised their eyebrows.

"Perhaps there is some misunderstanding here," said Skelder, speaking so swiftly as to give the impression of swooping down vulturelike upon Mrs. Kri. "Some difference in definition, or in language, perhaps. A god, as we understand the term, does not die."

Tand, who had come into the kitchen in time to

catch the last few words, said, "Was not your god slain upon a cross?"

Skelder bit his lip, then smiled, and said, "I must ask you to forgive me. And I must confess that I have been guilty of a lapse of memory, guilty because I allowed a second of anger to cloud my thinking. I forgot for the moment the distinction between the Human and the Divine Nature of Christ. I was thinking in purely pagan terms, and even there I was wrong because the pagans' gods died. Perhaps you Kareenians make the same distinction between the human and the divine nature of your god Yess. I do not know. I have not been on this planet long enough to determine that; there was so much else to assimilate before I could study the finer points of your theology."

He stopped, sucked in a deep breath, then, as if he were getting ready to dive into the sea, he thrust his head forward, hunched his bony shoulders, and said, "I still think that there is a vast difference between your conception of Yess and ours of Christ. Christ was resurrected and then went to Heaven to rejoin His Father. Moreover, His death was necessary if He were to take on the sins of the world and save mankind."

"If Yess dies, he will someday be born again."

"You do not understand. There is the very important difference that—"

"That your story is true and ours false, a pagan myth?" replied Tand, smiling. "Who may say what is fact, what is myth, or whether or not a myth is not as much fact as, say, this table here? Whatever operates to bring about action in this world is fact, and if a myth engenders action, then is it not a fact? The words spoken here and now will die out in ever-weakening vibrations, but who knows what undying effect they may cause?"

Suddenly the room darkened, and everybody in

it clutched for some hold, the top of a chair, the edge of a table, anything to keep oneself steady. Carmody felt that wave of heat sweep through him and saw the air before him harden, seeming to become glass.

Blood burst out of the mirror, shot as if from a hose nozzle into his face, blinded him, drenched him, filled his open mouth, drove its salty taste down his throat.

There was a scream, not from him but someone beside him. He jumped back, pulled his handkerchief out, wiped away the blood from his eyes, saw that the glassiness was gone and with it the spurt of blood, but that the table and the floor beside it were filmed in crimson. There must have been at least ten quarts of it, he thought, just what you would expect from a woman weighing one hundred pounds.

There was no chance to follow that up for he had to skip to one side to avoid Skelder and Mrs. Kri, who were wrestling across the kitchen, Mrs. Kri doing the pushing because she was heavier and, perhaps, stronger. Certainly, she was the more aggressive, for she was doing her best to strangle the monk. He was clutching at the hands around his neck and screaming. "Take your filthy hands off me, you . . . you *female!*"

Carmody roared with laughter, and the sound seemed to break the maniacal spell possessing Mrs. Kri. As if she were waking from a sleep, she stopped, blinked her eyes, dropped her hands, and said, "What was I doing?"

"You were choking the life out of me!" shouted Skelder. "What is the matter with you?"

"Oh, my," she said to no one in particular. "It's getting later than I thought. I'd better get to sleep at once. All at once it seemed to me that you were the most hateful man in the world, because of what you said about Yess, and I wanted to kill you. Really, I do get a little irked at what you say but not that much."

Tand said, "Apparently, your anger is much deeper than you thought, Mrs. Kri. You'd driven it into your unconscious, wouldn't admit it to yourself, and so—"

He didn't get to finish. She had turned to look at Carmody and had seen for the first time that blood covered him and was everywhere in the kitchen. She screamed.

"Shut your damn mouth!" said Carmody, quite passionlessly, and he struck her across the lips. She stopped screaming, blinked again, and said, in a quivering voice, "Well, I'd better clean up this mess. I'd hate to wake up and try to scrub off this stuff after it's dried. You're sure you're not hurt?"

He didn't answer her but instead walked out of the kitchen and upstairs to his room, where he began to take off the wet clothing. Ralloux, who had followed him, said, "I am beginning to get scared. If such things can happen, and they obviously are not hallucinations, then who knows what will become of us?"

"I thought we had a little device that would make us quite safe?" said Carmody, peeling off the last of his sticky clothes and heading for the shower. "Or are you not sure of it?" He laughed at Ralloux's expression of despair and spoke from behind the veil of hot water hurtling over his head. "What's the matter? You really scared?"

"Yes, I am. Aren't you?"

"I, frightened? No, I have never been afraid of anything in my whole life. I'm not saying that to cover up, either. I don't really know what it is to feel fear."

"I strongly suspect you don't know what it is to feel *anything*," said Ralloux. "I wonder sometimes if you *do* have a soul. It must be there somewhere but thrust down so deep that nobody, including yourself, can see it. Otherwise . . ."

Carmody laughed and began soaping his hair.

"The headthumper at Johns Hopkins said I was a congenital psychopath, that I was born incapable of even understanding a moral code, I was beyond guilt, beyond virtue, not born with an illness of the mind, you understand, just lacking something, whatever it is that makes a human being human. He made no bones about telling me that I was one of those rare birds before which the science of the Year of Our Lord 2256 is completely helpless. He was sorry, he said, but I would have to be committed for the rest of my life, probably kept under mild sedation so I would be harmless and cooperative, and undoubtedly would be the subject of thousands of experiments in order to determine what it is that makes a constitutional psychopath."

Carmody paused, stepped from the shower, and began drying himself.

"Well," he continued, smiling, "you can see that I couldn't put up with that. Not John Carmody. So—I escaped from Hopkins, escaped from Earth itself, got to Springboard—on the edge of the Galaxy, farthest colonized planet of the Federation, stayed there a year, made a fortune smuggling sodompears, was almost caught by Raspold—you know, the galactic Sherlock Holmes—but eluded him and got here where the Federation has no jurisdiction. But I don't intend to stay here; not that it wouldn't be a bad world, because I could make money here, too, the food and liquor are good, and the females are just unhuman enough to attract me. But I want to show Earth up for what it is, a stable for stupid asses. I intend to go back to Earth to live there in complete immunity from arrest. And to do pretty well what I please, though I shall be discreet about some things."

"If you think you can do that, you must be crazy. You would be arrested the moment you stepped off the ship."

Carmody laughed. "You think so? You know, don't you, that the Federal Anti-Social Bureau depends for its information and partly for its directives upon the Boojum?"

Ralloux nodded.

"Well, the Boojum after all is only a monster protein memory bank and probability computer. It has stored away in its cells all the available information about one John Carmody and it undoubtedly has issued orders that all ships leaving Dante's Joy should be searched for him. But what if proof comes that John Carmody is dead? Then the Boojum cancels all directives concerning Carmody, and it retires the information to mechanical files. Then, when a colonist from, say, Wildenwooly, who has made his pile there and wants to spend it on Earth, comes to the home planet, who is going to bother him, even if he does look remarkably like John Carmody?"

"But that's preposterous! In the first place, how is the Boojum going to get proof positive that you are dead? In the second place, when you land on Earth, your fingers, retina, and brainwaves will be printed and identified."

Carmody grinned joyfully. "I wouldn't care to tell you how I'll manage the first. As for the second, so what if my prints are filed? They won't be cross-checked; they'll just be those of some immigrant, who was born on a colony-planet and who is being recorded for the first time. I won't even bother to change my name."

"What if someone recognizes you?"

"In a world of ten billion population? I'll take my chance."

"What is to prevent my telling the authorities?"

"Do dead men tell?"

Ralloux paled but did not flinch. His expression was still the grave-faced gentle monk's, his large shining black eyes staring honestly at Carmody but giving him a slightly ludicrous appearance because of their unexpectedness in that snub-nosed freckled big-lipped pitcher-eared setting. He said, "Do you intend to kill me?"

Carmody laughed uproariously. "No, it won't be necessary. Do you think for one moment either you or Skelder will come through the Night alive or in your right mind? You've seen what has happened during the few brief flickers we've had. Those were preludes, tunings up. What of the real Night?"

"What about what happened to you?" said Ralloux, still pale.

Carmody shrugged his shoulders, ran his hand through his blue-black porcupinelike hair, now clean of blood. "Apparently my unconscious or whatever you call it is projecting pieces of Mary's body, reconstructing the crime, you might say. How it can take a strictly subjective phenomenon and turn it into objective reality, I don't know. Tand says there are several theories that attempt to explain the whole thing scientifically, that leave the supernatural out. It doesn't matter. It didn't bother me when I cut up Mary into little pieces, and it won't bother me to have pieces of her come floating back into my life. I could swim through her blood, or anybody else's, to reach my goal."

He paused, looked narrow-eyed but still grinning at Ralloux and said, "What did *you* see during those flickers?"

Ralloux, even paler, gulped. He made the sign of

the cross.

"I don't know why I should tell you. But I will. I was in Hell."

"In Hell?"

"Burning. With the other damned. With ninety-nine percent of all those who had lived, are living, and will live. Billions upon billions."

Sweat poured out of his face. "It was not something imagined. I *felt* the agony. Mine, and the others'."

He fell silent, while Carmody cocked his head to one side like one puzzled bird trying to figure out another. Then Ralloux murmured, "Ninety-nine percent."

"So," Carmody said, "that is what you worry about most, that is the basic premise of your mind."

"If so, I did not know it," murmured the monk.

"How ridiculous can you get? Why, even your Church no longer insists upon the medieval conception of literal flames. Still, I don't know. From what I see of most people, they ought to fry. I'd like to be supervisor of the furnaces; there are some I've met in my short life whose fat egotism I'd like to burn right out of them. . . ."

Ralloux said, incredulously, "*You* resent egotists?"

Carmody, clean and dressed, grinned and started downstairs.

The mess, Mrs. Kri announced, was cleaned up and now she was going down into the vault to Sleep. She would leave the house open for their convenience, she said, but she hoped that when she awoke she wouldn't find everything too dirty, that they would wipe their feet before they came in and would empty the ashtrays and wash their dishes. The she insisted upon giving each of them a peace-kiss, and broke down and cried, saying she might never see any of them again, and she asked Skelder's forgiveness for her attack upon him. He was quite gracious about it and gave her his blessing.

Five minutes later, Mrs. Kri, having injected herself with the necessary hibernatives, slammed the big iron door of the basement vault and locked herself in.

Tand bade them goodby. "If I'm caught before I get to my own vault, I'll have to go through the Night, willy-nilly. And once started, there's no holding back. It's all black and white then; you either get through or you don't. At the end of the seventh day, you are god, corpse, or monster."

"And what do you do with the monsters?" asked Carmody.

"Nothing, if they're harmless, like Mrs. Kri's husband. Otherwise, we kill them."

After a few more remarks, he shook hands, knowing this was an Earth custom, wishing them, not luck, but a suitable reward. He said goodby to Carmody last, holding his hand the longest and looking into his eyes. "This is your last chance ever to become anything. If the Night does not break up the frozen deeps of your soul, if you remain iceberg from top to bottom, as you now are, then you are done for. If there exists the least spark of warmth, of humanity, then let it burst into flame and consume you, no matter what the pain. The god Yess once said that if you would gain your life you must lose it. Nothing original in it—other gods, other prophets, everywhere there are sentient beings, have said so. But it is true in many ways, unimaginable ways."

As soon as Tand had left, the three Earthmen silently walked upstairs and took from a large trunk three helmets, each with a small box on its top, from which nodded a long antenna. These they put over their heads, then turned a dial just above the right ear.

Skelder smacked his thin lips doubtfully and said, "I certainly hope the scientists at Jung were correct in their theory. They said that the moment an electromagnetic wave is detected by this device, it will set up a canceling wave; that no matter how vast the energies of the magnetic storm, we will be able to walk through them unaffected."

"I hope so," said Ralloux, looking downcast. "I see now that in thinking I could conquer what better men than I have found invincible, I was committing the worst sin of all, that of spiritual pride. May God forgive me. I thank Him for these helmets."

"I thank Him, too," said Skelder, "though I think that we should not have to have recourse to them. We two should put our full trust in Him and bare our heads, and our souls, to the evil forces of this heathen planet."

Carmody smiled cynically. "There is nothing holding you back. Go ahead. You might earn yourself a halo."

"I have my orders from my superiors," Skelder replied stiffly.

Ralloux rose and began pacing back and forth. "I don't understand it. How could magnetic storms, even if of unparalleled violence, excite the atomic nuclei of beings on a planet eighty million miles away, and at the same time probe and stir the unconscious mind, cause it to fasten an iron grip upon the conscious, provoke inconceivable psychosomatic changes. The sun turns violet, extends its invisible wand, rouses the image of the beast that lives in the dark caves of our minds, or else wakens the sleeping golden god. Well, I can understand some of that. Changes in electromagnetic frequencies on Earth's sun not only influence our climate and weather, they control human behavior. But how could this star act upon flesh and blood so that skin tension lessens, bones grow soft, bend, harden into alien shapes that are not found in the genes . . . ?"

"We still don't know enough about genes to say what shapes are implicit in them," interrupted Carmody. "When I was a medical student at Hopkins, I saw some very strange things." He fell silent, thinking about those days.

Skelder sat upright and thinlipped on a chair, his helmet making him look more like a soldier than a monk.

"It won't be long," said Ralloux, still pacing, "before the Night will start. If what Tand says is true, the first twenty hours or so will put everybody who has stayed up—except us, who are protected by our helmets—into a deep coma. Seemingly, the bodies of the sleepers then build up a partial resistance so that they later wake up. Once awakened, they are so charged with energy or some sort of drive, that they cannot sleep until the sun is over its violent phase. It is while they are sleeping that we—"

"—shall do our dirty work!" said Carmody joyfully.

Skelder rose. "I protest! We are here on a scientific investigation, and we are allied with you only because there is certain work that we—"

"—don't want to soil our lily-white hands with," said Carmody.

At that moment the light in the room became dark, a heavy violet. There was dizziness, then a fading away of the senses. But it lasted only a second, though long enough to weaken their knees and send them crashing to the floor.

Carmody got up shakily on all fours, shook his

head like a dog struck by a club, and said, "Wow, what a jolt that was! Good thing we had these helmets. They seem to have pulled us through."

He rose to his feet, his muscles aching and stiff. The room seemed to be hung with many violet veils, it was so dark and silent.

"Say, Ralloux, what's the matter with you?" he said.

Ralloux, white as a ghost, his face twisted with agony, leaped to his feet, screamed, tore the helmet off his head, and ran out the door. His footsteps could be heard pounding down the hall, down the steps. And the front door banged hard.

Carmody turned to the other monk. "He . . . now what's the matter with you?"

Skelder's mouth was open and he was staring at the clock on the wall. Suddenly, he whirled on Carmody. "Get away from me," he snarled.

Carmody blinked, then smiled and said, "Sure, why not? I never thought you had the skin I loved to touch, anyway."

He watched amusedly as Skelder began to edge along the wall towards the door. "Why are you limping?"

Skelder replied with an obscenity that set back even Carmody for a moment. "If I could do that," he replied, "I'd be ye compleat closed feedback. Why, what's happened to St. Skelder?"

The monk did not reply but walked crabwise from the room. A moment later the front door banged again. Carmody, quite alone, stood a moment in thought, then examined the clock at which the monk had been staring. Like most Kareenian timepieces, it told the time of the day, the day, month, and year. The attack of violet had taken place at 17:25. It was now 17:30.

Five minutes had elapsed.

Plus twenty-four hours.

"No wonder my every muscle aches! And I'm so hungry!" Carmody said aloud. He took the helmet off and dropped it on the floor.

"Well, that's that. Noble experiment." He went downstairs into the kitchen, half-expecting to be struck in the face with more blood. But there was nothing untoward. Whistling to himself, he took food and milk from the refrigerator, made himself sandwiches, ate heartily, then checked the action of his gun. Satisfied, he rose and walked towards the front door.

The telephone rang.

He hesitated, then decided to answer it. Wothehll, he said to himself. *Toujours gai.*

He lifted the receiver. "Hello!"

"John!" said a lovely female voice.

His head jerked away as if the receiver were a snake.

"John?" repeated the voice, now sounding far away, ghostly.

He sucked in a deep breath, squared his shoulders, resolutely put the phone to his ear again.

"John Carmody speaking. Who is this?"

There was no answer.

Slowly, he put the phone back on the hook.

When he left the house, he found himself in a darkness lit only by the streetlamps, islanded at hundred feet intervals, and by the huge moon, hanging dim and violet and malevolent above the horizon. The sky was clear, but the stars seemed far away blobs straining to pierce the purplish haze. The buildings were like icebergs looming in a fog, threatening with their suddenness, seeming about to topple over. Only when he got close to them did they crystallize into stability.

The city lay silent. No bark of dog, no shrill of nighthawk, no toot of horn, no coughing, no slamming of door, no hard heels ringing on the sidewalks, no shout of laughter. If sight was muffled, sound was dead.

Carmody hesitated, wondering if he shouldn't commandeer a car he'd found parked by the curb. Four miles to the temple was a long walk when you thought about what might be roaming the violet-hazed darkness. Not that he was scared, but he didn't care for unnecessary obstacles. A car would give him speed for a getaway; on the other hand, it was much more noticeable.

Deciding he would ride it for the first two miles, then walk, he opened the door. He recoiled, and his hand grabbed for his gun. But it dropped. The occupant, lying face up on the seat was dead. Carmody's flashlight, briefly turned upon the man's face, showed a mass of dried sores. Apparently, the driver had either been one who'd taken the Chance or else put off too long going to Sleep. Something, maybe an explosion of cancer, had eaten him up, had even devoured the eyeballs and gulped away half of his nose.

Carmody pulled the body out and let it lie in the street. It took several minutes to get the water in the boiler heated up, then he drove off slowly, the headlights extinguished. As he cruised along, peering from side to side for strangers, keeping close to the curb on his left so he'd have contact with something solid, he kept thinking about the voice over the phone, trying to analyze how this thing could have come about.

To begin with, he thought, he must accept absolutely that he, John Carmody, through the power of his mind, out of the thin air, was creating something solid and objective. At least, he was the transmitter of energy. He didn't think his own body contained nearly enough power for the transmutation of energy into matter; if his own cells had to furnish it, they would burn up before the process was barely begun. Therefore, he must be, not the engine, but the transmitter, the transformer. The sun was supplying the energy; he, the blueprint.

Granted. So, if something he couldn't control—what a hateful but not to be denied thought!—if something he couldn't control was refashioning his dead wife, he at least was the engineer, the sculptor. What she was depended on him.

He didn't understand how it worked. Reconstructing a human body was a process a billion times more complex than fashioning a statue. A statue was all stone, from human-seeming surface to its rocky heart. But a living being required, literally, the knowledge of a god or the totality of a universe to construct. He, John Carmody, having been just about to get his M.D. when he'd killed Mary, had considerable knowledge of cell structure and of its electrochemical contents. But he didn't have enough for what was taking place. No one did, not even the great Doctor Zangrets, who had created the brain of the Boojum and who had recently announced the creation of his laboratory of self-producing starfish, the next step to be a more complex mollusc with an octopus's eye and with male and female organs. But this would take him and fifty assistants ten years and twenty million dollars to complete. And John Carmody was playing god in the space of a few minutes, apparently charge-free. Or, he thought, perhaps on credit.

The only explanation he could find was that this process somehow utilized, not his conscious knowledge of the human body, but his body's unconscious self-knowledge. Through some means, his cells reproduced themselves directly in Mary's newly born body. Were the cells in her body, then, mirror-images, as the cells of one twin were to the other's?

That he could understand. But what about those organs that were peculiarly female? It was true that his memory contained a minute file on interior female anatomy. He'd dissected enough corpses; and as far as her own particular organs went, he knew those well enough, having taken her apart quite scientifically and carefully before feeding the pieces to the garbage disposal. He had even examined the four-months embryo, the prime cause of his anger and revulsion towards her, the swelling thing within her that was turning her from the most beautiful creature in the world to a huge-bellied monster, that would inevitably demand at least a small share of her love for John Carmody. Even a little bit was too much; he possessed the most precious, exquisite, absolutely unflawed thing of beauty; she was his, nobody else's.

And then, when he had proposed that they get rid of this flawing growth, and she had said no, and he had insisted, and had tried to force her, and she had fought him, then she had cried that she did not love him as she once had, that this child was not even his but that of a man who was a *man*, not a monster of egotism; then, for the first time in his life, as far as he remembered, he had been angry. Angry was an understatement. He had completely lost himself, had, literally, seen red, thought red, drowned in a crimson flood.

Well, that was the first, and last, time. He was here because of that time. Or was he? Even if he'd not gone insane with passion, wouldn't he have killed her anyway, later on, simply because logic would demand it? And simply because he could not stand the idea of the most beautiful being in the universe soiled and swollen, monstrous . . .

Maybe. It didn't matter what might have happened. What did happen was the only thing for a realist to consider.

There was the matter of her cells, which should be female but would not be if they were mirror-images of his. And there was the matter of her brain. Even if her body could be created female because of his knowledge of organs and of structure of genes, the brain would not be Mary's. Its original shaping, plus the billions of sub-microscopic groovings her memories would make, these would be beyond his power, conscious or unconscious.

No, if she had a brain, and she must have, then it would be his, John Carmody's brain. And if his, then it must contain his memories, his attitudes. It would be bewildered at finding itself in Mary's body, would not know what to do, to think. But, being John Carmody, it would find a way to make the most of the situation.

He laughed at the thought. Why didn't he find her? He would then have the perfect woman, her flawless beauty plus his mind, which would agree absolutely with him. Sublime self-abuse.

Again he laughed. Mary had used that term herself in that last blazing moment before he went completely under. She had said that to him she was not a woman, a wife, but merely a superior instrument for making love to himself. She had never had that glorious feeling of being one flesh that should rightfully come to a loving and passionate wife, no, she had always felt alone. And she had had to go to another man, and then she had never really experienced the wonder of the two-made-one because she knew all the time that she was sinning and would have to cleanse herself through confession and repentance. Even that rightful sensation was spoiled for her. Nevertheless, she had felt more like a wife and a woman with this man than with her own husband.

Well, as he'd said, that was that. Dismiss the past. Think of the thing that looks like Mary.

(He was glad that this thing was taking place outside him, not in him, as it did with the others. Perhaps he did have a frozen soul, but if so, it was good to have one. The iciness repelled subjectivity, made the unconscious happen outside him, and he could deal with that, with a host of Marys, whereas he'd have been helpless if he'd been like that epileptic girl or Mrs. Kri's husband or the cancer-devoured owner of this car.)

Think of the thing that looks like Mary.

If she—it—was conceived out of your head, like Athena from Zeus's—then at the moment of birth she had, as far as you know, your mind. But from that moment on, she becomes an independent being, one with thoughts and motivations of her own. Now, John Carmody, if you somehow found yourself dispossessed of your native body, lodged in the flesh of a woman you had murdered, and knew at the same time that the other *you* was in your first body, what would you do?

"I" he said, murmuring to himself, "would accept at once the fact that I was where I was, that I could not get out. I would define the limitations I had to work within, and would then set to work. And what would I do? What would I want? I would want to get off Dante's Joy and go to Earth or some Federation planet, where I could easily find myself a rich husband, could insist on being his number one wife. Why not? I'd be the most beautiful woman in the world."

He chuckled at that thought. More than once

he'd imagined himself as a woman, wondering what it would really be like, envious as far as it was possible for him to envy, because a lovely woman with his brain would have the universe by the tail, as tight a hold as you could get on the tail of this wildly bucking universe.

He'd—

And then his hands tightened on the steering wheel and he sat up straight as if the new idea had been a hot poker rammed into him.

"Why didn't I think of that sooner?" he said loudly. "My God, if she and I can come to some arrangement—and even if we can't, I'll find some way of forcing her—why, why, she is the perfect alibi! I never did confess that I killed her, not to the authorities, anyway. And they never found the slightest trace of her. So, if I come back to Earth with her and say, 'Gentlemen, here is my wife. It's as I told you, she'd disappeared, and it turns out that she had an accident, was hit on the head, lost her memory, and somehow found her way to Dante's Joy . . . well, sure it sounds like a romantic novel, but remember such a thing does happen every now and then. What, you don't believe it? Well, gentlemen, take her fingerprints, photograph the pattern of blood vessels in her retina, type her blood, give her an EEG . . . Ah . . .!"

Ah, but wouldn't all those identification marks be John Carmody's if her cells were mirror-images of his? Possibly. But there was also the chance that she might have her own. He had seen the photographs of all of them, more than once, and while he couldn't consciously reproduce them, it might be that his unconscious, which presumably held an exact file of them, would have reconstructed them in this Mary-thing.

But the EEG. If that gray pulse in her skull were

his . . .

Well, sometimes the pattern did change if the brain had been injured, and that disconcerting feature might be the thing to verify her story. But what about the zeta wave? That would indicate she was a male, and one glance from the authorities or anybody else would be enough to disprove that. Their next step would be to hold her for examination. The only time the zeta wave changed its rhythm from female to masculine or vice versa was when the subject changed sex. And examination would show that she was female, that her hormones were predominantly female. Or would it? If her cells were mirror-images of his, then the genes would be masculine, and perhaps the hormones, too. And what about an internal search? Would it expose female organs or would she internally be his duplicate?

For a second he was downcast, but his racing brain seized upon another alibi. Of course! She'd been on Dante's Joy during the seven days of the Chance, hadn't she? And that meant that she would probably undergo some strange change, didn't it? So, the discrepancies turned up in the laboratory, the brain waves, the hormones, even the contradictory internal organs, all these would be the result of her taking the Chance. She might attract considerable publicity, and she'd have to have a definite, unshakable story, but if she had his rigid will and iron nerves (and she would), then she'd stick it through and would demand her rights as a citizen of the Federation, and however reluctant, they'd have to allow her her freedom. After that, what a team she and John Carmody would make!

If she were inclined to be cooperative, though, why hadn't she kept her telephone contact with him, arranged to meet him? If she had his brain, wouldn't she have thought of the same thing he had?

He frowned and whistled softly through his teeth. There was always one possibility he couldn't afford to ignore, even if he didn't like it. Perhaps she was *not* a female John Carmody.

Perhaps she *was* Mary.

He'd have to find out when he met her. In the meantime, his original plans were changed only slightly, to adjust to the realities of the situation. The gun in his coat pocket would still be used to give him the original, the unique, thrill he had promised himself.

At this moment he dimly saw, through the purplish halo cast by a streetlamp, a man and a woman. The woman was clothed, but the man was nude. They were locked in each other's arms, the woman leaning against the iron pillar of the lamp, forced back by the man's passionate strength. Forced? She was cooperating to the full.

Carmody laughed.

At that harsh sound, slapping the heavy silence of the night across the face, the man jerked his head upwards, gazed wide-eyed at the Earthman.

It was Skelder, but a Skelder scarcely recognizable. The long features seemed to have become even more elongated, the shaven skull had sprouted a light fuzz that looked golden even in this dark light, and the body, which had shed the monkish robes, showed a monstrous deformity of leg, a crookedness halfway between a man's limb and an animal's. Almost it was as if the bones had become flaccid and during the softness the legs had begun growing backwards. The naked feet themselves were extended from the legs so that he walked on tiptoe, like a ballerina, and they seemed to be covered with a light yellow shell that glistened like a hoof.

"The goat's foot!" said Carmody loudly, unable to restrain his delight.

Skelder loosed the woman and turned completely towards Carmody, revealing in his face the definitely caprine lines and in his body the satyr's abnormal yet fascinating repulsiveness.

Carmody threw back his head to laugh again, but stopped, his mouth open, suddenly choking.

The woman was Mary.

While he stared at her, paralyzed, she smiled at him, waved her hand gaily, then took Skelder's hand and started to walk off into the darkness with him, her hips swaying exaggeratedly in the age-old streetwalker's rhythm. The effect was, or would have been in other circumstances, half-comical, because of the six-months fat around waist and buttocks.

At the same time, Carmody was struck with a feeling he'd never had before, a melting heart-beating-wildly sensation directed towards Skelder, mixed with a cold laughter at himself. He felt a terrible invincible longing for the monstrous priest but knew also that he was standing off to one corner and laughing sneeringly at himself. And underneath this was a slowly rising tide, threatening to overwhelm in time the other feelings, a not-to-be denied lust for Mary, tinged with a horror at himself for that lust and the strangeness of being ripped apart.

Against this host of invaders there was but one defense, and he took it immediately, springing out of the car, running around the hood, raising his gun, firing through the red mist that had replaced the purple.

Skelder, whinnying, threw himself to the ground and rolled over and over, a long bundle of gray-white laundry in the uncertain light, blown by the winds of desperation, disappearing in the darkness of the shadow of a tremendous flying buttress.

Mary whirled around, her open mouth a dark O in her pale face, her hands white birds imploring for mercy, then she dropped heavily.

And John Carmody staggered as he was struck one heavy blow after another in the chest and the stomach, felt his heart and viscera blasted apart, felt himself falling, falling, blood cascading all over him, falling into a darkness.

Someone had suddenly opened fire upon him, he thought, and this was the end and goodby and good riddance and the universe had the last laugh. . . .

And then he found he was awake, on his back, thinking these thoughts, staring straight up at the purple glove of the moon, a monstrous gauntlet flung into the sky by a monstrous knight. Come on, Sir John Carmody, fat little man clad in thin-skinned armor, enter the lists.

"Always game," he muttered to himself and rose unsteadily to his feet, his hands going unbelievingly over his body, groping for the great holes that he could have sworn were there. But they weren't; the flesh was unbroken, and his clothes were innocent of blood. Wet, yes, but with his sweat.

So that is how it is to die, he thought. It is horrible because it makes you feel so helpless, like a baby in the grip of an adult squeezing the life out of you, not because it hates you but because it must kill in the order of things, and squeezing is the only way it knows to carry out its order.

Stupefied at first, he was beginning to think clearly now. Obviously, those strange to-be-avoided-at-all-costs-even-to-losing-one's-temper sensations were those felt by Skelder and the Mary-thing, and the impact of the bullets tearing into her body had somehow been communicated to him, the shock so great that he'd lost consciousness or else his body had for that moment been fooled into thinking it was dead.

What if it had insisted on thinking so? Then he'd really be dead, wouldn't he?

Well, what of it?

"Don't fool yourself, Carmody," he said. "Whatever you do, don't fool yourself. You felt scared . . . to death. You called out for somebody to help you. Who? Mary? I don't think so, though it may have been. My mother? But her name is Mary. Well, it doesn't matter; the thing is that *I*, this thing up here" he said, tapping his skull, "was not responsible, it was John Carmody buried in me that used to cry for Mommy, in vain, because Mommy was usually out somewhere, working, or out with some man, anyway, always out, and I, I was alone and she wouldn't have come except to tell me what a little monster I was. . . ."

He walked over to Mary and turned her over.

"You won't bother me any more. It is too bad this had to happen, Mary, because we could have gone back to Earth, scot-free."

A cry from the darkness made him jump. He whirled, his gun ready, but saw no one. "Skelder?" he called.

For answer he got another terrible cry, more like an animals' than a man's.

The street ran straight for a hundred yards ahead of him, then turned at a right angle. On the corner was a tall building, each of whose six stories overhung the one beneath, making it look like a telescope whose small end was stuck in the ground. Out of its shadows dashed Ralloux, his face twisted in agony. Seeing Carmody, he slowed to a walk.

"Stand to one side, John!" he cried. "You don't

have to be in it, even if I do. Get out of it! I will take your place! I want to be in it! There's room for only one, and that space is reserved for me!"

"What the hell are you talking about?" growled Carmody. Warily, he kept his automatic pointed at the monk. No telling what maneuver this chaotic talk was supposed to cover up.

"Hell! I am taking about Hell. Don't you see that flame, feel it? It burns me when I am in it, and it burns others when I am not in it. Stand to one side, John, and let me relieve you of its pain. It will hold still long enough to consume me entirely, then, as I begin to adjust myself to it, it runs off and I must chase it down, because it settles around some other tortured soul and will not leave him unless I offer to dive into it again. And I do, no matter what the pain."

"You really are crazy," said Carmody. "You—"

And then he was screaming, had flung away his gun, was beating at his clothes, was rolling on the ground.

Just as suddenly as it had come, it was gone. He sat up, shaking, sobbing uncontrollably.

"God, I thought I was on fire!"

Ralloux had stepped forward onto the space occupied by Carmody and was standing there with his fists clenched and his eyes roaming desperately as if looking for some escape from his invisible prison. But seeing Carmody walking towards him, he fixed his gaze upon him and said, "Carmody, nobody deserves this, no matter how wicked! Not even you!"

"That's nice," replied Carmody, but there was little of the old mocking tone in his voice. He knew now *what* the monk was suffering from. It was the *how* that bothered him. *How* could Ralloux project a subjective hallucination into another person, and make that person feel it as intensely

as he did? The only thing he could think of was
that the sun's curious action developed
enormously in certain persons their ESP powers,
or, if he discounted that, that it could transmit the
neural activities of one person to another without
direct contact. No mystery in that, certainly; it
was within the known limitations of the universe.
Radio transmitted sound, in a manner of speaking,
just as TV did pictures; what you heard wasn't the
original person, but the effect was the same, or
just as good. However this was done, it was
effective. He remembered now how he had felt in
himself the bullets smashing into Mary, and had
experienced the terror of death—whether it was
his terror or Mary's didn't matter, and . . . would
everybody he met during the seven nights transmit to him their feelings, and he be helpless to
resist them?

No, not helpless; he could kill the authors of the
emotions, the generators and broadcasters of this
power.

"Carmody," shouted Ralloux, seemingly trying
by the loudness of his voice to deafen the pain of
the fire, "Carmody, you must understand that I do
not have to stand in this flame. No, the flame does
not follow me, I follow it and will not allow it to
escape. I *want* to be in hell.

"But you must not understand by that that I
have lost my faith, have rejected my religion, and
therefore have been flung headlong into the place
where the flames are. No, I believe even more
firmly in the teachings of the Church than before!
I cannot disbelieve! But . . . I voluntarily have
consigned myself to the flame, for I cannot believe
that it is right to doom ninety-nine percent of God-
created souls to hell. Or, if it is right, then I will be
among the wrong.

"Believing absolutely every iota of the Creed, I

still refuse to go to my rightful place among the blest, if such a place was ever reserved for me! No, Carmody, I range myself among the eternally damned, as a protest against divine injustice. If a fraction only are to be spared, or even if things were reversed, and ninety-nine point nine nine nine to the ninety-ninth place souls were to be saved, and one solitary soul were to have Hell all to itself, I should renounce Heaven and stand in the flames with that piteous soul, and I should say, 'Brother, you are not alone, for I am here with you to eternity or until God relents.' But you would not hear one word of blasphemy from me, nor one word of pleading for mercy. I should stand and burn until that one soul were freed of its torment and could go to join the ninety-nine point nine nine nine to the ninety-ninth place. I . . .''

''Raving mad,'' said Carmody, but he was not so sure. Though Ralloux's face was contorted in agony, the look of dissonance, the splitting effect, as of two warring forces, was gone. He now appeared, though in pain, to be at one with himself. Whatever it was that had seemed to tear him apart from within was gone.

Carmody could not think of what it was that could cause the cleavage to vanish, especially now when, under the circumstances, he would have thought it'd be even more stressed. Shrugging, he turned to walk back towards the car. Ralloux yelled something else, something warning yet at the same time entreating. The next second, Carmody felt that terrible searing heat at his back; his clothes seemed to smoke and his flesh gave a silent scream.

He whirled, firing his gun in the general direction of the monk, unable to see him because of the glare of flame.

Suddenly, the dazzling light and the scorching

heat were whisked away. Carmody blinked, re-adjusting his eyes to the dim purple, looking for Ralloux's body, thinking that the hallucination must have died with the projector of it. But there was only one corpse, Mary's.

Down the street, something black-looking slipped around the corner. A scream drifted back. Ralloux in hot pursuit of his torture and justification.

"Let him go," said Carmody, "as long as he takes the flame with him." But, he thought, it was the flame that was dragging the monk after it.

Now, now that Mary was dead, was a good time to determine for himself something about which he'd wondered very much.

It took him a little time. He had to get out of the car's toolbox a hammer and a dull chisel-like instrument that was probably used to pry the hub cap and the tire from the wheel. With these he managed to split her skull open. Putting the tools down, he picked up the flashlight and on his knees bent over close to the open cranium, holding his coat over him to give some cover for the beam. He pressed the light's button, shining it straight into the hole, his face close as possible to the brain. It was not, he knew, that he would be able to dis-tinguish between a man's brain, his, and a woman's brain, Mary's. But he was curious to see if she did have a brain or if, perhaps, there was just a large knot of nerves, a nexus for the tele-pathic orders that he gave it. If her life and her behavior were somehow dependent upon the workings of his own unconscious, then . . .

The light sprang into being.

There was no brain that he could see. Just what it was he had no time then to determine, only time to see a coiled shape, glittering red eyes, a gaping white-fanged mouth, and than a blur as it struck.

He fell back, the light falling from his hand and rolling away, its beam shining out into the night. He didn't care or even think about it, for his face had begun puffing up at once. It was like a balloon, swelling as if air were being pumped into it at a very fast rate. And at the same time, an intense pain spread from it, ran down his neck and into his veins. Fire invaded his body, spreading through him as if his blood were turning into molten silver.

There was no running away from this flame, as there had been from Ralloux's.

He screamed again and again, leaped to his feet, and, half out of his mind, drove his heel in hysterical fury and pain against the snake whose fangs had bitten into his cheek and whose tail merged into the cluster of nerves at the base of Mary's spine, growing from it. It had been living coiled up in her skull, surely waiting for the time when John Carmody would open its bony nest. And it had released its deadly poison into the flesh of the man who had created it.

Not until the horrible thing had been crushed beneath his heel, smashed into a blob from which two long curved broken fangs still stuck out, did Carmody cease. Then he fell to the ground beside Mary, the tissue of his body seeming like dry wood that had burst into flame, and the terror of dissolving forever wrenching a choked cry from a throat that had seemed too full of a roaring fear to utter ever again. . . .

There was one thought, the only shape in the chaos, the only cool thing in the fire. He had killed himself.

Somewhere in the moon-tinged purple mist a bell was ringing.

Far off, the referee was chanting slowly, "... *five, six, seven* ..."

Somebody in the crowd—Mary?—was scream-
ing, "Get up, Johnny, get up! You've got to win,
Johnny boy, get up, knock that big brute down!
Don't let him count you out, Joh-oh-oh-oh-neeee!"

"*Eight!*"

John Carmody groaned, sat up and tried, in vain,
to get on his feet.

"*Nine!*"

The bell was still ringing. Why should he get up
when he was saved by the bell?

But then why hadn't the ref quit counting?

What kind of a fight was this where the round
wasn't over even if the bell did ring?

Or was it announcing the opening of a new
round, not the closing of an old?

"Gotta get up. Fight. Whale hell outa that big
bastard," he muttered.

"*Nine*" still hung in the air, as if it had jelled in
the mist and was glowing there, faintly, violently
phosphorescent.

Who was he fighting? he asked, and he rose,
shakily, his eyes opening for the first time, his
body crouching, his left fist sticking out, probing,
his chin behind his left shoulder, his right hand
held cocked, the right that had once won him the
welterweight championship.

But there was no one there to fight. No referee.
No crowd. No Mary screaming encouragement.
Only himself.

Somewhere, though, there *was* a bell ringing.

"Telephone," he muttered, and looked around.
The sound came from the massive granite public
phone booth half a block away. Automatically, he
began walking towards it, noticing at the same
time what a headache he had and how stiff his
muscles were and how his guts writhed uneasily
within him, like sleepy snakes being awakened by
the heat of the morning sun.

He lifted the receiver. "Hello," he said, at the same time wondering why he was answering, knowing that it couldn't possibly be for him.

"John?" said Mary's voice.

The receiver fell, swung, then it and the phone box erupted into many fragments as Carmody emptied a clip at them. Pieces of the red plastic struck him in the face, and blood, real blood, his, trickled down his cheeks and dripped off his chin and made warm channels down the sides of his neck.

Stiffly, almost falling, he ran away, reloading his gun but saying over and over, "You stupid fool, you might have blinded yourself, killed yourself, stupid fool, stupid fool. To lose your head like that."

Suddenly, he stopped, put the gun back into his pocket, took out a handkerchief, and wiped the blood off his face. The wounds, though many, were only surface-deep. And his face was no longer swollen.

Not until then did he perceive the full significance of the voice.

"Holy Mother of God!" he moaned.

Even in his distress, one part of him stood off, cool observer, and commented that he'd not sworn since childhood, but now he was on Dante's Joy he seemed to be doing it at every turn. He had long ago given up using any blasphemous terms because, in the first place, almost everybody did, and he didn't want to be like everybody, and, in the second place, if you blasphemed, you showed you believed in what you were blaspheming against, and he certainly didn't believe.

The cool observer said, "Come on, John, get a grip on yourself. You're letting this shake you. We don't let anything shake us, do you?''

He tried to laugh, but succeeded only in bringing out a croak, and it sounded so horrible that he quit.

"But I killed her," he whispered to himself.

"Twice," he said.

He straightened up, put his hand in his pocket, gripped the gun's butt tightly. "OK, OK, so she can come back to life, so I'm responsible for it, too. So what? She can be killed, again and again, and when the seven nights are up, then she's done forever, and I'll be rid of her forever. So, if I have to litter this city from one end to the other with her corpses, I'll do it. Of course, there'll be a tremendous stink afterwards"—he managed a feeble laugh—"but I won't have to clean up the mess, let the garbage department do that."

He went back to the car but decided first to look at the old body of Mary.

There were huge pools of black blood on the pavement and bloody footprints leading off into the night, but the dead woman was gone.

"Well, why not?" he whispered to himself. "If your mind can produce flesh and blood and bone from the thin air, why can't it even more easily repair blasted flesh and blood and bone and re-spark the dead body? After all, that's the Principle of Least Resistance, the economy of Nature, Occam's razor, the Law of Minimum Effort. No miracles in this, John, old partner. And everything's taking place outside you, John. The inner you is secure, unchanged!"

He got into the car and drove on. Because the night seemed a little brighter, he drove a little faster. His mind, too, seemed to be coming out of the slowness induced in it by the recent shocks, and he was thinking with his former quick fluidity.

"I say, 'Arise from the dead,' and they arise," he said, "like Jairus' daughter. *Talitha cumi*. Am I not a god? If I could do this on some other planet, I would *be* a god. But here," he added, chuckling with some of his old vigor, "here I am just a bum, one of the boys, prowling the night with the other monsters."

He passed the street corner on which stood the statue of Ban Dremon, a great man of Kareena, but dead these hundred years. From the statue to the Temple of Boonta was a straight mile and a half. Normally, he'd have been able to see it clearly but now, despite the enormous globe of the moon, halfway up the sky, he could discern the temple only as a bulk looming in the purple, hinting vaguely that it was formed of stone and not of shade, that it was itself the substance, not the shadow.

There was something lying on the road in his path. He steered the car around it, then stopped it and got out to look. The thing resembled a man, but there was a stiff and hard quality about it and its rigid limbs that aroused his curiosity.

It was the life-sized statue of Ban Dremon, tumbled from its pedestal.

He looked up at the pedestal. Dremon—another one—stood there in what should have been an empty place.

"If curiosity killed the cat," he muttered, "I'd have been dead a million times."

He gripped the edge of the marble base, which was a foot above his head, and with one easy powerful graceful motion pulled himself up and then over. The next moment, gun in hand, he was eye to eye with the statue.

No statue. A man, a native.

He was in the same attitude as the dislodged Ban Dremon, the right arm held out in salute, the left holding a baton, the mouth open as if to give a command.

Carmondy touched the skin of the face, so much darker than the normal Kareenian's, yet not so dark as the bronze of the statue.

It was hard, smooth and cold. If it was not metal, it would pass for it. As near as he could determine in the uncertain light, the eyeballs had lost their light color. He pressed his thumbs in on them and found that they resisted like bronze. But when he stuck his finger in the open mouth, he felt the back part of the tongue give a little, as if the flesh beneath the metallic covering were still soft. The mouth, however, was dry as any statue's.

Now how, he thought, could a man turn his protoplasm, which had only a very minute trace of copper and, as far as he remembered, no tin, into a solid alloy? Even if those elements were present in large enough quantities to form bronze, what of the heat needed?

The only explanation he could think of was that the sun was furnishing the energy and the human body was furnishing the blueprints and, somehow, the machinery necessary. The psyche had free scope during the seven nights of the Chance; it utilized, however unconsciously, forces that must exist at all times around it but of which it had no knowledge.

If that were so, he thought, then man must be, potentially, a god. Or if god was a term too strong, then he must be a titan. A rather stupid titan, however, blind, a Cyclops with a cataract.

Why couldn't a man have this power at other times than the Night? This vast power to bend the universe to *his* will? Nothing would be impossible, nothing. A man could move from one planet to the next without a spaceship, could step from the Avenue of the Temple of Boonta on Dante's Joy some 10,000 light-years to Broadway in Manhattan on Earth. Could become anything, do anything, perhaps hurl suns through space as easily as a boy hurled a baseball. Space and time and matter would no longer be walls, would be doorways to step through.

A man could become anything. He could become a tree, like Mrs. Kri's husband. Or, like this man, a statue of bronze, somehow digging with invisible hands into the deep earth, abstracting minerals, fusing them without the aid of furnace walls and heat, with no knowledge of chemical composition, and depositing them directly in his cells without killing himself at once.

There was one drawback. Eventually, having gotten what he wanted, he would die. Though able to bring about the miracle of metamorphosis, he could not bring about the miracle of living on.

This half-statue would die, just as Skelder would die when his insane lust swelled that monstrous member which he'd grown to complete his lust, swelled it until it became larger than he and he, now its appendage, would find himself immobile, unable to do anything but feed himself and it and wear his heart out trying to pump blood to keep himself, and it, the parasite grown larger than the host, alive. He would die, just as Ralloux would die in the heat of an imagined flame of hell. They would all die unless they reversed the leap of mind and flow of flesh that hurtled them into such rich sea-changes.

And what, he thought, what about you, John Carmody? Is Mary what you want? Why should you? And what harm can her resurrection do to you? The others are obviously suffering, doomed, but you can see no doom to you in yourself giving birth to Mary again, no suffering. Why are you an exception?

I am John Carmody, he whispered. *Always have been, am, will be an exception.*

From behind and below him came a loud roar like a lion's. Men shouted. Another roar. A snarling. A man screamed as if in a death agony. Another roar. Then a strange sound as if a great bag had burst. Vaguely, Carmody felt that his ankles were wet.

He looked around in surprise and saw that the moon had gone down and the sun had risen. What had he been doing all night? Standing here on this pedestal dreaming away the purple hours.

He blinked and shook his head. He had allowed himself to be caught up in the bronze thoughts of this statue, had felt as it did, had slowed time and let it lap around him gently and dreamily, just as he had experienced the hard scarlet lust of Skelder, Mary's meltingness and liquid movements toward the satyr-priest, the impact of bullets tearing into her, her terror of death, of dissolvingness, and Ralloux's agony of flesh in his sheet of flame and agony of soul over man's damnation—just as he had felt all these, so now he had fallen prey to this creature's mineral philosophy. And might perhaps have ended as it had if something had not jarred him out of the fatal contemplation. Even now, coming out of his—coma?—he felt the temptation of the silent peace, of letting time and space flow by you, sweetly and softly.

But in the next second he came fully awake. He had tried to move away and found that he was anchored more than mentally. The finger he'd put into the statue's mouth was clamped tight between its teeth. No matter how violently he pulled away, he could not get it loose. There was no pain at all, only a numbness. This, he supposed, was because the circulation was cut off. Still, there should be some pain. If this sharing of thoughts had gone so far that his own flesh had changed . . .

The man-statue must not have been completely transformed; there must have been feeling left in the soft back part of the tongue. Reacting automatically—or maybe maliciously—it had slowly closed its jaws during the night, and when the sun saw the process of casting flesh into bronze complete, its jaws were almost shut. Now they would never open, for the soul within it was gone. Or, at least, Carmody could detect no thoughts or feeling emanating from it.

He looked around him, anxious not only because he did not know yet how to get free of this trap but because of his exposed position. What made things worse was that he'd dropped the gun. It lay at his feet, but, though he bent his knees and reached down for it with his left hand, his fingertips were several inches away.

Straightening up, he allowed himself the luxury of a firecracker-string of curses. It was ridiculous, this verbal explosion, of no practical use whatever. But he certainly felt a little less tense.

He looked up and down the street. Nobody in sight.

He looked down, remembering then that he'd had the impression his legs had been wetted during the night. Dried blood caked his sandals and stained the green and white stripes of his fashionably painted legs.

He muttered, "Oh, no, not again," thinking of the shower of blood in Mrs. Kri's kitchen. But a further examination showed him that Mary was not responsible. The stuff had spurted from wounds made in the body of a monster, which lay at the base of the pedestal, face up, its dead eyes staring at the purplish sky. It was twice as tall as

the average Kareenian and was covered with a
bluish feathery hair. Apparently its body hairs,
once no thicker than those of an Earthman, had
sprouted into a dense mat. Its legs and feet had
broadened, like an elephant's, to support its
weight. From the hips grew a long thick tapering
tail that would in time have resembled that of a
tyrannosaurus rex. The hands had degenerated
into talons, and the face had assumed a bestial
angle, slanting out, the jawbones thickening,
powered with great muscles, equipped with sharp
teeth. These were fastened down on an arm that it
had torn from some unlucky man, supposedly one
of those who had killed it during the fight that
must have taken place. But of the others there was
no sign except great stains on the street and
sidewalk.

Then suddenly six men walked around the
corner and halted staring at him. Though they
seemed unarmed, there was something in the
concentration of their expressions that alarmed
him. Violently he jerked upon his finger, again and
again until, panting, sweating, he could only look
into the rigid grin and fixed eyes of the statue and
swear at it. Once, he thought, this thing was
human and therefore could have been dealt with,
being of weak flesh and blood. But now, dead and
of unyielding, *uncaring* metal, it was past
argument, past cunning words.

For the first time, he saw that it was not only his
finger that had become bronze. His whole hand,
and even a part of his wrist, had solidified.

He ground his teeth in silent agony, and he
thought, *If they won't help me, and there's no
reason why they should, then I must sacrifice my
hand. That's logical; that is that if I want to get free
again. It is possible to get my knife from my pocket
and . . .*

One of the men said, mockingly, and as if he'd been reading Carmody's thoughts, "Go ahead, Earthman, cut it off! That is, if you can possibly endure to mutilate your precious flesh!"

For the first time, Carmody recognized the man as Tand.

He had no chance to reply, for the others began to jeer, making fun of his having been caught in such a ridiculous way, asking him if he always made a public spectacle of himself like this. They hooted and laughed and slapped their thighs and each other's backs in typically uninhibited Kareenian fashion.

"This is the pipsqueak who thought he would kill a god!" howled Tand. "Behold the great deicide, caught like any baby with his finger in the jam jar!"

Keep cool, Carmody, they can't touch you. Sticks and stones may break your bones, but . . .

That was a fine thing to say, and it meant exactly nothing. He was tired, tired, his proud bristling-forward-bearing gone with the strength that seemed to have drained from his body. If his hand did not hurt because it was a frozen metal, his feet certainly made up for it. They felt as if he'd been standing on them for days.

Suddenly he felt panic. How long had he been upon this pedestal? How much time had flowed by? How much time did he have left before the Night of Light was over!

"Tand," said one of the men, "do you honestly think that this would-be statue might have the power?"

"Look at what he has done so far," replied Tand. He spoke to Carmody: "You were a little late, friend. The god Yess gave up the ghost on the first day of the Chance. Before he died, he told me to find six others who would qualify as lovers of the

Great Mother and fathers of the babe."

"So you lied to me!" snarled Carmody. "You
weren't going to Sleep, then?"

"If you will recall my exact words," said Tand,
"you will see that I did not lie. I told you the truth
but ambiguously. You chose the particular
interpretation."

"Friends," spoke another man, "I think we are
wasting our time here and giving the Enemy an
advantage we may not be able to overcome. This
man, despite his tremendous power, which I can
sense in him even without probing—this man, I
say, is one of the dirty-souled. In fact, I doubt if he
does have a soul. Or, if he does, it is such a
fragment, a rag, a minuscule, a tiny little thing
cowering in the deep and the darkness, afraid to
have anything to do with the body, allowing the
body to operate as it will, refusing to take any
responsibility, refusing to admit even its own
existence."

The others seemed to find this very funny, for
they laughed uproariously and added remarks of
their own.

Carmody trembled. Their amused contempt
struck him like six hammers, one after the other,
then all at once, then one after the other, like an
anvil chorus. It was intensified many times
because he shared in it at the same time that he
felt its impact, as if he were both transmitter and
receiver. He who had always thought he was *above*
being affected by anyone's contempt or laughter
had suddenly found that it was not altitude that
protected him but a barrier built up *around* him.
And the defense had crumbled.

Wearily, hopelessly, he began jerking on the
finger, then, as he saw six other strangers walking
down the street towards him, he gave up. These
men were also unarmed and walked with the same

proud bearing possessed by the other group. They, too, stopped before him but ignored the first-comers.

"Is this the man?" said one.

"This is the man," replied another.

"Should we release him?"

"No. If he wishes to be one of us, he will release himself."

"But if he wishes to be one of *them* he will also release himself."

"Earthman," said a third, "you are being honored above all others—indeed you are the first man not born on this planet ever to be so honored."

"Come," said a fourth, "let us go to the Temple and there lie with Boonta and so father Algul, the true prince of this world."

Carmody began to feel less humiliated. Apparently, he was important, not only to the second group but to the first. Though, if the first wanted him for something, they had a strange way of enlisting him.

What made the procedure so peculiar was that no man in the two groups was distinguished by any conventional marks of good or evil. All were handsome, vigorous, and seemingly self-confident. The only difference in their bearing was that the first, those who spoke for Yess, seemed to be having a good time, and were not afraid to lose their dignity in laughter. The second were uniformly grave and somewhat stiff.

They must need me badly, he thought.

"What will you give me?" he said very loudly, encompassing both groups in one glance.

The men of the first group looked at each other, shrugged their shoulders, and Tand said, "We will give you nothing you can't give yourself."

The spokesman for the newcomers, a tall young man, almost too handsome, said, "When we go into the Temple and there lie with Boonta as the Dark Mother, and father Algul her Dark Son, you will experience an ecstasy that cannot be described because you have never felt anything like it before. And during the years that it will take the babe to grow into manhood and godhood, you will be one of his regents, and there will be nothing in this world denied you—"

"Even," broke in Tand, "the fear of these others killing you so they may not have to share any of the riches which they cannot possibly spend during their lifetime. For it is true that when the seven evil fathers triumph, they always plot against each other after Algul is born. They are forced to, because they cannot trust each other. And it has always happened that only one survives, and when Algul comes to manhood, he kills that one, because he cannot endure having a mortal father."

"What is to prevent Algul from being killed by one of his fathers?" asked Carmody.

Even in the violet light, he could see the men of the second group turn pale. They looked at each other. "Though he is a baby who must be fed and have his diapers changed, Algul is yet a god," said Tand. "That is, being a god, he is the sum and essence of the spirit of those who created him. And, as most men wish for immortality, he, representing them, is immortal. That is, he would live forever if his creators did, too. But, being evil, he cannot trust his fathers, and so they must die. And when they do, he begins to age and eventually dies. Though potentially immortal, he is dead the day he is born because the seeds of evil are in him, and the seeds flower into distrust and hate."

"This is all very fine," said Carmody. "Why, then, does Yess, the supposedly good god, also age and die?"

The men of Algul laughed, and their leader said, "Well, spoken, Earthman."

Patiently, as if talking to a child, Tand replied, "Yess, though a god, is also a man, a being of flesh and blood. As such he is limited, and he works within the bounds set for flesh and blood. Like all men, he must die. Furthermore, he is the sum and essence of the predominating spirit of the people who lived at the time he was born—or created, whichever term you prefer. Those who Sleep have as much to do with the formation and tempering of his body and spirit as we seven Wakers do. The Sleepers dream, and the collective force of their dreaming decides which god shall be born during the Night, and also what his spirit—or what you call his personality—shall be. If the inclination of the people who Sleep has been towards evil during the years preceding the Night, then it is likely that Algul will be born. If towards good, then it is likely that Yess will be born. We would-be fathers are not actually the determining factors. We are the agents, and the Sleepers, the two billion people of our world, are the will."

Tand paused, stared hard at Carmody as if trying to impress his sincerity upon him, and said, "I will be frank. You are so important partly because you *are* an Earthman; a man from another star. Only lately have we Kareenians become very much aware that the Great Mother, or God, or the Prime Cause, or whatever you wish to term the Creator of the universe, is not restricted in Her interest to our little cloud of dust, that She has scattered Her creatures everywhere.

"Therefore, the Sleepers, knowing that man is not alone, that he has blood-brothers everywhere

that life may be, outwards to infinity and to
eternity, wish to have as a father one of these
strangers from the stars. Yess, reborn, will not be
the old Yess. He will be as different from the old
man who died, his predecessor, as any baby is
from his father. He will be, we hope, part alien,
because of his alien heritage. And during his
princehood over us, he will enable us to understand and become one with these strangers from
the stars, and we will be better men because of
him and his heritage. That is one reason, Carmody,
why we desire you."

Tand pointed at his Enemies.

"And these six want you also as seventh, but not
for quite the same reason. If you are one of the
fathers of Algul, then perhaps Algul may extend
his dominion past this planet and to the stars. And
they, through Algul, will share in this cosmic
loot."

Carmody felt hope—and craving—surge within
him, bringing him strength from somewhere in his
exhausted flesh. To take for yourself the richest
planets, as you would the biggest diamonds for a
necklace! String them around your neck! With the
vast powers he would undoubtedly have as Algul's
regent, he could do anything! Nothing barred!

It was then that the second group must have
decided that the right moment had come, for they
suddenly launched at him the collective force of
their feelings. And he, being wide open, reeled
beneath them.

Dark, dark, dark . . .

Ecstasy . . .

He, John Carmody, would be forever John
Carmody as he now knew him, inviolate, strong,
defiant, bending or destroying anything in the way
of what he wanted. No danger here of his changing, of becoming something other than what he

now was. Body, mind, and soul, he would in the flame of this dark ecstasy become hard as a diamond, resisting all change, permanent, forever John Carmody. The race of man might die around him, suns grow cold, planets slow and fall into their parent suns, but he, John Carmody, would travel outwards with the expanding universe, landing upon freshly born planets, living there until they grew old and died, then setting out again. And always and forever himself, today and tomorrow, unchanging, the same hard-and-bright-as-a-diamond John Carmody.

Then the first group opened themselves up. But instead of launching at him their concentrated essence, like a spear, they merely lowered the wall and allowed him to attack or do whatever he wished. There was not the slightest hint of assault or force, nor the feeling the fathers of Algul gave of withholding something deep within themselves in reserve. They were wide open and transparent to the depths of their beings. Nothing withheld. Do with us what you may.

John Carmody could no more resist attacking than a hungry tiger who sees a goat tethered to a tree.

Light, light, light . . .

Ecstasy . . .

But not the hardening, setting-forever ecstasy of the others. This was threatening, frightening, for it exploded him, dissolved, sent him flying in a thousand bits outwards.

Screaming silently, in mental anguish, he tried to collect the hundred thousand fragments, to bring them back, fused again into the image of the old John Carmody. The pain of destroying himself was unendurable.

Pain? It was the same as the ecstasy. How could pain and ecstasy be the same thing?

He didn't know. All he did know was that he had recoiled from the seven of Yess. Their lack of walls was their defense. Not for anything would he again attack them. Destroy John Carmody?

"Yes," said Tand, though Carmody had not spoken. "You must die first; you must dissolve that image of the old John Carmody, and build a new image, a better one, just as the newly born Yess will be better than the old god who died."

Abruptly, Carmody turned from both groups and, reaching in his pocket, drew out the switchknife. His thumb pressed the button in the handle and the blade shot out like a blue-gray tongue, like the tongue of the snake that had bitten him.

There was but one way to get loose from the bronze jaws.

He did it.

It hurt, but not so badly as he thought it would. Nor did he bleed so much as he had expected. He mentally ordered the blood vessels at the end of the stump to close. And they, like flowers at the approach of night, obeyed.

But the work of sawing through flesh and bone left him panting as if he'd run a mile. His legs trembled, and the faces below him blurred, and ran into two broad white featureless faces. He couldn't last long.

The leader of the men of Algul stepped forward and held out his arms. "Jump, Carmody," he called joyfully. "Jump! I will catch you; my arms are strong. Then we will scatter this weak, sniveling brood, and go to the temple and there—"

"Wait!"

The woman's voice, coming from behind them, loud and commanding, yet at the same time musical, froze them.

He looked up, over the heads of the men.

Mary.

Mary, alive and whole again, as he had seen her before he emptied his gun into her face. Unchanged, except for one thing. Her belly was swollen enormously; it had grown since he had last seen her and was now ripe to give birth to the life within her.

The leader of the men of Algul said to Carmody, "Who is this Earthwoman?"

Carmody, standing on the edge of the base, ready to leap down, hesitated and opened his mouth to reply. But Tand spoke first.

"She is his wife. He killed her upon Earth and fled here. But he created her the first night of the Sleep."

"Ahhhh!"

The seven of Algul sucked in their breath and drew back.

Carmody blinked at them. Apparently, Tand's information held implications he didn't see.

"John," she said, "it is no use your murdering me again and again. I always rise. I always will. And I am ready to bear the child you did not want; he will be here within the hour. At dawn."

Quietly, but with a tremor in his voice that betrayed the great strain he felt, Tand said, "Well, Carmody, which shall it be?"

"Which?" said Carmody, sounding stupid even to himself. Automatically, he tried to rub his finger against his nose in the old nervous gesture, but drew the stump of his arm back just in time.

"Yes," said the leader of Algul, stepping back beneath the pedestal. "Which shall it be? Shall the baby be Yess or Algul?"

"So that is it!" said Carmody. "The economy of the Goddess, of Nature, of What-have-you. Why create a baby when one is at hand?"

"Yes," said Mary loudly, her voice still musical but demanding, like a bronze bell. "John, you do

not want our baby to be as you were, do you? A
frozen dark soul? You do want him to be of heat
and light, don't you?"

"Man," said Tand, "don't you see that you have
already chosen who the babe shall be? Don't you
know that she has no brain of her own, that what
she says is what you think, really think and truly
desire in the depths of your soul? Don't you know
that you are putting her words into her mouth,
that her lips move as you direct them?"

Carmody almost fainted, but not from weakness
and hunger of body.

Light, light, light . . . Fire, fire, fire . . . Let
himself dissolve. Like the phoenix, he would rise
again. . . .

"Catch me, Tand," he whispered.

"Jump," said Tand, laughing loudly. A roar of
laughter and of cries that sounded like hallelujahs
burst from the men of Yess.

But the men of Algul shouted in alarm and
began running away in all directions.

At the same time the dark purplish haze began
to grow lighter, to turn pale violet. Then,
suddenly, the ball of fire was above the horizon,
and the violet light was white again, as if someone
had yanked aside a veil.

And those of the men of Algul who were still in
sight staggered, fell to the ground, and died in the
midst of convulsions that threw them from side to
side and that broke their bones. For a time they
thrashed like chickens with their heads cut off,
then, bloody-mouthed, lay still.

"Had you chosen otherwise," said Tand, still
embracing Carmody after his leap downwards,
"we would be lying in the dust of the street."

They began walking towards the temple,
forming a circle around Mary, who walked slowly
and stopped now and then as the pains struck her.

Carmody, walking behind her, gritted his teeth
and moaned softly, for he too felt the pangs. He
was not alone; the others were biting their lips and
holding their hands tight upon their bellies.

"And what happens afterwards to her—to it?"
he whispered to Tand. He whispered because,
even if he knew that this Mary-thing was not self-
conscious, was really manipulated by his
thoughts—and now by those of the others, too—he
had become suddenly sensitive to the feelings of
other people. He did not want to take a chance on
hurting her, even if such a thing did not seem
possible.

"Her work will be done when Yess is born," said
the Kareenian. "She will die. She is dying now,
began dying when the Sleep ended. She is being
kept alive by our combined energies and by the
unconscious will of the infant within her. Let us
hurry. Soon the wakers will be coming from their
vaults, not knowing if this time Yess or Algul won,
not knowing if they must rejoice or weep. We must
not leave them long in doubt, but must get to the
Temple. There we will enter the holy chamber of
the Great Mother, will lie in mystical love and
procreation with Her, in that act that cannot be
described but can only be experienced. The
swollen body of this creation of your hate and
your love will deliver the baby and will die. And
then we must wash and wrap the baby and have
him ready to show the adoring people."

He squeezed Carmody's hand affectionately,
then tightened his grip as the pangs struck again.
But Carmody did not feel the bone-squeezing
strength because he was fighting his own pain, hot
and hard in his own belly, rising and falling in
waves, the terrible hurt and awful ecstasy of
giving birth to divinity.

That pain was also the light and fire of himself

still exploding and dissolving into a million pieces. But now there was no panic, only a joy he had never known in accepting this light and fire and in the sureness that he would at the end of this destruction be whole, be one as few men are.

Through this pain, this joy, this sureness was a lacing of determination that he would pay for what he had done. Not pay in the sense that he would forever be plunged into self-punishment, into gloom and remorse and self-hate. No, that was a sickness, that was not the healthy way to pay. He must make up for what he had been and had done. Now he believed that this universe, though it still ran like a hard cold machine and presented no really sweet-smiling face to mankind, this world could be changed.

What means he would employ and just what sort of goal he would choose, he did not know just now. That would come later. At this moment, he was too busy carrying out the final act of the drama of the Sleep and the Awakening.

Suddenly he saw the faces of two men he had never expected to see any more. Ralloux and Skelder. The same, yet transfigured. Gone was the agony on Ralloux's face, replaced by serenity. Gone was the harshness and rigidity on Skelder's face, replaced by the softness of a smile.

"So you two came through all right," Carmody said throatily.

Wonderingly, he noted that one was still clad in his monk's robes but that the other had cast them off and was dressed in native clothes. He would have liked to find out just why this man accepted and the other rejected, but he was sure that both had their good and sufficient reasons, otherwise they would not have survived. The same look was on both their faces, and at the monent it did not matter which path either had chosen for his future.

"So you both came through," Carmody murmured, still scarcely able to believe it.

"Yes," replied one of them, which Carmody couldn't determine, so dreamlike did everything seem, except for the reality of the waves of pain within his bowels. "Yes, we both came through the fire. But we were almost destroyed. On Dante's Joy, you know, you get what you really want."

A FEW MILES

Brer John Carmody was bent over, pulling out the carrots from the garden soil, when he heard his name called.

He straightened up, saying "Ough!" as he did so and putting the palm of his hand to his aching back. He waited for Brer Francis because Brer Francis had not told him to come but had merely named him.

Brer John was a short heavily built man with a square face, one drooping eyelid and a shock of blueblack hair that bristled like porcupine quills. Lay brothers of the order of St. Jairus, to which he belonged, did not shave their heads. He wore an ankle-length robe of maroon fiberglass and maroon plastic sandals. A broad plastleather belt circled his bulging stomach, and from it hung a cross and a small maroon book.

Brer Francis, a tall thin man with a narrow face and a ski-slope nose, halted before the fat man. He pointed at the bunch of carrots in the fat man's hand and said, "What happened to those, Brer?"

"Rabbits," said Brer John. He looked upwards

and gestured furiously, though it was evident by his half-grin that his anger was mock.

"Rabbits! How do you explain that, heh? We live in cities that are completely roofed over and walled, and the walls go deep into the ground. Yet rabbits and mice and rats manage to get under the walls and raid our gardens and pantries. And squirrels somehow climb into our trees, and birds, who must squeeze themselves through the interstices of the molecules of the roof, nest on every tree. And insects, who don't know how to burrow, only to fly or hop, are here at hand."

He swatted at a fly and said, "And on my nose, too. That pesky creature of Satan has been tickling my bulbous proboscis for the last past hour. However, I have refused to kill it on the grounds that it might have been sent to tempt me to anger and violence. And it has nearly succeeded, too, I might add."

"Brer John, you talk too much," said Brer Francis. "Far too much. However, I did not come here to reprimand you for that . . ."

"Though you have stayed to do so," said Brer John; and then, quickly, before Brer Francis, reddening face exploded into words, "Forgive me for that last remark. And the previous ones, too. As you said, I talk too much. It is a very grave fault, or, if not a fault, at least a characteristic to be frowned upon, and . . ."

"Brer John!" said Brer Francis. "Will you keep quiet long enough to allow me to tell you why I am here? I did not come out here to satisfy my curiosity, you know."

"Forgive me," said Brer John. "I'm all ears."

"The bishop wishes to see you. At once," said Brer Francis very quickly as if he were afraid Brer John would interrupt if he breathed between words.

Brer John turned and threw the rabbit-damaged carrots into a cart and the good carrots into another. Then he set off towards the main building, a long low structure of pressed earth-blocks painted a dark maroon. Its high-pitched roof was raised several feet above the walls by thin poles, and a grillework of maroon metal filled the space between roof and wall. The entrances had no doors, for it was the tradition of the order never to have a locked door, and here in the controlled environment of the enclosed city, it was not necessary to keep out the weather. The roof was there only to give privacy from people flying overhead.

Brer John entered the main building and, without bothering to clean his dirty hands and face, went straight to the office of the Father Superior. When the chief called, no man loitered.

The rooms within the building did have doors, though they were unlocked. As the door to the Father Superior's office was closed, Brer John knocked.

"Come in!" said a voice within, and Brer John, not for the first time since he had joined the order as a lay brother, entered the large triangular room. He stood at the base of the triangle, and the Father Superior sat behind a large translucent desk at the apex of the triangle. The top of the desk was loaded with piles of tapes, a stenowriter, and a vuephone. The Father Superior, however, was not dwarfed by the mountainous mass before him; he was a very tall man.

He was broad-faced with long rusty-red hair and a full rusty-red beard, which he and only he in the "inn" was entitled to wear. He was puffing on a huge Havana cigar.

Brer John, who had given up smoking for a month as a penance for one of his several sins, sniffed hungrily at the green smoke roiling around him.

The Father Superior flicked off the toggle of the stenowriter into which he had been dictating.

"Good morning, Brer John," he said. He waved a cartridge at the fat man.

"I have here an order which just came in via spaceship. You are to go to the planet of Wildenwooly at once and report to the Bishop of Breakneck. We will miss you in more ways than one, but we love you. God speed you, and our blessing."

Brer John's blue eyes widened. He did not move, and for the first time in a long time he could not talk.

The Father Superior, however, had closed his eyes and leaned back on his tiling chair while he dictated out of one corner of his mouth and puffed cigar smoke out of the other. It was evident that he considered that he had given all orders necessary.

For a moment Brer John stared at the long ash on the end of the Father Superior's cigar. Obviously, the ash was just about to fall, and he wondered if it would fall on the long red beard beneath it.

However, the Father Superior, without opening his eyes, removed the cigar and flicked the ashes onto the stone floor.

Brer John shrugged and left the room, but the wonder was still on his face.

Outside the room, he hesitated for a few minutes. Then, sighing, he walked outside and crossed the garden to Brer Francis.

"Brer Francis, may I speak?"

"Yes," said the thin man. "If you confine yourself to the matter at hand and do not take the opportunity to run off at the tongue as usual."

"Where is Wildenwooly?" said Brer John with a tone that bordered on the pathetic.

"Wildenwooly? It is, I believe, the fourth planet of Tau Caesari. Our order has a church and an inn there," he said.

Brer John did not think that the order had a tavern on the planet. The dwellings of the order were customarily called inns because they had been so designated by the founder, St. Jairus.

"Why do you ask?" continued Brer Francis.

"I have just been ordered to go to Wildenwooly by the Father Superior." He looked hopefully at the other man.

But Brer Francis merely said, "Then you must go at once. God speed you, Brer John. Go with my love. I may have reprimanded you many times, but it has been for your good."

"I thank you for your love," said Brer John. "But I am at a loss."

"Why?"

"Why? To whom do I go to get a ticket for berth on a spaceship? Who gives me a draft on the order for travel expenses? What about a letter of introduction to the Bishop at Breakneck? I don't even know his name. I don't even know when a spaceship might leave for Wildenwooly or how long I might have to wait for it or where to wait for it. I don't even know where the spaceport is!"

"You talk too much," said Brer Francis. "You have been given all the orders you will get. Or need. As for the spaceport, it's only a few miles outside the city. And the inn on Wildenwooly is only a few miles outside the city of Breakneck. With good luck you might be there by this afternoon."

"That's all you have to say?" said Brer John unbelievingly.

"Only a few miles," repeated Brer Francis. "You must leave at once. Orders, you know."

Brer John looked hard at Brer Francis. Was he

imagining or was a grin about to break out on that long lean rarely smiling face? No, he must be mistaken. The face was grim and unmoving.

"Don't be distressed," said Brer Francis. "I was once given just such an order. And so have others."

Brer John's eyes narrowed. "This is a test of some sort?"

"The order wouldn't send you forty thousand light years away *just* to test you," said Brer Francis. "You are wanted and needed at Wildenwooly. So go."

Brer John Carmody seldom hesitated. Once he had decided upon a course, and it did not customarily take him long to decide, he acted. Now he walked swiftly to the communal shower, entered the room, removed his robe, revealing a white body and legs painted black to the groin. He inserted the robe into a rectangular hole in the wall, and then he entered the shower. He did not stay long, for though the order had installed an entirely automatic shower, it had insisted that only cold water would be provided for the discomfort of its members. Once a month the order was treated to a warm shower.

He stepped out, shivering, and dried off in a blast of air, also cold, which blew from vents in the wall. Then he took out his robe from a receptable below the one in which he had inserted the robe and put it on. And he gave a short thanksgiving that the order had at least installed a cleaning apparatus. When he got to the frontier planet of Wildenwooly, he would have to wash his clothes by hand. And probably, considering his humble position, the robes of the other members, too.

Putting on his robe, he went to his cell. This was a room, six feet by seven feet, with luminescent

walls, a crucifix attached to the wall, a hammock
which was rolled into a bag during the day, a desk
which folded down from the wall, and a niche in
the wall where he kept all his worldly possessions.
These, a missal, a history of the Church from 1
A.D. to 2260 A.D., a Latin grammar, and a Life of
Saint Jairus, he put into the sack formed by the
hood hanging down over his shoulders. Then he
got down onto his knees before the crucifix, said,
"Lord and Master, let me know what I am doing.
Amen," rose and walked to the door of his cell.
Just before leaving, and without breaking his
stride, he reached out and took a long shepherd's
staff from its peg on the wall. All lay brothers
were required to take that crook with them when
they went into the outside world, if the encapsul-
ated city of Fourth of July could be called the outside world.

It was past noon, and the Arizona summer sun
was sliding downhill. Brer John found the
temperature only a little warmer than inside the
inn. The plastic roof over the city was, at this time
of the day, opaqued enough to reflect most of the
rays. Even so, Brer John looked forward to getting
outside the walls, even if it meant being immersed
in the staggering heat of midsummer Arizona. He
had long felt cooped up, and, though he had never
openly complained, he had felt the urge to do so.
And had accordingly confessed and made his
penance.

For a moment he paused. He knew there was a
spaceport near Fourth of July, but he had no idea
in which direction. So he went to a cop.

The cop was one of the new types, a Mark LIV.
Its face and body were made of a tantalum alloy,
but the eyes were of protoplasm, copied from
those of some long-dead corpse and grown in the
laboratory. And it had a semi-independent action,

for the brain in its metallic belly was not a mechanism controlled remotely from headquarters below the ground. Its brain was a grey protoplasmic shape like a man's, twice as large and half as intelligent. It could not carry on a decent conversation, much less an indecent one, but it could handle its job quite well, and it could not be bribed or influenced. And, unlike its predecessors, it got around on legs instead of wheels. Its feet were flat.

Brer John looked at the name on its chest, and then said, "Officer O'Malley, where is the space-port?"

"What spaceport?" replied the cop. The voice was loud and toneless and sent shivers down Brer John's spine. It was like talking with a man deprived of his soul.

"Ah, yes, I forgot," said Brer John. "It's been so long since I talked to a cop. And they were usually shooting at me. I must ask direct questions, *n'est-ce pas?*"

"*N'est-ce pas?*" echoed the cop. "What language do you speak? I will refer you to Headquarters," and the cop reached with a huge grey-scaled hand for the microphone attached to the side of its head.

"I speak American," said Brer John hastily. "I wish to know how to get to the Fourth of July Spaceport from here."

"Are you going by tubeway or private car?" said the cop.

Brer John put his hand into the huge pockets of his robe and then withdrew them, empty. "Shank's mare," he said sadly.

"You told me you spoke American," said the cop. "Please speak American."

"I mean, I am going to the spaceport on foot," said Brer John. "I am walking."

The cop stood silent for a moment. Its face was expressionless as metal, but Brer John, who had a vivid imagination, thought he saw puzzlement film the features and then flit away.

"I can't tell you how to get there if you walk," said the cop. "Just a moment. I'll refer you to Headquarters."

"That won't be necessary," said Brer John hastily. He could visualize himself going into a lengthy explanation to Headquarters just why he was *walking* to a city exit from this distant point. And perhaps being delayed to wait while a human cop was sent to investigate him on the spot.

"I can follow the tubeway to its end," he said. He pointed to a line of tall metal rods, each of which was surmounted by an enormous loop of metal.

"Which way do I go to the exit closest to the spaceport? Fourth of July," he added.

The cop was silent for two seconds. Then it said, "You don't mean on the date of the Fourth of July? You mean the spacesport called Fourth of July, right?"

"Right," said Brer John.

The cop pointed to the closest tubeway. "Take a North car on Number Ten Tubeway. Get off at the exit to the city. Go outside the city. Take a taxi from there to the spaceport of Fourth of July."

"Thank you," said Brer John.

"You're welcome to the services of the city," said the cop.

Brer John hurried away. The living eyes in the dead face made him uncomfortable. But he could not help wondering if the cop was truly incorruptible. Ah, if it had been the old John Carmody talking to the cop, then things might have been different! Not a humble lay brother of St. Jairus asking directions, but the cleverest crook in the cosmos trying to see if finally here was a cop who couldn't be bribed, tricked or coerced.

"John Carmody," said Brer John to himself, "you're a long way from being pure in thought. And you've just added another penance to suffer. God preserve you! You've barely left the cloister, just ventured into the outside world, and already you're thinking of the old days as the good old days. Yet you were a monster, John Carmody, a hideous monster who should have been obliterated. Not at all the lovable rogue you were picturing yourself as."

He walked below the tubeway. Overhead, a bus shot through the loops at the ends of the poles, then paused a hundred yards ahead of him and discharged its passengers. He wished he had a deci-credit, vulgarly called "dessy," as fare. One decicredit would take him to the city exit and spare him the ten miles of shank's mare he had ahead of him.

He sighed, and said, "John, if wishes were horses..." and then he chuckled, visioning himself on a horse in this city. What a panic that would create! People running to stare at this monster seen now only on tridi or in the zoo! People running away in fright, the cops being called, and he ... hauled off to jail. And guilty not only of secular crime but of ecclesiastical. A humble lay brother anything but humble, prancing pridefully on a horse, or was it a horse that pranced? Guilty of public display, inciting to riot and God knew what else.

He sighed again and began walking. Fortunately, he thought, a man was able to walk from one end of the city to the other if he followed the narrow path created by the poles of the tubeway. Unlike the old days, when there had been streets for a man to walk on, the city was one maze of narrow yards with high fences and a single family room in the middle of each strip of fence and grass, the main quarters being underground. And underneath the houses, the factory or offices where the house dwellers earned their living. If you could call it living.

He walked and walked, while overhead the citizens traveled in the tubeway bus or flew in their private cars (rented to them by the clutch to which they belonged). Once a robin flew over him, and Brer John said, "Ah, John, if you believed in the pernicious doctrine of transmigration, you would wish to enter the cycle of karma again as a bird. But of course, you don't, so why sigh for the ecstasy of wings? It is your aching feet that make you think these dangerous thoughts. Go, John, go! Plod on like the weary ass that you are."

He walked for perhaps two more miles and then to his delight he saw a park open up before him. It was one of the two large parks afforded by the city, where the citizens flocked to get a facsimile of the outdoors world. Here were winding dirt paths and rocks heaped up to resemble small mountains and caves in the mountains and trees and birds and squirrels and lakes on which swans and geese and ducks swam and every now and then a fish leaped up from beneath the surface.

It was, compared to the geometric jungle from which he had just come, a paradise. Alas! this paradise had no snakes, but it had too many Adams and Eves. They swarmed everywhere with their little Abels and Cains, lolling, drinking, screaming, bellowing, lovemaking, quarreling, laughing, scowling.

Appalled, Brer John halted. He had been shut up so long inside the walls of Our Lady of Fourth of July that he had forgotten the manswarm.

He paused, and at the same time he heard a sound that shut up the uproar. A fire siren whooping in the distance.

He turned and saw the smoke pouring from an eathouse on the edge of the park. And overhead, shooting through the air, the red needle shape of a fire engine.

Brer John ran towards the eathouse. It was one of the few aboveground dining places in the city, a building constructed to resemble the Early American loghouse. Here the picknickers could go to eat in "atmosphere" and get away from the vast and dismally clean and bright cafeterias of the clutches where they habitually ate.

The owner of the YE OLDE ARIZONA LOGHAUS stood in the doorway and barred Brer John's entrance.

"No looting!" he shouted. "I'll kill the first man that tries to come in!" He held in his big meaty hands a butcher's cleaver.

Brer John halted and said, between gasps, "I've no wish to loot, my friend. I ran to see if I could help."

"No help needed," said the owner, still holding his cleaver poised. "I had a fire a couple of years ago, and the mob broke in and stole everything before the cops could get here. I'll have no more of that."

Brer John felt himself pushed from behind. He looked over his shoulder and saw that he was being urged forward by the pressure of many men and women behind him. Obviously, they wanted to burst in and steal everything they could lay their hands on and wreck the eathouse before the police arrived. It was the custom when anything broke down in the city, an expression of the resentment they felt at their hemmed-in lives and at the non-human representatives of the authorities.

The owner stepped back inside the doorway and shouted, "So help me, I'll split the skull of the first man or woman who tries to get in!"

The mob yelled with fury, and it snarled at him for having the affrontery to spoil their sport. It thrust forth a pseudopod of force, and Brer John found himself, willy-nilly, the vanguard and vicar of violence.

Luckily, at that moment, the shadow of the fire engine fell on the crowd, and the next moment a spray of foam drenched them. They fell back, panting, the oxygen suddenly cut from around their noses and mouths. Brer John himself almost strangled before he could fight his way out of the foam that roiled hipdeep around him.

Immediately afterwards, the copcars, sirens screaming, slid down out of the sky. And the cops poured out of the cars, light gleaming from the metal rings of their legs and round metal chests and the living black eyes, wet in the dead metal faces, moving back and forth. Their voices roared above the crowd's, and in a short time they had returned order to the park. The firemen walked into the eathouse, and in ten minutes came out. Most of them took off in their fire engines; one company stayed behind to clean up the foam. A lone cop recorded a report from the owner, and then he, too, left.

The owner was a short dark beefy man of about fifty. He had a thick black walrus moustache, through which he cursed fluently and loudly in American, Lingo, and Mexican for five minutes. Then he began locking the doors of the eathouse.

Brer John, one of the few people who had remained to watch, said, "Why are you closing? Hasn't the place been cleaned up?"

He was not really worried about *why*; he hoped that somehow he would be able to get a meal from the man. His stomach had been growling like a starving dog for half an hour.

"Oh, it's clean enough," said the man. "But the autochef is out of order. It started smoking; that's why I called the firemen."

"Can't you have it repaired?" said Brer John.

"Not until I sign a new contract with the Electrical Maintenance Union," growled the man. "And that I won't do. They're on strike now for higher wages. Well, I don't give a damn. I'll go out of business before I deal with them. Or wait until my brother Juan gets here from Mexico. He's an electronics tech; he's going into business with me, and he can keep the autochef going. But he won't get here until next week. When he does, we'll show the bastards."

"It just so happens," said Brer John, grinning, his mouth watering at the thought of all the goodies within, "that I am an electronics expert, among other things. I could repair the chef for you."

The man looked at him from under thick brows. "And just what's in it for you?"

"A good meal," said Brer John. "And enough busfare and taxi fare to get me to the spaceport."

The man looked around, then said, "Ain't you worried about the union? They'll be down on us like a bus whose antigrav has given out."

Brer John hesitated. The growling of his belly was loud. He said, "I don't wish to be called a scab. But if it is true that your brother is going to fix it anyway, then I see no harm in repairing the machinery a few days before he gets here. Besides, I'm hungry."

"O.K." said the owner. "It's your funeral. But I oughta warn you that there's a picket stationed in the kitchen."

"Will he resort to violence?" asked Brer John.

The owner took the cigar out of his mouth and stared at the brother. Then he said, "Where you been all your life?"

"I was gone from Earth quite a few years," said Brer John. "And my life here on Earth has been quite cloistered since my return."

He did not think it necessary to add that the first year had been spent at John Hopkins, where he had been undergoing rehabilitation therapy after surrendering himself to the police.

The owner shrugged and led Brer John through the dining rooms into the kitchen. There he pointed at a large painting hanging from the wall, Trudeau's *Morning On Antares II*. "Looks like a picture," he said. "It's the picket. A TV receiver. The union monitors it from its headquarters. Once they see you working on the chef, they'll be down on us like the wolf on the fooled."

"I don't wish to suggest anything illegal or unethical," said Brer John. "But what would happen if we—I—turned off the picket's power?"

"You can't turn it off unless you was to smash it," said the owner gloomily. "The power switch is remote-controlled by the union."

"What about hanging a sheet over it?" said Brer John.

"An alarm would go off at union headquarters," replied the owner. "And I'd be hauled off to jail by one of those stinking zombie cops. It's against the law for me to interfere with the vision of the picket in any way. I even have to keep the lights on in the kitchen day and night. And what's worse, *I* have to pay the light bill, not the fucking union."

The use of the four-letter word did not bother Brer John. Such words had long ago ceased to be equated with vulgarity or immorality; it made no difference whether one used words of English or Latin origin in describing bodily functions or as expletives. Twenty-third century culture, however, did have other taboo words, and the owner could have offended Brer John by using them.

The brother asked for pliers, cutters, a screwdriver, and insulating tape. Then he stuck his head into the hole left by the removal of the wall-panels by the firemen. The owner began pacing back and forth, his big cigar puffing like signals sent by an Indian frantically asking for money from home.

"Maybe I shouldn't ought to of let you start doing this," he said. "The union'll have its goon squad on the way. Myabe they'll try to wreck the place. Maybe they'll start a lawsuit against me. It ain't as if you was my brother fixing that damn chef. They can't do nothing if the repairman is part-owner of the place."

Brer John wished he had insisted upon being fed before beginning work. His stomach rumbled louder than ever, and his intestines felt as if they had turned cannibal.

"Why not call a cop?" he said. "He can maintain order."

"I hate those metal-bellied zombies," said the owner. "So does any decent man. It's got so people won't call a cop unless they absolutely have to. People are beginning to take the law in their own hands 'cause they hate to deal with the cops. I'd rather have the joint wrecked and pay for it than ask them damn zombies for help."

"Impersonal uncorruptible law enforcement has always been an ideal," said Brer John. "So, now we have it . . ."

"Brer John, if you wasn't a man of the cloth, I'd tell you where to stick it," said the owner. "But you get the message. Say, tell me, how come you monks are called Brer instead of Brother?"

"Because that is the way our founder, St. Jairus,

pronounced brother," said Brer John. "He was
born on the planet of Hawaiki, where the
Polynesian colonists developed their own brand of
American. Ah, here's the trouble! Burned-out
transformer in the high voltage power supply.
Lucky for us the malfunction is so obvious. Maybe
not so lucky unless we can replace the transformer. Do you have spare parts? Or do you, I
suppose, depend upon the maintenance men to
supply the parts?"

The owner grinned and said, "Usually I do. But
my brother phoned me and said to lay in all the
parts I'd need before the union caught on he was
coming. You see, once they knew I was using him,
the union'd fix it up with the suppliers in L.A. not
to sell me any stuff. Oh, those bastards! One way
or another, they'll turn off your switch!"

"Ah well, they must ensure their living, too,"
said Brer John. "There's something to be said for
both sides in a labor-management dispute."

"The hell there is!" said the owner, clamping
down on his cigar. "Besides, I ain't no
management. I'm a proprietor who has to pay
highway robbery prices to keep my electronic
stuff going, that's what."

"Show me where you keep those parts," said
Brer John.

He paused. A loud knocking had penetrated the
kitchen from the front of the eathouse.

The owner scowled and said, "They're here. But
they can't get in unless I unlock the doors. Or they
bust 'em down."

He hurried into a room behind the kitchen. Brer
John followed, and there he picked out the transformer he needed. When he came back into the
kitchen, the knocking was louder and more
furious.

"Do you intend to let them in?" asked Brer John.

"If I don't, they'll kick the door open," said the owner. "And I can't do a damn thing about it. According to the law, they got a perfect right to make sure nobody except the owner fixes up the electronic equipment. And they're trying to get a law passed to keep a man from doing that."

"Yes, it's true that a man has increasingly little liberty and rights," said Brer John. "On Earth, that is. That is why the individualist and non-conformist leave Earth in such great numbers for the frontier planets."

He paused, frowned as if he were thinking deeply, and said, "Perhaps that is why I am being sent to Wildenwooly." He sighed and added, "Though it looks as if I may not be getting there."

He turned to the open panel and said, "You keep them out as long as you can without resorting to violence. Perhaps, by the time they get here, I can have this repaired."

It did not take him long, for the transformer needed only to be clipped onto the circuit board and the terminals plugged in. He laughed. It was so simple that the owner, if he had taken the time to examine the situation, could easily have done the repair work himself. But he, like many, thought of electronics as being such a highly mysterious and complex science, that he needed an expert. Though there were many things that only a highly trained technician could trouble-shoot, this was not one of them.

He withdrew the upper part of his body from the opening just in time to see the owner being pushed by four maintenance men into the kitchen. These were dressed in scarlet coveralls and electric-blue caps and wore their emblems on their chests and backs, a lightning streak crossed by a screwdriver.

On seeing Brer John they halted in astonish-

ment; apparently they had not seen him on the
picket but had been told to go to Ye Olde Arizona
Loghaus and stop the scab.

Their leader, a six-foot-six man with the protruding brows and thick jaw of a pugilist, stepped
forward. "I don't know what you're doing here,
brother," he said. "But you better have a good
reason."

Another man, shorter than the first but broader,
said, "Perhaps the Father didn't know what he
was doing?"

The big man whirled on the broad man. "He
ain't no Father!" he snarled. "If you was one of
our faith, you'd know that. He's a monk or a friar
or a lay brother, something like that. But he ain't
no priest!"

"I'm a lay brother of the Order of St. Jairus,"
said Brer John. "Brer John is the name."

"Well, Brer John," said the big man. "Maybe
you've been shut up behind those walls so long
meditating that you don't know that you're
scabbing on us, taking the bread out of our
mouths."

"I knew what I was doing," said Brer John. "By
not fixing the autochef, I was taking the bread out
of this man's mouth—," he pointed to the owner.
"And I was also depriving many people of the
chance to get away from those ghastly soulless
clutch cafeterias."

"All this capitalist has to do is pay us what we
want, and he can feed as many people as he can
handle," snarled the big man.

"Well," said Brer John, "the trouble has been
fixed."

The big man turned purple and clenched his
fists.

"Shame on you," said Brer John. "You are ready
to strike a man of your own faith, a member of a

holy order, too. And yet that man—" he pointed to
the broad man— "a man of another faith, if any, is
ready to take a reasonable attitude."

"He's one of them damn Universal Light
people," said the big man. "Always ready to
consider the other fellow's side, even if it's to his
own injury."

"Then the more shame to you," said Brer John.

"I didn't come here to be shamed!" roared the
big man. "I come here to get rid of a sneaky little
scab hiding behind a robe! More shame to you, I
say!"

"And just what do you propose to do?" said Brer
John. He was shaking all over, not from fear of
injury but from the fear that he might lose his self-
control and attack the big man. And thus betray
his own principles. Not to mention the principles
of the order to which he belonged. What if they
heard of this incident! What would they say, what
action take?

"I propose first to throw you out," said the big
man. "And then I propose to take out that
transformer you put in."

"You can't do that!" bellowed the owner.
"What's done is done!"

"Wait a minute," said Brer John to the owner.
"No use getting upset. Let them take the
transformer out. You can put it back in yourself,
and there's not a thing they can do."

Again the big man purpled, and his eyes bulged
out. "He will like hell!" he said. "If the picket sees
him do anything like that, or even try to, we'll be
down on him like the roof of the city fell in!"

"There ain't a thing you can do about it," said
the owner, smiling smugly. "Go ahead. Take the
transformer out. I'll just stand here and watch
how you do it so's I'll know how to, too."

"He's right," said the broad man. "We can't do a

thing if the trouble's that simple."

"Say, who's side you on?" roared the big man. "You a scab?"

"No. I just want to be legal," said the broad man. "Anyway, we can hire human pickets to picket the place."

"Are you out of your skull?" said the big man. "You know the Human Picket Union just upped their hourly rates, and we can't afford to hire any. And we don't have enough men to our own to spare for picketing. Besides, them damn pickets are pushing through a law to make it illegal for anybody except a picket union member to picket. The nerve of them guys!"

Brer John smiled and shook his head and tsk-tsked.

"I'm warning you!" shouted the big man, shaking his fist in the direction of the owner and Brer John. "If you re-repair the autochef, you won't have an eathouse to run!"

The owner, whose own face had been purpling, suddenly jumped on the big man and bowled him over. The two went down together, locked in furious, if not deadly, combat. Another of the goon squad took a poke at Brer John. Brer John ducked, and before he could think, his reflexes took over. He threw up his left to block the fellow's punch, and seeing him wide open, slammed him in the belly with a hard right.

A fierce joy ran through him. Before he could recollect what he should be doing, he had done what he should not. Excellent student of karate, judo, sabate, *akrantu*, and *vispexwun*, and a veteran of a hundred bar-room and back alley brawls, he went into action like a maddened lynx mother who thought her kittens were in danger. A chop of the palm-edge against a neck, a thrust of stiff fingers into a soft gut, a hard heel of a foot against a chin, a knee in the groin and an elbow in the throat, and all except the big man were out of the fight. Following the Biblical precept of saving the best for the last, Brer John incapacitated the big man by pulling him from the owner and working him over with palm, fingers, knee, foot, and elbow. The big man went down like a tree attacked by a thousand woodpeckers.

The owner struggled to his feet and was astonished to see Brer John on his knees, eyes closed, praying.

"What's the matter?" said the owner. "You hurt?"

"Not physically," said Brer John, getting to his feet. He did not believe in long prayers when they were informal. "I am hurt because I failed."

"Failed?" said the owner, looking around at the unconscious or groaning men. "Did one of them get away?"

"No," said Brer John. "Only it should be I who am on the floor, not they. I lost my temper, and also my self-respect. I should have let them do what they wanted to with me but never lifted a finger."

"Shit!" cried the owner. "Look at it this way. You saved these men from being murderers! Believe me, they'd have had to kill me before I would have let them mess up my autochef. No, you've done them, and me, a great service. Though I don't know what's going to happen once they go back to headquarters. There'll be hell to pay."

"There usually is," said Brer John. "What will you do?"

"Don't say that," said the owner. "The last time you asked that, we had a free-for-all. But I'll tell you what. I'm going to drag these goons out—and I could use some help from you—and then I'm going to lock the door, and then, much as I hate to have

anything to do with those metal-bellies, I'm going
to call the cops. They can station a flatfoot here
and keep the goons from bombing or wrecking the
place. I'll say that much for the zombies, they can't
be scared by threats or influence."

Brer John began helping the owner carry the
men out of the eathouse. They had, however, no
sooner placed the four on the sidewalk and locked
the door than they heard the siren of a police car.

"I have to go now," said Brer John. "I can't
afford to have my name on the police records or in
the papers. My superiors would frown on such un-
favorable publicity. And it wouldn't do me any
good either," he added, thinking of his pre-
Christian days. It was possible that he might be
taken back to John Hopkins for further
observation.

"What will I tell the cops?" wailed the owner.

"Tell the truth," said Brer John. "Always tell the
truth. I'm sorry I failed you so miserably. I have a
lot to learn yet. And I'm still hungry," he said, but
it was doubtful if the owner heard the last phrase,
for Brer John was running in his shapeless
maroon robe like a frightened bear for the shelter
of a copse of trees in the park.

Once inside the grove, he stopped. Not because
he had planned to, but because he ran across a
picnic blanket and his feet slipped on a bowl of
potato salad. He fell face forward in a plate of fish
eggs. And lay there, half-stunned, vaguely aware of
the howls and shrieks of laughter around him.

When he managed to sit up and look around, he
saw that he was surrounded by six teenage boys
and girls. Luckily for him, they were in a holiday
mood. If they'd been in an ugly mood, they might
have been able to harm or perhaps even kill him.
They were dressed in the uniform of the "skunks"
as others called them and as they called them-

selves. These were black-and-white striped jumpers with close-fitting hoods, and their legs were painted with vertical black and white stripes. The eyes of the girls were ringed with black paint, and the eyes of the boys were painted with black semi-circles.

"Gimp the high priest!" screamed one of the boys. He pointed with red-painted fingernails. "Ain't him a dudu!"

"A real dong-dong," said one of the girls. She bent over Brer John and pulled a little string hanging from the side of her jumper. Her breasts leaped out of the low-cut bodice and stared at him with two red-pupilled blue-rimmed eyes. The rest howled and screamed and threw themselves gasping on the grass.

Brer John averted his eyes. He had heard of the trick the juveniquent girls liked to play; the false breasts which leaped out at the startled stranger like a jack-in-a-box. But he wasn't sure that these were false.

The girl stuffed the device back into her grotesquely out-thrust bosom. She smiled at Brer John, and he saw that she would have been a pretty girl if it hadn't been for the absurdly painted face. "What's ionizing, Willie?" she said to him.

Brer John rose, and, while he wiped his face with a handkerchief he took from his pocket, he said, "I am running from the cops."

He couldn't have said anything else that would have more quickly gained their sympathy.

"Hophopping the deadpans? Ain't him a dudu? Don't him look some priest? Scratch one, him's some monk, nothing a priest, you short-cut to zero."

Home among my own, thought Brer John, and hot on the heels of that thought a fierce denial. No, they are not my own. My brothers and sisters, sons and daughters, sinners, too, but I am not home. I can understand them, how and why they are, but I will not be one of them. I will hurt no man with malice aforethought.

"Pink some me," said the girl who had popped out her bosom, false or otherwise. "Me'll straight you some hole." Brer John interpreted that to mean that he was to give her his hand and she would lead him to a hiding place.

"Me'll stick my nose along," said a youth who was distinguished from the others by his tallness and the closeness of his black eyes.

"Some poxy," said the girl, which seemed to mean that the boy was to come along. She led Brer John out of the grove and down a winding grove where they stepped over couples in various degrees of passion, and then up over an artificial hill and under an artificial waterfall and into another collection of trees. Brer John looked overhead from time to time. A police car was still hanging in the air, but evidently they hadn't spotted him yet. Suddenly, the girl pulled him into a thick collection of bushes and sat down in the middle of them. The youth forced his body between the girl and Brer John and began drinking from the bucket of beer which he had brought along.

The girl handed Brer John a sandwich, and he devoured it. His stomach growled, and his mouth salivated. By the time he'd eaten it, the boy had put the bucket down, and the girl handed the bucket to Brer John. He drank it eagerly in great gulps. But the boy tore the bucket from his hands.

"Don't no road," he said, which freely translated meant, "Don't be a hog."

"Some you dudo," said the girl. "Frwhat you jet some?"

Brer John interpreted this to mean that she wanted to know from what he was running. He told them that he was a lay brother of the order of St. Jairus, one who had not yet taken his final vows. As a matter of fact, inside a week his year would be up, and if he then wished to quit the society, he could do so. He didn't even have to notify his superiors.

He did not tell them that he suspected that this order to go to Wildenwooly at the same time that his year was up had been authorized so he could make up his mind whether he wished to remain with the order of St. Jairus.

He told them that there was a possibility that he might go into the priesthood, but he wasn't sure that he wouldn't be happier by remaining a simple brother. He would get all the dirty menial tasks, true, but he also would not have the tremendous responsibilities that came with being a priest.

Also, though he did not say so, he did not want the humiliation of being refused permission to enter the priesthood. He was not sure that he was worthy.

There was silence except for the loud gulpings of the youth as he drank from the bucket. Brer John looked out through the bushes and saw that they were next to a fence. Just beyond the fence was a narrow strip of dirt and then a deep moat. On the other side of the moat was a large bare space of rock and, beyond it, a cave. Evidently this was the cage of some animal, and it had been prepared to resemble the natural habitat of the animal.

He looked for the animal but could not see it. Then, he saw a sign by the fence.

HOROWITZ

A fierce meat-eating giant
bird of the planet Feral.
Highly intelligent. Named
after its discoverer, Alexander
Horowitz. Please do not tease.
This area monitored.

The girl reached out a hand and stroked Brer John's chin. "Some scratch," she said.

She turned to the youth and jerked her thumb in an invitation for him to leave.

"Whyn't some ionize?" she said.

He narrowed his eyes and said, "Me? Summun want rigor mortis?"

"Me never so monk-monk before," said the girl, and she laughed, while her blue eyes looked at Brer John with a look he knew too well.

The boy snarled, "Monk-monk?" and then Brer John understood that the girl was punning. Monk-monk, he remembered now, was an extremely vulgar word which had replaced one of the formerly tabooed four-letter words.

"Monk-monk the monk-monk," said the boy. "Me monk-monk summun if summun ain't getting the monk-monk off the pad."

He turned to Brer John. "Ionize, gutbutt!"

Suddenly, a knife was in the girls' hand, and the point was at the boy's throat. "Me seesaw rigor mortis," she said crooningly.

"Some?" said the boy amazedly, jerking his thumb at Brer John.

The girl nodded her head. "Me some. Never no monk-monk a monk-monking monk, comprendo? You ionize sooner than later. Some seesaw rigor mortis, no?"

The boy put his hands on the ground behind him and tried to back away from her. She followed him, the knife held to his throat.

As she did so, Brer John's hand flashed out and knocked the knife from her grasp. All three dived for it, and their heads came together. Brer John saw stars; by the time he recovered, the youth had grabbed him by the throat and was trying to strangle him. Brer John fought back; his stiff fingers plunged into the boy's stomach, the boy said, "Oof!" and released his hold. The girl, knife in hand, leaped at the boy. He turned and hit her on the jaw with his fist and knocked her unconscious to the ground. Then, before Brer John could move in close enough, the boy grabbed him by the front of the robe and lifted him high and helpless in the air. And the next Brer John knew, he was flying over the fence. He hit the ground hard, rolled over, felt the world slipping away beneath him, knew briefly that he was falling into the moat, fell backwards, and then . . . heard a voice shrieking, "Hey, John, hey, John! Here I am, John!"

He woke to hear the same voice calling, "Hey, John! Here I am!"

He was flat on his back, staring upwards past the gray walls of the moat and up at the roof of the city. The roof was no longer transparent, allowing the blue of the Arizona sky to come through undiminished. Night had fallen outside the roof, and now the roof itself was a glow bright as day, shining with energy stored during the day and released at sunset.

Brer John groaned and tried to sit up to see if he had any broken bones. But he could not move.

"Holy Mother!" he breathed. "I'm paralyzed! St. Jairus preserve me!"

But he was not totally paralyzed. He could move his legs and his arms. It was just that his chest felt as if it were crushed against the earth by a great weight.

He turned his head, and he almost fainted with fright. It was a weight that was holding him down. A huge bird, larger than a man . . .

It had been squatting by his side, its giant claw placed on his chest, pinning him to the ground. Now that it saw the man had his eyes open, it rose to one foot, still keeping the other placed on him.

"Hey, John!" it screamed. "Here I am, John!"

"So you are," said Brer John. "Would you mind letting me up?" But he did not expect anything, for it was obvious that the huge bird—if it was a bird—had a parrot's power to mimic.

Slowly, he moved his arms, not wishing to alarm the horowitz, for that must be what it was. It could have torn him open at any moment with its tremendous three-toed foot or with its moa-sized beak. Evidently it had leaped down into the moat after him, with what purpose, he didn't know.

His arms bent at the elbows, he lowered the upper parts to feel his chest. He had wondered what it was that lay on his chest, which was bare, probably because the big bird had ripped his robe open.

He felt sick. An egg lay on his chest.

It was a small egg, not much larger than a barnyard hen's. He couldn't imagine why a creature that large would lay such a small egg, why it would lay it on him. But it was and it had.

The horowitz, seeing the man's hands feel the egg, screamed with protest. Its huge beak stabbed down at his face. Brer John closed his eyes, and breathed in the rotten breath of the meat-eating creature. But the beak did not touch him, and after a moment he opened his eyes. The beak was poised a few inches above his face, ready to complete its descent if he harmed the egg.

Brer John gave a longer than usual prayer, then

he tried to think of a way to get out of his predicament.

And could not. He dared not try to escape by
force, and he could not, for one of the few times in
his life, talk his way out. He did turn his head to
look up at the edge of the moat from which he had
fallen, supposing that some spectators would
notice him. But there were none. And in a moment
he realized why. The people who had been in the
park probably had gone home to supper or to
work, and the second shift at the clutches had not
yet come into the park. And, of course, it was
possible that nobody would come by for a long
time. Nor did he dare to shout for fear of alarming
the horowitz.

He was forced to lie motionless on his back and
wait until the big bird left him. If it intended to
leave him. It did not seem likely that it would. For
some reason it had jumped into the moat to lay its
egg on him. And it could not jump back out. Which
meant that in time it would get hungry.

"Who would have thought that when I was told
to go to Wildenwooly that I might perish in the
city zoo only halfway out of the city. Strange and
wondrous are the ways of the Lord," he muttered.

He lay, staring upwards at the glowing roof, at
the huge beak and black red-rimmed eyes of the
bird, and occasionally at the top of the moat,
hoping for a passerby.

After a time he felt his chest tickling beneath the
egg. The tickling grew stronger with every minute,
and he had an insane desire to scratch, insane
because to indulge would be to die.

"Holy Mother," he said, "if you are torturing me
to make me think on my sins before I die, you are
certainly succeeding. Or would be if I weren't so
concerned with the tickling and itching itself. I
can barely think of my most grievous faults

because of the disturbing everlasting damnable itching. I have to scratch! I must!"

But he did not dare. To do so would have been to commit suicide, and that, the unpardonable sin because it could not be regretted, was unthinkable. Or perhaps not unthinkable because he *was* thinking of it; what *was* the correct word—undoable? No, but it did not matter. If he could only scratch!

Presently, after what seemed hours but probably was not more than fifteen minutes, the itching quit. Life again became endurable, even if not pleasant.

It was at that precise minute that the youth who had thrown him into the moat appeared above him.

"Grab time!" called the youth. "Me'll drop a rope!"

Brer John watched the boy tie one end of a rope to the fence and then throw the other end down into the moat. He wondered if the youth expected him to walk over and draw himself up, meanwhile blithely ignoring the huge bird. He wanted to call out and tell him he couldn't even sit up, but he was afraid his voice might alarm the creature.

However, he did not have to initiate any action. The second the rope touched the floor of the moat the horowitz released its hold on the man and ran to the rope. It seized it in its two small hands and, bracing its feet against the side of the moat, swarmed up.

Brer John jumped up and shouted, "Don't let it get out of the moat, son! It'll kill you!"

The youth stared at the creature coming swiftly up the rope. Just as the bird's head came over the edge of the moat, the youth came out of his paralysis. He stepped up to the bird and kicked savagely at the beaked head. The bird gave a cry, loosed its hold on the rope, and fell backwards. It struck the earth, rolled a few feet, and lay stunned, its eyes glazed.

Brer John did not hesitate. He ran to the rope and began hauling himself up hand over hand on it. Halfway up, he felt the rope straighten out beneath him. Looking down, he saw the horowitz had recovered and was following him up the rope. It began squawking furiously, intermingling its cries with screams of "Hey, John! Here I am, John!"

Brer John climbed a few feet higher, then hung there while he kicked at the crested head beneath him. His foot drove solidly into the creature's skull, and once again the bird lost its hold and fell backwards to the ground. Gasping for breath, it lay there long enough for Brer John to pull the rope out of its reach.

"We must notify the zoo personnel," he said. "Otherwise, the poor creature might starve to death. Besides, I have something that is the property of the zoo."

"Me don't scratch you," said the youth. Brer John interpreted this to mean that he didn't understand him. "Dum-dum some rigor mortised summum."

"The bird was only obeying the dictates of its nature," said Brer John. "Unlike you or me, it doesn't have free will."

"Will-swill," said the youth. "Gimp the baldun."

"You mean, look at the egg?" replied Brer John. He looked down to examine the strange situation of the egg. It had not fallen off his chest when he rose but had clung to his skin as if glued on. He pulled it away from his chest, and the skin stretched with it.

"Curioser and curioser," he said. "Perhaps the bird secretes an adhesive when it lays an egg. But why should it?"

Then he thought of his manners and his gratitude, and he said, "I thank you for coming to my rescue. Though I must admit I was surprised since—forgive me for mentioning it—you were the one who threw me down there."

"Goed out of me frying-pan," said the youth, meaning that he had lost his head. "Goed monk-monk gimping the trangle smack-smacking summun. Her's no monk-monking good. Gived her the ivory-doctor."

"Knocked her teeth out?" said Brer John.

"Scratch," said the youth. "Telled the trangle ionize. Daily dozen gived me cross-gimps."

"You told the girl to get lost because she was always getting you in trouble?"

"Scratch. Rigor mortis summun; me get sing-singed gray fat fried."

"You might kill someone and get sent to an institution where your personality would be changed? Possibly. However, your act in coming back shows you have promise. I wish I could repay you, but I have nothing to give you."

Suddenly, he began scratching furiously, and he added, "Except for these monk-monking lice that bird gave me. Is there anything I could do for you?"

The youth shrugged hopelessly. "Round-round. You going to Wildenwooly?"

Brer John nodded. The youth looked up at the glowing roof overhead.

"Bye-bye, maybe me go some there. Nothing but daily dozen in-and-out on The Antheap. Is a different dummy out in deep space."

"Yes, getting off Earth and on a frontier planet might make a new man of you," said Brer John. "And you might learn to speak American, too. Well, God bless you, my boy. I must go. And if you

should get to Wildenwooly before I do, tell them
I'm doing my best to get there. Holy Mary, it's only
a few miles, said Brer Francis!''

He began walking away. Behind him rose a
harsh wail of "Hey, John! Here I am, John! Your
old buddy, John!''

He shuddered and crossed himself and
continued walking. But he could not forget the
monster in the moat. The vermin that now
swarmed under his robe and drove him almost
frantic would not allow him to forget. Neither
would the egg attached to his chest.

It was the combination of the two which decided
him to find a secluded spot on the lagoon and
bathe. He had hopes he could drown the bird-lice
and unglue the adhesive which made the egg stick
so tightly. Finding a place where he would not be
seen was not, however, so easy. The first shift was
streaming from the clutches into the park and was
lying on the sandy beaches or swimming. Brer
John did his best to avert his eyes from the naked
as he passed through them. But it was impossible
not to catch more than a glimpse of the women as
they lay on the sand or ran before him. And, after a
while, he quit trying. After all, he told himself, he
had been accustomed all his life to seeing them all
undressed at the beach and in his own home
before he had gone into the order of St. Jairus.
And all the fulminations of the Church had not
been able to stop the faithful from following the
custom any more than it had been able in the
previous centuries to keep them from swimming
in the abbreviated bathing suits. The Church had
long ceased protesting against nude public
bathing, but it still denounced the appearance of
nudes in the streets. Though what its policy would
be twenty years from now was unpredictable.
Occasionally, a nude did venture on the street or

in the markets and was arrested for indecent exposure, just as women in shorts or bathing suits outside of the beach had been arrested in the early part of—the Twentieth Century? The laity might go undressed in the public bathing places, but the clergy did not. In fact, they were forbidden even to be at such places. And he, Brer John, was disobeying the rules of his order, not to mention the Church as a whole, by being here.

But expediency sometimes dictated the breaking of rules, and the bird-lice biting madly into him demanded that he get rid of them at once before he made a spectacle of himself.

Brer John went halfway around the lagoon before he found what he was looking for. This was a high bank which was shielded from view by a group of bushes. He pushed through the foliage, and almost put his foot on a couple who must have thought they were alone in the Garden of Eden. He stepped over them and plunged on until he could not see them, though he was still distressed by the sounds.

Quickly, he slid his robe off and then let himself down the high bank of mud into the water. He shivered as the relatively cold water hit him, then after a moment he felt quite comfortable. Remembering the fable of how the fox rid himself of fleas, he slowly immersed himself. He had a hope that the insects would climb up his body as the water came towards them and that when he had ducked his head, they would be left to shift for themselves.

His head went under, and he held his breath while he counted one hundred and eighty seconds. Then he lifted his head above the water. He didn't see the collection of insects floating before his nose that he had expected. But the lice must have gone somewhere, for he no longer was being bitten.

Then he tried to pull the egg away from his skin and allow the water to soften the glue. But he had no success.

"It's as if it had put out tendrils into my skin," he said.

His eyes widened, and he paled. "Good St. Jairus! Maybe that's what *did* happen!"

He forced himself to push back the rising panic and to think, if not calmly, at least coherently. Perhaps the horowitz had egg-laying habits analogous to that of the wasp. It might be its instinct to place the egg on a corpse or even living creature. And the egg might send forth small fleshy roots to hook into the bloodstream of its host. And through the roots it would draw the nourishment it needed to grow larger and to develop into an embryo. The horowitz might have taken an evolutionary step which would place it among placental creatures, the difference being that the embryo would develop on the *outside* of the body of its host instead of *inside*.

Brer John didn't feel much like taking a strictly biological and zoological attitude. This thing attached to his body was a monstrous leech, and it was sucking the blood from him.

It might not be necessarily fatal. And he could kill the egg now, and, presumably, the roots would dissolve.

But there was the ethical view to consider. The egg was not his property to dispose of as he wished. It belonged to the zoo.

Brer John squelched his desire to rip out the thing by the bloody tendrils and to throw it away as far as possible. He must return it to the zoo authorities. Even if that would involve much time while he told the long and complex story of just how he had happened to be in a situation where he could have an egg laid on him.

He scrambled back up the bank. And stood dismayed. His robe was gone.

Brer John had always thought of himself as a strong man. But tears ran down his cheeks, and he groaned, "Worse and worse! Every step I take towards Wildenwooly puts me back two steps! How will I ever get out of this mess?"

He looked up at the sky. No sky, just a blaze of light from a man-made roof. Light but no revelation.

He thought of the motto of the order of St. Jairus. *Do as he would do.*

"Yes, but he was never in such a situation!" he said aloud.

However, he thought, consideration of the life of St. Jairus did show that he had always taken the lesser of two evils, unless doing so might lead to an evil even greater than the one rejected. In which case one chose the greater evil, if one had to choose.

"John," he said to himself, "you are not a philosopher. You are a man of action, however ill-advised that action may be. You have never really thought your way out of a mess. Which is why you may be in this particular one. But you have always trusted to the wisdom of your feeling to extricate yourself. So, act!"

The first thing he had to do was to clothe himself. He could remain nude while he searched the beach for whoever might have stolen his clothes. But he did not think it likely that the thief, or prankster, would be in evidence. And he had no means for covering the egg on his chest. That would lead to an intense curiosity and probable trouble for him before he had gotten far. The cops might be called, he might go to jail. And he would have much explaining to do, not only to the secular authorities but to his superior.

No. He must find clothing. Then he must get money to call the director of the zoo and get rid of the egg. Then, somehow, he must get the money for fare to Wildenwooly.

Cautiously, he pushed back into the bushes. The couple over whom he had stumbled were still there, but they now seemed to be asleep in each other's arms. Muttering under his breath, "Only a loan. I will see you get it back," he reached out and took the man's clothes from the bush on which they hung. Then he retreated to the edge of the bank and put them on.

He found the experience distasteful for several reasons. One, he was giving the police another reason to look for him. Two, when the man woke up, he would be in Brer John's difficult position of getting off the beach and home without his clothes, though, doubtless, he could send the woman after some. Three, the puffkilt he was putting on was covered with garish mustard-yellow circles with pink dots. This was not only an esthetic crime in itself but, four, the puffkilt was soiled and smelly. Five, the dickey which he put on his chest was an electric-blue with crystal sequins.

"Horrible taste," said Brer John, shuddering. He was aware that he made a ridiculous figure.

"Better than having an egg hanging from our chest," he said, and he set off across the park towards the city.

He intended to enter a public phone booth and there find out the address of the zoo director. Then he would walk to the zoo director's house and tell him about the egg. What would happen then, he told himself, would be up to God and the agile (?) wits of Brer John. But somehow, he must also contrive to get the stolen (borrowed) clothes back to the owner with some recompense.

Brer John walked swiftly towards the edge of the park. He did not look behind him as he passed the white-fleshed bodies and many-colored legs of the beach-people. But he felt what he had not felt for a long time, the prickling frightening half-exhilarating sensation that at any moment the cry of "Stop, thief!" would ring out. And he would be in full flight ahead of the pack.

Not that there was much chance of that. The man had been sleeping too deeply.

"Stop, thief!" rang the cry.

Automatically, Brer John increased his pace, but he did not start running yet. Instead, he pointed dramatically to one side at a man who was running by a happy coincidence away from those beside him.

"There he goes!" he yelled. And the crowd surged around him, running after the innocent who fled when every man was pursuing. Unfortunately, the crowd by Brer John ran into the crowd behind the man who was running after Brer John and the stolen clothes. Somebody pushed somebody, and within two seconds a full-scale brawl had spread through this section of the park.

A cop's whistle blew; a number of men piled upon the cop and bore the metal man under by sheer weight. Brer John decided that now was as good as time as any to run.

He reached the edge of the park and began running through a narrow alley formed by the fences around the small yards of private houses. It was a twisting labyrinthian alley in which he could easily lose any ground pursuit. But a cop's car was scooting overhead towards the riot in the park, so Brer John vaulted over a fence lithely as a cat despite his round-stomached bulk. He landed easily and crouched against the fence, hugging it to avoid observance from the air.

The footsteps of a man running went by the fence and faded into the distance. Brer John smiled, then the smile froze as a low growl came from behind him.

Slowly, he turned his head. He was inside the yard of a typical house. The fence encircled a small plot of grass in the center of which was a roofed patio. The patio held a table and a few chairs and a *chaise-longue* and the entrance to the house underneath the ground. No human beings were in evidence, but a dog was very much so. It was a huge Doberman-Pinscher, and it was ready to charge.

Back over the fence went Brer John, the dog so close to him that he felt its jaws clash at the edge of his puffkilt. Then he was running again.

However, after he had spurted for a hundred yards and looked behind him to make sure that the dog hadn't come over the fence after him, he slowed to a fast walk. He saw a public phone booth and made for it. Before he was at its door, a man stepped up to him and seized his elbow.

"Wanta talk to you," he said. "Me can solve all your problems for you in a micro."

Brer John looked at the man closely. He was small and thin and had a ratty face. His legs were painted barber-pole fashion with red and white stripes, his kilt and dickey were sequined with imitation diamonds, and he wore a tricorne hat with a long plume. These were enough to identify him as one of the lower classes; the plastic imitation bone stuck through the septum of his nose marked him at once as a lower-class criminal.

"Me got switches," the man said, meanwhile darting glances from side to side and turning his head like a robin afraid the cat was sneaking up on him. "Heard 'bout ya quick as ya robe was

snatched. Heard 'bout the egg, too. That's what
wanta talk ta ya 'bout. Ya sell the egg ta me; me
sell the egg to a rich beast in Phoenix. Him's
queer, get it? Eats, uh, rare delicacies, gets his
rockets off. Been vine out long time good zoola
horowitz egg. Scratch?"

"Scratch," said Brer John. "You mean a rich
man in Phoenix pays big prices for food hard to
get, like the ancient Chinese paid high for so-
called thousand year old eggs?"

"Scratch. Know ya need ticket to Wildenwooly.
Can finger."

"I'm tempted, *friend*," said Brer John. "You
would solve my temporal difficulties."

"Do? Buzz-buzz. Only drag is, have to go ta
Phoenix first. Slice egg off here, no buzz-buzz. Egg
rigor mortis; no carry from fat beast."

"You tempt me, *friend*," said Brer John. "But,
fortunately I remember that I will also have
eternal difficulties if I deal with you. Moreover,
this egg so fondly clutching my breast is not my
property. It belongs to the zoo."

The man's eyes narrowed. "No buzz-buzz. Come
anyway."

He pulled a whistle from a pocket on his puffkilt
and blew. No sound issued, but three men stepped
out from the corner of a tavern. All three held airguns, which doubtless contained darts whose tips
were smeared with a paralytic.

Brer John leaped like an uncoiling rattler
striking. The ratty little man squawked with
terror, and his hand darted towards his pocket.
But Brer John chopped him into unconsciousness
with the edge of his palm, and he thrust the man
before him. There was a whacking sound as two
darts hit the sagging form. Then Brer John,
holding the man into the air before him, managed
to run towards the three gunmen. Another dart

thwacked into the flesh of his shield, and then he was on them. Or they were on him; it was hard to tell. He went down; he was up; airguns hissed in the air and missed; one man cried out as a dart hit him; another folded as stiff fingers drove into his soft belly; then the butt of a gun came down on Brer John's temple.

Stars . . . blackness.

He woke to find himself lying on a couch in a strange room. And a strange man was looking down at him.

"I protest against this high-handed misuse of a fellow human being," said Brer John. "If you think you can get away with this, you're mistaken. I was once known as John Carmody, the only man who ever gave the famous detective Leopardi the slip. I'll hunt you down and I'll . . . turn you over to the authorities," he ended mildly.

The man smiled and said, "I'm not what you think, Brer John. The crooks who tried to snatch you were caught by a police car immediately after you were knocked out. They were injected, and they made a full confession. And you were injected, too. We know the full story. A most amazing one, too, and I've heard some weird ones."

Brer John sat up and felt dizzy. The man said, "Take it easy. Allow me to introduce myself. I'm John Richards, the director of the zoo."

Brer John felt at his chest. The egg was still attached.

"Wait a minute," he said. "The horowitz has a parrot's mimicking powers. Just as a guess, you taught it to call you by your name, John? Scratch? I mean, right?"

"Right," said John Richards. "And if it'll make you feel any better, I can solve your problem."

"The last time I heard that, I almost got kidnapped," said Brer John. But he smiled. "All right. What is this solution?"

"Just this. We have been waiting for a long time for the horowitz to lay its egg; we even had a host animal ready. Your appearance upset everything. But it doesn't necessarily ruin everything. If you would be willing to sign a contract to go to Feral, the native planet of the horowitz, and there allow yourself to be studied until the egg fully develops, then—"

"You give me hope, Mr. Richards. But there is something about your tone I don't like. What will this involve? Especially how much time will it take?"

"We—the Feral Study Grant group—would like you to go to Feral and there live as one of them while—"

"As one of them? How? They'd kill me!"

"Not at all. They don't kill the host animal until after the embryo is—uh—born. But we would step in just before that time. You'll be under close observance all the time. I wouldn't try to deceive you into thinking it couldn't involve danger. But if you agree, you'll be doing science a marvelous service. You can give us a much more detailed, and personal, account than we could get by watching through long-distance scopes.

"And, Brer John, at the end of your service, we'll guarantee you immediate passage to Wilden-wooly. Plus a substantial contribution to your order there."

"How long will it be before I get to Wilden-wooly?"

"About four months."

Brer John closed his eyes. Richards could not tell if he were praying or thinking. Probably, he decided, it was both.

Then Brer John opened his eyes, and he smiled.

"If I took a job on Earth, I'd have to work two years to pay for the passage. I might be able to do something else, but offhand I can't think of anything. And from the strange course of events, I think I was *led* into that moat and thence into your hands. At least, I choose to think so.

"I'll go to Feral for four months. The best route is not necessarily the straightest one. Success in circuit lies."

Brer John was sitting in the waiting room of the spaceport, meditating and also thanking God that the loose robe of his order allowed the egg attached to his breast to be well hidden. Within a few minutes a bell would sound, and it would be time to board the *Rousehound*.

A man came in, placed his traveling bag on the floor, and sat down next to him. The man fidgeted a while, looking at Brer John every now and then. Brer John smiled whenever his eye was caught, and he said nothing. He was learning the value of silence. Presently, the man said, "Going frontier, Father?"

"Call me Brer," said Brer John. "I am not a priest but a lay brother. Yes, I am going frontier. To Wildenwooly."

"Wildenwooly? Me, too! Thank God, I'll be off Earth! What a dull restricted place! Nothing exciting ever happens here. Same old in-and-out, up-and-down, day after day. Now, you take Wildenwooly! There's a place calling to every red-blooded freedom-loving adventurous man! Why, I understand you can't walk more than a mile or two before more strange and wonderful things happen to you than in a lifetime on this grey globe."

"Bless you!" said Brer John.

The man looked at the brother and moved away. He never did understand why Brer John's face turned red and his hand doubled up as if to strike a blow.

PROMETHEUS

The man with the egg growing on his chest stepped out of the spaceship.

In the light of dawn the veldt of Feral looked superficially like an African plain before the coming of the white man. It was covered with a foot-high brown grass. Here and there were tall thick-trunked trees standing alone or in groves of from five to thirty. Everywhere were herds of animals. These were cropping the grass or else drinking from a waterhole a quarter of a mile away. At this distance, some resembled antelopes, gnus, giraffes, pigs, and elephants. There were other creatures that looked as if they had come out of Earth's Pliocene. And others that had no terrestrial parallels.

"No mammals," said a voice behind the man with the egg attached to his chest. "They're warm-blooded descendants of reptiles. But not mammals."

The speaker walked around John Carmody. He was Doctor Holmyard, sapientologist, zoologist, chief of the expedition. A tall man of about sixty

with a lean body and leaner face and brown hair
that had once been a bright red.

"The two previous studies established that
mammals either never developed or were wiped
out early. Apparently, the reptiles and birds
jumped the gun in the evolutionary race. But they
have filled the ecological niche the mammals
occupied on Earth."

Carmody was a short rolypoly man with a big
head and a long sharp nose. His left eye had a lid
that tended to droop. Before he had gotten off the
ship he had been wearing a monk's robe.

Holmyard pointed at a clump of trees due north
and a mile away. "There is your future home until
the egg hatches," he said. "And, if you want to stay
after that, we'll be very happy."

He gestured at two men who had followed him
out of the ship, and they approached Carmody.
They removed his kilt and fastened a transparent
belt around his protruding stomach. Then they
attached it to a sporran of feathers, barred red
and white. Over his shaven head went a wig with a
tall crest of red and white feathers. Next, a false
beak edged with teeth was fitted over his nose. His
mouth, however, was left free. Then, a bustle from
which projected a tail of red and white plumage
was fitted to the belt.

Holmyard walked around Carmody. He shook
his head. "These birds—if they are birds—won't
be fooled one bit when they get a close look at you.
On the other hand, your general silhouette is
convincing enough to allow you to get fairly close
to them before they decide you're a fake. By then,
they may be curious enough to permit you to join
them."

"And if they attack?" said Carmody. Despite the
seriousness of what might happen, he was
grinning. He felt such a fool, togged out like a man

going to a masquerade party as a big rooster.

"We've already implanted the mike into your throat," said Holmyard. "The transceiver is flat, fitted to curve with your skull. You can holler for help, and we'll come running. Don't forget to turn the transceiver off when you're not using it. The charge won't last for more than fifty operational hours. But you can renew the charge at the cache."

"And you'll move camp to a place five miles due south of here?" said Carmody. "Then the ship takes off?"

"Yes. Don't forget. If—after—you've established yourself, come back to the cache and get the cameras. You can put them in the best locations for taking films of the horowitzes."

"I like that *if*," said Carmody. He looked across the plains at his destination, then shook hands with the others.

"God be with you," said the little monk.

"And with you, too," said Holmyard, warmly pumping his hand. "You're doing a great service for science, John. Perhaps for mankind. And for the horowitzes, too. Don't forget what I've told you."

"Among my many failings, a bad memory is not numbered," said John Carmody. He turned and began walking off across the veldt. A few minutes later, the great vessel lifted silently to a height of twenty feet, then shot off towards the south.

A lonely little man, ridiculous in his borrowed feathers, looking less like a man than a rooster that had lost a fight, and feeling like one at the moment, John Carmody set off through the grass. He was wearing transparent shoes, so the occasional rocks he stepped on did not hurt his feet.

A herd of equine creatures stopped feeding to

look at him, to sniff the air. They were about the size of zebras and were completely hairless, having a smooth yellowish skin mottled with squares of a pale red. Lacking tails, they had no weapons of defense against the flies that swarmed around them, but their long nonreptilian tongues slid out and licked the flies off each other's flanks. They gave horsy snorts and whinnied. After watching Carmody for about sixty seconds, they suddenly broke and fled to a position about a hundred yards away. Then, they wheeled almost as a unit and faced him again. He decided that it must be his strange odor that had spooked them, and he hoped that the horowitzes would not also be offended.

At that moment, he was beginning to think that he had been foolish to volunteer for this job. Especially, when a huge creature, lacking only long tusks to resemble an elephant, lifted its trunk and trumpeted at him. However, the creature immediately began pulling down fruit from a tree and paid no more attention to him.

Carmody walked on, not without many sidewise glances to make sure it was keeping its air of indifference. By now, however, his characteristic optimism had reasserted itself. And he was telling himself that he had been guided to this planet for a very definite purpose. What the purpose was, he didn't know. But he was certain of Who had sent him.

The chain of events that had dragged him here was made of too strange a series of links to be only coincidences. Or so, at least, he believed. Only a month ago he had been fairly happy to be a simple monk working in the garden of the monastery of the Order of St. Jairus in the city of Fourth of July, Arizona, North American Department. Then, his abbot had told him that he was to transfer to a parish on the planet of Wildenwooly. And his troubles had begun.

First, he was given no money with which to buy a ticket for passage on a spaceship, no letters of introduction or identification or any detailed orders at all. He was just told to leave at once. He did not even have enough money to buy a bus ticket which would take him to the spaceport outside the domed city. He began walking and, as seemed to be his fate wherever he was, he got into one trouble after another. He finally found himself in the city park, where he was thrown by a hoodlum into a moat in the city zoo. Here a female horowitz, a giant bird of the planet Feral, had leaped into the moat and, holding him down with one foot, proceeded to lay her egg on his chest. Later, Carmody had escaped from the moat, only to find that the egg had put out tendrils of flesh and attached itself permanently to his chest.

When the zoo authorities located Carmody, they told him that the female horowitz, when she had no available male or other female on whom to attach her eggs, would attach it to a host animal. Carmody had been unlucky enough—or, from the viewpoint of the zoologists, lucky enough—to be a host. Lucky because now they would have an opportunity to study closely the development of the embryo in the egg and the manner in which it drew sustenance from its host. Moreover, if Carmody would go to Feral and attempt to pass as a horowitz, he would be the means for furnishing the zoologists with invaluable data about these birds. The zoologists believed the horowitzes to be the Galaxy's most intelligent nonsentient beings. There was even speculation they might be advanced enough to have a language. Would Carmody work with the zoologists if they paid for his trip to Wildenwooly after the study was made?

So, the lonely little man walked across the veldt with a leathery-skinned egg attached to his bloodstream. He was filled with apprehension which even his prayers did little to still.

Flocks of thousands of birds flew overhead. A creature large as an elephant, but with a long neck and four knobbly horns on its muzzle, browsed off the leaves of a tree. It paid no attention to him, so Carmody did not veer away but walked in a straight line which took him only fifty yards from it.

Then, out of a tall clump of grass stepped an animal which he knew at once was one of the great carnivores. It was lion-colored, lion-sized, and was built much like a lion. However it was hairless. Its feline face wrinkled in a silent snarl. Carmody stopped and made a half-turn to face it. His hand slid among his tailfeathers and closed around the butt of the gun hidden there.

He had been warned about this type of meat-eater.

"Only if they're very hungry or too old to catch fleeter prey will they attack you," Holmyard had said.

This creature didn't look old, and its sides were sleek. But Carmody thought that if its temperament was as catlike as its looks, it might attack just because it was annoyed.

The leonoid blinked at him and yawned. Carmody began to breathe a trifle easier. The creature sat down on its haunches and gazed at him for all the world like a curious, but oversize, pussycat. Slowly, Carmody edged away.

The leonoid made no move to follow. Carmody was congratulating himself, when, on his left, a creature burst loose from a clump of grass.

He saw that it was a half-grown horowitz, but he had no more time to look at it. The leonoid, as

startled as Carmody, leaped forward in pursuit of
the runner. The horowitz cried in fear. The leonoid
roared. Its pace increased.

Suddenly, out of the same clump from which the
young bird had run, an adult darted. This one held
a club in its hand. Though it was no match for the
carnivore, it ran towards it, waving its club in its
humanlike hand and yelling.

By then Carmody had drawn the pistol from its
holster, and he directed the stream of bullets at
the leonoid. The first missile exploded in the
ground a few feet ahead of the creature; the
remainder raked its side. Over and over the animal
turned, and then it fell.

The adult horowitz dropped the club, scooped
up the young bird in its arms, and began running
towards the grove of trees about a half a mile
ahead, its home.

Carmody shrugged, reloaded the gun, and
resumed his walk.

"Perhaps, I can put this incident to good use,"
he said aloud to himself. "If they are capable of
gratitude, I should be received with open arms. On
the other hand, they may fear me so much they
might launch a mass attack. Well, we shall see."

By the time he had neared the grove, the
branches of the trees were alive with the females
and the young. And the males had gathered to
make a stand outside the grove. One, evidently a
leader, stood ahead of the group. Carmody was
not sure, but he thought that this was the one who
had run with the child.

The leader was armed with a stick. He walked
stiff-leggedly and slowly towards him. Carmody
stopped and began talking. The leader also
stopped and bent his head to one side to listen in a
very birdlike gesture. He was like the rest of his
species, though larger—almost seven feet tall. His

feet were three-toed, his legs thick to bear his weight, his body superficially like an ostrich's. But he had no wings, rudimentary or otherwise. He had well-developed arms and five-fingered hands, though the fingers were much longer in proportion than a man's. His neck was thick, and the head was large with a well-developed brain-case. The brown eyes were set in the front of his broad head like a man's; the corvine beak was small, lined with sharp teeth, and black. His body was naked of plumage except for red-and-white-barred feathers in the loin region, on the back, and on the head. There a tall crest of feathers bristled, and around his ears were stiff feathers, like a horned owl's designed to focus sound.

Carmody listened for a minute to the sounds of the leader's voice and those behind him. He could make out no definite pattern of speech, no distinguishing rhythm, no repetition of words. Yet, they were uttering definite syllables, and there was something familiar about their speaking.

After a minute, he recognized its similarity, and he was startled. They were talking like a baby when he is at the stage of babbling. They were running the scale of potential phonemes, up and down, at random, sometimes repeating, more often not.

Carmody reached up slowly to his scalp so he wouldn't alarm them with a sudden movement. He slid the panel-switch on the skull-fitting transceiver under his crest, thus allowing the zoologists at the camp to tune in.

Carmody spoke in a low tone, knowing that the microphone implanted in his throat would clearly reproduce his voice to the listeners at the camp. He described his situation and then said, "I'm going to walk into their home. If you hear a loud crack, it'll be a club breaking my skull. Or vice versa."

He began walking, not directly towards the leader but to one side. The big horowitz turned as the man went by, but he made no threatening move with his club. Carmody went on by, though he felt his back prickle when he could no longer see the leader. Then he had walked straight at the mob, and he saw them step to one side, their heads cocked to one side, their sharp-toothed bills emitting the infantile babblings.

He passed safely through them to the middle of the grove of cottonwoodlike trees. Here the females and males and young looked down at him. The females resembled the males in many respects, but they were smaller and their crests were brown. Almost all of them were carrying eggs on their chests or else held the very young in their arms. These were covered from head to thigh with a golden-brown chicklike fuzz. The older children, however, had lost the down. The female adults looked as puzzled as the males, but the children seemed to have only curiosity. The older children climbed out on the branches above him and looked down at him. And they, too, babbled like babies.

Presently, a half-grown horowitz, a female by her all-brown crest, climbed down and slowly approached him. Carmody reached into the pouch in his tail feathers, and he brought out a lump of sugar. This he tasted himself to show her it wasn't poisonous, and then he held it out in his hand and made coaxing sounds. The young girl—he was already thinking of these beings as human—snatched the cube from his hand and ran back to the trunk of the tree. Here she turned the sugar lump over and over, felt its texture with the tips of her fingers, and then barely touched the cube with the tip of her long broad tongue.

She looked pleased. This surprised Carmody,
for he had not thought of the possibility that
humanoid expressions could take place on such an
avian face. But the face was broad and flat and
well-equipped with muscles and able as a man's to
depict emotion.

The girl put all of the cube in her bill, and she
looked ecstatic. Then she turned to the big
horowitz—who had neared the two—and uttered a
series of syllables. There was evident pleasure in
her voice.

Carmody held out another lump of sugar to the
leader, who took it and popped it into his bill. And
over his face spread pleasure.

Carmody spoke out loud for the benefit of the
men in the camp. "Put a good supply of sugar in
the cache," he said, "plus some salt. I think it's
likely that these people may be salt-starved, too."

"People!" exploded the ghostly voice in his ear.
"Carmody, don't start making anthropocentric
errors regarding these creatures."

"You've not met them," said Carmody. "Perhaps
you could maintain a zoologist's detachment. But
I can't. Human is as human does."

"O.K., John. But when you report, just give a
description, and never mind your interpretations.
After all, I'm human, and therefore, open to
suggestion."

Carmody grinned and said, "O.K. Oh, they're
starting to dance now. I don't know what the
dance means, whether it's something instinctive
or something they've created."

While Carmody had been talking, the females
and the young had climbed down out of the trees.
They formed a semicircle and began clapping
their hands together in rhythm. The males had
gathered before them and were now hopping,
jumping, spinning, bowing, waddling bent-kneed

like ducks. They gave weird cries and occasionally flapped their arms and leaped into the air as if simulating the flight of birds. After about five minutes, the dance suddenly ceased, and the horowitzes formed a single-file line. Their leader, at the head of the line, walked towards Carmody.

"Oh, oh," said Carmody. "I think we're seeing the formation of the first breadline in the non-history of these people. Only it's sugar, not bread, that they want."

"How many are there?" said Holmyard.

"About twenty-five."

"Got enough sugar?"

"Only if I break up the cubes and give each a slight taste."

"Try that, John. While you're doing that, we'll rush more sugar to the cache on a jeep. Then you can lead them there after we leave."

"Maybe I'll take them there. Just now I'm worried about their reaction if they don't get a complete lump."

He began to break up the cubes into very small pieces and to put one into each extended hand. Every time, he said, "Sugar." By the time the last one in line—a mother with a fuzzy infant in her arms—had stuck out her hand, he had only one fragment left.

"It's a miracle," he said, sighing with relief. "Came out just right. They've gone back to what I presume are their normal occupations. Except for their chief and some of the children. These, as you can hear, are babbling like mad at me."

"We're recording their sounds," said Holmyard. "We'll make an attempt to analyze them later, find out if they've a speech."

"I know you have to be scientific," replied Carmody. "But I have a very perceptive ear, like all people who run off at the mouth, and I can tell you now they don't have a language. Not in the sense we think of, anyway."

A few minutes later, he said, "Correction. They at least have the beginning of a language. One of the little girls just came up and held out her hand and said, 'Sugar.' Perfect reproduction of English speech, if you ignore the fact that it couldn't have come from a human mouth. Sounded like a parrot or crow."

"I heard her! That's significant as hell, Carmody! If she could make the correlation so quickly, she must be capable of symbolic thinking." He added, in a more moderate tone, "Unless it was accidental, of course."

"No accident. Did you hear the other child also ask for it?"

"Faintly. While you're observing them, try to give them a few more words to learn."

Carmody sat down at the base of a thick tree-trunk in the shade of branches, for the sun was beginning to turn the air hot. The tree had thick corrugated bark like a cottonwood, but it bore fruit. This grew high up on the branches and looked from a distance like a banana. The young girl brought him one and held it out to him, saying at the same time, "Sugar?"

Carmody wanted to taste the fruit, but he didn't think it would be fair to receive it without giving her what she wanted. He shook his head no, though he didn't expect her to interpret the gesture. She cocked her head to one side, and her face registered disappointment. Nevertheless, she did not withdraw the fruit. And, after making sure she knew he was out of sugar, he took the gift. The shell had to be rapped against the side of the tree to be broken, and it came apart in the middle, where it creased. He took a small bite from the interior and reported to Holmyard that it tasted like a combination of apple and cherry.

"They not only feed on this fruit," he said.
"They're eating the tender shoots of a plant that
resembles bamboo. I also saw one catch and eat a
small rodentlike animal which ran out from under
a rock she turned over. And they pick lice off each
other and eat insects they find around the roots of
the grass. I saw one try to catch a bird that was
eating the bamboo shoots.

"Oh, the leader is pounding a club on the
ground. They're dropping whatever they're doing
and clustering around him. Looks as if they're
getting ready to go some place. The females and
young are forming a group. The males, all armed
with clubs, are surrounding them. I think I'll join
them."

Their destination, he was to find out, was a
waterhole about a mile and a half away. It was a
shallow depression about twenty feet across filled
with muddy water. There were animals gathered
about it: gazellelike creatures, a giant porcine
with armor like an armadillo, several birds that
seemed at first glance and far off to be horowitzes.
But when Carmody got closer, he saw they were
only about two and a half feet high, their arms
were much longer, and their foreheads slanted
back. Perhaps, these filled the ecological niche
here that monkeys did on Earth.

The animals fled at the approach of the
horowitzes. These established guards, one at each
cardinal point of the compass, and the rest drank
their fill. The young jumped into the water and
splashed around, throwing water in each other's
face and screaming with delight. Then they were
hauled out, protesting, by their mothers. The
guards drank their fill, and the group prepared to
march back to their home, the grove.

Carmody was thirsty, but he didn't like the looks

or odor of the water, which smelled as if something had died in it. He looked around and saw that the dozen trees around the waterhole were a different type. These were fifty-feet high slim plants with a smooth lightbrown bark and only a few branches, which grew near the top. Clusters of gourds also grew among the branches. At the bottom of the trees lay empty gourds. He picked up one, broke in the narrow end, and dipped it in the water. Then he dropped in the water an antibiotic pill which he took from the bustle under his tailfeathers. He drank, making a face at the taste. The young girl who had first asked him for sugar approached, and he showed her how to drink from the gourd. She laughed a quite human-sounding laugh and poured the water down her open beak.

Carmody took advantage of the curiosity of the others to show them that they, too, could fill their gourds and transport water back to the grove.

Thus, the first artifact was invented—or given—on Feral. In a short time, everyone had gourds and filled them. And the group, babbling like babies, began the march back to home.

"I don't know if they're intelligent enough to learn a language yet," said Carmody to Holmyard. "It seems to me that if they were, they'd have created one. But they are the most intelligent animal I've yet encountered. Far superior to the chimpanzee or porpoise. Unless they just have a remarkable mimetic ability."

"We've run off samples of their speech in the analyzer," said Holmyard. "And there's no distribution to indicate a well-organized language. Or even an incipient language."

"I'll tell you one thing," replied Carmody. "They at least have identifying sounds for each other. I've noticed that when they want the leader's

attention, they say 'Whoot!', and he responds.
Also, this girl who asked for sugar responds to the
call of Tutu. So, I'm identifying them as such."

The rest of the day Carmody spent observing the
horowitzes and reporting to Holmyard. He said
that, during times of danger or during a joint
undertaking such as going for water, the group
acted as a whole. But most of the time they
seemed to operate in small family units. The
average family consisted of a male, the children,
and anywhere from one to three females. Most of
the females had eggs attached to their chests or
bellies. He was able to settle for Holmyard the
question of whether, generally, the females laid
their eggs on each other, and so raised foster-
families, or transferred the eggs to their own skin
immediately after laying. Towards dusk he saw a
female deposit an egg and then hold it against the
chest of another female. In a few minutes, little
tendrils crept forth from the leathery-skinned
ovum and inserted themselves into the
bloodstream of the hostess.

"That, I would take it, is the general course of
action," Carmody said. "But there is one male
here who, like me, carries an egg. I don't know
why he was singled out. But I would say that, at
the time the egg was produced, the female and her
mate were separated from the others. So the
female took the lesser alternative. Don't ask me
why the females just don't attach the eggs to their
own bodies. Maybe there's a chemical factor that
prevents the egg from attaching itself to its own
mother. Perhaps some sort of antibody setup. I
don't know. But there is some reason which, up to
now, only the Creator of the horowitzes knows."

"It's not a general pattern for all the birds of
this planet," said Holmyard. "There are
oviparous, oviviparous, and viviparous species.

But the order of birds of which the horowitzes are the highest in development, the order of Aviprimates, all have this feature. From highest to lowest, they lay their eggs and then attach them to a host."

"I wonder why this particular line of creatures didn't develop viviparism?" said Carmody. "It seems obvious that it's the best method for protecting the unborn."

"Who knows?" said Holmyard, and Carmody, mentally, could see him shrugging. "That's a question that may or may not be answered during this study. After all, this planet is new to us. It's not had a thorough study. It was only by a lucky accident that Horowitz discovered these birds during his brief stay here. Or that we were able to get a grant to finance us."

"One reason for this externalism may be that even if the embryo is injured or killed, the hostess is not," said Carmody. "If the embryo of a viviparous mother is destroyed, then the mother usually is, too. But here, I imagine, though the embryo may be more susceptible to death and injury, the bearer of the unborn is relatively unaffected by the wound."

"Maybe," said Holmyard. "Nature is an experimenter. Perhaps, she's trying this method on this planet."

He is, you mean, thought Carmody, but he said nothing. The gender of the Creator did not matter. Both he and the zoologist were talking about the same entity.

Carmody continued to give his observations. The mothers fed the very young in the traditional manner of birds, by regurgitating food.

"That seemed probable," said Holmyard. "The reptiles developed a class of warmblooded animals, but none of these have hair or even rudimentary mammaries. The horowitz, as I told you, evolved from a very primitive bird which took up arboreal life at the time its cousins were learning to glide. The fleshy fold of skin hanging down between arm and rib is a vestige of that brief period when it had begun to glide and then changed its mind and decided to become a lemuroid-type.

"Or so it seems to us. Actually, we haven't unearthed enough fossils to speak authoritatively."

"They do have certain cries which can be interpreted by the others. Such as a cry for help, a cry for pick-my-fleas, a rallying cry, and so on. But that's all. Except that some of the children now know the word for sugar and water. And they identify each other. Would you say that that is the first step in creating a language?"

"No, I wouldn't," said Holmyard firmly. "But if you can teach them to take an assemblage of independent words and string them together into an intelligible sentence, and if they become capable of reassembling these words in different patterns and for different situations, then I'd say they are in a definite lingual stage. But your chance for doing that is very remote. After all, they might be in a prelingual stage, just on the verge of becoming capable of verbal symbolism. But it might take another ten thousand years, maybe fifty thousand, before their kind develop that ability. Before they take the step from animal to human being."

"And maybe I can give them the nudge," said Carmody. "Maybe . . ."

"Maybe what?" said Holmyard after Carmody had been silent for several minutes.

"I'm confronted with the theological question the Church raised some centuries before interstellar travel became possible," said Carmody. "At what moment did the ape become a man? At what moment did the ape possess a soul, and . . ."

"Jesus Christ!" said Holmyard. "I know you're a monk, Carmody! And it's only natural you should be interested in such a question! But, I beg of you, don't start muddling around with something as divorced from reality as the exact moment when a soul is inserted into an animal! Don't let this—this how-many-angels-on-a-pinpoint absurdity begin to color your reports. Please try to keep a strictly objective and scientific viewpoint. Just describe what you see; no more!"

"Take it easy, Doc. That's all I intend to do. But you can't blame me for being interested. However, it's not for me to decide such a question. I leave that up to my superiors. My order, that of St. Jairus, does not do much theological speculation; we are primarily men of action."

"O.K., O.K., said Holmyard. "Just so we understand each other. Now, do you intend to introduce fire to the horowitzes tonight?"

"Just as soon as dusk falls."

Carmody spent the rest of the day in teaching little Tutu the word for tree, egg, gourd, a few verbs which he acted out for her, and the pronouns. She caught on quickly. He was sure that it was not the purely mimetic speech ability of a parrot. To test her, he asked her a question.

"You see the tree?" he said, pointing at a large sycamore-like fruit tree.

She nodded, a gesture she had learned from him, and she replied in her strange birdlike voice, "Yes. Tutu see the tree."

Then, before he could frame another question, she said, pointing at the chief, "You see Whoot? Tutu see Whoot. Him horowitz. Me horowitz. You . . .?"

For a moment Carmody was speechless, and

Holmyard's voice screeched thinly, "John, did you
hear her? She can speak and understand English!
And in such a short time, too! John, these people
must have been ready for speech! We gave it to
them! We gave it to them!"

Carmody   could   hear   Holmyard's   heavy
breathing as if the man stood next to him. He said,
"Calm down, my good friend. Though I don't
blame you for being excited."

Tutu cocked her head to one side and said, "You
talk to . . .?"

"Me a man," said Carmody, replying to her
previous question. "Man, man. And me talk to a
man . . . not me. The man far away." Then,
realizing she didn't know the meaning of the
words *far away*, he indicated distance with a
sweep of his arm and a finger pointing off across
the veldt.

"You talk to . . . a man . . . far away?"

"Yes," said Carmody, wishing to get off that
subject. She wasn't ready to understand any
explanation he could give her for his ability to
communicate across long distances, so he said,
"Me tell you some time . . ." And he stopped again,
for he didn't have enough words with which to
explain time. That would have to come later.

"Me make fire," he said.

Tutu continued to look puzzled, as she understood only the first word of his sentence. "Me
show you," he said, and he proceeded to gather
long dried grasses and punk from a dead tree.
These he piled together, and then tore off some
twigs and smaller dead branches, which he laid by
the first pile. By this time many of the children
and some of the adults had collected around him.

He pulled from his bustle under the tailfeathers
a flint and a piece of iron pyrite. These he had
brought from the spaceship because the zoologists

had told him this area was poor in both minerals. He showed the two pieces to them and then, after six tries, struck a spark. The spark fell on the grass but did not set fire to it. He tried three more times before a spark took root. In the next few seconds he had enough of a fire going to be able to throw on twigs and then branches.

When the first jet of flame arose, the wide-eyed assembly gasped. But they did not run, as he had feared. Instead, they made sounds which attracted the others. Shortly, the entire tribe was gathered around him.

Tutu, saying, "Au! Au!"—which Carmody interpreted as a sound of amazement or of delight in beauty—put out her hand to seize the flame. Carmody opened his mouth to say, "No! Fire bad!" But he closed his lips. How to tell her that something could be very harmful and at the same time be a great good?

He looked around and saw that one of the youngsters standing at the back of the crowd was holding a mouse-sized rodent in her hand. So fascinated was she by the fire that she had not yet popped the living animal into her beak. Carmody went to her and pulled her close to the fire, where everybody could see her. Then, not without having to overcome the reluctance of the child with many reassuring gestures, he got her to give him the rodent. Distastefully, he dashed its life out by snapping its head against a rock. He took his knife and skinned and gutted and decapitated the creature. Then he sharpened a long stick and stuck it through the rodent. After which, he took Tutu by her slender elbow and guided her close to the fire. When she felt its intense heat, she drew back. He allowed her to do so, saying, "Fire hot! Burn! Burn!"

She looked at him with wide eyes, and he smiled

and patted her feathery top. Then he proceeded to
roast the mouse. Afterwards, he cut it in three
parts, allowed the bits to cool, and gave one to the
girl from whom he had taken the mouse, one to
Tutu, and one to the chief. All three gingerly tasted
it and at the same time breathed ecstasy, "Ah!"

Carmody didn't get much sleep that night. He
kept the fire going while the whole tribe sat
around the flames and admired them. Several
times, some large animals, attracted by the
brightness, came close enough for him to see their
eyes glowing. But they made no attempt to get
closer.

In the morning, Carmody talked to Holmyard.
"At least five of the children are only a step behind
Tutu in learning English," he said. "so far, none of
the adults has shown any inclination to repeat any
of the words. But their habit patterns may be too
rigid for them to learn. I don't know. I'll work on
the chief and some others today. Oh, yes, when
you drop off some ammunition at the cache,
would you leave me a holster and ammo belt for
my gun? I don't think they'll find it strange.
Apparently, they know I'm not a true horowitz.
But it doesn't seem to matter to them.

"I'm going to kill an antelope today and show
them how to cook meat on a big scale. But they'll
be handicapped unless they can find some flint or
chert with which to fashion knives. I've been
thinking that I ought to lead then to a site where
they can find some. Do you know of any?"

"We'll go out in the jeep and look for some,"
said Holmyard. "You're right. Even if they are
capable of learning to make tools and pottery,
they're not in an area suited to develop that
ability."

"Why didn't you pick a group which lived near a
flint-rich area?"

"Mainly, because it was in this area that Horowitz discovered these creatures. We scientists are just as apt to get into a rut as anybody, so we didn't look into the future. Besides, we had no idea these animals —uh—people, if they do deserve that term—were so full of potential."

Just then Tutu, holding a mouse-sized grasshopper in her hand, came up to Carmody.

"This . . . ?"

"This is a grasshopper," said Carmody.

"You burn . . . the fire."

"Yes. Me burn *in* fire. No, not burn. Me cook *in* fire."

"You cook in the fire," she said. "You give to me. Me eat; you eat."

"She's now learned two prepositions—I think," said Carmody.

"John, why this pidgin English?" said Holmyard. "Why the avoidance of *is* and the substitution of the nominative case for the objective with the personal pronouns?"

"Because *is* isn't necessary," replied Carmody. "Many languages get along without it, as you well know. Moreover, there's a recent tendency in English to drop it in conversational speech, and I'm just anticipating what may become a general development.

"As for teaching them lower-class English, I'm doing that because I think that the language of the illiterates will triumph. You know how hard the teachers in our schools have to struggle to overcome the tendency of their high-class students to use button-pusher's jargon."

"O.K.," said Holmyard. "It doesn't matter, anyway. The horowitzes have no conception—as far as I know—of the difference. Thank God, you're not teaching them Latin!"

"Say!" said Carmody. "I didn't think of that!
Why not? If the horowitzes ever become civilized
enough to have interstellar travel, they'd always
be able to talk to priests, no matter where they
went."

"Carmody!"

Carmody chuckled and said, "Just teasing,
Doctor. But I do have a serious proposition. If
other groups should show themselves as capable
of linguistic learning, why not teach each group a
different language? Just as an experiment? This
group would be our Indo-European school;
another, Sinitic; another, our Amerindian; still
another, Bantu. It would be interesting to see how
the various groups developed socially, tech-
nologically, and philosophically. Would each
group follow the general lines of social evolution
that their prototypes did on Earth? Would the
particular type of language a group used place it
on a particular path during its climb uphill to
civilization?"

"A tempting idea," said Holmyard. "But I'm
against it. Sentient beings have enough barriers to
understanding each other without placing the
additional obstacles of differing languages in their
way. No, I think that all should be taught English.
A single speech will give them at least one unifying
element. Though, God knows, their tongues will
begin splitting into dialects soon enough."

"Bird-English I'll teach them," said Carmody.

One of the first things he had to do was
straighten out Tutu concerning the word *tree*. She
was teaching some of the younger horowitzes
what language she'd mastered so far and was
pointing to a cottonwood and calling out, "Tree!
Tree!"

Then she pointed to another cottonwood, and
she became silent. Wonderingly, she looked at

Carmody, and he knew in that moment that she thought of that cottonwood as tree. But that word to her meant an individual entity or thing. She had no generic concept of tree.

Carmody tried by illustration to show her. He pointed at the second cottonwood and said, "Tree." Then he pointed at one of the tall thin trees and repeated the word.

Tutu cocked her head to one side, and an obvious puzzlement settled on her face.

Carmody further confused her by indicating the two cottonwoods and giving each their name. Then, on the spot, he made up a name for the tall thin trees and said, "Tumtum."

"Tumtum," said Tutu.

"Tumtumtree," said Carmody. He pointed at the cottonwood. "Cottonwoodtree." He pointed out across the veldt. "Thorntree." He made an all-inclusive gesture. "All tree."

The youngsters around Tutu did not seem to grasp his meaning, but she laughed—as a crow laughs—and said, "Tumtum. Cottonwood. Thorn. All tree."

Carmody wasn't sure whether she grasped what he'd said or was just mimicking him. Then she said, swiftly—perhaps she was able to interpret his look of frustration—"Tumtumtree. Cottonwoodtree. Thorntree."

She held up three fingers and made a sweeping gesture with the other hand. "All tree."

Carmody was pleased, for he was fairly certain she now knew tree as not only an individual but a generic term. But he didn't know how to tell her that the last-named was not a thorn but was a thorntree. He decided that it didn't matter. Not for the time being, at least. But when the time came to name a thorn as such, he would have to give the thorn another nomenclature. No use confusing them.

"You seem to be doing famously," said Holmyard's voice. "What's next on the agenda?"

"I'm going to try to sneak away to the cache and pick up some more ammo and sugar," said Carmody. "Before I do, could you drop off a blackboard and some paper and pencils?"

"You won't have to take notes," said Holmyard. "Everything you say is being recorded, as I think I once told you," he added impatiently.

"I'm not thinking of making memos," said Carmody. "I intend to start teaching them how to read and write."

There was a silence for several seconds, then, "*What?*"

"Why not?" replied Carmody. "Even at this point, I'm not absolutely certain they really understand speech. Ninety-nine per cent sure, yes. But I want to be one-hundred per cent certain. And if they can understand written speech, then there's no doubt.

"Besides, why wait until later? If they can't learn now, we can try later. If they do catch on now, we've not wasted any time."

"I must apologize," said Holmyard. "I lacked imagination. I should have thought of that step. You know, John, I resented the fact that you had, through pure accident, been chosen to make this first venture among the horowitzes. I thought a trained scientist, preferably myself, should have been the contact man. But I see now that having you out there isn't a mistake. You have what we professionals too often too quickly lose: the enthusiastic imagination of the amateur. Knowing the difficulties or even the improbabilities, we allow ourselves to be too cautious."

"Oh, oh!" said Carmody. "Excuse me, but it looks as if the chief is organizing everybody for some big move. He's running around, gabbling his nonsense syllables like mad and pointing to the north. He's also pointing at the branches of the trees. Oh, I see what he's getting at. Almost all of the fruit is eaten. And he wants us to follow him."

"Which direction?"

"South. Towards you."

"John, there's a nice valley about a thousand miles north of here. We found it during the last expedition and noted it because it's higher, cooler, much better watered. And it not only contains flint but iron ores."

"Yes, but the chief evidently wants us to go in the opposite direction."

There was a pause. Finally, Carmody sighed and said, "I get the message. You want me to lead them north. Well, you know what that means."

"I'm sorry, John. I know it means conflict. And I can't order you to fight the chief. That is, if it's necessary for you to fight."

"I rather think it will be. Too bad, too; I wouldn't exactly call this Eden, but at least no blood has been shed among these people. And now, because we want to plumb their potentiality, lead them on to higher things . . ."

"You don't have to, John. Nor will I hold it against you if you just tag along and study them wherever they go. After all, we've gotten far more data than I ever dreamed possible. But . . ."

"But if I don't try to take over the reins of leadership, these beings may remain at a low level for a long long time. Besides, we have to determine if they are capable of any technology. So . . . the end justifies the means. Or so say the Jesuits. I am not a Jesuit, but I can justify the premise on which we're basing the logic of this argument."

Carmody did not say another word to

Holmyard. He marched up to the big leader, took a
stand before him, and, shaking his head fiercely
and pointing to the north, he shouted, "Us go this
way! No go that way!"

The chief stopped his gabbling and cocked his
head to one side and looked at Carmody. His face,
bare of feathers, became red. Carmody could not
tell, of course, if it was the red of embarrassment
or of rage. So far as he could determine, his
position in this society had been a very peculiar
one—from the society's viewpoint. It had not
taken him long to see that a definite peck-order
existed here. The big horowitz could bully anyone
he wanted to. The male just below him in this
unspoken   hierarchy   could   not—or   would
not—resist the chief's authority. But he could
bully everybody below him. And so forth. All the
males, with the exception of one weak character,
could push the females around. And the females
had their own system, similar to the males, except
that it seemed to be more complex. The top female
in the peck-order system could lord it over all but
one female, and yet this female was subject to the
authority of at least half the other females. And
there were other cases whose intricacy defied
Camrody's powers of analysis.

One thing he had noticed, though, and that was
that the young were all treated with kindness and
affection. They were, in fact, very much the
spoiled brats. Yet, they had their own give-and-
take-orders organization.

Carmody had up to this time held no position in
the social scale. They seemed to regard him as
something apart, a *rara avis*, an unknown
quantity. The chief had made no move to establish
Carmody's place here, so the others had not dared
to try. And, probably, the chief had not dared
because he had been witness to Carmody's killing

of the leonoid.

But now the stranger had placed him in such a position that he must fight or else step down. And he must have been the top brass too long to endure that idea. Even if he knew Carmody's destructive potential, he did not intend to submit meekly.

So Carmody guessed from the reddened skin, the swelling chest, the veins standing out on his forehead, the glaring eyes, the snapping beak, the clenched fists, the sudden heavy breathing.

The chief, Whoot, was impressive. He stood a foot and a half taller than the man, his arms were long and muscular, his chest huge, and his beak with its sharp meat-eater's teeth and his three-toed legs with their sharp talons looked as if they could tear the heart out of Carmody.

But the little man knew that the horowitz didn't weigh as much as a man his height, for his bones were the half-hollow bones of a bird. Moreover, though the chief was undoubtedly a capable and vicious fighter, and intelligent, he did not have at his command the sophisticated knowledge of infighting of a dozen worlds. Carmody was as deadly with his hands and feet as any man alive; many times, he had killed and crippled.

The fight was sharp but short. Carmody used a melange of all his skills and very quickly had the chief reeling, bloody-beaked, and glassy-eyed. He gave the *coup de grace* by chopping with the edge of his palm against the side of the thick neck. He stood over the unconscious body of Whoot, breathing heavily, bleeding from three wounds delivered by the point of the beak and pointed teeth and suffering from a blow of a fist against his ribs.

He waited until the big horowitz had opened his eyes and staggered to his feet. Then, pointing north, he shouted, "Follow me!"

In a short time, they were walking after him as
he headed for a grove of trees about two miles
away. Whoot walked along in the rear of the
group, his head hung low. But after a while he
regained some of his spirit. And, when a large
male tried to make him carry some of the water
gourds, he jumped on the male and knocked him
to the ground. That re-established his position in
the group. He was below Carmody but still higher
than the rest.

Carmody was glad, for the little Tutu was
Whoot's child. He had been afraid that his defeat
of her father might make her hostile to him.
Apparently, the change in authority had made no
difference, unless it was that she stayed even more
by his side. While they walked together, Carmody
pointed out more animals and plants, naming
them. She repeated the words, sound-perfect,
after him. By now she had even adopted his style
of speaking, his individual rhythm pattern, his
manner of saying, "Heh?" when a strong thought
seized him, his habit of talking to himself.

And she imitated his laugh. He pointed out a
thin, shabby-looking bird with its feathers sticking
out all round and looking like a live mop.

"That a borogove."

"That a borogove," she repeated.

Suddenly, he laughed, and she laughed, too. But
he could not share the source of his mirth with
her. How could he explain *Alice in Wonderland* to
her? How could he tell her that he had wondered
what Lewis Carroll would think if he could see his
fictional creation come to life on a strange planet
circling around a strange star and centuries after
he had died? Or know that his works were still
alive and bearing fruit, even if weird fruit?
Perhaps, Carroll would approve. For he had been a
strange little man—like Carmody, thought Car-

mody—and he would consider the naming of this bird the apex of congruous incongruity.

He sobered immediately, for a huge animal resembling a green rhinoceros with three knobbed horns, trotted thunderingly towards them. Carmody took his pistol out from his bustle, causing Tutu's eyes to widen even more than at the sight of the tricorn. But, after stopping only a few feet from the group and sniffing the wind, the tricorn trotted slowly away. Carmody replaced the pistol, and he called Holmyard.

"You'll have to forget about caching the stuff I ordered in that tree," he said. "I'm leading them on the exodus as of now. I'll build a fire tonight, and you can relocate about five miles behind us. I'm going to try to get them to walk past this grove ahead, go on to another. I plan to lead them on a two mile and a half trek every day. I think that's about as far as I can push them. We should reach the valley of milk and honey you described in nine months. By then, my child," he tapped the egg on his chest, "should be hatched. And my contract with you will be terminated."

He had less trouble than he thought he would. Though the group scattered as soon as they reached the grove, they reassembled at his insistence and left the tempting fresh fruits and the many rodents to be found under the rocks. They did not murmur while he led them another mile to another grove. Here he decided they'd camp for the rest of the day and night.

After dusk fell, and he had supervised Tutu's building of a fire, he sneaked away into the darkness. Not without some apprehension, for more carnivores prowled under the two small moons than in the light of the sun. Nevertheless, he walked without incident for a mile and there met Doctor Holmyard, waiting in a jeep.

After borrowing a cigarette from Holmyard, he described the events of the day more fully than he had been able to do over the transceiver. Holmyard gently squeezed the egg clinging to Carmody's chest, and he said, "How does it feel not only to give birth to a horowitz, but to give birth to speech among them? To become, in a sense, the father of all the horowitzes?"

"It makes me feel very odd," said Carmody. "And aware of a great burden on me. After all, what I teach these sentients will determine the course of their lives for thousands of years to come. Maybe even further.

"Then again, all my efforts may come to nothing."

"You must be careful. Oh, by the way, here's the stuff you asked for. A holster and belt. And, in a knapsack, ammo, a flashlight, more sugar, salt, paper, pen, a pint of whiskey."

"You don't expect me to give them firewater?" said Carmody.

"No," chuckled Holmyard. "This bottle is your private stock. I thought you might like a nip now and then. After all, you must need something to buck up your spirits, being without your own kind."

"I've been too busy to be lonely. But nine months is a long time. No, I don't really believe I'll get unbearably lonely. These people are strange. But I'm sure they have spirits kindred to mine, waiting to be developed."

They talked some more, planning their method of study for the year to come. Holmyard said that a man would always be in the ship and in contact with Carmody, if an emergency should come up. But everybody would be busy, for this expedition had many projects in the fire. They would be collecting and dissecting specimens of all sorts, making soil and air and water analyses, geological surveys, digging for fossils, etc. Quite often the ship would take a trip to other regions, even to the other side of this planet. But when that happened, two men and a jeep would be left behind.

"Listen, Doc," said Carmody. "Couldn't you take a trip to this valley and get some flint ore? Then leave it close to us, so my group could find it? I'd like to find out *now* if they're capable of using weapons and tools."

Holmyard nodded and said, "A good idea. Will do. We'll have the flint for you before the week's up."

Holmyard shook Carmody's hand, and the little monk left. He lit his way with the flashlight, for he hoped that, though it might attract some of the big carnivores, it might also make them wary of getting too close.

He had not gone more than a hundred yards when, feeling as if he were being stalked, and also feeling foolish because he was obeying an irrational impulse, centered on the small figure of Tutu.

"What you do here?" he said. She approached slowly, as if fearing him, and he rephrased his question. There were so many words that she did not know that he could not, at this point, fully communicate with her.

"Why you here?"

Never before had he used *why*, but he thought that now, under the circumstances, she might understand it.

"Me . . ." she made a motion of following.

"Follow."

"Me follow . . . you. Me no . . . want you hurt. Big meat-eaters in dark. Bite, claw, kill, eat you. You die; me . . . how you say it?"

He saw what she meant, for tears were filling

her large brown eyes.

"Cry," he said. "Ah, Tutu, you cry for me?"

He was touched.

"Me cry," she said, her voice shaking, on the edge of sobs. "Me . . ."

"Feel bad. Feel bad."

"John die after now . . . me want to die. Me . . ."

He realized that she had just coined a term for the future, but he did not try to teach her the use of the future tense. Instead, he held out his arms and embraced her. She put her head against him, the sharp edge of her beak digging into the flesh between his ribs, and she burst into loud weeping.

Stroking the plumage on top of her round head, he said, "No feel bad, Tutu. John love you. You know . . . me love you."

"Love. Love," she said between sobs. "Love, love. Tutu love you!"

Suddenly, she pushed herself away from him, and he released her. She began to wipe the tears from her eyes with her fists and to say, "Me love. But . . . me 'fraid of John."

" 'Fraid? Why you 'fraid of John?"

"Me see . . . uh . . . horowitz . . . by you. You look like him, but not look like him. Him . . . how say . . . funny-looking, that right? And him fly like vulture, but no wing . . . on . . . me no able to say on what him fly. Very . . . funny. You talk to him. Me understand some words . . . no some."

Carmody sighed. "All me able to tell you now that him no horowitz. Him man. Man. Him come from stars." He pointed upwards.

Tutu also looked up, then her gaze returned to him, and she said, "You come from . . . star?"

"Child, you understand that?"

"You no horowitz. You place on beak and feathers. But . . . me understand you no horowitz."

"Me man," he said. "But enough of this, child. Some day . . . after soon . . . me tell you about the stars."

And, despite her continued questioning, he refused to say another word on the subject.

The days and then weeks and then months passed. Steadily, walking about two and a half to three miles a day, progressing from grove to grove, the band followed Carmody northwards. They came across the flints left by the ship. And Carmody showed them how to fashion spearheads and arrowheads and scrapers and knives. He made bows for them and taught them to shoot. In a short time, every horowitz who had the manual skill was making weapons and tools for himself. Fingers and hands were banged and cut, and one male lost an eye from a flying chip. But the group began to eat better; they shot the cervinoid and equinoid animals and, in fact, anything that wasn't too big and looked as if it might be edible. They cooked the meat, and Carmody showed them how to smoke and dry the meat. They began to get very bold, and it was this that was the undoing of Whoot.

One day, while with two other males, he shot a leonoid that refused to move away from their approach. The arrow only enraged the beast, and it charged. Whoot stood his ground and sent two more arrows into it, while his companions threw their spears. But the dying animal got hold of Whoot and smashed in his chest.

By the time the two had come for Carmody, and he had run to Whoot, Whoot was dead.

This was the first death among the group since Carmody had joined them. Now he saw that they did not regard death dumbly, as animals did, but as an event that caused outcries of protest. They wailed and wept and beat their chests and cast

themselves down on the ground and rolled in the
grass. Tutu wept as she stood by the corpse of her
father. Carmody went to her and held her while
she sobbed her heart out. He waited until their
sorrow had spent itself, then he organized a burial
party. This was a new thing to them; apparently,
they had been in the custom of leaving their dead
on the ground. But they understood him, and they
dug a shallow hole in the ground with sharp-
pointed sticks and piled rocks over the grave.

It was then that Tutu said to him, "Me father.
Where him go now?"

Carmody was speechless for several seconds.
Without one word from him, Tutu had thought of
the possibility of afterlife. Or so he supposed, for
it was easy to misinterpret her. She might just be
unable to conceive of the discontinuity of the life
of one she loved. But, no, she knew death well. She
had seen others die before he had joined the
group, and she had seen the death and dissolution
of many large animals, not to mention the
innumerable rodents and insects she had eaten.

"What think the others?" he said, gesturing at
the rest of the group.

She looked at them. "Adults no think. Them no
talk. Them like the animals.

"Me a child. Me think. You teached me to think.
Me ask you where Whoot go because you understand."

As he had many times since he met her,
Carmody sighed. He had a heavy and serious
responsibility. He did not want to give her false
hopes, yet he did not want to destroy her hopes—if
she had any—of living after death. And he just did
not know if Whoot had a soul or, if he did, what
provision might be made for it. Neither did he
know about Tutu. It seemed to him that a being
who was sentient, who had self-consciousness,

who could use verbal symbolism, must have a soul. Yet, he did not know.

Nor could he try to explain his dilemma to her. Her vocabulary, after only six months of contact with him, could not deal with the concepts of immortality. Neither could his, for even the sophisticated language at his command did not deal with reality but only with abstractions dimly comprehended, with vague hopes only stammered about. One could have faith and could try to translate that faith into effective action. But that was all.

Slowly, he said, "You understand that Whoot's body and the lion's body become earth?"

"Yes."

"And that seeds fall on this earth, and grass and trees grow there and feed from the earth, which Whoot and the lion becomed?"

Tutu nodded her beaked head. "Yes. And the birds and the jackals will eat the lion. Them will eat Whoot, too, if them able to drag the rocks from him."

"But at least a part of the lion and of Whoot become soil. And the grasses growing from them become partly them. And the grass in turn become eaten by antelopes, and the lion and Whoot not only become grass but beast."

"And if me eat the antelope," interrupted Tutu excitedly, her beak clacking, her brown eyes shining, "then Whoot become part of me. And me of him."

Carmody realized he was treading on theologically dangerous ground.

"Me no mean that Whoot live in you," he said. "Me mean . . ."

"Why him no live in me? And in the antelopes that eat grass and in the grass? Oh, understand! Because Whoot then become breaked into many pieces! Him live in many different creatures. That what you mean, John?"

She wrinkled her brow. "But how him live if all teared apart? No, him no! Him body go so many places. What me mean, John, where Whoot go?"

She repeated fiercely, "Where *him* go?"

"Him go wherever the Creator send him," replied Carmody, desperately.

"Cre-a-tor?" she echoed, stressing each syllable.

"Yes. Me teached you the word *creature*, meaning any living being. Well, a creature must become created. And the Creator create him. Create means to cause to live. Also mean to bring into becoming what no becomed before."

"Me mother me creator?"

She did not mention her father because she, like the other children and probably the adults, too, did not connect copulation with reproduction. And Carmody had not explained the connection to her because, as yet, she lacked the vocabulary.

Carmody sighed and said, "Worse and worse. No. You mother no you Creator. Her make the egg from her body and the food her eat. But her no create you. In the beginning . . ."

Here he boggled. And he wished that he had become a priest and had a priest's training. Instead, he was only a monk. Not a simple monk, for he had seen too much of the Galaxy and had lived too much. But he was not equipped to deal with this problem. For one thing, he just could not hand out a ready-made theology to her. The theology of this planet was in formation and would not even be born until Tutu and her kind had full speech.

"Me tell you more in the future," he said. "After many suns. For this time, you must become satisfied with the little me able to tell you. And that . . . well, the Creator make this whole world, stars, sky, water, animals, and the horowitzes. He make you mother and her mother and her mother's mother's mother. Many mothers many suns ago, he make . . ."

"*He*? That him name? *He*?"

Carmody realized he had slipped up in using the nominative case, but old habit had been too much for him.

"Yes. You can call him He."

"He the Mother of the first mother?" said Tutu. "He the Mother of all creatures? Mothers?"

"Here. Have some sugar. And run along and play. Me tell you more later."

After I have time to think, he said to himself.

He pretended to scratch his head and slid back the activating plate on the transceiver curved over his skull. And he asked the operator on duty to call Holmyard. In a minute, Holmyard's voice said, "What's up, John?"

"Doc, isn't a ship due in a few days to drop down and pick up the records and specimens you've collected so far? Will you have it take a message back to Earth? Notify my superior, the abbot of Fourth of July, Arizona, that I am in deep need of guidance."

And Carmody related his talk with Tutu and the questions that he had to answer in the future.

"I should have told him where I was going before I left," he said. "But I got the impression that he had put me on my own. However, I am now in a predicament which requires that wiser and better trained men help me."

Holmyard chuckled. He said, "I'll send on your message, John. Though I don't think you need any help. You're doing as well as anyone could. Anyone who tries to maintain objectivity, that is. Are you sure that your superiors will be able to do that? Or that it may not take them a hundred years to arrive at a decision? Your request might even cause a council of the Church heads. Or a dozen councils."

Carmody groaned, and then he said, "I don't know. I think I'll start teaching the kids how to read and write and do arithmetic. There, at least, I'll be navigating in safe waters."

He shut off the transceiver and called Tutu and the other young who seemed capable of literacy.

In the days and nights that followed, the young made exceptional progress, or so it seemed to Carmody. It was as if the young had been fallow, just waiting for the touch of somebody like Carmody. Without too much trouble, they learned the relation between the spoken and the written word. To keep them from being confused, Carmody modified the alphabet as it was used on Earth and made a truly phonetic system so that every phoneme would have a parallel notation. This was something that had been talked about for two hundred years among the English-speakers of Earth but had not, so far, been done. Orthography there, though it had changed, still lagged behind the spoken word and presented the same maddening and confusing picture to the foreigner who wished to learn English.

But reading and writing in short time led to Carmody's being forced to teach another art: drawing. Tutu, without any hint on his part that she should do so, one day began to make a sketch of him. Her efforts were crude, and he could have straightened her out very quickly. But, aside from later teaching her the principles of perspective, he made no effort to help her. He felt that if she, and the others who also began to draw, were influenced too much by terrestrial ideas of art, they would not develop a truly Feral art. In this decision he was commended by Holmyard.

"Man has a fundametally primate brain, and so he has worked out a primate's viewpoint through his art. So far, we've had no art produced by—forgive me—birdbrains. I'm with you, John, in allowing them to paint and sculpture in their own peculiar fashion. The world may some day be enriched by avian artistry. Maybe, maybe not."

Carmody was busy from the time he woke, which was dawn, until the time he went to sleep, about three hours after nightfall. He not only had to spend much time in his teaching, but he had to act as arbitrator—or rather dictator—of disputes. The disputes among the adults were much more trying than among the young, for he could communicate effectively with the latter.

The cleavage between the young and the adults was not as strong as he had expected. The adults were intelligent, and, though speechless, could learn to make flint tools and weapons and could shoot arrows and throw spears. They even learned to ride horses.

Halfway towards their destination, they began to encounter bands of animals that strongly resembled hairless horses. Carmody, as an experiment, caught one and broke it. He made reins from bone and a strong-fibered grass. He had no saddles as first but rode it bareback. Later, after the older children and the adults had caught their own horses and began to ride them, they were taught how to make saddles and reins from the thick skin of the tricorn.

Shortly after, he met his first resistance from the young. They came to a place where a lake was, where trees grew thickly, where a breeze blew most of the time from the nearby hills, and where the game was numerous. Tutu said that she and the others thought it would be a good idea if they built a walled village, such as Carmody had told them they would build when they got to the Valley.

"Many speechless ones live around here," she said. "Us able to take them young and raise them, make them us people. That way, us become stronger. Why travel every day? Us become tired of traveling, become footsore, saddlesore. Us able to make—barns?—for them horses, too. And us able to catch other animals, breed them, have plenty of meat to kill without hunting. Also, us able to plant seeds like you told us and grow crops. Here a good place. Just as good as that Valley you speaked of, maybe gooder. Us children talked it over, decided to stay here."

"This a good place," said Carmody. "But not the goodest. Me have knowledge that there many things this place no have. Such as flint, iron, which much gooder than flint, healthier climate, not so many big beasts that eat meat, gooder soil in which to grow crops, and other things."

"How you have knowledge of this Valley?" said Tutu. "You seed it? You goed there?"

"Me have knowledge of the Valley because someone who there once telled me of it," said Carmody. (And he wished that he had not avoided the use of the verb *know* to avoid confusion with the adjective and adverb *no*. So far he had not introduced any homonyms into the horowitz's vocabulary. But he determined at this moment to make use of know. He could, though, partially reinstate the original Old English pronunciation and have them pronounce the k. At the first chance, he would do that.)

"Who telled you of the Valley?" said Tutu. "No horowitz doed it, because none haved speech until you teached them how to talk. Who telled you?"

"The man doed it," replied Carmody. "Him goed there."

"The man who comed from the stars? The man me seed you talking to that night?

Carmody nodded, and she said, "Him have knowledge of where us go after death?"

He was caught by surprise and could only stare, open-mouthed, at her a few seconds. Holmyard was an agnostic and denied that there was any valid evidence for the immortality of man. Carmody, of course, agreed with him that there was no scientifically provable evidence, no facts. But there were enough indications of the survival of the dead to make any open-minded agnostic wonder about the possibility. And, of course, Carmody believed that every man would live forever because he had faith that man would do so. Moreover, he had a personal experience which had convinced him. (But that's another story.)

"No, the man no have knowledge of where us go after death. But me have knowledge."

"Him a man; you a man," said Tutu. "If you have knowledge, why no him?"

Again, Carmody was speechless. Then he said, "How you have knowledge that me a man?"

Tutu shrugged and said, "At first, you fool us. Later, everybody have knowledge. Easy to see that you put on beak and feathers."

Carmody began to remove the beak, which had chafed and irritated him for many months.

"Why no say so?" he said angrily. "You try to make fool of me?"

Tutu looked hurt. She said, "No. Nobody make fool of you, John. Us love you. Us just thinked you liked to put on beak and feathers. Us no have knowledge of why, but if you like to do so, O.K. with us. Anyway, no try to get off what we talk about. You say you have knowledge of where dead go. Where?"

"Me no supposed to tell you where. No just yet,

anyway. Later."

"You no wish to scare us? Maybe that a bad
place us no like? That why you no tell us?"

"Later, me tell. It like this, Tutu. When me first
comed among you and teached you speech, me no
able to teach you all the words. Just them you able
to understand. Later, teach you harder words. So
it now. You no able to understand even if me tell
you. You become older, have knowledge of more
words, become smarter. Then me tell. See?"

She nodded and also clicked her beak, an
additional sign of agreement.

"Me tell the others," she said. "Many times,
while you sleep, we talk about where us go after
us die. What use of living only short time if us no
keep on living? What good it do? Some say it do no
good; us just live and die, and that that. So what?
But most of us no able to think that. Become
scared. Besides, no make sense to us. Everything
else in this world make sense. Or seem to. But
death no make sense. Death that last forever no
do, anyway. Maybe us die to make room for
others. Because if us no die, if ancestors no die,
then soon this world become too crowded, and all
starve to death, anyway. You tell us this world no
flat but round like a ball and this force—what you
call it, gravity?—keep us from falling off. So us see
that soon no more room if us no die. But why no go
to a place where plenty of room? Stars, maybe?
You tell us there plenty of round worlds like this
among the stars. Why us not go there?"

"Because them worlds also have plenty of
creatures on them," said Carmody.

"Horowitzes?"

"No. Some have mans on them; other have
creatures as different from both man and
horowitz as me different from you. Or from a
horse or a bug."

"Plenty to learn. Me glad me no have to find out all that by meself. Me wait until you tell me everything. But me become excited thinking about it."

Carmody had a council with the older children, and the upshot was that he agreed they should settle down for a short period at this site. He thought that, when they began to chop down trees for a stockade and houses, they would break and dull their flint axes and in a short time would run out of flint. Not to mention that his descriptions of the Valley would influence the more restless among them to push on.

Meanwhile, the egg on his chest grew larger and heavier, and he found it an increasing burden and irritation.

"I just wasn't cut out to be a mother," he told Holmyard over the transceiver. "I would like to become a Father, yes, in the clerical sense. And that demands certain maternal qualities. But, literally, and physically, I am beginning to be bothered."

"Come on in, an we'll take another sonoscope of the egg," said Holmyard. "It's time that we had another record of the embryo's growth, anyway. And we'll give you a complete physical to make sure that the egg isn't putting too much strain on you."

That night, Carmody met Holmyard, and they flew back in the jeep to the ship. This was now stationed about twenty miles from Carmody, because of the far-ranging of the horowitzes on their horses. In the ship's laboratory, the little monk was put through a series of tests. Holmyard said, "You've lost much weight, John. You're no longer fat. Do you eat well?"

"More than I ever did. I'm eating for two now, you know."

"Well, we've found nothing alarming or even

mildly disturbing. You're healthier than you ever were, mainly because you've gotten rid of that flab. And the little devil you're carrying around is growing apace. From the studies we've made on horowitzes we've caught, the egg grows until it reaches a diameter of three inches and a weight of four pounds.

"This biological mechanism of attaching eggs to the bloodstream of hosts of another species is amazing enough. But what biological mechanism enables the foetus to do this? What keeps it from forming antibodies and killing itself? How can it accept the bloodstream of another totally different species? Of course, one thing that helps is that the blood cells are the same shape as a man's; no difference can be detected with microscopic examination. And the chemical composition is approximately the same. But even so . . . yes, we may be able to get another grant just to study this mechanism. If we could discover it, the benefit to mankind might be invaluable."

"I hope you do get another grant," said Carmody. "Unfortunately, I won't be able to help you. I must report to the abbot of the monastery of Wildenwooly."

"I didn't tell you when you came in," said Holmyard. "Because I didn't want to upset you and thus bollix up your physical. But the supply ship landed yesterday. And we got a message for you."

He handed Carmody a long envelope covered with several official-looking seals. Carmody tore it open and read it. Then he looked up at Holmyard.

"Must be bad news, judging from your expression," said Holmyard.

"In one way, no. They inform me that I must live up to my contract and cannot leave here until the egg is hatched. But the day my contract expires, I must leave. And, furthermore, I am not to give the horowitzes any religious instruction at all. They must find out for themselves. Or rather, they must have their peculiar revelation—if any. At least, until a council of the Church has convened and a decision arrived at. By then, of course, I'll be gone."

"And I'll see to it that your successor has no religious affiliations," said Holmyard. "Forgive me, John, if I seem anticlerical to you. But I do believe that the horowitzes, if they develop a religion, should do it on their own."

"Then why not their speech and technology?"

"Because those are tools with which they may deal with their environment. They are things which, in time, they would have developed on lines similar to those of Earth."

"Do they not need a religion to ensure that they do not misuse this speech and technology? Do they not need a code of ethics?"

Holmyard smiled and gave him a straight and long look. Carmody blushed and fidgeted.

"All right," said Carmody, finally. "I opened my big mouth and put both my feet in it. You don't need to recite the history of the various religions on Earth. And I know that a society may have a strong and workable code of ethics with no concept of a divinity who will punish transgressors temporally or eternally.

"And the point is, religions may change and evolve. The Christianity of the twelfth century is not exactly like that of the twentieth century, and the spirit of the religion of our time differs in more than one aspect from that of the twentieth. Besides, I wasn't intending to convert the horowitzes. My own Church wouldn't permit me to do so. All I have done so far is tell them that there is a Creator."

"And even that they misunderstood," said Holmyard, laughing. "They refer to God as He but classify Him as a female."

"The gender doesn't matter. What does is that I am in no position to reassure them of immortality."

Holmyard shrugged to indicate he couldn't see what difference it made. But he said, "I sympathize with your distress because it is causing you pain and anxiety. However, there is nothing I can do to help. And, apparently, your Church is not going to, either."

"I made a promise to Tutu," Carmody said, "and I don't want to break that. Then she would lose faith."

"Do you think they regard you as God?"

"Heaven forbid! But I must admit that I have worried about that happening. So far, there has been no indication on their part that they do so regard me."

"But what about after you leave them?" said Holmyard.

Carmody could not forget the zoologist's parting reply. He had no difficulty getting to sleep that night. For the first time since he had joined the group, he was allowed to sleep late. The sun had climbed halfway towards its zenith before he woke. And he found the partially constructed village in an uproar.

Not that of chaos but of purposeful action. The adults were standing around looking bewildered, but the young were very busy. Mounted on their horses, they were herding ahead of them, at the point of their spears, a group of strange horowitzes. There were some adults among these, but most were youngsters between the ages of seven and twelve.

"What mean what you do?" said Carmody indignantly to Tutu.

The smile-muscles around her beak wrinkled, and she laughed.

"You no here last night, so us no able to tell you what us planned to do. Anyway, nice surprise, heh? Us decide to raid them wild horowitzes that live near here. Us catch them sleeping; drive away adults, forced to kill some, too bad."

"And why you do this?" said Carmody, aware that he was about to lose his temper.

"You no understand? Me thinked you understand everything."

"Me no God," said Carmody. "Me told you that often enough."

"Me forget sometimes," said Tutu, who had lost her smile. "You angry?"

"Me no angry until you tell me why you did this."

"Why? So us able to make us tribe bigger. Us teach the little ones how to talk. If them no learn, them grow up to become adults. And adults no learn how to talk. So them become like the beasts. You no want that, surely?"

"No. But you killed!"

Tutu shrugged. "What else to do? Them adults tried to kill us; us killed them, instead. Not many. Most runned off. Besides, you say O.K. to kill animals. And adults same as animals because them no able to talk. Us no kill childs because them able to learn to talk. Us—what you say? adopt—yes, us adopt them. Them become us brothers and sisters. You told me that every horowitz me brother and sister, even if me never see them."

She regained her smile and, bending eagerly towards him, she said, "Me haved a good thought while on raid. Instead of eating eggs that mothers hatch when no enough adults to attach eggs to, why not attach eggs to childs and to horses, and other animals, too? That way, us increase us tribe much faster. Become big fastly."

And so it was. Within a month's time, every horowitz large enough to carry the weight, and every horse, bore an egg on his/her chest.

Carmody reported this to Holmyard. "I see now the advantage of extra-uterine development of the embryo. If the unborn aren't as well protected from injury, it does furnish a means for a larger number to be born."

"And who's going to take care of all these young?" said Holmyard. "After all, the horowitz chick is as helpless as and requires as much care as the human infant."

"They're not going hog-wild. The number to be produced is strictly regulated. Tutu has it figured out how many chicks each mother can adequately care for. If the mothers can't furnish enough regurgitated food, they will prepare a paste of fruit and meat for the chicks. The mothers no longer have to spend a good part of their time hunting for food; the males are doing that now."

"This society of yours is not developing quite along the lines of those of Paleolithic Earth," said Holmyard. "I see an increase towards a communistic trend in the future. The children will be produced *en masse*, and their raising and education will have to be done collectively. However, at this stage, in order to gain a large enough population to be stable, it may be well for them to organize on an assembly-line basis.

"But there's one thing you've either not noticed or have purposely neglected to mention. You said the attaching of the eggs will be strictly regulated. Does that mean that any eggs for which there is no provision will be eaten? Isn't that a method of birth control?"

Carmody was silent for a moment, then he said, "Yes."

"Well?"

"Well, what? I'll admit I don't like the idea. But I don't have any justification for objecting to the horowitzes. These people don't have any Scriptural injunctions, you know. Not yet, anyway. Furthermore, under this system, many more will be given a chance for life."

"Cannibalism and birth control," said Holmyard. "I'd think you'd be glad to get out of this, John."

"Who's talking about the anthropocentric attitude now?" Carmody retorted.

Nevertheless, Carmody was troubled. He couldn't tell the horowitzes not to eat the surplus eggs, for they just would not have understood. Food wasn't so easy to get that they could pass up this source of supply. And he couldn't tell them that they were committing murder. Murder was the illegal slaying of a being with a soul. Did the horowitzes have souls? He didn't know. Terrestrial law maintained that the illegal killing of any member of a species capable of verbal symbolism was murder. But the Church, though it enjoined its members to obey that law or be punished by the secular government, had not admitted that that definition had a valid theological basis. The Church was still striving to formulate a rule which could be applied towards recognition of a soul in extra-terrestrial beings. At the same time, they admitted the possibility that sapients of other planets might not have souls, might not need them. Perhaps the Creator had made other provisions for assuring their immortality—if any.

"It's all right for *them* to sit around a table and discuss their theories," said Carmody to himself.

"But I am in the field of action; I must work by rule of thumb. And God help me if my thumb slips!"

During the next month he did many things in the practical area. He arranged with Holmyard to send the ship to the Valley and there dig up and transport to the outskirts of the village several tons of iron ore. The following morning he took the children to the place where the ore lay. They gave cries of astonishment, cries which increased as he told them what they were to do with it.

"And where this iron ore come from?" asked Tutu.

"Mans bringed it from the Valley."

"On horses?"

"No. Them bringed it in a ship which comed from the stars. The same ship that carried me from the stars."

"Me able to see it some day?"

"No. You forbidden. No good for you to see it."

Tutu wrinkled her brow with disappointment and clacked her beak. But she made no further reference to it at that time. Instead, she and the others, with Carmody's help and some of the more cooperative adults, built furnaces to smelt the ore. Afterwards, they built a furnace to add carbon from charcoal to the iron, and they made steel weapons, bridle braces and bits, and tools. Then they began to construct steel parts for wagons. Carmody had decided that it was time now to teach them to construct wagons.

"This fine," said Tutu, "But what us do when all the iron ore gone, and the steel us make rust and wear out?"

"There more in the Valley," said Carmody. "But us must go there. The starship bring no more."

Tutu cocked her head and laughed. "You shrewd man, John. You know how to get us to go to Valley."

"If us to go, us must get a move on soon," said Carmody. "Us must arrive before winter come and snow fall."

"Hard for any of us to imagine winter," she said. "This cold you talk about something us no able to understand."

Tutu knew what she was talking about. When Carmody called another council and exhorted them to leave at once for the Valley, he met resistance. The majority did not want to go; they liked it too well where they were. And Carmody could see that, even among the horowitzes, and as young as they were, the conservative personality was the most numerous. Only Tutu and a few others backed Carmody; they were the radicals, the pioneers, pushers-ahead.

Carmody did not try to dictate to them. He knew he was held in high regard, was, in fact, looked upon almost as a god. But even gods may be resisted when they threaten creature comforts, and he did not want to test his authority. If he lost, all was lost. Moreover, he knew that if he became a dictator, these people would not learn the basics of democracy. And it seemed to him that democracy, despite its faults and vices, was the best form of secular government. Gentle coercion was to be the strongest weapon he would use.

Or so he thought. After another month of vainly trying to get them to make the exodus, he became desperate. By now the stick-in-the-muds had another argument. Under Carmody's tutelage, they had planted vegetable gardens and corn, the seeds of which came from seed brought by the supply ship on Carmody's request. If they moved now, they would not be able to profit by their hard work. All would go to waste. Why did Carmody have them break their backs digging and plowing

and planting and watering, and chasing off the
wild life, if he intended them to move on?

"Because me wanted to show you *how* to grow
things in the soil," he said. "Me no intend to
remain with you forever. When us get to the
Valley, me leave."

"No leave us, beloved John!" they cried. "Us
need you. Besides, now us have another reason for
no go to the Valley. If us no go, then you no leave
us."

John had to smile at this child-like reasoning,
but he became stern immediately thereafter.
"Whether you go or no go, when this egg hatch, me
go. In fact, me go now, anyway. You no go, me
leave you behind. Me call on all of you who want to
go with me to follow me."

And he gathered Tutu and eleven other
adolescents, plus their horses, wagons, weapons,
food, and twenty chicks and five adult females. He
hoped that the sight of his leaving would cause the
others to change their minds. But, though they
wept and begged him to stay, they would not go
with him.

It was then that he lost his temper and cried,
"Very well! If you no do what me know the
goodest for you to do, then me destroy you village!
And you must come with me because you no have
any place else to go!"

"What you mean?" they shouted.

"Me mean that tonight a monster from the stars
come and burn up the village. You see!"

Immediately afterwards, he spoke to Holmyard.
"You heard me, Doc! I suddenly realized I had to
put pressure on them! It's the only way to get
them off their fannies!"

"You should have done it long ago," replied
Holmyard. "Even if all of you travel fast now,
you'll be lucky to get to the Valley before winter."

That night, while Carmody and his followers stood on top of a high hill outside the village, they watched the spaceship suddenly appear in the dim light cast by the two small moons. The inhabitants of the village must all have been looking up for the promised destroyer, for a shriek from a hundred throats arose. Immediately, there was a mad rush through the narrow gates, and many were trampled. Before all the children, chicks, and adults could get out, the monster loosed a tongue of flame against the log-walls surrounding the village. The walls on the southern side burst into flame, and the fire spread quickly. Carmody had to run down the hill and reorganize the demoralized horowitzes. Only because he threatened them with death if they didn't obey him, would they go back into the enclosure and bring out the horses, wagons, food, and weapons. They then cast themselves at Carmody's feet and begged forgiveness, saying they would never again go against his wishes.

And Carmody, though he felt ashamed because he had scared them so, and also distressed because of the deaths caused by the panic, nevertheless was stern. He forgave them but told them that he was wiser than they, and he knew what was good for them.

From then on, he got very good behavior and obedience from the adolescents. But he had also lost his intimacy with them, even with Tutu. They were all respectful, but they found it difficult to relax around him. Gone were the jokes and the smiles they had formerly traded.

"You have thrown the fear of God into them," said Holmyard.

"Now, Doc," said Carmody. "You're not suggesting that they think I am God. If I really believed that, I'd disabuse them."

"No, but they believe you're His representative. And maybe a demi-god. Unless you explain the whole affair from beginning to end, they'll continue to think so. And I don't think the explanation will help much. You'd have to outline our society in all its ramifications, and you've neither the time nor ability to do that. No matter what you said, they'd misunderstand you."

Carmody attempted to regain his former cordial relations with them, but he found it impossible. So he devoted himself to teaching them all he could. He either wrote or else dictated to Tutu and other scribes as much science as he had time for. Though the country they had crossed so far was lacking in any sulfur or saltpeter deposits, Carmody knew that the Valley contained them. He wrote down rules for recognizing, mining, and purifying the two chemicals and also the recipe for making gunpowder from them. In addition, he described in great detail how to make rifles and pistols and mercury fulminate, how to find and mine and process lead.

These were only a few of the many technological crafts he recorded. In addition, he wrote down the principles of chemistry, physics, biology, and electricity. Furthermore, he drew diagrams of an automobile which was to be driven by electric motors and powered by hydrogen-air fuel cells. This necessitated a detailed procedure for making hydrogen by the reaction of heated steam with zinc or iron as a catalyst. This, in turn, demanded that he tell them how to identify copper ore and the processes for refining it and making it into wire, how to make magnets, and the mathematical formulae for winding motors.

To do this, he had to call frequently on Holmyard for help. One day, Holmyard said, "This has gone far enough, John. You're working yourself to a shadow, killing yourself. And you're attempting to do the impossible, to compress one hundred thousand years of scientific progress into one. What it took humanity a hundred millenia to develop, you're handing to the horowitzes on a silver platter. Stop it! You've done enough for them by giving them a speech and techniques in working flint and agriculture. Let them do it on their own from now on. Besides, later expeditions will probably get into contact with them and give them all the information you're trying to forcefeed them.'

"You are probably right," groaned Carmody. "But what bothers me most of all is that, though I've done my best to give them all I can to enable them to deal with the material universe, I've done scarcely anything to give them an ethics. And that is what I should be most concerned with."

"Let them work out their own."

"I don't want to do that. Look at the many wrong, yes, evil, avenues they could take."

"They will take the wrong ones, anyway."

"Yes, but they will have a right one which they can take if they wish."

"Then, for Christ's sake, give it to them!" cried Holmyard. "Quit belly-aching! Do something, or shut up about it!"

"I suppose you're right," said Carmody humbly. "At any rate, I don't have much time left. In a month, I have to go to Wildenwooly. And this problem will be out of my hands."

During the next month, the party left the hot plains and began to travel over high hills and through passes between mountains. The air became cooler, the vegetation changed to that which superficially resembled the vegetation of the uplands of Earth. The nights were cool, and the horowitzes had to huddle around roaring fires. Carmody instructed them how to tan skins with which to clothe themselves, but he did not allow

them to take time out to hunt and skin the animals
and make furs from them. "You able to do that
when you reach the Valley," he said.

And, two weeks before they were to reach the
pass that would lead them to the Valley, Carmody
was awakened one night. He felt a tap-tapping in
the egg on his chest and knew that the sharp beak
of the chick was tearing away at the double-walled
leathery covering. By morning a hole appeared in
the skin of the egg. Carmody did what he had
observed the mothers do. He grabbed hold of the
edges of the tear and ripped the skin apart. It felt
as if he were ripping his own skin, so long had the
egg been a part of him.

The chick was a fine healthy specimen, male,
covered with a golden down. It looked at the world
with large blue eyes which, as yet, were un-
coordinated.

Tutu was delighted. "All of us have brown eyes!
Him the first horowitz me ever see with blue eyes!
Though me hear that the wild horowitzes in this
area have blue eyes. But him have eyes just like
you eyes. You make him eyes blue so us know him
you son?"

"Me have nothing to do with it," said Carmody.
He did not say that the chick was a mutation, or
else had carried recessive genes from mating by
ancestors with a member of the blue-eyed race.
That would have required too lengthy an
explanation. But he did feel uncomfortable. Why
had this happened to the chick that *he* was
carrying?

By noon the tendrils holding the egg to his flesh
had dried up and the empty skin fell to the ground.
Within two days, the many little holes in his chest
had closed; his skin was smooth.

He was cutting his ties to this world. That afternoon, Holmyard called him and said that his
request for an extension of his stay on Feral had

been denied. The day his contract ended, he was to leave.

"According to our contract, we have to furnish a ship to transport you to Wildenwooly," said Holmyard. "So, we're using our own. It'll only take a few hours to get you to your destination."

During the next two weeks, Carmody pushed the caravan, giving it only four hours sleep at night and stopping only when the horses had to have rest. Fortunately, the equine of Feral had more endurance, if less speed, than his counterpart on Earth. The evening of the day before he had to leave, they reached the mountain pass which would lead them to the promised Valley. They built fires and bedded down around the warmth. A chilly wind blew from the pass, and Carmody had trouble getting to sleep. It was not so much the cold air as it was his thoughts. They kept going around and around, like Indians circling a wagon train and shooting sharp arrows. He could not keep from worrying about what would happen to his charges after he left them. And he could not quit regretting that he had not given them any spiritual guidance. Tomorrow morning, he thought, tomorrow morning is my last chance. But my brain is numb, numb. If it were left up to me, if my superiors had not ordered me to be silent . . . but then they know best. I would probably do the wrong thing. Perhaps it is best to leave it up to divine revelation. Still, God works through man, and I am a man. . . .

He must have dozed away, for he suddenly awakened as he felt a small body snuggling next to his. It was his favorite, Tutu.

"Me cold," she said. "Also, many times, before the village burn, me sleep in your arms. Why you no ask me to do so tonight? You last night!" she said with a quavering voice, and she was crying. Her shoulders shook, and her beak raked across his chest as she pressed the side of her face against him. And, not for the first time, Carmody regretted that these creatures had hard beaks. They would never know the pleasure of soft lips meeting in a kiss.

"Me love you, John," she said. "But ever since the monster from the stars destroyed us village, me scared of you, too. But tonight, me forget me scared, and me must sleep in you arms once more, so me able to remember this last night the rest of me life."

Carmody felt tears welling in his own eyes, but he kept his voice firm. "Them who serve the Creator say me have work to do elsewhere. Among the stars. Me must go, even if no wish to. Me sad, like you. But maybe someday me return. No able to promise. But always hope."

"You no should leave. Us still childs, and us have adults' work ahead of us. The adults like childs, and us like adults. Us need you."

"Me know that true," he said. "But me pray to He that He watch over and protect you."

"Me hope He have more brains than me mother. Me hope He smart as you."

Carmody laughed and said, "He is infinitely smarter than me. No worry. What come, come."

He talked some more to her, mainly advice on what to do during the coming winter and reassurances that he might possibly return. Or, if he did not, that other men would. Eventually, he drifted into sleep.

But he was awakened by her terrified voice, crying in his ear.

He sat up and said, "Why you cry, child?"

She clung to him, her eyes big in the reflected light of the dying fire. "Me father come to me, and him wake me up! Him say, 'Tutu, you wonder where us horowitzes go after death! Me know, because me go to the land of beyond death. It a beautiful land; you no cry because John must leave.

Some day, you see him here. Me allowed to come see you and tell you. And you must tell John that us horowitzes like mans. Us have souls, us no just die and become dirt and never see each other again.

"Me father told me that. And him reached out him hand to touch me. And me become scared, and me waked up crying!"

"There, there," said Carmody, hugging her. "You just dream. You know your father no able to talk when him alive. So how him able to talk now? You dreaming."

"No dream, no dream! Him not in me head like a dream! Him standing outside me head, between me and fire! Him throw a shadow! Dreams no have shadows! And why him no able to talk? If him can live after death, why him no talk, too? What you say, 'Why strain at a bug and swallow a horse?' "

"Out of the mouths of babes," muttered Carmody, and he spent the time until dawn talking to Tutu.

At noon of that same day, the horowitzes stood upon the rim of the pass. Below them lay the Valley, flashing with the greens, golds, yellows, and reds of the autumnal vegetation. In a few more days the bright colors would turn brown, but today the Valley glittered with beauty and promise.

"In a few minutes," said Carmody, "the mans from the skies come in the starwagon. No become frightened; it will not harm you. Me have a few words to say, words which me hope you and you descendants never forget.

"Last night, Tutu seed her father, who had died. Him told her that all horowitzes have souls and go to another place after them die. The Creator have maked a place for you—so say Whoot—because you He's childs. He never forget you. And so you must become good childs to He, for He . . ."

Here he hesitated, for he had almost said

Father. But, knowing that they had fixed in their minds the maternal image, he continued . . . "for He you Mother.

"Me have telled you the story of how the Creator maked the world from nothing. First, space. Then, atoms created in space. Atoms joined to become formless matter. Formless matter becomed suns, big suns with little suns circling around them. The little suns cooled and becomed planets, like the one you now live on. Seas and land formed.

"And He created life in the seas, life too small to see with the naked eye. But He see. And some day you, too, see. And out of the little creatures comed big creatures. Fish comed into being. And some fish crawled onto the land and becomed air-breathers with legs.

"And some animals climbed trees and lived there, and their forelimbs becomed wings, and they becomed birds and flyed.

"But one kind of tree-creature climbed down out of the trees before it becomed a bird. And it walked on two legs and what might have becomed wings becomed arms and hands.

"And this creature becomed you ancestor.

"You know this, for me have telled you many times. You know you past. Now, me tell you what you must do in the future, if you wish to become a good child of He. Me give you the law of the horowitz.

"This what He wish you to do every day of you lives.

"Love you Creator even gooder than you own parents.

"Love each other, even the one who hate you.

"Love the animals, too. You able to kill animals for food. But no cause them pain. Work the animals, but feed them and rest them well. Treat the animals as childs.

"Tell the truth. Also, seek hard for the truth.

"Do what society say you must do. Unless

society say what He no wish you to do. Then, you may defy society.

"Kill only to keep from becoming killed. The Creator no love a murderer or a people who make war without good cause.

"No use evil means to reach a good goal.

"Remember that you horowitzes no alone in this universe. The universe filled with the childs of He. Them no horowitzes, but you must love them, too.

"No fear death, for you live again."

John Carmody looked at them for a moment, wondering upon what paths of good and of evil this speech would set them. Then he walked to a large flat-topped rock on which sat a bowl of water and a loaf of bread made from baked acorn flour.

"Each day at noon, when the sun highest, a male or female choosed by you must do this before you and for you."

He took a piece of bread and dipped it in the water and ate the piece, and then he said, "And the Chooses One must say so all able to hear.

" 'With this water, from which life first comed, me thank me Creator for life. And with this bread, me thank me Creator for the blessings of this world and give me self strength against the evils of life. Thanks of He.' "

He paused. Tutu was the only one not looking at him, for she was busily writing down his words. Then, she looked up at him as if wondering if he meant to continue. And she gave a cry and dropped her pencil and tablet and ran to him and put her arms around him.

"Starship come!" she cried. "You no go!"

There was a moan of fear and astonishment from the beaks of the crowd as they saw the shining monster hurtle over the mountain towards them.

Gently, Carmody loosed her embrace and stepped away from her.

"Come a time when the parent must go, and the

child must become adult. That time now. Me must go because me wanted elsewhere.

"Just remember, me love you, Tutu. Me love all of you, too. But me no able to stay here. However, He always with you. Me leave you in the care of He."

Carmody stood within the pilothouse and looked at the image of Feral on the screen. It was now no larger to him than a basketball. He spoke to Holmyard.

"I will probably have to explain that final scene to my superiors. I may even be severely rebuked and punished. I do not know. But I am convinced at this moment that I did rightly."

"You were not to tell them they had a soul," said Holmyard. "Not that I myself care one way or another. I think the idea of a soul is ridiculous."

"But you can think of the idea," said Carmody. "And so can the horowitzes. Can a creature capable of conceiving a soul be without one?"

"Interesting question. And unanswerable. Tell me, do you really believe that that little ceremony you instituted will keep them on the straight and narrow?"

"I'm not all fool," said Carmody. "Of course not. But they do have correct basic instruction. If they pervert it, then I am not to blame. I have done my best."

"Have you?" said Holmyard. "You have laid the foundations for a mythology in which you may become the god, or the son of the god. Don't you think that, as time blurs the memory of these events you initiated, and generations pass, that myth after myth and distortion after distortion will completely alter the truth?"

Carmody stared at the dwindling globe. "I do not know. But I have given them something to raise them from beasts to men."

"Ah, Prometheus!" breathed Holmyard. And they were silent for a long time.

FATHER

The first mate of the *Gull* looked up from the navigation desk and pointed to the magnified figures cast upon the information screen by the spoolmike.

"If this is correct, sir, we're a hundred thousand kilometres from the second planet. There are ten planets in this system. Luckily, one is inhabitable. The second one."

He paused. Captain Tu looked curiously at him, for the man was very pale and had ironically accented the *luckily*.

"Sir, the second planet must be Abatos."

The captain's swarthy skin whitened to match the mate's. His mouth opened as if to form an oath, then clamped shut. At the same time his right hand made an abortive gesture towards his forehead, as if he had meant to touch it. His hand dropped.

"Very well, Mister Givens. We shall make an attempt to land. That is all we can do. Stand by for further orders."

He turned away so none could see his face.

"Abatos, Abatos," he murmured. He licked his dry lips and locked his hands behind his back.

Two short buzzes sounded. Midshipman Nkrumah passed his hand over an activating plate and said, "Bridge," to a plate that sprang into life and colour on the wall. A steward's face appeared.

"Sir, please inform the captain that Bishop Andre and Father Carmody are waiting for him in cabin 7."

Captain Tu glanced at the bridge clock and tugged at the silver crucifix that hung from his right ear. Givens, Nkrumah, and Merkalov watched him intently, though they looked to one side when their eyes met his. He smiled grimly when he saw their expressions, unlocked his hands, and straightened his back. It was as if he knew his men were depending on him to preserve a calm that would radiate confidence in his ability to get them to safety. So, for a half minute, he posed monolithic in his sky-blue uniform that had not changed since the Twenty-First Century. Though it was well known that he felt a little ridiculous when he wore it planetside, when he was on his ship he walked as a man clad in armour. If coats and trousers were archaic and seen only at costume balls or in historical stereos or on officers of interstellar vessels, they did give a sense of apartness and of glamour and helped enforce discipline. The captain must have felt as if he needed every bit of confidence and respect he could muster. Thus, the conscious striking of the pose; here was the thoughtful and unnervous skipper who was so sure of himself that he could take time to attend to social demands.

"Tell the bishop I'll be in to see him at once," he ordered the midshipman.

He strode from the bridge, passed through several corridors, and entered the small lounge.

There he paused in the doorway to look the passengers over. All except the two priests were there. None of them as yet was aware that the *Gull* was not merely going through one of the many transitions from normal space to perpendicular space. The two young lovers, Kate Lejeune and Pete Masters, were sitting in one corner on a sofa, holding hands and whispering softly and every now and then giving each other looks that ached with suppressed passion. At the other end of the room Mrs. Recka sat at a table playing double solitaire with the ship's doctor, Chandra Blake. She was a tall voluptuous blonde whose beauty was spoiled by an incipient double chin and dark halfmoons under her eyes. The half-empty bottle of bourbon on the table told of the origin of her dissipated appearance; those who knew something of her personal history also knew that it was responsible for her being on the *Gull*. Separated from her husband on Wildenwooly, she was going home to her parents on the faraway world of Diveboard on the Galaxy's rim. She'd been given the choice of him or the bottle and had preferred the simpler and more transportable item. As she was remarking to the doctor when the captain entered, bourbon never criticized you or called you a drunken slut.

Chandra Blake, a short dark man with prominent cheekbones and large brown eyes, sat with a fixed smile. He was very embarrassed at her loud conversation but was too polite to leave her.

Captain Tu touched his cap as he passed the four and smiled at their greetings, ignoring Mrs. Recka's invitation to sit at her table. Then he went down a long hall and pressed a button by the door of cabin 7.

It swung open and he strode in, a tall stiff gaunt man who looked as if he were made of some dark inflexible metal. He stopped abruptly and performed the seeming miracle of bending forward. He did so to kiss the bishop's extended hand, with a lack of grace and a reluctance that took all the meaning out of the act. When he straightened up, he almost gave the impression of sighing with relief. It was obvious that the captain liked to unbend to no man.

He opened his mouth as if to give them at once the unhappy news, but Father Carmody pressed a drink into his hand.

"A toast, captain, to a quick trip to Ygdrasil," said Father John in a low gravelly voice. "We enjoy being aboard, but we've reason for haste in getting to our destination."

"I will drink to your health and His Excellency's," said Tu in a harsh clipped voice. "As for the quick trip, I'm afraid we'll need a little prayer. Maybe more than a little."

Father Carmody raised extraordinarily thick and tufted eyebrows but said nothing. This act of silence told much about his inner reactions, for he was a man who must forever be talking. He was short and fat, about forty, with heavy jowls, a thick shock of blue-black slightly wavy hair, bright blue and somewhat bulging eyes, a drooping left eyelid, a wide thick mouth, and a long sharp rocket-shaped nose. He quivered and shook and bounced with energy; he must always be on the move lest he explode; must be turning his hand to this and that, poking his nose here and there, must be laughing and chattering; must give the impression of vibrating inside like a great tuning fork.

Bishop Andre, standing beside him, was so tall and still and massive that he looked like an oak turned into a man, with Carmody the squirrel that raced around at his feet. His superb shoulders, arching chest, lean belly, and calves bursting with muscle told of great strength rigidly controlled and kept at a prizefighter's peak. His features did justice to the physique; he had a large high-cheek-boned head topped by a mane of lion-yellow hair. His eyes were a glowing golden-green, his nose straight and classical in profile though too narrow and pinched when seen from the front; his mouth full and red and deeply indented at the corners. The bishop, like Father John, was the darling of the ladies of the diocese of Wildenwooly, but for a different reason. Father John was fun to be around. He made them giggle and laugh and made even their most serious problems seem not insurmountable. But Bishop Andre made them weak-kneed when he looked into their eyes. He was the kind of priest who caused them regret that he was not available for marrying. The worst part of that was that His Excellency knew the effect he had and hated it. At times he had been downright curt and was always just a little standoffish. But no woman could long remain offended at him. Indeed, as was well known, the bishop owed some of his meteoric rise to the efforts of the ladies behind the scenes. Not that he wasn't more than capable; it was just that he'd attained his rank faster than might have been expected.

Father John poured out a drink from a wine bottle, then filled two glasses with lemonade.

"I shall drink of the wine," he said. "You, Captain, will be forced to gag down this non-alcoholic beverage because you are on duty. His Excellency, however, refuses the cup that cheers, except as a sacrament, for reasons of principle. As for me, I take a little wine for my stomach's sake."

He patted his large round paunch. "Since my belly constitutes so much of me, anything I take for it I also take for my entire being. Thus, not

only my entrails benefit, but my whole body glows
with good health and joy and calls for more tonic.
Unfortunately, the bishop sets me such an unen-
durably good example, I must restrain myself to
this single cup. This, in spite of the fact that I am
suffering from a toothache and could dull the pain
with an extra glass or two."

Smiling, he looked over the rim of his glass at
Tu, who was grinning in spite of his tension, and at
the bishop, whose set features and dignified bearing made him look like a lion deep in thought.

"Ah, forgive me, Your Excellency," said the
padre. "I cannot help feeling that you are most im-
moderate in your temperance, but I should not
have intimated as much. Actually, your asceticism
is a model for all of us to admire, even if we
haven't the strength of character to imitate it."

"You are forgiven, John," said the Bishop
gravely. "But I'd prefer that you confine your rail-
lery—for I cannot help thinking that that is what it
is—to times when no one else is around. It is not
good for you to speak in such a manner before
others, who might think you hold your bishop in
some measure of contempt."

"Now, God forgive me, I meant no such thing!"
cried Carmody. "As a matter of fact, my levity is
directed at myself, because I enjoy too much the
too-good things of this life, and instead of putting
on wisdom and holiness, add another inch to my
waistline."

Captain Tu shifted uneasily, then suppressed his
telltale movements. Obviously, this mention of
God outside of church walls embarrassed him.
Also, there just was no time to be chattering about
trivial things.

"Let's drink to our good healths," he said. He
gulped his ale. Then, setting the glass on the table
with an air of finality as if he would never get a

chance to drink again, he said, "The news I have is bad. Our translator engine cut out about an hour ago and left us stranded in normal space. The chief says he can't find a thing wrong with it, yet it won't work. He has no idea of how to start it again. He's a thoroughly competent man, and when he admits defeat, the problem is unsolvable."

There was silence for a minute. Then Father John said, "How close are we to an inhabitable planet?"

"About a hundred thousand kilometers," replied Tu, tugging at the silver crucifix hanging from his ear. Abruptly realizing that he was betraying his anxiety, he let his hand fall to his side.

The padre shrugged his shoulders. "We're not in free fall, so there's nothing wrong with our interplanetary drive. Why can't we set down on this planet?"

"We're going to try to. But I'm not confident of our success. The planet is Abatos."

Carmody whistled and stroked the side of his long nose. Andre's bronzed face paled.

The little priest set down his glass and made a moue of concern.

"That is bad." He looked at the bishop. "May I tell the captain why we're so concerned about getting to Ygdrasil in a hurry?"

Andre nodded, his eyes downcast as if he were thinking of something that concerned the other two not at all.

"His Excellency," said Carmody, "left Wildenwooly for Ygdrasil because he thought he was suffering from hermit fever."

The captain flinched but did not step back from his position close to the bishop. Carmody smiled and said, "You needn't worry about catching it. He doesn't have it. Some of his symptoms matched those of hermit fever, but an examination failed to disclose any microbes. Not only that, His Excellency didn't develop a *typical* antisocial behaviour. But the doctors decided he should go to Ygdrasil, where they have better facilities than those on Wildenwooly, which is still rather primitive, you know. Also, there's a Doctor Ruedenbach there, a specialist in epileptoid diseases. It was thought best to see him, as His Excellency's condition was not improving."

Tu held out his palms in a gesture of helplessness.

"Believe me, 'Your Excellency, this news saddens me and makes me regret even more this accident. But there is nothing . . .''

Andre came out of his reverie. For the first time he smiled, a slow, warm, and handsome smile. "What are my troubles compared to yours? You have the responsibility of this vessel and its expensive cargo. And, far more important, the welfare of twenty-five souls."

He began pacing back and forth, speaking in his vibrant voice.

"We've all heard of Abatos. We know what it may mean if the translator doesn't begin working again. Or if we meet the same fate as those other ships that tried to land on it. We're about eight light years from Ygdrasil and six from Wildenwooly, which means we can't get to either place in normal drive. We either get the translator started or else land. Or remain in space until we die."

"And even if we are allowed to make planetfall," said Tu, "we may spend the rest of our lives on Abatos."

A moment later, he left the cabin. He was halted by Carmody, who had slipped out after him.

"When are you going to tell the other passengers?"

Tu looked at his watch.

"In two hours. By then we'll know whether or not Abatos will let us pass. I can't put off telling them any longer, because they'll know something's up. We should have been falling to Ygdrasil by now."

"The bishop is praying for us all now," said Carmody. "I shall concentrate my own request on an inspiration for the engineer. He's going to need it."

"There's nothing wrong with that translator," said Tu flatly, "except that it won't work."

Carmody looked shrewdly at him from under his thatched eyebrows and stroked the side of his nose.

"You think it's not an accident that the engine cut out?"

"I've been in many tough spots before," replied Tu, "and I've been scared. Yes, scared. I wouldn't tell any man except you—or maybe some other priest—but I have been frightened. Oh, I know it's a weakness, maybe even a sin . . ."

Here Carmody raised his eyebrows in amazement and perhaps a little awe of such an attitude.

". . . but I just couldn't seem to help it, though I swore that I'd never again feel that way, and I never allowed anyone to see it. My wife always said that if I'd allow myself now and then to show a little weakness, not much, just a little . . . Well, perhaps that may have been why she left me, I don't know, and it doesn't really matter any more, except . . ."

Suddenly realizing that he was wandering, the captain stopped, visibly braced himself, squared his shoulders, and said, "Anyway, Father, this set-up scares me worse than I've ever been scared. Why, I couldn't exactly tell you. But I've a feeling that something caused that cut-out and for a purpose we won't like when we find out. All I have to base my reasoning on is what happened to those other three ships. You know, everybody's read about them, how the *Hoyle* landed and was never heard of again, how the *Priam* investigated its disappearance and couldn't get any closer than fifty kilometres because her normal space drive failed, and how the cruiser *Tokyo* tried to bull its way in with its drive dead and only escaped because it had enough velocity to take it past the fifty kilo limit. Even so, it almost burned up when it was going through the stratosphere."

"What I can't understand," said Carmody, "is how such an agent could affect us while we're in translation. Theoretically, we don't even exist in normal space then."

Tu tugged at the crucifix. "Yes, I know. But we're *here*. Whatever did this has a power unknown to man. Otherwise it wouldn't be able to pinpoint us in translation so close to its home planet."

Carmody smiled cheerfully. "What's there to worry about? If it can haul us in like fish in a net, it must want us to land. So we don't have to fret about planetfall."

Suddenly he grimaced with pain. "This rotten molar of mine," he explained. "I was going to have it pulled and a bud put in when I got to Ygdrasil. And I'd sworn to quit eating so much of the chocolate of which I'm perilously overfond and which has already cost me the loss of several teeth. And now I must pay for my sins, for I was in such a hurry I forgot to bring along any painkiller, except for the wine. Or was that a Freudian slip?"

"Doctor Blake will have pain pills."

Carmody laughed. "So he does! Another convenient oversight! I'd hoped to confine myself to the natural medicine of the grape, and ignore the

tasteless and enervating laboratory-born
nostrums. But I have too many people looking out
for my welfare. Well, such is the price of
popularity."

He slapped Tu on the shoulder. "There's
adventure awaiting us, Bill. Let's get going."

The captain did not seem to resent the
familiarity. Evidently, he'd known Carmody for a
long time.

"I wish I had your courage, Father."

"Courage!" snorted the priest. "I'm shaking in
my hair shirt. But we must take what God sends
us, and if we can like it, all the better."

Tu allowed himself to smile. "I like you because
you can say something like that without sounding
false or unctuous or—uh—priestly. I know you
mean it."

"You're blessed well right I do," answered
Carmody, then shifted from cheeriness to a more
grave tone. "Seriously, though, Bill, I do hope we
can get going soon. The bishop is in a bad way. He
looks healthy, but he's liable at any moment to
have an attack. If he does, I'll be pretty busy with
him for a while. I can't tell you much more about
him because he wouldn't want me to. Like you, he
hates to confess to any weakness; he'll probably
reprimand me when I go back to the cabin for
having mentioned the matter to you. That's one
reason why he has said nothing to Doctor Blake.
When he has one of his . . . spells, he doesn't like
anyone but me to take care of him. And he resents
that little bit of dependency."

"It's pretty bad, then? Hard to believe. He's
such a healthy-looking man; you wouldn't want to
tangle with him in a scrap. He's a *good* man, too.
Righteous as they make them. I remember one
sermon he gave us at St. Pius' on Lazy Fair. Gave
us hell and scared me into living a clean life for all

of three weeks. The saints themselves must have thought they'd have to move over for me, and then . . ."

Seeing the look in Carmody's eyes, Tu stopped, glanced at his watch, and said, "Well, I've a few minutes to spare and I've not been doing as well as I might, though I suppose we all could say that, eh, Father? Could we step into your cabin? There's no telling what might happen in the next few hours and I'd like to be prepared."

"Certainly. Follow me, my son."

Two hours later, Captain Tu had told crew and passengers the truth over the bridge-viser. When his voice died and his grim gaunt face faded off the screen in the lounge, he left behind him silence and stricken looks. All except Carmody sat in their chairs as if the captain's voice had been an arrow pinning them to the cushions. Carmody stood in the centre of the lounge, a soberly clad little figure in the midst of their bright clothes. He wore no rings on his ears, his legs were painted a decent black, his puffkilts were only moderately slashed, and his quilted dickie and suspenders were severe, innocent of golden spangles or jewels. Like all members of the Jairusite Order, he wore his Roman collar only when on planetside in memory of the founder and his peculiar but justified reason for doing so.

He shrewdly watched his passengers. Rocking back and forth on his heels, his forefinger tracing the length of his nose, he seemed to be interested in the announcement only from the viewpoint of how it was affecting them. There was no sign that he was concerned about himself.

Mrs. Recka was still sitting before her cards, her head bent to study them. But her hand went out more often to the bottle, and once she upset it with a noise that made Blake and the two young lovers jump. Without bothering to get up from her chair, she allowed the fifth to spill on the floor while she rang for the steward. Perhaps the significance of the captain's words had not penetrated the haze in her brain. Or perhaps she just did not care.

Pete Masters and Kate Lejeune had not moved or spoken a word. They huddled closer, if that were possible, and squeezed hands even more tightly—pale-faced, their heads nodded like two white balloons shaken by an internal wind, Kate's red painted mouth, vivid against her bloodless skin, hanging open like a gash in the sphere and by some miracle keeping the air inside her so her head did not collapse.

Carmody looked at them with pity, for he knew their story far better than they realized. Kate was the daughter of a rich 'pelterpiper' on Wilden-wooly. Pete was the son of a penniless 'tinwood-man', one of those armoured lumberjacks who venture deep into the planet's peculiarly dangerous forests in search of wishing-wood trees. After his father had been dragged into an underwater cavern by a snoligoster, Pete had gone to work for Old Man Lejeune. That he had courage was quickly proved for it took guts to pipe the luxuriously furred but savage-tempered agro-pelters out of their hollow trees and conduct them into the hands of the skinners. That he was also foolhardy was almost as swiftly demonstrated for he had fallen as passionately in love with Kate as she had with him.

When he had summoned up enough bravery to ask her father for her hand—Old Man Lejeune was as vicious and quickly angered as an agropelter itself and not to be charmed by any blowing on a pipe—he had been thrown out bodily with several bruises and contusions, a slight brain concussion, and a promise that if he got within speaking distance of her again he would lose both life and limb. Then had followed the old and inevitable story. After getting out of the hospital Pete had sent Kate messages through her widowed aunt. The aunt disliked her brother and was moreover such an intense devotee of the stereo romance-serials that she would have done almost anything to smooth the path of true love.

Thus it was that a copter had suddenly dropped on to the port outside Breakneck just before the *Gull* was to take off. After identifying themselves and purchasing tickets—which was all they had to do to get passage for there were no visas or passports for human beings who wanted transportation between the planets of the Commonwealth—they had entered cabin 9 next to the bishop's, and there stayed until just before the translator had broken down.

Kate's aunt had been too proud of her part as Cupid to keep her mouth shut. She'd told a half dozen friends in Breakneck after getting their solemn promises not to tell anyone. Result: Father Carmody had all the facts and some of the lies about the Master-Lejeune affair. When the couple had slipped aboard he'd known at once what had happened and indeed was waiting for the outraged father to follow them with a band of tough skinners to take care of Pete. But the ship had flashed away, and now there was little chance they'd be met at Ygdrasil port with an order for the couple's detention. They'd be lucky if they ever arrived there.

Carmody walked to a spot before them and halted. "Don't be frightened, kids," he said. "The captain's private opinion is that we won't have any trouble landing on Abatos."

Pete Masters was a red-haired hawk-nosed youth with hollow cheeks and a too large chin. His frame was large but he'd not yet filled out with a man's muscles nor got over the slouch of the adolescent who grows too fast. He covered the delicate long-fingered hand of Kate with his big bony hand and said, glaring up at the priest, "And I suppose he'll turn us over to the authorities as soon as we land?"

Carmody blinked at the brassiness of Pete's voice and leaned slightly forward as if he were walking against the wind of it.

"Hardly," he said softly. "If there's an authority on Abatos, we haven't met him yet. But we may, we may."

He paused and looked at Kate. She was pretty and petite. Her long wheaten hair was caught up in the back with a silver circlet; her large violet eyes turned up to meet his with a mixture of guilelessness and pleading.

"Actually," said the padre, "your father can't do a thing—legally—to stop you two unless you commit a crime. Let me see, you're nineteen, aren't you, Pete? And you, Kate, are only seventeen, right? If I remember the clauses in the Free Will Act, your being under age will not hamper your moving away from your father's house without his permission. You're of mobile age. On the other hand, according to law, you're not of nubile age. Biology, I know, contradicts that, but we also live in a social world, one of manmade laws. You may not get married without your father's consent. If you try to do so, he may legally restrain you. And will, no doubt."

"He can't do a thing," said Pete, fiercely. "We're not going to get married until Kate is of age."

He glared from under straw-coloured eyebrows. Kate's paleness disappeared under a flood of red, and she looked down at her slim legs, painted canary yellow with scarlet-tipped toenails. Her free hand plucked at her Kelly-green puffkilt.

Carmody's smile remained.

"Forgive a nosy priest who is interested because he doesn't want to see you hurt. Or to have you hurt anybody. But I know your father, Kate. I know he's quite capable of carrying out his threat against Pete. Would you want to see him kidnapped, brutally beaten up, perhaps killed?"

She raised her large eyes to him, her cheeks still flaming. She was very beautiful, very young, very intense.

"Daddy wouldn't dare!" she said in a low but passionate voice. "He knows that if anything happens to Pete, I'll kill myself. I said so in the note I left him, and he knows I'm just as stubborn as he. Daddy won't hurt Pete because he loves me too much."

"Just don't bother talking to him, honey," said Pete. "I'll handle this. Carmody, we don't want any interference, well meant or not. We just want to be left alone."

Father John sighed. "To be left alone is little enough to desire. Unfortunately, or perhaps fortunately, it's one of the rarest things in this universe, almost as rare as peace of mind or genuine love for mankind."

"Spare me your cliches," said Pete. "Save them for church."

"Ah, yes, I did see you once at St. Mary's, didn't I?" replied Father John, stroking the side of his nose. "Two years ago during that outbreak of hermit fever. Hmm."

Kate put her hand on the young man's wrist. "Please, darling. He means well, and what he says is true, anyway."

"Thank you, Kate."

Carmody hesitated, then, looking thoughtful and sad, he reached into the puffkilt's pocket and pulled out a slip of yellow paper. He held it out to Kate, who took it with a trembling hand.

"This was given to the steward just before our ship took off," he said. "It was too late then for anything to be done; unless it's a matter of supreme importance, the ship's schedule is adhered to."

Kate read the message and paled again. Pete, reading over her shoulder, became red, and his nostrils flared. Tearing the paper from her, he jumped up.

"If Old Man Lejeune thinks he can jail me by accusing me of stealing his money, he's crazy!" he snarled. "He can't prove it because I didn't do it! I'm innocent, and I'll prove it by volunteering for chalarocheil! Or any truth drug that they want to give me! That'll show him up for the liar he is!"

Father John's eyes widened. "Meanwhile, you two will be held, and Kate's father will take steps to get her back or at least remove her to the other end of the Galaxy. Now, I'd like to suggest . . ."

"Never mind your needlenosing suggestions," barked Pete.

He crumpled the paper and dropped it on the floor. "Come on, Kate, let's go to our cabin."

Submissively, she rose, though she shot a look at Pete as if she'd like to express her opinion. He ignored it.

"Do you know," he continued, "I'm glad we're being forced to land on Abatos. From what I've read, the *Tokyo* determined that it's a habitable planet, perhaps another Eden. So Kate and I ought to be able to live fairly easy on it. I've got my Powerkit in my cabin; with it we can build a cabin and till the soil and hunt and fish and raise our children as we wish. And there'll be no interference from anyone—no one at all."

Father John cocked his head to one side and let his left eyelid droop. "Adam and Eve, heh? Won't you two become rather lonely? Besides, how do you know what dangers Abatos holds?"

"Pete and I need nobody else," replied Kate quietly. "And no interference from anyone—no one at all."

"Except your father."

But the two were walking away hand in hand; they might not have heard him.

He leaned over to pick up the paper, grunting as he did so. Straightening up with a sigh, he smoothed it out and read it.

Doctor Blake rose from the table and approached him. He smiled with a mixture of affability and reproach.

"Aren't you being a little bit too officious?"

Carmody smiled. "You've known me for a long time, Chandra. You know that this long sharp nose of mine is an excellent sign of my character, and that I would not put my hand in the flame to deny that I an a needlenosing busybody. However, my excuse is that I am a priest and that that is a professional attribute. No escaping it. Moreover, I happen to be interested in those kids; I want them to get out of this mess without being hurt."

"You're likely to get the shape of your nose changed. That Pete looks wild enough to swing on you."

Father John rubbed the end of his nose. "Won't be the first time it's been busted. But I doubt if Pete'd hit me. One good thing about popping off if you're a priest. Even the roughest hesitate about hitting you. Almost like striking a woman. Or God's representative. Or both. We cowards sometimes take advantage of that."

Blake snorted. "Coward?" Then, "Kate's not

even of your religion, Father, and Pete might as
well not be."

Carmody shrugged and spread his palms out as
if to show that his hands were for anybody who
needed them. A few minutes later, he was pressing
the buzzer by the bishop's door. When he heard no
answering voice, he turned as if to go, then
stopped, frowning. Abruptly, as if obeying an
inner warning, he pushed in on the door. Unlocked, it swung open. He gasped and ran into the
room.

The bishop was lying face up on the middle of
the floor, his arms and legs extended crucifix-
wise, his back arched to form a bow, his eyes open
and fixed in a stare at a point on the ceiling. His
face was flushed and glistening with sweat; his
breath hissed; bubbles of foam escaped from his
lax mouth. Yet there was nothing of the classic
seizure about him, for the upper part of his body
seemed to be immobile, almost as if it were
formed of wax just on the verge of melting from
some internal heat. The lower part, on the contrary, was in violent movement. His legs thrashed
and his pelvis stabbed upwards. He looked as if a
sword had cut an invisible path through the region
of his abdomen and severed the nerves and
muscles that connected the two halves. The trunk
had cast off the hips and legs and said, "What you
do is no concern of mine."

Carmody closed the door and hastened to do
that which needed doing for the bishop.

The *Gull* chose to settle upon a spot in the centre
of the only continent of Abatos, a globe-encirling
mass large as Africa and Asia put together, all of it
in the northern hemisphere.

"Best landing I ever made," said Tu to his first

mate. "Almost as if I were a machine, I set her down so easy." Aside, he muttered, "Perhaps I've saved the best for the last."

Carmody did not come from the bishop's cabin until twenty-four hours later. After telling the doctor and the captain that Andre was resting quietly and did not wish to be disturbed, Carmody asked what they'd found out so far. Obviously, he'd been eaten up with curiosity while locked in the cabin, for he had a hundred questions ready and could not fire them out fast enough.

They could tell him little, though their explorations had covered much territory. The climate seemed to be about what you'd find in midwest America in May. The vegetation and animal life paralleled those of Earth, but of course there were many unfamiliar species.

"Here's something strange," said Doctor Blake. He picked up several thin disks, cross-sections of trees, and handed them to the priest. "Pete Masters cut these with his Power-kit. Apparently he's been looking for the best kind of wood with which to build a cabin—or maybe I should say a mansion; he has some rather grandiose ideas about what he's going to do here. Notice the grain and the distance between the rings. Perfect grain. And the rings are separated by exactly the same length. Also, no knots or worm-holes of any kind.

"Pete pointed out these interesting facts, so we cut down about forty trees of different types with the ship's Survival Kit saw. And all specimens showed the same perfection. Not only that, but the number of rings, plus the Mead method of photostatic dating, proved that every tree was exactly the same age. All had been planted ten thousand years ago!"

"The only comment I could make would be an understatement," said Carmody. "Hmmm. The even spacing of the growth rings would indicate that the seasons, if any, follow a regular pattern, that there have been no irregular stretches of wetness and dryness but a static allotment of rain and sunshine. But these woods are wild and untended. How account for the lack of damage from parasites? Perhaps there are none."

"Don't know. Not only that, the fruit of these trees is very large and tasty and abundant—all looking as if they'd come from stock carefully bred and protected. Yet we've seen no signs of intelligent life."

Blake's black eyes sparkled, and his hands seesawed with excitement.

"We took the liberty of shooting several animals so we could examine them. I did a fast dissection on a small zebra-like creature, a wolf with a long copper-coloured snout, a yellow red-crested corvine, and a kangarooish non-marsupial. Even my hasty study turned up several astonishing facts, though one of them could have been determined by any layman."

He paused, then burst out, "All were females! And the dating of their bones indicated that they, like the trees, were ten thousand years old!"

Father John's tufted eyebrows could rise no higher; they looked like untidy wings flapping heavily with a freight of amazement.

"Yes, we've detected no males at all among any of the millions of beasts that we've seen. Not a one. All, all females!"

He took Carmody's elbow and escorted him towards the woods.

"Ten thousand years old the skeletons were. But that wasn't all that was marvellous about them. Their bones were completely innocent of evolutionary vestiges, were perfectly functional. Carmody, you're an amateur paleontologist, you should know how unique that is. On every planet where we've studied fossil and contemporary skeletons, we've found that they display tag-ends of bones that have degenerated in structure because of loss of function. Consider the toes of a dog, the hoofs of a horse. The dog, you might say, walks on his fingers and has lost his big toe and reduced his thumb to a small size. The horse's splint bones were once two toes, the hoof representing the main toe that hardened and on which the fossil horse put his main weight. But this zebra had nó splint bones, and the wolf showed no vestiges of toes that had lost their function. The same with the other creatures I studied. Functionally perfect."

"But, but," said Father John, "you know that evolution on other planets doesn't follow exactly the same pattern laid down on Earth. Moreover, the similarity between a terrestrial and a non-terrestrial type may be misleading. As a matter of fact, likenesses between Earth types may be deceiving. Look how the isolated Australian marsupials developed parallels to placentals. Though not at all related to the higher mammals of the other continents, they evolved dog-like, mouse-like, mole-like, and bear-like creatures."

"I'm quite aware of that," replied Blake, a little stiffly. "I'm no ignoramus, you know. There are other factors determining my opinion, but you talk so much you've given me no chance to tell you."

Carmody had to laugh. "I? Talk? I've hardly got in a word. Never mind. I apologize for my gabbiness. What else is there?"

"Well, I had some of the crewmen do some looking around. They brought in hundreds of specimens of insects, and of course I'd no time for anything except a hasty glance. But there were none with any correspondence to larval forms as we know them on Earth. All adult forms. When I thought of that, I realized something else we'd all seen but hadn't been impressed by, mostly, I suppose, because the deductions were too over-whelming or because we just weren't looking for such a thing. We saw no young among the animals."

"Puzzling, if not frightening," said Carmody. "You may release my elbow, if you wish. I'll go with you willingly. Which reminds me, where are you taking me?"

"Here!"

Blake stopped before a redwoodish tree tower-ing perhaps two hundred feet. He indicated a very large hole in the trunk, about two feet from the ground. "This cavity is not the result of damage by some animal. It obviously is part of the tree's structure."

He directed the beam of a flashlight into the dark interior. Carmody stuck his head into the hole and after a moment withdrew it, looking thoughtful.

"There must be about ten tons of that jelly-like substance inside," he said. "And there are bones embedded deep within it."

"Wherever you go, you find these jelly trees, as we now call them," said Blake. "About half of them hold animal skeletons."

"What are they? A sort of Venusian fly-trap?" asked the priest, involuntarily taking a backward step. "No, they couldn't be that, or you'd not have allowed me to stick my head in. Or does it, like many men, find theological subjects distasteful?"

Blake laughed, then sobered quickly.

"I've no idea *why* these bones are there nor what purpose the jelly serves," he said. "But I can tell you *how* they got there. You see, while we were flying around, mapping and observing, we witnessed several killings by the local carnivora. There are two types we were glad we didn't run into on the ground, though we've means to repel them if we see them soon enough. One's a cat about the size of a Bengal tiger, leopard-like except for big round ears and tufts of grey fur on the backs of its legs. The other's a ten-foot-high black-furred mammal built like a tyrannosaurus with a bear's head. Both prey on the zebras and the numerous deer and antelope. You'd think that their fleet-footed prey would keep the killer swift and trim, but they don't. The big cats and the struthiursines are the fattest and laziest meateaters you ever saw. When they attack, they don't sneak up through the grass and then make a swift but short run. They walk boldly into view, roar a few times, wait until the majority of the herd have dashed off, then select one from the several submissive animals that have refused to flee, and kill it. Those that have been spared then drift off. They're not frightened by the sight of the killer devouring one of their sisters. No, they just appear uneasy.

"As if that weren't extraordinary enough, the sequel positively astounds you. After the big killer has gorged himself and leaves, the small carrion-eaters then descend, yellowish crows and brown-and-white foxes. The bones are well cleaned. But they aren't left to bleach in the sun. Along comes a black ape with a long lugubrious face—the under-taker ape, we call him—and he picks the bones up and deposits them in the jelly inside the nearest jelly tree. Now, what do you think of that?"

"I think that, though it's a warm day, I have a sudden chill. I . . . oh, there's His Excellency. Excuse me."

The priest hurried across the daisy-starred

meadow, a long black case in his hand. The bishop did not wait for him but stepped from the shadow of the ship into the light. Though the yellow sun had risen only an hour ago above the purplish mountains to the east, it was very bright. When it struck the bishop's figure, it seemed to burst into flame around him and magnify him, almost as if its touch were that of a golden god imparting some of his own magnificence to him. The illusion was made all the stronger by the fact that Andre showed no signs of his recent illness. His face glowed, and he strode swiftly towards the crowd at the forest's edge, his shoulders squared and his deep chest rising and falling as if he were trying to crowd all the planet's air into his lungs.

Carmody, who met him half-way, said, "You may well breathe this superb air, Your Excellency. It has a tang and freshness that is quite virginal. Air that has never been breathed by man before."

Andre looked about him with the slowness and sure majesty of a lion staking out a new hunting territory. Carmody smiled slightly. Though the bishop made a noble figure of a man, he gave at that moment just the hint of a poseur, so subtle that only one with Carmody's vast experience could have detected it. Andre, catching the fleeting indentations at the corners of the little priest's lips, frowned and raised his hands in protest.

"I know what you are thinking."

Carmody bent his neck to gaze at the bright green grass at their feet. Whether he did so to acknowledge that the reprimand was just or to hide another emotion, he managed to veil his eyes. Then, as if realizing it was not good to conceal his thoughts, he raised his head to look his bishop in the eyes. His gesture was similar to Andre's and had dignity but none of the other man's beauty, for Carmody could never look beautiful, except with the more subtle beauty that springs from honesty.

"I hope you can forgive me, Your Excellency. But old habits die hard. Mockery was so long a part of me before I was converted—indeed, was a necessity if one was to survive on the planet where I lived, which was Dante's Joy, you know—that it dug deep into my nervous system. I believe that I am making a sincere effort to overcome the habit; but, being human, I am sometimes lax."

"We must strive to be more than human," replied Andre, making a gesture with his hand which the priest, who knew him well, interpreted as a sign to drop the subject. It was not peremptory, for he was always courteous and patient. His time was not his; the lowliest were his masters. Had Carmody persisted in dwelling on that line of thought, he would have allowed it. The priest, however, accepted his superior's decision.

He held out a slender black case six feet long.

"I thought that perhaps Your Excellency would like to try the fishing here. It may be true that Wildenwooly has a Galaxy-wide reputation for the best fishing anywhere, but there's something about the very looks of Abatos that tells me we'll find fish here to put a glow in our hearts—not to mention a whale of an appetite in our mouths. Would you care to try a few casts? It might benefit Your Excellency."

Andre's smile was slow and gentle, ending in a huge grin of delight. "I'd like that very much, John. You could have suggested nothing better."

He turned to Tu. "Captain?"

"I think it'll be safe. We've sent out survey copters. They reported some large carnivores but none close. However, some of the herbivores may be dangerous. Remember, even a domestic bull may be a killer. The copter crews did try to get some of the larger beasts to charge and failed. The animals either ignored them or ambled away. Yes, you may go fishing, though I wish the lake weren't so far off. What about a copter dropping you off there and picking you up later?"

Andre said, "No thank you. We can't get the feel of this planet by flying over it. We'll walk."

The first mate held out two pistols of some sort. "Here you are, Reverends. Something new. Sonos. Shoots a subsonic beam that panics man or beast, makes 'em want to get to hell and away as fast as they can, if you'll pardon the expression."

"Of course. But we can't accept them. Our order is never permitted to carry arms, for any reason."

"I wish you'd break the rule this time," said Tu. "Rules aren't made to be broken; no captain would subscribe to that proverb. But there are times when you have to consider their context."

"Absolutely not," replied the bishop, looking keenly at Carmody, who'd stretched out his hand as if to take a sono.

At the glance, the priest dropped his hand. "I merely wished to examine the weapon," said Carmody. "But I must admit I've never thought much of that rule. It's true that Jairus had his peculiar power over beasts of prey. However, that fact didn't necessarily endow his disciples with a similar gift. Think of what happened on Jimdandy because St. Victor refused a gun. Had he used one, he'd have saved a thousand lives."

The bishop closed his eyes and murmured so that only Carmody could hear. "*Even though I walk in the dark valley . . .*"

Carmody murmured back, "But the dark is sometimes cold, and the hairs on the back of the neck rise with fear, though I become hot with shame."

"Hmm. Speaking of shame, John, you always manage, somehow, while deprecating yourself, to leave me discomfited and belittled. It's a talent which, perhaps, should be possessed by the man who is most often with me, for it cuts down my inclination to grow proud. On the other hand . . ."

Carmody waved the long case in his hand. "On the other hand, the fish may not wait for us."

Andre nodded and began walking towards the woods. Tu said something to a crewman, who ran after the two priests and gave the little one a ship-finder, a compass that would always point in the *Gull's* direction. Carmody flashed a grin of thanks and, shoulders set jauntily, bounced after the swiftly striding bishop, the case whipping behind him like a saucy antenna. He whistled an old old tune—'My Buddy.' Though seemingly carefree, his eyes looked everywhere. He did not fail to see Pete Masters and Kate Lejeune slipping hand in hand into the woods in another direction. He stopped in time to keep from bumping into the bishop, who had turned and was frowning back towards the ship. At first Carmody thought he, too, had noticed the young couple, then saw he was gazing at Mrs. Recka and First Mate Givens. They were standing to one side and talking very intensely. Then they began walking slowly across the meadow towards the towering hemisphere of the *Gull*. Andre stood motionless until the couple went into the ship and, a moment later, came out. This time Mrs. Recka had her pocketbook, a rather large one whose size was not enough to conceal the outlines of a bottle within. Still talking, the two went around the curve of the vessel and presently came into sight of the priests again, though they could not be seen by Tu or the crew members.

Carmody murmured, "Must be something in the

air of this planet . . ."

"What do you mean by that?" said the bishop, his features set very grim, his green eyes narrowed but blazing.

"If this is another Eden, where the lion lies down with the lamb, it is also a place where a man and woman . . ."

"If Abatos is fresh and clean and innocent," growled the bishop, "it will not remain so very long. Not while we have people like those, who would foul any nest."

"Well, you and I will have to content ourselves with fishing."

"Carmody, don't grin when you say that! You sound almost as if you were blessing them instead of condemning!"

The little priest lost his half-smile. "Hardly. I was neither condemning nor blessing. Nor judging them beforehand, for I don't actually know what they have in mind. But it is true that I have too wide a streak of the earth earthy, a dabble of Rabelais, perhaps. It's not that I commend. It's just that I understand too well, and . . ."

Without replying, the bishop turned away violently and resumed his longlegged pace. Carmody, somewhat subdued, followed at his heels, though there was often room enough for the two to walk side by side. Sensitive to Andre's moods, he knew that it was best to keep out of his sight for a while. Meanwhile, he'd interest himself in his surroundings.

The copter survey crews had reported that between the mountains to the east and the ocean to the west the country was much alike: a rolling, sometimes hilly land with large prairies interspersed with forests. The latter seemed more like parks than untamed woods. The grass was a succulent kind kept cropped by the herbivores; many of the trees had their counterparts among the temperate latitudes of Earth; only here and there were thick tangled stretches that might properly be called wild. The lake towards which the two were headed lay in the centre of just such a 'jungle.' The widely spaced oaks, pines, cypresses, beeches, sycamores, and cedars here gave way to an island of the jelly-containing redwoods. Actually, they did not grow close together but gave that impression because of the many vines and lianas that connected them and the tiny parasitic trees, like evergreens, that grew horizontally out of cracks in their trunks.

It was darker under these great vegetation-burdened limbs, though here and there shafts of sunlight slanted, seeming like solid and leaning trunks of gold themselves. The forest was alive with the colour and calls of bright birds and the dark bodies and chitterings of arboreal animals. Some of these looked like monkeys; when they leapt through the branches and came quite close, the resemblance was even more amazing. But they were evidently not sprung from a protosimian base; they must have been descended from a cat that had decided to grow fingers instead of claws and to assume a semi-upright posture. Dark brown on the back, they had grey-furred bellies and chests and long prehensile tails tufted at the end with auburn. Their faces had lost the pointed beastish look and become flat as an ape's. Three long thick feline whiskers bristled from each side of their thin lips. Their teeth were sharp and long, but they picked and ate a large pear-shaped berry that grew on the vines. Their slitted pupils expanded in the shade and contracted in the sunlit spaces. They chattered among themselves and behaved in general like monkeys, except that they seemed to be cleaner.

"Perhaps they've cousins who evolved into humanoid beings," said Carmody aloud, partly because he'd the habit of talking to himself, partly to see if the bishop were out of his mood.

"Heh?" said Andre, stopping and also looking at the creatures, who returned his gaze just as curiously. "Oh, yes, Sokoloff's Theory of the Necessary Chance. Every branch of the animal kingdom as we know it on Earth seems to have had its opportunity to develop into a sentient being some place in the Galaxy. The vulpoids of Kubeia, the avians of Albiero IV, the cetaceoids of Oceanos, the molluscs of Baudelaire, the Houyhnhnms of Somewhere Else, the so-called lying bugs of Munchausen, the . . . well, I could go on and on. But on almost every Earth-type planet we find that this or that line of life seized the evolutionary chance given by God and developed intelligence. All, with some exceptions, going through an arboreal simian stage and then flowering into an upright creature resembling man."

"And all thinking of themselves as being in God's image, even the porpoise-men of Oceanos and the land-oysters of Baudelaire," added Carmody. "Well, enough of philosophy. At least, fish are fish, on any planet."

They had come out of the forest on to the lake shore. It was a body of water about a mile wide and two long, fed by a clear brook to the north. Grass grew to the very edge, where little frogs leaped into the water at their approach. Carmody uncased their two rods but disengaged the little jet mechanisms that would have propelled their bait-tipped lines far out over the lake.

"Really not sporting," he said. "We ought to give these foreign piscines a chance, eh?"

"Right," replied the bishop, smiling. "If I can't do anything with my own right arm, I'll go home with an empty basket."

"I forgot to bring along a basket, but we can use some of those broad leaves of the vines to wrap our catch in."

An hour later they were forced to stop because of the pile of finny life behind them, and these were only the biggest ones. The rest had been thrown back. Andre had hooked the largest, a magnificent trout of about thirty pounds, a fighter who took twenty minutes to land. After that, sweating and breathing hard but shining-eyed, he said, "I'm hot. What do you say to a swim, John?"

Carmody smiled at the use of his familiar name again and shouted, "Last one in is a Sirian!"

In a minute two naked bodies plunged into the cold clear water at exactly the same time. When they came up, Carmody sputtered, "Guess we're both Sirians, but you win, for I'm the ugliest. Or does that mean that I win?"

Andre laughed for sheer joy, then sped across the lake in a fast crawl. The other did not even try to follow him but floated on his back, eyes closed. Once he raised his head to determine how the bishop was getting along but lay back when he saw that he was in no trouble. Andre had reached the other shore and was returning at a slower but easy pace. When he did come back and had rested for a while on the beach, he said, "John, would you mind climbing out and timing me in a dive? I'd like to see if I'm still in good form. It's about seven feet here, not too deep."

Carmody climbed on to the grassy shore, where he set his watch and gave the signal. Andre plunged under. When he emerged he swam back at once. "How'd I do?" he called as he waded out of the water, his magnificent body shining wet and golden brown in the late afternoon sun.

"Four minutes, three seconds," said Carmody.

"About forty seconds off your record. But still better, I'll bet, than any other man in the Galaxy. You're still the champ, Your Excellency."

Andre nodded, smiling slightly. "Twenty years ago I set the record. I believe that if I went into rigorous training again, I could equal it again or even beat it. I've learned much since then about control of my body and mind. Even then I was not entirely at ease in the pressure and gloom of the underwater. I loved it, but my love was tinged just a little with terror. An attitude that is almost, you might say, one's attitude towards God. Perhaps too much so, as one of my parishioners was kind enough to point out to me. I think he meant that I was paying too much attention to what should have been only a diversion for my idle moments.

"He was correct, of course, though I rather resented his remarks at the time. He couldn't have known that it was an irresistible challenge to me to float beneath the bright surface, all alone, feel myself buoyed as if in the arms of a great mother, yet also feel her arms squeezing just a little too tight. I had to fight down the need to shoot to the surface and suck in life-giving air, yet I was proud because I could battle that panic, could defeat it. I felt always as if I was in danger but because of that very danger was on the verge of some vital discovery about myself—what, I never found out. But I always thought that if I stayed down long enough, could keep out the blackness and the threat of loss of consciousness, I would find the secret.

"Strange thought, wasn't it? It led me to study the neo-Yoga disciplines which were supposed to enable one to go into suspended animation, death-in-life. There was a man on Gandhi who could stay buried alive for three weeks, but I could never determine if he was faking or not. He was some help to me, however. He taught me that if I would, as he put it, go dead here, first of all," and Andre touched his left breast, "then here," and he touched his loins, "the rest would follow. I could become as an embryo floating in the amniotic sac, living but requiring no breath, no oxygen except that which soaked through the cells, as he put it. An absurd theory, scientifically speaking, yet it worked to some extent. Would you believe it, I now have to force myself to rise because it seems so safe and nice and warm under there, even when the water is very cold, as in this lake?"

While he talked, he'd been wiping the water from his skin with his quilted dickie, his back turned to Carmody. The priest knew his bishop was embarrassed to expose himself. He himself, though he knew his body looked ugly and grotesque beside the other's perfect physique, was not at all ill-at-ease. In common with most of the people of his time, he'd been raised in a world where nudity on the beach and in the private home was socially accepted, almost demanded. Andre, born in the Church, had had a very strict up-bringing by devout parents who had insisted that he follow the old pattern even in the midst of a world that mocked.

It was of that he spoke now, as if he'd guessed what Carmody was thinking.

"I disobeyed my father but once," he said. "That was when I was ten. We lived in a neighborhood composed mainly of agnostics or members of the Temple of Universal Light. But I had some very good pals among the local gang of boys and tomboys, and just once they talked me into going swimming in the river, skin-style. Of course my father caught me; he seemed to have an instinct for detecting when sin was threatening any of his family. He gave me the beating of my life—may his

soul rest in peace," he added without conscious
irony.

" 'Spare the rod and spoil the child' was ever his
favourite maxim, yet he had to whip me just that
one time in my life. Or rather, I should say
twice, because I tore loose from him while he was
strapping me in front of the gang, plunged into the
river, and dived deep, where I stayed a long time
in an effort to frighten my father into thinking I'd
drowned myself. Eventually, of course, I had to
come up. My father resumed the punishment. He
was no more severe the second time, though. He
couldn't have been without killing me. As a matter
of fact, he almost did. If it weren't for modern
science's ability to do away with scars, I'd still
bear them on my back and legs. As it is, they're
still here," and he pointed to indicate his heart.

He finished drying himself and picked up his
puffkilt. "Well, that was thirty-five years ago and
thousands of light years away, and I dare say the
beating did me a tremendous amount of good."

He looked at the clear sky and at the woods,
arched his deep chest in a great breath, and said,
"This is a wonderful and unspoiled planet, a
testimony to God's love for the beauty of His
creatures and His generosity in scattering them
across the universe, almost as if He had had to do
so! Here I feel as if God is in His heaven and all's
right with the world. The symmetry and fruitful-
ness of those trees, the clean air and waters, the
manifold songs of those birds and their bright
colours . . ."

He stopped, for he suddenly realized what Carmody had just previously noticed. There were
none of the noisy but melodious twitterings and
chirpings and warblings nor the chattering of the
monkeys. All was hush. Like a thick blanket of
moss, a silence hung over the forest.

"Something's scared those animals," whispered Carmody. He shivered, though the westering sun was yet hot, and he looked around. Near them, on a long branch that extended over the lake's edge, sat a row of catmonkeys that had appeared as if from nowhere. They were grey-furred except for a broad white mark on their chests, roughly in the form of a cross. Their head-hair grew thick and forward and fell over their foreheads like a monk's cowl. Their hands were placed over their eyes in a monkey-see-no-evil attitude. But their eyes shone bright between their fingers, and Carmody, despite his sense of uneasiness, felt a prickling of laughter and murmured, "No fair peeking."

A deep cough sounded in the forest; the monk-monks, as he'd tagged them, cowered and crowded even closer together.

"What could that be?" said the bishop.

"Must be a big beast. I've heard lions cough: they sounded just like that."

Abruptly, the bishop reached out a large square hand and closed Carmody's little pudgy hand in it.

Alarmed at the look on Andre's face, Carmody said, "Is another seizure coming on?"

The bishop shook his head. His eyes were glazed. "No. Funny, I felt for a moment almost as I did when my father caught me."

He released the other's hand and took a deep breath. "I'll be all right."

He lifted his kilt to step into it. Carmody gasped. Andre jerked his head upright and gave a little cry. Something white was looming in the shadow of the trees, moving slowly but surely, the focus and cause of the silence that spread everywhere. Then it grew darker as it stepped into the sunshine and stopped for a moment, not to adjust its eyes to the dazzle but to allow the beholders to adjust their eyes to him. He was eight feet tall and looked much like a human being and moved with such dignity and such beauty that the earth seemed to give way respectfully at each footstep. He was long-bearded and naked and massively male, and the eyes were like those of a granite statue of a god that had become flesh, too terrible to look straight into.

He spoke. They knew then the origin of that cough that had come from the depth of lungs deep as an oracle's well. His voice was a lion's roar; it made the two pygmies clasp each other's hands again and unloosed their muscles so that they thought they'd come apart. Yet they did not think of how amazing it was that he should speak in their tongue.

"Hello, my sons!" he thundered.

They bowed their heads.

"Father."

An hour before sunset, Andre and Carmody ran out of the woods. They were in a hurry because of the tremendous uproar that had aroused the forest for miles around. Men were yelling, and a woman was screaming, and something was growling loudly. They arrived just in time to see the end. Two enormous beasts, bipedal heavily tailed creatures with bearish heads, were racing after Kate Lejeune and Pete Masters. Kate and Pete were running hand in hand, he pulling her so fast that she seemed to fly through the air with every step. In his other hand he carried his power saw. Neither had a sono-gun with which to defend themselves, although Captain Tu had ordered that no one be without the weapon. A moment later it was seen that the gun would have made no difference, for several crewmen who had been standing by the ship had turned their sonos against the beasts. Undeterred by the panicking effects of the beams, the monsters sprang after the couple and caught them half-way across the meadow.

Though unarmed, Andre and Carmody ran at the things, their fists clenched. Pete turned in his captor's grasp and struck it across the muzzle with the sharp edge of his saw. Kate screamed loudly then fainted. Suddenly, the two were lying in the grass, for the animals had dropped them and were walking almost leisurely towards the woods. That neither the sonos nor the priests had scared them off was evident. They brushed by the latter without noticing them, and if the former had affected their nervous systems at all, they gave no signs.

Carmody looked once at the young woman and yelled, "Doctor Blake! Get Blake at once!"

Like a genie summoned by the mention of his name, Blake was there with his little black kit. He at once called for a stretcher; Kate, moaning and rolling her head from side to side, was carried into the ship's hospital. Pete raged until Blake ordered him out of the room.

"I'll get a gun and kill those beasts. I'll track them down if it takes me a week. Or a year! I'll trap them and . . ."

Carmody pushed him out of the room and into the lounge, where he made the youth sit down. With a shaking hand, he lit two cigarettes.

"It would do you no good to kill them," he said. "they'd be up and around in a few days. Besides, they're just animals who were obeying their master's commands."

He puffed on his cigarette while with one hand he snapped his glow-wire lighter shut and put it back in his pocket.

"I'm just as shaken up as you. Recent events have been too fast and too inexplicable for my nervous system to take them in stride. But I wouldn't worry about Kate being hurt, if I were you. I know she looked pretty bad, but I'm sure she'll be all right and in a very short time, too."

"You blind optimistic ass!" shouted Pete. "You *saw* what happened to her!"

"She's suffering from hysterics, not from any physical effects of her miscarriage," replied Carmody calmly. "I'll bet that in a few minutes, when Blake has her calmed down with a sedative, she'll walk out of the hospital in as good a condition as she was in this morning. I know she will. You see, son, I've had a talk with a being who is not God but who convinces you that *he* is the nearest equivalent."

Pete became slack-jawed "What? What're you talking about?"

"I know I sound as if I were talking nonsense. But I've met the owner of Abatos. Or rather *he* has talked to me, and what *he* has shown the bishop and me is, to understate, staggering. There are a hundred things we'll have to let you and everybody else know in due time. Meanwhile, I can give you an idea of *his* powers. They range in terrible spectrum from such petty, but amazing, deeds as curing my toothache with a mere laying on of hands, to bringing dead bones back to life and reclothing them with flesh. I have seen the dead arise and go forth. Though, I must admit, probably to be eaten again."

Frowning, he added, "The bishop and I were permitted to perform—or should I say commit?—a resurrection ourselves. The sensation is not indescribable, but I prefer not to say anything about it at present."

Pete rose with clenched fists, his cigarette

shredding under the pressure.

"You must be crazy."

"That would be nice if I were, for I'd be relieved of an awful responsibility. And if the choice were mine, I'd take incurable insanity. But I'm not to get off so easily."

Suddenly, Father John lost his calmness; he looked as if he were going to break into many pieces. He buried his face in his hands, while Pete stared, stunned. then the priest as abruptly lowered his hands and presented once again the sharp-nosed, round and smiling features the world knew so well.

"Fortunately, the ultimate decision will not be mine but His Excellency's. And though it is cowardly to be glad because I may pass the buck on to him, I must confess that I will be glad. His is the power in this case, and though power has its glory, it also has its burdens and griefs. I wouldn't want to be in the bishop's shoes at this moment."

Pete didn't hear the priest's last words. He was gazing at the hospital door, just opening. Kate stepped out, a little pale but walking steadily. Pete ran to her; they folded each other in their arms; then she was crying.

"Are you all right, honey?" Pete kept saying over and over.

"Oh, I feel fine," she replied, still weeping. "I don't understand why, but I do. I'm suddenly healed. There's nothing wrong down there. It was as if a hand passed over me, and strength flowed out of it, and all was well with my body."

Blake, who had appeared behind her, nodded in agreement.

"Oh, Pete," sobbed Kate, "I'm all right, but I lost our baby! And I know it was because we stole that money from Daddy. It was our punishment. It was bad enough running away, though we had to do that because we loved each other. But we should never have taken that money!"

"Hush, honey, you're talking too much. Let's go to our cabin where you can rest."

Gently he directed her out of the lounge while he glared defiantly at Carmody.

"Oh, Pete," she wailed, "all that money, and now we're on a planet where it's absolutely no good at all. Only a burden."

"You talk too much, baby," said Pete, a roughness replacing the gentleness in his voice. They disappeared down the corridor. Carmody said nothing. Eyes downcast, he, too, walked to his cabin and shut the door behind him.

A half hour later, he came out and asked for Captain Tu. Told that Tu was outside, he left the *Gull* and found an attentive group at the edge of the meadow on the other side of the ship. Mrs. Recka and the first mate were the centre of attraction.

"We were sitting under one of those big jelly trees and passing the bottle back and forth and talking of this and that," said Givens. "Mostly about what we'd do if we found out we were stranded here for the rest of our lives."

Somebody snickered. Givens flushed but continued evenly.

"Suddenly, Mrs. Recka and I became very sick. We vomited violently and broke out into a cold sweat. By the time we'd emptied our stomachs, we were sure the whisky had been poisoned. We thought we'd die in the woods, perhaps never to be found, for we were quite a distance from the ship and in a rather secluded spot.

"But as suddenly as it had come, the illness went away. We felt completely happy and healthy. The only difference was, we both were absolutely certain that we'd never again want to touch a drop of whisky."

"Or any other alcoholic drink," added Mrs. Recka, shuddering.

Those who knew of her weakness gazed curiously and somewhat doubtfully at her. Carmody tapped the captain's elbow and drew him off to one side.

"Is the radio and other electronic equipment working by now?" he asked.

"They resumed operation about the time you two showed up. But the translator still refuses to budge. I was worried when you failed to report through your wrist radios. For all I knew, some beast of prey had killed you, or you'd fallen into the lake and drowned. I organized a search party, but we'd not gone half a mile before we noticed the needles on our ship-finders whirling like mad. So we returned. I didn't want to be lost in the woods, for my primary duty is to the ship, of course. And I couldn't send out a copter crew, for the copters simply refused to run. They're working all right now, though. What do you think of all this?"

"Oh, I know *who* is doing this. And *why.*"

"For God's sake, man, *who?*"

"I don't know if it is for God's sake or not . . ." Carmody glanced at his watch. "Come with me. There is someone you must meet."

"Where are we going?"

"Just follow me. *He* wants a few words with you because you are the captain, and your decision will have to be given also. Moreover, I want you to know just what we are up against."

"Who is *he?* A native of Abatos?"

"Not exactly, though *he* has lived here longer than any native creature of this planet."

Tu adjusted the angle of his cap and brushed dust flakes from his uniform. He strode through the corridors of the noisy jungle as if the trees were on parade and he were inspecting them.

"If *he* has been here longer than ten thousand years," said the captain, unconsciously stressing the personal pronoun as Carmody did, "then *he* must have arrived long before English and its descendant tongue, Lingo, were spoken, when the Aryan speech was still only the property of a savage tribe in Europe. How can we talk with him? Telepathy?"

"No. *He* learned Lingo from the survivor of the crash of the *Hoyle*, the only ship *he* ever permitted to get through."

"And where is this man?" asked Tu, annoyedly glancing at a choir of howling monkeys on an overhead branch.

"No man. A woman, a medical officer. After a year here, she committed suicide. Built a funeral pyre and burned herself to death. There was nothing left of her but ashes."

"Why?"

"I imagine because total cremation was the only way she could put herself beyond *his* reach. Because otherwise *he* might have placed her bones in a jelly tree and brought her back to life."

Tu halted. "My mind understands you, but my sense of belief is numb. Why did she kill herself when, if you are not mistaken, she had eternal life before her or at least a reasonable facsimile thereof?"

"*He—Father—*says that she could not endure the thought of living forever on Abatos with him as her only human, or humanoid, companion. I know how she felt. It would be like sharing the world with only God to talk to. Her sense of inferiority and her loneliness must have been overwhelming."

Carmody stopped suddenly and became lost in

thought, his head cocked to one side, his left eyelid drooping.

"Hmm. That's strange. *He* said that we, too, could have *his* powers, become like *him*. Why didn't *he* teach her? Was it because *he* didn't want to share? Come to think of it, *he's* made no offer of dividing *his* dominions. Only wants substitution. Hmm. All or none. Either *he* or . . . or what?"

"What the hell are you talking about?" barked Captain Tu irritatedly.

"You may be right at that," said Carmody absently. "Look, there's a jelly tree. What do you say we do a little poking and prying, heh? It's true that *he* forbade any needlenosing on the part of us extra-Abatosians; it's true that this may be another garden of Eden and that I, a too true son of Adam, alas, may be re-enacting another fall from grace, may be driven out with flaming swords—though I—may even be blasted with lightning for blaspheming against the local deity. Nevertheless, I think a little delving into the contents of that cavity may be as profitable as any dentist's work. What do you say, Captain? The consequences could be rather disastrous."

"If you mean am I afraid, all I can say is that you know better than that," growled Tu. "I'll let no priest get ahead of me in guts. Go ahead. I'll back you up all the way."

"Ah," said Carmody, walking briskly up to the foot of the enormous redwood, "ah, but you've not seen and talked to the Father of Abatos. It's not a matter of backing me up, for there's little you could do if we should be discovered. It's a matter of giving me moral courage, of shaming me with your presence so that I won't run like a rabbit if *he* should catch me red-handed."

With one hand he took a small vial out of his pocket and with the other a flashlight, whose beam he pointed into the dark O. Tu looked over his shoulder.

"It quivers, almost as if it were alive," said the captain in a low voice.

"It emits a faint humming, too. If you put your hand lightly on its surface, you can feel the vibration."

"What are those whitish things embedded in it? Bones?"

"Yes, the hollow goes rather deep, doesn't it? Must be below the surface of the ground. See that dark mass in one corner? An antelope of some sort, I'd say. Looks to me as if the flesh were being built up in layers from the inside out; the outer muscles and skin aren't re-created yet."

The priest scooped out a sample of the jelly, capped the vial, and put it back in his pocket. He did not rise but kept playing his beam over the hollow.

"This stuff really makes a Geiger counter dance. Not only that, it radiates electromagnetic waves. I think that radio waves from this jelly damped out our wrist speakers and sonos and played havoc with our ship-finders. Hey, wait a minute! Notice those very minute white threads that run through the whole mass. Nerve-like, aren't they?"

Before Carmody could protest, Tu stooped and dipped out a handful of the quivering gelatinous mass. "Do you know where I've seen something like this before? This stuff reminds me of the protein transistors we used in the translator."

Carmody frowned. 'Aren't they the only living parts of the machine? Seems to me I read that the translator won't rotate the ship through perpendicular space unless these transistors are used.'

"Mechanical transistors could be used," corrected Tu. "But they would occupy a space as large as the spaceship itself. Protein transistors take up very little area; you could carry the *Gull*'s on your back. Actually, that part of the translator is not only a series of transistors but a memory bank. Its function is to "remember" normal space. It has to retain a simulacrum of real or "horizontal" space as distinguished from perpendicular. While one end of the translator is "flopping us over," as the phrase goes, the protein end is reconstructing an image of what the space at our destination looks like, down to the last electron. Sounds very much like sympathetic magic, doesn't it? Build an effigy, and shortly you establish an affinity between reality and counterfeit."

"What happened to the protein banks?"

"Nothing that we could tell. They functioned normally."

"Perhaps the currents aren't getting through. Did the engineer check the synapses or just take a reading on the biostatic charge of the whole? The charge could be normal, you know, yet any transmission could be locked."

"That's the engineer's province. I wouldn't dream of questioning his work, any more than he would mine."

Carmody rose. "I'd like to talk to the engineer. I've a layman's theory, but like most amateurs I may be overly enthusiastic because of my ignorance. If you don't care, I'd rather not discuss it now. Especially here, where the forest may have ears, and . . ."

Though the captain had not even opened his mouth, the priest had raised his finger for silence in a characteristic gesture. Suddenly, it was apparent that he *did* have his silence, for there was not a sound in the woods except the faint soughing of the wind through the leaves.

"*He* is around," whispered Carmody. "Throw that jelly back in, and we'll get away from this tree."

Tu raised his hand to do so. At that moment a rifle shot cracked nearby. Both men jumped. "My God, what fool's doing that?" cried Tu. He said something else, but his voice was lost in the bedlam that broke out through the woods, the shrieks of birds, the howling of monkeys, the trumpetings, neighings, and roarings of thousands of other animals. Then, as abruptly as it had begun, it stopped, almost as if by signal. Silence fell. Then, a single cry. A man's.

"It's Masters," groaned Carmody.

There was a rumble, as of some large beast growling deep in its chest. One of the leopard-like creatures with the round ears and grey tufts on its legs padded out from the brush. It held Pete Masters' dangling body between its jaws as easily as a cat holds a mouse. Paying no attention to the two men, it ran past them to the foot of an oak, where it stopped and laid the youth down before another intruder.

Father stood motionless as stone, one nailless hand resting upon his long red-gold beard, his deeply sunken eyes downcast, intent on the figure on the grass. He did not move until Pete, released from his paralysis, writhed in a passion of abjectness and called out for mercy. Then he stooped and touched the youth briefly on the back of his head. Pete leaped to his feet and, holding his head and screaming as if in pain, ran away through the trees. The leopardess remained couchant, blinking slowly like a fat and lazy housecat.

Father spoke to her. While he stalked off into the woods, she turned her green eyes upon the two men. Neither felt like testing her competence as a guard.

Father stopped under a tree overgrown with vines from which hung fat heavy pods like white hairless coconuts. Though the lowest was twelve feet high, he had no difficulty in reaching up and squeezing it in his hand. It cracked open with a loud report, and water shot from the crushed shell. Tu and Carmody paled; the captain muttered, "I'd rather tackle that big cat than him."

The giant wheeled, and, washing his hands with the water, strode towards them. "Would you like to crush coconuts in one hand too, Captain?" he thundered. "That is nothing. I can show you how you may also do that. I can tear that young beech tree out of the ground by the roots, I can speak a word to Zeda here, and she will heel like a dog. That is nothing. I can teach you the power. I can hear your whisper even at a distance of a hundred yards, as you realize by now. And I could catch you within ten seconds, even if you had a head start and I were sitting down. That is nothing. I can tell instantly where any of my daughters are on the face of Abatos, what state of health they are in, and when they've died. That is nothing. You can do the same, provided you become like that priest there. You could even raise my dead, if you had the will to be like Father John. I may take your hand and show you how you could bring life again to the dead body, though I do not care to touch you."

"For God's sake, say no," breathed Carmody. "It's enough that the bishop and I should have been exposed to that temptation."

Father laughed. Tu grabbed hold of Carmody's hand. He could not have answered the giant if he had wished, for his mouth opened and closed like a fish's out of water, and his eyeballs popped.

"There's something about his voice that turns the bowels to water and loosens the knees," said the priest, then fell silent. Father stood above them, wiping his hands on his beard. Aside from that magnificent growth and a towering roach on his head, he was absolutely bald. His pale red skin was unblemished, glowing with perfect blood beneath the thin surface. His high-bridged nose was septumless, but the one nostril was a flaring Gothic one. Red teeth glistened in his mouth; a blue-veined tongue shot out for a moment like a flame; then the black-red lips writhed and closed. All this was strange but not enough to make these star-travelled men uncomfortable. The voice and the eyes stunned them, the thunder that seemed to shake their bones so they rattled, and the black eyes starred with silver splinters. Stone come to flesh.

"Don't worry, Carmody. I will not show Tu how to raise the dead. Unlike you and Andre, he'd not be able to do it, anyhow. Neither would any of the others, for I've studied them, and I know. But I have need of you, Tu. I will tell you why, and when I have told you, you will see there is nothing else for you to do. I will convince you by reason, not by force, I hate violence, and indeed am required by the nature of my being not to use it. Unless an emergency demands it."

Father talked. An hour later, he stopped. Without waiting for either of them to say a word, even if they'd been capable, he turned and strode away, the leopardess a respectable distance behind his heels. Presently, the normal calls of the wood animals began. The two men shook themselves and silently walked back to the ship. At the meadow's edge, Carmody said, "There's only one thing to do. Call a Council of the Questions of Jairus. Fortunately, you fill the bill for the kind of layman required as moderator. I'll ask the bishop's permission, but I'm sure he'll agree it's the only thing to do. We can't contact our superiors and refer a decision to their judgment. The responsibility rests on us."

"It's a terrible burden," said the captain.

At the ship they asked about the bishop, to be

told he had walked away into the forest only a short time before. The wrist radios were working, but no answer came from Andre. Alarmed, the two decided to go back into the forest to search for him. They followed the path to the lake, while Tu checked every now and then through his radio with a copter circling overhead. They'd reported the bishop was not by the lakeshore, but Carmody thought he might be on his way to it or perhaps was just sitting some place and meditating.

About a mile from the *Gull* they found him lying at the foot of an exceptionally tall jelly tree. Tu halted suddenly.

"He's having an attack, Father."

Carmody turned away and sat down on the grass, his back to the bishop. He lit a cigarette but dropped it and crushed it beneath his heel.

"I forgot *he* doesn't want us to smoke in the woods. Not for fear of fire. *He* doesn't like the odour of tobacco."

Tu stood by the priest, his gaze clinging to the writhing figure beneath the tree. "Aren't you going to help him? He'll chew off his tongue or dislocate a bone."

Carmody hunched his shoulders and shook his head. "You forget that *he* cured our ills to demonstrate *his* powers. My rotten tooth, Mrs. Recka's alcoholism. His Excellency's seizures."

"But, but . . ."

"His Excellency has entered into this so-called attack voluntarily and is in no danger of breaking bones or lacerating his tongue. I wish that were all there were to it. Then I'd know what to do. Meanwhile, I suggest you do the decent thing and turn your back, too. I didn't care for this the first time I witnessed it; I still don't."

"Maybe you won't help, but I sure as hell am going to," said Tu. He took a step, halted, sucking in his breath.

Carmody turned to look, then rose. "It's all right. Don't be alarmed."

The bishop had given a final violent spasm, a thrusting of the pelvis that raised his arched body completely off the ground. At the same time he gave a loud racking sob. When he fell back, he crumpled into silence and motionlessness.

But it was not towards him but towards the hollow in the tree that Tu stared. Out of it was crawling a great white snake with black triangular markings on its back. Its head was large as a watermelon; its eyes glittered glassy green; its scales dripped with white-threaded jelly.

"My God," said Tu, "isn't there any end to it? It keeps coming and coming. Must be forty or fifty feet long."

His hand went to the sono-gun in his pocket. Carmody restrained him with another shake of his head.

"That snake intends no harm. On the contrary, if I understand these animals, it knows dimly that it has been given life again and feels a sense of gratitude. Perhaps *he* made them aware that *he* resurrects them so that *he* may warm himself in their automatic worship. But, of course, *he* would never stand for what that beast is doing. *He*, if you've not noticed, can't endure to touch *his* secondhand progeny. Did you preceive that after *he* had touched Masters, *he* washed *his* hands with coconut water? Flowers and trees are the only things *he* handles."

The snake had thrust its head above the bishop's and was touching his face with its flickering tongue. Andre groaned and opened his eyes. Seeing the reptile, he shuddered with fear, then grew still and allowed it to caress him. After determining that it meant him no harm, he stroked it back.

"Well, if the bishop should take over from Father, he at least will give these animals what they have always wanted and have not got from *him*, a tenderness and affection. His Excellency does not hate these females. Not yet."

In a louder voice, he added, "I hope to God that such a thing does not come to pass."

Hissing with alarm, the snake slid off into the grass. Andre sat up, shook his head as if to clear it, rose to greet them. His face had lost the softness it had held while he was caressing the serpent. It was stern, and his voice was challenging.

"Do you think it is right to come spying upon me?"

"Your pardon, Your Excellency, we were not spying. We were looking for you because we have decided that the situation demands a Council of the Question of Jairus."

Tu added, "We were concerned because Your Excellency seemed to be having another attack."

"Was I? Was I? But I thought that *he* had done away . . . I mean . . ."

Sadly, Carmody nodded, "*He* has. I wonder if Your Excellency would forgive me if I gave an opinion. I think that you were not having an epileptoid seizure coincidentally with sparking the snake with its new life. Your seeming attack was only a mock-up of your former illness.

"I see you don't understand. Let me put it this way. The doctor on Wildenwooly had thought that your sickness was psychosomatic in origin and had ordered you to Ygdrasil where a more competent man could treat it. Before you left, you told me that he thought that your symptoms were symbolic behaviour and pointed the way to the seat of your malady, a suppressed . . ."

"I think you should stop there," said the bishop

coldly.

"I had intended to go no further."

They began walking back to the ship. The two priests dropped behind the captain, who strode along with his eyes fixed straight ahead of him.

The bishop said, hesitantly, "You too experienced the glory—perhaps perilous, but nevertheless a glory—of bringing the dead back to life. I watched you, as you did me. You were not unmoved. True, you did not fall to the ground and become semi-conscious. But you trembled and moaned in the grip of ecstasy."

He cast his eyes to the ground, then, as if ashamed of his hesitancy, raised them to glare unflinchingly.

"Before your conversion, you were very much a man of this world. Tell me, John, is not this fathering something like being with a woman?"

Carmody looked to one side.

"I want neither your pity nor your revulsion," said Andre. "Just the truth."

Carmody sighed deeply.

"Yes, the two experiences are very similar. But the fathering is even more intimate because, once entered upon, there is no control at all, absolutely no withdrawal from the intimacy; your whole being, mind and body, are fused and focused upon the event. The feeling of oneness—so much desired in the other and so often lacking—is inescapable here. You feel as if you were the recreator and the recreated. Afterwards, you have a part of the animal in you—as you well know—because there is a little spark in your brain that is a piece of its life, and when the spark moves you know that the animal you raised is moving. And when it dims you know it is sleeping, and when it flares you know it is in panic or some other intense emotion. And when the spark dies, you know the beast has died too.

"Father's brain is a constellation of such sparks, of billions of stars that image brightly their owner's vitality. *He* knows where every individual unit of life is on this planet, *he* knows when it is gone, and when *he* does, *he* waits until the bones have been refleshed, and then *he* fathers forth . . ."

"*He fathers-forth whose beauty is past change: Praise him!*" Andre burst out.

Startled, Carmody raised his eyes. "Hopkins, I think, would be distressed to hear you quoting his lines in this context. I think perhaps he might retort with a passage from another of his poems.

"Man's spirit will be fleshbound when found at best,

But uncumbered: meadow-down is not distressed

For a rainbow footing it nor he for his bones risen."

"Your quite supports mine. *His bones risen.* What more do you need?"

"*But uncumbered.* What is the penalty for this ecstasy? This world is beautiful, yes, is it not sterile, dead-ended? Well, never mind that now. I wished to remind Your Excellency that this power and glory come from a sense of union and control over brutes. The world is *his* bed, but who would lie forever in it? And why does *he* now wish to leave it, if it is so desirable? For good? Or for evil?"

An hour later, the three entered the bishop's cabin and sat down at the bare round table in its centre. Carmody was carrying a little black bag, which he put under his chair without commenting on it. All were dressed in black robes, and as soon as Andre had given the opening ritual prayer, they

put on the masks of the founder of the order. For a
moment there was silence as they looked at each
other from behind the assumed anonymous safety
of identical features; brown skin, kinky hair, flat
nose, thick lips, and with the intense West
Africanness of the face, the maker of the masks
had managed to impart to them the legendary
gentleness and nobility of soul that had belonged
to Jairus Cbwaka.

Captain Tu spoke through rigid lips.

"We are gathered here in the name of His love
and of His love to formulate the temptation, if any,
that confronts us, and take action, if any, against
it. Let us speak as brothers, remembering each
time we look across the table and see the face of
the founder that he never lost his temper except
upon one occasion nor forgot his love except on
one occasion. Let us remember his agonies caused
by that forgetfulness and what he has directed us,
priest and layman, to do. Let us be worthy of his
spirit in the presence of the seeming of his flesh."

"I would like it better if you didn't rattle
through the words so fast," said the bishop. "Such
a pace destroys the spirit of the thing."

"It doesn't remedy anything for you to criticize
my conducting."

"Rebuke well taken. I ask you to forgive me."

"Of course," Tu said, somewhat uncomfortably.
"Of course. Well to business."

"I speak for Father," said the bishop.

"I speak against Father," said Carmody.

"Speak for Father," said Tu.

"Thesis: Father represents the forces of good.
He has offered the Church the monopoly of the
secret of resurrection."

"Antithesis."

"Father represents the forces of evil, for *he* will
unloose upon the Galaxy a force which will

destroy the Church if she tries to monopolize it. Moreover, even if she should refuse to have anything to do with it, it will destroy mankind everywhere and consequently our Church."

"Development of thesis."

"All *his* actions have been for good. Point. *He* has cured our illnesses major and minor. Point. *He* stopped Masters and Lejeune from carnal intercourse and perhaps did the same to Recka and Givens. Point. *He* made the former confess they had stolen money from Lejeune's father, and since then Lejeune has come to me for spiritual advice. She seemed to consider very seriously my suggestion that she have nothing to do with Masters and to return to her father, if the chance came, in an attempt to solve their problems with his consent. Point. She is studying a manual I gave her and may be led to the Church. That will be Father's doing and not Masters', who has neglected the Church though he is nominally a member of our body. Point. Father is forgiving, for *he* didn't allow the leopardess to harm Masters, even after the youth's attempt at killing *him*. And *he* has said that the captain may as well release Masters from the brig, for *he* fears nothing, and our criminal code is beneath his comprehension. *He* is sure that Masters won't try again. Therefore, why not forget about his stealing a gun from the ship's storeroom and let him loose? We are using force to get our goal of punishment, and that is not necessary, for according to the laws of psychodynamics which *he* has worked out during ten thousand years of solitude, a person who uses violence as a means to an end is self-punished, is robbed of a portion of his powers. Even *his* original act of getting the ship down here has hurt *him* so much that it will be some time before he recovers the full use of *his* psychic energies.

"I enter a plea that we accept *his* offer. There can be no harm because *he* wishes to go as a passenger. Though I, of course, possess no personal funds, I will write out an authorization on the Order for *his* ticket. And I will take *his* place upon Abatos while *he* is gone.

"Remember, too, that the decision of this particular Council will not commit the Church to accept *his* offer. We will merely put *him* under our patronage for a time."

"Antithesis."

"I have a blanket statement that will answer most of thesis's points. That is, that the worst evil is that which adopts the lineaments of good, so that one has to look hard to distinguish the true face beneath the mask. Father undoubtedly learned from the *Hoyle* survivor our code of ethics. He has avoided close contact with us so we may not get a chance to study his behaviour in detail.

"However, these are mostly speculations. What can't be denied is that this act of resurrection is a drug, the most powerful and insidious that mankind has ever been exposed to. Once one has known the ecstasies attendant upon it, one wishes for more. And as the number of such acts is limited to the number of dead available, one wishes to enlarge the ranks of the dead so that one may enjoy more acts. And Father's set-up here is one that 'combines the maximum of temptation with the maximum of opportunity.' Once a man has tasted the act, he will seriously consider turning his world into one like Abatos.

"Do we want that? I say no. I predict that if Father leaves here, *he* will open the way to such a possibility. Won't each man who has the power begin thinking of himself as a sort of god? Won't he become as Father, dissatisfied with the original unruly rude chaotic planet as he found it? Won't he find progress and imperfection unbearable and remodel the bones of his creatures to remove all evolutionary vestiges and form perfect skeletons? Won't he suppress mating among the animals —and perhaps among his fellow human beings—while allowing the males to die unresurrected until none but the more pliable and amenable females are left and there is no chance of young being born? Won't he make a garden out of his planet, a beautiful but sterile and unprogressive paradise? Look, for example, at the method of hunting that the fat and lazy beasts of prey use. Consider its disastrous results, evolutionarily speaking. In the beginning they picked out the slowest and stupidest herbivores to kill. Did this result in the survivors breeding swifter and more intelligent young? Not at all. For the dead were raised, and caught and killed again. And again. So that now when a leopardess or bitch wolf goes out to eat, the unconditioned run away and the conditioned stand trembling and paralysed and meekly submit to slaughter like tame animals in a stockyard. And the uneaten return to graze unconcernedly within leaping distance of the killer while she is devouring their sister. This is a polished planet, where the same event slides daily through the same smooth groove.

"Yet even the lover of perfection, Father, has become bored and wishes to find a pioneer world where *he* may labour until *he* has brought it to the same state as Abatos. Will this go on for ever until the Galaxy will no longer exhibit a multitude of worlds, each breathtakingly different from the other, but will show you everywhere a duplicate of Abatos, not one whit different? I warn you that this is one of the very real perils.

"Minor points. *He* is a murderer because *he*

caused Kate Lejeune to miscarry, and . . ."

"Counterpoint. *He* maintains that it was an accident that Kate lost her foetus, that *he* had *his* two beasts chase her and Masters out of the woods because they were having carnal intercourse. And *he* could not tolerate that. Point. Such an attitude is in *his* favour and shows that *he* is good and on the side of the Church and of God."

"Point. It would not have mattered to *him* if Pete and Kate had been bound in holy matrimony. Carnal intercourse *per se* is objectionable to *him*. Why, I don't know. Perhaps the act offends his sense of property because *he* is the sole giver of life on this world. But I say *his* interference was evil because it resulted in the loss of a human life, and that *he* knew it would . . ."

"Point," said the bishop, somewhat heatedly. "This is, as far as we know, a planet without true death and true sin. We have brought those two monsters with us, and *he* cannot endure either one."

"Point. We did not ask to come but were forced."

"Order," said the moderator. "The Question first, then the formulation of the temptation, as laid down in the rules. If we say yes, and Father goes with us, one of us must remain to take *his* place. Otherwise, so *he* insists, this world will go to wrack and ruin in *his* absence."

The moderator paused, then said, "For some reason, *he* has limited choice of *his* substitutes to you two."

"Point," said the bishop. "We are the only candidates because we have sworn total abstinence from carnal intercourse. Father seems to think that women are even greater vessels of evil than men. *He* says that bodily copulation involves a draining of the psychic energy needed for the act

of resurrection and implies also that there is
something dirty—or perhaps I should say, just too
physical and animal—about the act. I do not, of
course, think *his* attitude entirely justified, nor do
I agree at all that women are on the same plane
with animals. But you must remember that *he* has
not seen a woman for ten thousand years, that
perhaps the female of *his* own species might
justify *his* reaction. I gathered from *his*
conversation that there is a wide gap between the
sexes of *his* kind on *his* own planet. Even so, *he* is
kind to our women passengers. *He* will not touch
them, true, but *he* says that any physical contact
with us is painful to *him*, because it robs *him* of
his, what shall I say, sanctity? On the other hand,
with flowers and trees . . ."

"Point. What you have told us indicates *his*
aberrated nature."

"Point, point. You have confessed you dare not
say such a thing to *his* face, that you are awed by
the sense of the power that emanates from *him*.
Point. *He* acts as one who has taken a vow of
chastity; perhaps *his* nature is such that too close
a contact does besmirch him, figuratively speaking. I take this religious attitude to be one more
sign in *his* favour."

"Point. The devil himself may be chaste. But for
what reason? Because he loves God or because he
fears dirt?"

"Time," said Tu, "time for the chance of
reversal. Has thesis or antithesis altered his mind
on any or all points? Do not be backward in
admitting it. Pride must fall before love of truth."

The bishop's voice was firm. "No change. And
let me reaffirm that I do not think Father is God.
But *he* has Godlike powers. And the Church
should use them."

Carmody rose and gripped the table's edge. His

head was thrust aggressively forward, his stance was strange in contrast to the tender melancholy of the mask.

"Antithesis reports no change, too. Very well. Thesis has stated that Father has Godlike powers. I say, so has man, within limits. Those limits are what he may do to material things through material means. I say that Father is limited to those means, that there is nothing at all supernatural about *his* so-called miracles. As a matter of fact, man can do what Father is doing, even if on a primitive scale.

"I have been arguing on a spiritual level, hoping to sway thesis with spiritual points before I revealed to you my discoveries. But I have failed. Very well. I will tell you what I have found out. Perhaps then thesis will change his mind."

He stopped and picked up the little black bag and laid it on the table before him. While he spoke, he kept one hand upon it, as if to enforce attention towards it.

"Father's powers, I thought, might be only extensions of what we humans may do. *His* were more subtle because *he* had the backing of a much older science than ours. After all, we are able to rejuvenate the old so that our life span is about a hundred and fifty. We build organs of artificial flesh. Within a limited period we may revive the dead, provided we can freeze them quickly enough and then work on them. We've even built a simple brain of flesh—one on the level of a toad's. And the sense of the numinous and of panic is nothing new. We have our own sonobeams for creating a like effect. Why could he not be using similar methods?

"Just because we saw *him* naked and without a machine in *his* hand didn't mean that *his* effects were produced by mental broadcast. We couldn't conceive of science without metal mechanisms. But what if *he* had other means? What about the jelly trees, which display electromagnetic phenomena? What about the faint humming we heard?

"So I borrowed a microphone and oscilloscope from the engineer, rigged up a sound detector, put it in the bag, and set out to nose around. And I observed that His Excellency was also making use of his time before the Question, that he was talking again to *him*. And while doing so, the jelly trees nearby were emitting subsonics at four and thirteen cycles. You know what those do. The first massages the bowels and causes peristalsis. The second stimulates a feeling of vague overpowering oppression. There were other sonics, too, some sub, some super.

"I left Father's neighbourhood to investigate elsewhere. Also, to do some thinking. It's significant, I believe, that we have had little chance or inclination to do any meditating since we've been here. Father has been pushing us, has kept us off balance. Obviously, *he* wants to keep our minds blurry with too rapid a pace of events.

"I did some fast thinking, and I concluded that the resurrection act itself was not touched off by *his* spark of genesis. Far from it. It is completely automatic, and it comes when the newly formed body is ready for a shock of bio-electricity from the protoplasm-jelly.

"But *he* knows when it is ready and taps the wave-lengths of life blooming anew, feeds upon them. How? There must be a two-way linkage between *his* brainwaves and the jelly's. We know that we think in symbols, that a mental symbol is basically a complex combination of brainwaves issuing as series of single images. *He* triggers off certain pre-set mechanisms in the jelly with *his* thoughts, that is, with a mental projection of a symbol.

"Yet not anyone may do it, for we two priests, dedicated to abstention from carnal intercourse, were the only ones able to tap in on the waves. Evidently, a man has to have a peculiar psychosomatic disposition. Why? I don't know. Maybe there is something spiritual to the process. But don't forget that the devil is spiritual. However, the mind-body's actions are still a dark continent. I can't solve them, only speculate.

"As for *his* ability to cure illnesses at a distance, *he* must diagnose and prescribe through the medium of the tree-jelly. It receives and transmits, takes in the abnormal or unhealthy waves our sick cells broadcast and sends out the healthy waves to suppress or cancel the unhealthy. There's no miracle about the process. It works in accordance with materialistic science.

"I surmise that when Father first came here, *he* was fully aware that the trees originated the ecstasy, that *he* was merely tuning in. But after millennia of solitude and an almost continuous state of drugging ecstasy, *he* deluded *himself* into thinking that it was *he* who sparked the new life.

"There are a few other puzzling points. How did *he* catch our ship? I don't know. But *he* knew about the translator motor from the *Hoyle* survivor and was thus able to set up the required wavelengths to neutralize the workings of the protein "normal space" memory banks. *He* could have had half the jelly trees of Abatos broadcasting all the time, a trap that would inevitably catch a passing ship."

Tu said, "What happened to *his* original spaceship?"

"If we left the *Gull* to sit out in the rain and sun for ten thousand years, what would happen to it?"

"It'd be a heap of rust. Not even that."

"Right. Now I suspect strongly that Father, when *he* first came here, had a well-equipped laboratory on *his* ship. *His* science was able to mutate genes at will, and *he* used his tools on the native trees to mutate them into these jelly trees. That also explains why *he* was able to change the animals' genetic pattern so that their bodies lost their evolutionary vestiges, became perfectly functional organisms."

The little man in the mask sat down. The bishop rose. His voice was choked.

"Admitting that your researches and surmises have indicated that Father's powers are unspiritual gimmickry—and in all fairness it must be admitted that you seem to be right—admitting this, then, I still speak for Father."

Carmody's mask cocked to the left. "What?"

"Yes. We owe it to the Church that she get this wonderful tool in her hands, this tool which, like anything in this universe, may be used for evil or for good. Indeed, it is mandatory that she gets control of it, so that she may prevent those who would misuse it from doing so, so that she may become stronger and attract more to her fold. Do you think that eternal life is no attraction?

"Now—you say that Father has lied to us. I say *he* has not. *He* never once told us that *his* powers were purely spiritual. Perhaps, being of an alien species, *he* misunderstands our strength of comprehension and took it for granted that we would see how *he* operates.

"However, that is not the essence of my thesis. The essence is that we must take Father along and give the Church a chance to decide whether or not to accept *him*. There is no danger in doing that, for *he* will be alone among billions. And if we should leave *him* here, then we will be open to rebuke, perhaps even a much stronger action from the Church, for having been cowards enough to turn down *his* gift.

"I will remain here, even though my motives are questioned by those who have no right to judge me. I am a tool of God as much as Father is; it is right that we both be used to the best of our abilities; Father is doing no good for Church or man while isolated here; I will endure my loneliness while waiting for your return with the thought that I am doing this as a servant who takes joy in his duty."

"What a joy!' Carmody shouted. "No! I say that we reject Father once and for all. I doubt very much that *he* will allow us to go, for *he* will think that, faced with spending the rest of our lives here and then dying—for I don't think *he*'ll resurrect us unless we say yes—we will agree. And *he*'ll see to it that we are cooped up inside the ship, too. We won't dare step outside, for we'll be bombarded with panic-waves or attacked by *his* beasts. However, that remains to be seen. What I'd like to ask thesis is this: Why can't we just refuse *him* and leave the problem of getting *him* off Abatos to some other ship? *He* can easily trap another. Or perhaps, if we get to go home, we may send a government craft to investigate."

"Father has explained to me that we represent *his* only sure chance. *He* may have to wait another ten millennia before another ship is trapped. Or forever. It works this way. You know that translation of a vessel from one point in normal space to the other occurs simultaneously, as far as outside observers are affected. Theoretically, the ship rotates the two coordinates of its special axis, ignoring time, disappears from its launching point, reappearing at the same time at its destination. However, there is a discharging effect, a simulacrum of the ship, built of electromagnetic fields, which radiates at six points from the starting place, and speeds at an ever-accelerating rate at six right-angles from there. These are called 'ghosts.' They've never been seen, and we've no instrument that can detect them. Their existence is based on Guizot's equations, which have managed to explain how electromagnetic waves may exceed the speed of light, though we know from Auschweigh that Einstein was wrong when he said that the velocity of light was the absolute.

"Now, if you were to draw a straight line from Wildenwooly to Ygdrasil, you would find that Abatos does not lie between, that it is off to one side of the latter. But it is at right-angles to it, so that one of the 'ghosts' passes here. The electromagnetic net that the trees sent up stopped it cold. The result was that the *Gull* was literally sucked along the line of power, following this particular ghost to Abatos instead of to Ygdrasil. I imagine that we appeared for a flickering millisecond at our original destination, then were yanked back to here. Of course, we were unaware of that, just as the people on Ygdrasil never saw us.

"Now—the voyages between Ygdrasil and Wildenwooly are infrequent, and the field has to mesh perfectly with the ghost, otherwise the ghost passes between the pulses. So that *his* chances of catching another are very few."

"Yes, and that is why *he* will never allow us to leave. If we go without him and send a warship back to investigate, it may be able to have defences built in to combat his trees' radiations. So we represent *his* sole ticket. And I say *no* even if we must remain marooned!"

So the talk raged for two hours until Tu asked for the final formulations.

"Very well. We have heard. Antithesis has stated the peril of the temptation as being one that will make man a sterile anarchistic pseudo-god.

"Thesis has stated that the peril is that we may reject a gift which would make our Church once again the universal, in numbers as well as in claim, because she would literally and physically hold the keys to life and death.

"Thesis, please vote."

"I say we accept Father's offer."

"Antithesis."

"No. Refuse."

Tu placed his large and bony hands on the table. "As moderator and judge, I agree with antithesis."

He removed his mask. The others, as if reluctant to acknowledge both identity and responsibility, slowly took off their disguises. They sat glaring at each other, and ignored the captain when he cleared his throat loudly. Like the false faces they had discarded, they had dropped any pretence of brotherly love.

Tu said, "In all fairness, I must point out one thing. That is, that as a layman of the Church, I may concur in the agreement to reject Father as a passenger. But as a captain of the Saxwell Company's vessel, it is my duty when landing upon an unscheduled stop to take on any stranded non-active who wishes to leave, provided he has passage money and there is room for him. That is Commonwealth law."

"I don't think we need worry about anybody paying for *his* passage," said the padre. "Not now. However, if *he* should have the money, *he*'d present you with a nice little dilemma."

"Yes, wouldn't *he*? I'd have to report my refusal, of course. And I'd face trial and might lose my captaincy and would probably be earthbound the rest of my life. Such a thought is—well, unendurable."

Andre rose. "This has been rather trying. I think I'll go for a walk in the woods. If I meet Father, I will tell *him* our decision."

Tu also stood up. "The sooner the better. Ask *him* to reactivate our translator at once. We won't even bother leaving in orthodox style. We'll translate and get our fixings later. Just so we get away."

Carmody fumbled in his robe for a cigarette. "I think I'll talk to Pete Masters. Might be able to drive some sense into his head. Afterwards, I'll take a walk in the woods, too. There's much hereabouts to learn yet."

He watched the bishop walk out and grimly shook his head.

"It went hard to go against my superior," he said to Tu. "But His Excellency, though a great man, is lacking in the understanding that comes from having sinned much yourself."

He patted his round paunch and smiled as if all were right, though not very convincingly.

"It's not fat alone that is stuffed beneath my belt. There are years of experience of living in the depths packed solidly there. Remember that I survived Dante's Joy. I've had my belly full of evil. At its slightest taste, I regurgitate it. I tell you, Captain, Father is rotten meat, ten thousand years old."

"You sound as if you're not quite certain."

"In this world of shifting appearances and lack of true self-knowledge, who is?"

Masters had been released after he had promised Tu that he would make no more trouble. Carmody, not finding the youth inside, walked out and called him over the wrist radio. No reply.

Still carrying his black bag, the padre hurried into the woods as fast as his short legs would go. He hummed as he passed beneath the mighty branches, called out to the birds overhead, stopped once to bow gravely to a tall heron-like bird with dark purple mask-markings over its eyes, then staggered off laughing and holding his sides when it replied with a call exactly like a plunger withdrawing from a stopped drain, finally sat down beneath a beech to wipe his streaming face with a handkerchief.

"Lord, Lord, there are more things in this universe . . . surely You must have a sense of humour," he said out loud. "But then, I mustn't identify a purely human viewpoint with You and make the anthropomorphic fallacy."

He paused, said in a lower tone as if not wanting Anyone to hear, "Well, why not? Aren't we, in one sense, the focus of creation, the Creator's image? Surely He too likes to feel a need for relief and finds it in laughter. Perhaps His laughter does not come out as mere meaningless noise but is manifested on a highly economical and informative level. Perhaps He tosses off a new galaxy, instead of having a belly-laugh. Or sub-stitutes a chuckle with a prodding of a species up the Jacob's ladder of evolution towards a more human state.

"Or, old-fashioned as it sounds, indulges in the sheer joy of a miracle to show His children that His is *not* an absolutely orderly clockwork universe. Miracles are the laughter of God. Hmm, not bad. Now, where did I leave my notebook? I knew it. Back in my cabin. That would have made such a splendid line for an article. Well, no matter. I shall probably recall it, and posterity won't die if I don't. But they'll be the poorer, and . . ."

He fell silent as he heard Masters and Lejeune nearby. Rising, he walked towards them, calling out so they wouldn't think he was eavesdropping.

They were facing each other across a tremen-dous fringe-topped toadstool. Kate had quit talking, but Pete, his face red as his hair, continued angrily as if the priest did not exist. He gestured wildly with one fist, while the other hung by his side clenching a powersaw handle.

"That's final! We're not going back to Wildenwooly. And don't think I'm afraid of your father, 'cause I'm afraid of nobody. Sure, he won't press charges against us. He can afford to be noble-hearted. The Commonwealth will prosecute us for him. Are you so stupid you don't remember that it's the law that the Board of Health must take into custody anyone who's been put on notice as guilty of unhealthy practices? Your father must have sent word on to Ygdrasil by now. We'll be detained as soon as we put foot on it. And you and I will be sent to an institution. We won't even get to go together to the same place. They never send partners-in-misdoing to the same resort. And how do I know that I won't have lost you then? Those rehabilitation homes do things to people, change their outlooks. You might lose your love for me. Probably that would be fine with them. They'd say you were gaining a healthy attitude in getting rid of me."

Kate raised her large violet eyes to his. "Oh, Pete, that would never ever happen. Don't talk such stuff. Besides, Daddy wouldn't report us. He knows I'd be taken away for a long time, and he couldn't stand that. He won't inform the government; he'll send his own men after us."

"Yeah? What about that telegram to the *Gull* just before we left?"

"Daddy didn't mention the money. We'd have been held for a juvenile misdemeanour only."

"Sure, and then his thugs would have beaten me up and dropped me off in the Twogee Woods. I suppose you'd like that?"

Tears filled Kate's eyes. "Please, Pete, don't. You know I love you more than anybody else in the world."

"Well, maybe you do, maybe you don't. Anyway, you forget that this priest knows about the money, and his duty is to report us."

"Perhaps I am a priest," said Carmody, "but that doesn't automatically classify me as non-human. I wouldn't dream of reporting you. Needlenose though I am, I am not a malicious trouble-maker. I'd like to help you out of your predicament, though just now I must confess to a slight inclination to punch you in the nose for the way you are talking to Kate. However, that is neither here nor there. What is important is that I'm under no compulsion to tell the authorities, even though your act was not told to me in confession.

"But I do believe you should follow Kate's advice and go back to her father and confess all and try to come to an agreement. Perhaps he would consent to your marriage if you were to promise him to wait until you had proved yourself capable of supporting Kate happily. And proved that your love for her is based on more than sexual passion. Consider his feelings. He's as much concerned in this as you. More, for he's known her far longer, loved her a greater time."

"Ah, to hell with him and the whole situation!" shouted Pete. He walked off and seated himself under a tree about twenty yards away. Kate wept softly. Carmody offered her a handkerchief, saying, "A trifle sweaty, perhaps, but sanitary with sanctity." He smiled at his own wit with such self-evident enjoyment, mingled with self-mockery, that she could not help smiling back at him. While she dried her tears, she gave him her free hand to hold.

"You are sweet and patient, Kate, and very much in love with a man who is, I'm afraid, afflicted with a hasty and violent temper. Now,

tell me true, is not your father much the same?
Wasn't that part of the reason you ran away with
Pete, to get away from a too-demanding, jealous,
hot-headed father? And haven't you found out
since that Pete is so much like your father that you
have traded one image for its duplicate?"

"You're very perceptive. But I love Pete."

"Nevertheless, you should go home. Pete, if he
really loves you, will follow you and try to come to
an honest and open contract with your father.
After all, you must admit that your taking the
money was not right."

"No," she said, beginning to weep again, "it
wasn't. I don't want to be a weakling and put the
blame on Pete, for I did agree to take the money,
even if it was his suggestion. I did so in a weak
moment. And ever since, it's been bothering me.
Even when I was in the cabin with him and should
have been deliriously happy, that money bothered
me."

Masters jumped up and strode towards them,
the powersaw swinging in his hand. It was a
wicked-looking tool, with a wide thin adjustable
blade spreading out like a fan from a narrow
motorbox. He held the saw like a pistol, his hand
around the butt and one finger on the trigger.

"Take your paws off her," he said.

Kate withdrew her hand from Carmody's grip,
but she faced the youth defiantly. "He isn't
hurting me. He's giving me real warmth and
understanding, trying to help."

"I know these old priests. He's taking advantage
of you so he can hug and pinch you and . . ."

"Old?" exploded the padre. "Listen, Masters,
I'm only forty . . ."

He laughed. "Almost got me going, didn't you?"
He turned to Kate. "If we do get off Abatos, go
home to your father. I'll be stationed at Breakneck
for a while; you may see me as often as you wish,

and I'll do my best to help you. And though I
foresee some years of martyrdom for you, placed
between two fires like Pete and your father, I
think you're made of strong stuff."

His eyes twinkling, he added, "Even if you do
look fragile and exceedingly beautiful and very
huggable and pinchable."

At the moment a deer trotted into the little
glade. Rusty red, flecked with tiny white spots
edged in black, her large liquid black eyes unafraid, she danced up to them and held out her
nose inquiringly towards Kate. She seemed to
know that Kate was the only female there.

"Evidently one of those unconditioned to being
killed by the beasts of prey," said Carmody.
"Come here, my beauty. I do believe that I brought
along some sugar for just such an occasion. What
shall I call you? Alice? Everybody is mad at this
party, but we've no tea."

The girl gave a soft cry of delight and touched
the doe's wet black nose. It licked her hand. Pete
snorted with disgust.

"You'll be kissing it next."

"Why not?" She put her mouth on its snout.

His face became even redder. Grimacing, he
thrust the blade-edge of the saw against the
animal's neck, and pressed the trigger. The doe
dropped, taking Kate with it, for she had no
warning to remove her arms from around its neck.
Blood spurted over the saw and Pete's chest and
over her arm. The fan-edge of the tool, emitting
supersonic waves capable of eating through
granite, had sliced a thin plane through the beast's
cells.

Masters stared, white-faced now. "I only
touched it. I didn't really mean to pull the trigger.
I must have nicked its jugular vein. The blood, the
blood . . ."

Carmody's face was also pale, and his voice shook.

"Luckily, the doe won't remain dead. But I hope you keep the sight of this blood in your mind the next time you feel anger. It could just as easily be human, you know."

He quit talking to listen. The forest sounds had ceased, overcome by a rush of silence, like the shadow of a cloud. Then, the striding legs and stone eyes of Father.

His voice roared around them as if they were standing beneath a waterfall.

"Anger and death in the air! I feel them when the beast of prey are hungry. I came quickly, for I knew that these killers were not mine. And I also came for another reason, Carmody, for I have heard from the bishop of your investigations and of your mistaken conclusions and the decision which you forced upon the captain and the bishop. I came to show you how you have deceived yourself about my powers, to teach you humility towards your superiors."

Masters gave a choked cry, grabbed Kate's hand with his bloodied hand, and began half-running, half-stumbling, dragging her after him. Carmody, though trembling, stood his ground.

"Shut off your sonics. I know how you create awe and panic in my breast."

"You have your device in that bag. Check it. See if there are any radiations from the trees."

Obediently, the man fumbled at the lock at his case, managed after two tries to get it open. He twisted a dial. His eyes grew wide when it had completed its circuit.

"Convinced? There are no sonics at that level, are there? Now—keep one eye on the oscilloscope but the other on me."

Father scooped from the hole of the nearest tree

a great handful of the jelly and plastered it over
the bloodied area of the doe's neck. "This liquid
meat will close up the wound, which is small to
begin with, and will rebuild the devastated cells.
The jelly sends out probing waves to the surrounding parts of the wound, identifies their structure
and hence the structure of the missing or ruptured
cells, and begins to fill in. But not unless I direct
the procedure. And I can, if necessary, do without
the jelly. I do not need it, for my power is good
because it comes from God. You should spend ten
thousand years with no one to talk to but God.
Then you would see that it is impossible for me to
do anything but good, that I see to the mystical
heart of things, feel its pulse as nearer than that of
my body."

He had placed his hand over the glazed eyes.
When he withdrew it, the eyes were a liquid
shining black again, and the doe's flanks rose and
fell. Presently it got on its hoofs, thrust a nose
towards Father, was repelled by a raised hand,
wheeled, and bounded off.

"Perhaps you would like to call for another
Question," roared Father. "I understand that new
evidence permits it. Had I known that you were
filled with such a monkey-like curiosity—and had
reasoning powers on a monkey's level—I should
have shown you exactly what I am capable of."

The giant strode away, Carmody stared after
him. Shaken, he said to himself, "Wrong? Wrong?
Have I been lacking in humility, too contemptuous
of His Excellency's perceptiveness because he
lacked my experience . . . I thought. Have I read
too much into his illness, mistaken its foundations?"

He took a deep breath. "Well, if I'm wrong, I will
confess it. Publicly, too. But how small this makes
me. A pygmy scurrying around the feet of giants,

tripping them up in an effort to prove myself larger than they."

He began walking. Absently, he reached up to a branch from which hung large apple-like fruit.

"Hmm. Delicious. This world is an easy one to live in. One need not starve nor fear death. One may grow fat and lazy, be at ease in Zion, enjoy the ecstasy of re-creation. That is what you have wanted with one part of your soul, haven't you? God knows you are fat enough, and if you give others the impression of bursting with energy, you often do so with a great effort. You have to ignore your tiredness, appear bristling with eagerness for work. And your parishioners, yes, and your superiors, too, who should know better, take your labour for granted and never pause to wonder if you, too, are tired or discouraged or doubtful. Here there would be no such thing."

Half-eaten, the apple was discarded for red-brown berries from a bush. Frowning, muttering, he ate them, his eyes always on the retreating shoulders and golden-red roach of Father.

"Yet . . .?"

After a while, he laughed softly. "It is indeed a paradox, John I. Carmody, that you should be considering again the temptation after having talked Tu and Andre out of it. And it would be an everlasting lesson—one that you are not, I hope, too unintelligent to profit from—if you talked yourself into changing your mind. Perhaps you have needed this because you have not considered how strong was the bishop's temptation, because you felt a measure—oh, only a tinge, but nevertheless a tinge—of contempt for him because he fell so easily and you resisted so easily.

"Hah, you thought you were so strong, you had so many years of experience packed beneath your belt! It was grease and wind that swelled you out,

Carmody. You were pregnant with ignorance and
pride. And now you must give birth to humiliation.
No, humility, for there is a difference between the
two, depending on one's attitude. God give you in-
sight for the latter.

"And admit it, Carmody admit it. Even in the
midst of the shock at seeing the deer killed, you
felt a joy because you had an excuse to resurrect
the animal and to feel again that ecstasy which
you know should be forbidden because it *is* a drug
and *does* take your mind from the pressing business of your calling. And though you told yourself
you weren't going to do it, your voice was feeble,
lacking the authority of conviction.

"On the other hand, doesn't God feel ecstasy
when He creates, being The Artist? Isn't that part
of creating? Shouldn't we feel it, too? But if we do,
doesn't that make us think of ourselves as godlike? Still, Father says that *he* knows from whence
he derives his powers. And if *he* acts aloof, *noli me
tangere*, *he* could be excused by reason of ten
thousand years of solitude. God knows, some of
the saints were eccentric enough to have been
martyred by the very Church that later canonized
them.

"But it's a drug, this resurrection business. If it
is, you are correct, the bishop is wrong. Still,
alcohol, food, the reading of books, and many
other things may become drugs. The craving for
them can be controlled, they may be used
temperately. Why not the resurrection, once one
has got over the first flush of intoxication? Why
not, indeed?"

He threw away the berries and tore off a fruit
that looked like a banana with a light brown shell
instead of soft peelings.

"Hmm. *He* keeps an excellent cuisine. Tastes
like roast beef with gravy and a soupcon of onions.

Loaded with protein, I'll bet. No wonder Father
may be so massively, even shockingly, male, so
virile-looking, yet a strict vegetarian.

"Ah, you talk too much to yourself. A bad habit
you picked up on Dante's Joy and never got rid of,
even after *that* night when you were converted.
That was a terrible time, Carmody, and only by the
grace ... Well, why don't you shut up, Carmody?"

Suddenly, he dropped behind a bush. Father had
come to a large hill which rose from the forest and
was bare of trees except for a single giant crown-
ing it. The huge O at the base of its trunk showed
its nature, but where the others of its kind were
brown-trunked and light-green-leaved, this had a
shiny white bark and foliage of so dark a green
that it looked black. Around its monstrous white
roots, which swelled above the ground, was a
crowd of animals. Lionesses, leopardesses, bitch
wolves, struthiursines, a huge black cow, a rhino,
a scarlet-faced gorilla, a cow-elephant, a moa-like
bird capable of gutting an elephant with its beak, a
man-sized crested green lizard, and many others.
All massed together, moving restlessly but ignoring each other, silent.

When they saw Father, they gave a concerted,
muted roar, a belly-deep rumble. Moving aside for
him, they formed an aisle through which he
walked.

Carmody gasped. What he had mistaken for the
exposed roots of the tree were piles of bones, a
tumulus of skeletons.

Father halted before them, turned, addressed
the beasts in a chanting rhythm in an unknown
tongue, gestured, describing large and small
wheels that interwove. Then he stooped and began
picking up the skulls one by one, kissing them on
their grinning teeth, replacing them tenderly. All
this while the beasts crouched silently and

motionless, as if they understood what he was
saying and doing. Perhaps, in a way, they did, for
through them, like wind rippling fur, ran a current
of anticipation.

The padre, straining his eyes, muttered,
"Humanoid skulls. *His* size too. Did *he* come here
with them, and they died? Or did *he* murder them?
If so, why the ceremony of loving, the caresses?"

Father put down the last grisly article, lifted his
hands upwards and out in a sign that took in the
skies, then brought them in so they touched his
shoulders.

"*He*'s come from the heavens? Or *he* means *he*
identifies *himself* with the sky, the whole universe, perhaps? Pantheism? Or what?"

Father shouted so loudly that Carmody almost
jumped up from behind the bush and revealed
himself. The beasts growled an antiphony. The
priest balled his fists and raised his head, glaring
fiercely. He seemed to be gripped with anger. He
looked like a beast of prey, so much did his
snarling face resemble the assembled animals'.
They, too, had been seized with fury. The big cats
yowled. The pachyderms trumpeted. The cow and
bears bellowed. The gorilla beat her chest. The
lizard hissed like a steam engine.

Again Father shouted. The spell that held them
in restraint was shattered. *En masse*, the pack
hurled itself upon the giant. Without resistance,
he went down beneath the heaving sea of hairy
backs. Once, a hand was thrust above the screaming *melee*, making a circular motion as if it were
still carrying out the prescribed movement of a
ritual. Then it was engulfed in a lioness' mouth,
and the spurting stump fell back.

Carmody had been grovelling in the dirt, his
fingers hooked into the grass, obviously restrain-
ing himself from leaping up to join the slaughter.

At the moment he saw Father's hand torn off, he did rise, but his facial expression was different. Fright showed on it, and horror. He ran off into the woods, doubled over so the bush would conceal him from the chance gaze of the animals. Once, he stopped behind a tree, vomited, then raced off again.

Behind him rose the thunder of the blood-crazed killers.

The enormous melon-striped moon rose shortly after nightfall. Its bright rays glimmered on the hemisphere of the *Gull* and on the white faces gathered at the meadow's edge. Father John walked out of the forest's darkness. He stopped and called out, "What is the matter?"

Tu disengaged himself from the huddled group. He pointed at the open main port of the ship, from which light streamed.

Father John gasped. "*Him*? Already?"

The majestic figure stood motionless at the foot of the portable steps, waiting as if he could stand there patiently for another ten thousand years.

Tu's voice, though angry, was edged with doubt.

"The bishop has betrayed us! He's told *him* of the law that we must accept *him* and has given *him* passage money!"

"And what are you going to do about it?" said Carmody, his gravelly voice even rougher than usual.

"Do? What else can I do but take *him* on? Regulations require it. If I refuse—why, why, I'd lose my captaincy. You know that. The most I can do is put off leaving until dawn. The bishop may have changed his mind by then."

"Where is His Excellency?"

"Don't Excellency that traitor. He's gone off

into the woods and become another Father."

"We must find him and save him from himself!" cried Carmody.

"I'll go with you," said Tu. "I'd let him go his own way to hell, except that the enemies of our Church would mock us. My God, a bishop, too!"

Within a few minutes, the two men, armed with flashlights, ship-finders and sonobeams, walked into the forest. Tu also wore a pistol. They went alone because the padre did not want to expose his bishop to the embarrassment that would be his if confronted by a crowd of angry men. Moreover, he thought they'd have a better chance of talking him back into his senses if just his old friends were there.

"Where in hell could we find him?" groaned the captain. "God, it's dark in here. And look at those eyes. There must be thousands."

"The beasts know something extraordinary is up. Listen, the whole forest's awake."

"Celebrating a change of reign. The King is dead; long live the King. Where could he be?"

"Probably the lake. That's the place he loved best."

"Why didn't you say so? We could have been there in two minutes in a copter."

"There'll be no using the copter tonight."

Father John flashed his light on the ship-finder. "Look how the needle's whirling. I'll bet our wrist radios are dead."

"Hello, *Gull, Gull*, come in, come in . . . You're right. It's out. Christ, those eyes glowing, the trees are crawling with them. Our sonos are kaput too. Why don't our flashes go out?"

"I imagine because *he* knows that they enable *his* beasts to locate us more quickly. Try your automatic. Its mechanism is electrically powered, isn't it?"

Tu groaned again. "Doesn't work. Oh, for the old type!"

"It's not too late for you to turn back," said Carmody. "We may not get out of the woods alive if we do locate the bishop."

"What's the matter with you? Do you think I'm a coward? I allow no man, priest or not, to call me that."

"Not at all. But your primary duty is to the ship, you know."

"And to my passengers. Let's go."

"I thought I was wrong. I almost changed my mind about Father," said the priest. "Perhaps *he* was using *his* powers, which didn't depend entirely on material sources, for good. But I wasn't sure. So I followed *him*, and then, when I witnessed death, I knew I'd been right, that evil would come from any attempted use of *him*."

"*His* death? But *he* was at the *Gull* a moment ago."

Carmody hurriedly told Tu what he'd seen.

"But, but ... I don't understand. Father can't stand the touch of *his* own creatures, and *he* exercises perfect control over them. Why the mutiny? How could *he* have come back to life so quickly, especially if *he* were torn to pieces? Say, maybe there's more than one Father, twins, and *he*'s playing tricks on us. Maybe *he* just has control over a few animals. *He*'s a glorified lion tamer, and *he* uses his trained beasts when *he*'s around us. And *he* ran into a group *he* couldn't handle."

"You are half-right. First, it was a mutiny, but one that *he* drove them into, a ritual mutiny. I felt *his* mental command; it almost made me jump in and tear *him* apart, too. Second, I imagine *he* came back to life so quickly because the white tree is an especially powerful and swiftly acting one. Third, *he* is playing tricks on us, but not the kind you suggest."

Carmody, slowing his pace, puffed and panted. "I'm paying for my sins now. God help me, I'm going on a diet. I'll exercise, too, when this affair is over. I loathe my fat carcass. But what about when I'm seated hungry at a table piled high with the too-good things of life, created in the beginning to be enjoyed? What then?"

"I could tell you what then, but we've no time for talk like that. Stick to the point," Tu growled. His contempt for self-indulgers was famous.

"Very well. As I said, it was obviously a ritual of self-sacrifice. It was that knowledge which sent me scurrying off in an unsuccessful search for the bishop. I meant to tell him that Father was only half-lying when *he* said *he* derived *his* powers from God and that *he* worshipped God.

"*He* does. But the god is *himself!* In his vast egoism *he* resembles the old pagan deities of Earth, who were supposed to have slain themselves and then, having made the supreme sacrifice, resurrected themselves. Odin, for instance, who hung himself from a tree."

"But *he* wouldn't have heard of them. Why would *he* imitate them?"

"*He* doesn't have to have heard of our Earth myths. After all, there are certain religious rites and symbols that are universal, that sprang up spontaneously on a hundred different planets. Sacrifice to a god, communion by eating the god, sowing and reaping ceremonies, the concept of being a chosen people, like symbols of the circle and the cross. So Father may have brought the idea from *his* home world. Or *he* may have thought it up as the highest possible act *he* was capable of. Man must have a religion, even if it consists of worshipping himself.

"Also, don't forget that *his* ritual, like most, combined religion with practicality. *He*'s ten millenia old and has preserved *his* longevity by going from time to time into the jelly tree. *He* thought *he*'d be going with us, that it'd be some time before *he* could grow a tree on an alien world. The calcium deposit in your vascular system, the fatty deposits in your brain cells, the other degenerations that make you old, are left out of the process. You emerge fresh and young from the tree."

"The skulls?"

"The entire skeleton isn't necessary for the re-creation, though it's the custom to put it in. A sliver of bone is enough, for a single cell contains the genetic pattern. You see, I'd overlooked something. That was the problem of how certain animals may be conditioned into being killed by the carnivores. If their flesh is rebuilt around the bones according to the genetic record alone, then the animal should be without memory of its previous life. Hence, its nervous system would contain no conditioned reflexes. But it does. Therefore, the jelly must also reproduce the contents of the neural system. How? I surmise that at the very moment of dying the nearest jelly-deposit records the total wave output of the cells, including the complex of waves radiated by the 'knotted' molecules of the memory. Then it reproduces it.

"So, Father's skulls are left outside, and when *he* rises, *he* is greeted with their sight, a most refreshing vision to *him*. Remember, *he* kissed them during the sacrifice. *He* showed his love for *himself*. Life kissing death, knowing *he* had conquered death."

"Ugh!"

"Yes, and that is what will happen to the Galaxy

if Father leaves here. Anarchy, a bloody battle until only one person is left to each planet, stagnation, the end of sentient life as we know it, no goal . . . Look, there's the lake ahead!"

Carmody halted behind a tree. Andre was standing by the shore, his back turned to them. His head was bent forward as if in prayer or meditation. Or perhaps grief.

"Your Excellency," said the padre softly, stepping out from behind the tree.

Andre started. His hands, which must have been placed together on his chest, flew out to either side. But he did not turn. He sucked in a deep breath, bent his knees, and dived into the lake.

Carmody yelled, "No!" and launched himself in a long flat dive. Tu was not long behind him but stopped short of the edge. He crouched there while the little waves caused by the disappearance of the two spread, then subsided into little rings, moonlight haloed on a dark flat mirror. He removed his coat and shoes but still did not leap in. At that moment a head broke the surface and a loud whoosh sounded as the man took in a deep breath.

Tu called, "Carmody? Bishop?"

The other sank again. Tu jumped in, disappeared. A minute passed. Then three heads emerged simultaneously. Presently, the captain and the little priest stood gasping above the limp form of Andre.

"Fought me," said Carmody hoarsely, his chest rising and falling quickly. "Tried to push me off. So . . . put my thumbs behind his ears . . . where jaw meets . . . squeezed . . . went limp but don't know if he'd breathed water . . . or I'd made him unconscious . . . or both . . . no time to talk now . . ."

The priest turned the bishop over so he was face

downward, turned the head to one side, straddled the back on his knees. Palms placed outwards on the other's shoulders, he began the rhythmic pumping he hoped would push the water out and breath in.

"How could he do it?" said Tu. "How could he, born and raised in the faith, a consecrated and respected bishop, betray us? Who'd have thought it? Look what he did for the Church on Lazy Fair; he was a great man. And how could he, knowing all it meant, try to kill himself?"

"Shut your damn mouth," replied Carmody, harshly. "Were *you* exposed to *his* temptation? What do you know of his agonies? Quit judging him. Make yourself useful. Give me a count by your watch so I can adjust my pumpings. Here we go. One . . . two . . . three . . ."

Fifteen minutes later, the bishop was able to sit up and hold his head between his hands. Tu had walked off a little distance and stood there, back turned to them. Carmody knelt down and said, "Do you think you can walk now, Your Excellency? We ought to get out of this forest as quickly as possible. I feel danger in the air."

"There's more than just danger. There's damnation," said Andre feebly.

He rose, almost fell, was caught by the other's strong hand.

"Thank you. Let's go. Ah, old friend, why didn't you let me sink to the bottom and die where *he* would not have found my bones and no man would have known of my disgrace?"

"It's never too late, Your Excellency. The fact that you regretted your bargain and were driven by remorse . . ."

"Let's hurry back before it does become too late. Ah, I feel the spark of another life being born. You know how it is, John. It glows and grows and flares until it fills your whole body and you're about to burst with fire and light. This one is powerful. It must be in a nearby tree. Hold me. John. If I go into another seizure, drag me away, no matter how I fight.

"You have felt what I did, you seem to be strong enough to fight against it, but I have fought against something like it all my life and never revealed it to anyone, even denied it in my prayers—the worst thing I could do—until the too-long-punished body took over and expressed itself in my illness. Now I fear that . . . Hurry, hurry!"

Tu grabbed Andre's elbow and helped Carmody propel him onwards through the darkness, lit only by the priest's beam. Overhead was a solid roof of interlacing branches.

Something coughed. They stopped, frozen.

"Father?" whispered Tu.

"No. His representative, I fear."

Twenty yards away, barring their path, crouched a leopardess, spotted and tufted, five hundred pounds ready to spring. Its green eyes blinked, narrowing in the beam; its round ears were cocked forward. Abruptly, it rose and stalked slowly towards them. It moved with a comic mixture of feline grace and overstuffed waddle. At another time they might have chuckled at this creature, its fat sheathing its spring-steel muscles and its sagging swollen belly. Not now, for it could—and probably would—tear them to bits.

Abruptly, the tail, which had been moving gently back and forth, stiffened out. It roared once, then sprang at Father John, who had stepped out in front of Tu and Andre.

Father John yelled. His flashlight sailed through the air and into the brush. The big cat yowled and bounded off. There were two sounds: a large body crashing through the bushes and Father John cursing heartily, not with intended blasphemy but for the sake of an intense relief.

"What happened?" said Tu. "And what are you doing down on your knees?"

"I'm not praying. I'll save that for later. This perilous flashlight went out, and I can't find it. Get down here and help me and be useful. Get your hands dirty for once; we're not on your perilous vessel, you know."

"What happened?"

"Like a cornered rat," groaned Carmody, "I fought. Out of sheer desperation I struck with my fist and accidentally hit it on its nose. I couldn't have done better if I'd planned it. These beasts of prey are fat and lazy and cowardly after ten thousand years of easy living on conditioned victims. They have no real guts. Resistance scares them. This one would not have attacked if it hadn't been urged by Father, I'm sure. Isn't that so, Your Excellency?"

"Yes. *He* showed me how to control any animal on Abatos anywhere. I'm not advanced enough as yet to recognize the individual when she's out of sight and transmit mental commands, but I can do so at close range."

"Ah, I've found this doubly perilous flashlight."

Carmody turned the beam on and rose. "Then I was wrong in thinking my puny fist had driven off that monster? You instilled panic in it?"

"No. I cancelled out Father's wavelengths and left the cat on its own. Too late, of course—once it had begun an attack, its instinct would urge it on. We owe its flight to your courage."

"If my heart would stop hammering so hard, I'd believe more in my courage. Well, let's go. Does Your Excellency feel stronger?"

"I'll keep up with any pace you set. And don't

use the title. My action in defying the Question Council's decision constituted an automatic resignation. You know that."

"I know only what Tu has told me Father told him."

They walked on. Occasionally, Carmody flashed his light behind him. While doing this he became aware that the leopardess or one of its sisters was following them by some forty yards. "We are not alone," he said. Andre said nothing, and Tu, misunderstanding him, began to pray in a very low voice. Carmody did not elucidate but urged them to walk faster.

Suddenly, the shadow of the forest fell away before the brightness of the moon. There was still a crowd on the meadow, but it was away from the edge, gathered beneath the curve of the ship. Father was not in sight.

"Where is *he*?" called Father John. An echo answered from the meadow's other side, followed at once by the giant's appearance in the main port. Stooping, Father walked through it and down the steps to the ground, there to resume his motionless vigilance.

Andre muttered, "Give me strength."

Carmody spoke to the captain. "You must make a choice. Do what your faith and intelligence tell you is best. Or obey the regulations of Saxwell and the Commonwealth. Which is it to be?"

Tu was rigid and silent, cast into thought like bronze. Without waiting for a reply, Carmody started to walk towards the ship. Half-way across the meadow, he stopped and raised clenched fists and cried, "No use trying that panic trick on us, Father! Knowing what *you* are doing, and how, we may fight against it, for we are men!"

His words were lost to the people around the ship. They were yelling at each other and scrambling for a place on the steps so they could get inside. Father must have evoked a battery of waves from the surrounding trees, more powerful than anything used before. It struck like a tidal wave, carrying all before it. All except Carmody and Andre. Even Tu broke and ran for the *Gull*.

"John," moaned the bishop. "I'm sorry. But I can't stand it. Not the subsonics. No. The betrayal. The recognition of what I've been fighting against since manhood. It's not true that when you first see the face of your unknown enemy you have the battle half-won. I can't stand it. The need I have for this damnable communion . . . I'm sorry, believe me. But I must . . ."

He whirled and ran back into the forest. Carmody chased after him, shouting, but his legs were quickly out-distanced. Ahead of him, out of the darkness, came a coughing roar. A scream. Silence.

Unhesitatingly, the priest plunged on, his light stabbing before him. When he saw the cat crouching over the crumpled form, one grey-furred paw tearing at its victim's groin, he shouted again and charged. Snarling, the leopardess arched its back, seemed ready to rear on its hind legs and bat the man with its bloodied claws, then roared, turned, and bounded away.

It was too late. There'd be no bringing back the bishop this time. Not unless . . .

Carmody shuddered and lifted the sagging weight in his arms and staggered back across the meadow. He was met by Father.

"Give me the body," thundered the voice.

"No! You'll not put him in your tree. I'm taking him back to the ship. After we get home we'll give him a decent burial. And you might as well quit broadcasting your panic. I'm angry, not scared. And we're leaving in spite of you, and we're not taking you. So do your damnedest!"

Father's voice became softer. It sounded sad and puzzled.

"You do not understand, man. I went aboard your vessel and into the bishop's cabin and tried to sit down in a chair that was too small for me. I had to sit on the cold hard floor, and while I waited I thought of going out into vast and empty space again and to all the many strange and uncomfortable and sickeningly undeveloped worlds. It seems to me that the walls were getting too close and were collapsing in upon me. They would crush me. Suddenly, I knew I could not endure their nearness for any time at all, and that, though our trip would be short, I'd soon be in other too-small rooms. And there would be many of the pygmies swarming about me, crushing each other and possibly me in an effort to gape at me, to touch me. There would be millions of them, each trying to get his dirty little hairy paws on me. And I thought of the planets crawling with unclean females ready to drop their litters at a moment's notice and all the attendant uncleanliness. And the males mad with lust to get them with child. And the ugly cities stinking with refuse. And the deserts that scab those neglected worlds, the disorder, the chaos, the uncertainty. I had to step out for a moment to breathe again the clean and certain air of Abatos. It was then that the bishop appeared."

"You were terrified by the thought of change. I would pity you, except for what you have done to him," said Carmody, nodding down at the form in his arms.

"I do not want your pity. After all, I am Father. You are a man who will crumble into dust forever. But do not blame me. He is dead because of what he was, not because of me. Ask his real father why he did not give him love along with his blows and why he shamed him without justifying why he should be shamed and why he taught him to forgive others but not himself.

"Enough of this. Give me him. I liked him, could almost stand his touch. I will raise him to be my companion. Even I want someone to talk to who can understand me."

"Out of the way," demanded Carmody. "Andre made his choice. He trusted me to take care of him, I know. I loved the man, though I did not always approve of what he did or was. He was a great man, even with his weakness. None of us can say anything against him. Out of the way, before I commit the violence which you say you so dread but which does not keep you from sending wild beasts to bring about your will. Out of the way!"

"You do not understand," murmured the giant, one hand pulling hard upon his beard. The black, silver-splintered eyes stared hard, but he did not lift his hand against Carmody. Within a minute, the priest had carried his burden into the *Gull*. The port shut softly, but decisively, behind him.

Some time later, Captain Tu, having disposed of his major duties in translating the ship, entered the bishop's cabin. Carmody was there, kneeling by the side of the bed that held the corpse.

"I was late because I had to take Mrs. Recka's bottle away from her and lock her up for a while," he explained. He paused, then, "Please don't think I'm hateful. But right is right. The bishop killed himself and doesn't deserve burial in consecrated ground."

"How do you know?" replied Carmody, his head still bent, his lips scarcely moving.

"No disrespect to the dead, but the bishop had power to control the beasts, so he must have ordered the cat to kill him. It was suicide."

"You forget that the panic waves which Father caused in order to get you and me quickly into the ship also affected any animals in the area. The leopardess may have killed the bishop just because he got in the way of her flight. How are we to know any different?

"Also, Tu, don't forget this. The bishop may be a martyr. He knew that the one thing that would force Father to stay on Abatos would be for himself to die. Father would not be able to endure the idea of leaving *his* planet fatherless. Andre was the only one among us that could take over the position Father had vacated. He was ignorant at that time, of course, that Father had changed *his* mind because of *his* sudden claustrophobia.

"All the bishop could know was that his death would chain Father to Abatos and free us. And if he deliberately slew himself by means of the leopardess, does that make him any less a martyr? Women have chosen death rather than dishonour and been canonized.

"We shall never know the bishop's true motive. We'll leave knowledge of that to Another.

"As for the owner of Abatos, my feeling against *him* was right. Nothing *he* said was true, and *he* was as much a coward as any of *his* fat and lazy beasts. *He* was no god. *He* was the Father . . . of Lies."

ATTITUDES

Roger Tandem crouched behind his pinochle hand as if he were hiding behind a battery of shields. His eyes ran like weasels over the faces of the other players, seated around a table in the lounge of the interstellar liner, *Lady Luck*.

"Father John," he said, "I've got you all figured out. You'll be nice to me, you'll crack jokes, and you'll play pinochle with me, though not for money, of course. You'll even have a beer with me. And, after I begin thinking you're a pretty good guy, you'll lead me gradually to this and that topic. You'll approach them at an angle, slide away when I get annoyed or alarmed, but always circle back. And then, all of a sudden, when I'm not watching, you jerk the lid off hell's flames and invite me to take a look. And you think I'll be so scared I'll jump right back under the wing of Mother Church."

Father John raised his light blue eyes long enough from his cards to say, mildly, "You're right about the last half of your last sentence. As to the rest, who knows?"

"You're smart, Father, with this religious angle. But you'll get no place with me. Know why? It's because you haven't the right attitude."

The eyebrows of the other five players rose as

high as they could get. The captain of the *Lady
Luck*, Rowds, coughed until he was red in the face
and then, sputtering and blowing into a handkerchief, said, "Hang it all, Tandem, what—ah—do
you mean by saying that—ah—*he* hasn't got the
right attitude?"

Tandem smiled as one who is very sure of
himself and replied, "I know you're thinking I've a
lot of guts to say that. Here's Roger Tandem, a
professional gambler and a collector—and
seller—of interstellar *objets d'art*, reproaching a
padre. But I've got more to add to that. I not only
do not think Father John has the right attitude, I
don't think any of you gentlemen have."

Nobody replied. Tandem's lips curved to ap-
proximate a sneer, but his fellow-players could
not see them because he held his cards in front of
his mouth.

"You're all more or less pious," he said. "And
why? Because you're afraid to take a chance,
that's why. You say to yourself that you're not
sure there's life beyond this one, but there just
might be. So you decide it's playing safe if you
hitch a ride aboard one or another religion. None
of you gentlemen belong to the same one, but you
all have this in common. You think you have
nothing to lose if you profess to believe in this or
that god. On the other hand, if you deny one, you
might lose out altogether. So, why not profess?
It's safer."

He laid his cards down and lit up a cigarette and
quickly blew smoke out so it formed a veil before
his face.

"I'm not afraid to take a chance. I'm betting big
stakes. My so-called eternal soul against the belief
that there is nothing beyond this life. Why should I
always *not* do what I want to and thus make myself miserable and hypocritical, when I can enjoy
myself thoroughly?"

"That," said Father John Carmody, "is where you may be making a mistake. My opinion is that *you* have the wrong attitude. All of us are betting in a game where there is only one way in which we *can* win. That is by faith. But your method of placing your stakes is not, from my viewpoint, the sensible one. Even if you should be proved correct, you would not know it. How would you collect your wager?"

"I collect it while I live, Father," said Tandem. "That's enough for me. When I'm dead, I don't worry about anyone welshing on me. And I might point out, Father, that you had better have more luck with your faith than you do with your cards. You're not a very good player, you know."

The priest smiled. His round pudgy face was not at all handsome, but, when he was amused, he looked pleasant and likeable. You got the impression he had a tuning fork inside him, and it was shaking him with a mirth he invited you to share.

Tandem liked it except when the laughter seemed to be at his expense. Then his mouth curved into the expression it so often took when his cards hid it.

At that moment a loud voice came over the intercom, and a yellow light began flashing above the entrance to the lounge room. Captain Rowds rose and said, "Ah, pardon me, gentlemen. The—ah—pilot-room wants me. We're about to come out of Translation. Don't forget that we'll be—ah—in free fall as soon as the red light comes on."

The hand was not finished. The cards were put away in a box whose magnetized side would cling to an iron panel set in the table. The players leaned back to wait until the *Lady Luck* came out of Translation and went into free fall for a period of ten minutes while the automatic computer took its bearings.

If they had emerged from no-space at the desired point, they would then continue to their destination by normal space-drive.

Tandem looked around the lounge and sighed. Pickings had been slim during this trip. Most of his time had been spent playing for fun with Father John, Captain Rowds, the Universal Light missionary, and the two sociology professors. It was too bad his companions had no money and thought of themselves as gentlemen. Had they played for keeps, they would have been offended if anyone had insisted on suspending a PK or ESP indicator above the cardtable. And Tandem would, then, have had no second thoughts about using either of those talents. He reasoned that they had been given to him for a purpose. The question of from whom they had come did not shadow his mind.

He'd made some money during the hop from B Velorum to Y Scorpii when he had struck up an acquaintance with a rich young dice-enthusiast, the type who was insulted if you set an alarm on the floor. He was a *real* gambler. That is, he understood that one PKer could detect when another was using energies supposedly forbidden during a game. But he also understood that, nowadays, one of the most exciting risks was that of running up against somebody who might be as good as you. Or better.

Whatever happened, when two of the "talented" were in a game with a group of non-PKers, neither would divulge that the other was a cheater. Then it became a duel between the two who thought of themselves as the "aristocrats" of gambling. The plebs were left outside in the cold, and possessed neither wisdom nor money at the game's end.

Tandem had had the edge with the rich young man. But, just when he had jockeyed him to the verge of making some big bets, the *Lady Luck* [a

misnamed vessel if ever there was one!] had Translated outside their destination, the game had
ended, and the sucker had left shortly after.

Now, he was not only getting close to broke, he
was, far worse, bored. Even the long argument
with Father John—if you could call anything so
mild such—no longer titillated him. And now,
perhaps, it was that failure to be excited and the
vague feeling that the padre had gotten the better
of him that made him do what he did. For, as the
red light began flashing and the intercom warned
the passengers to watch themselves, Tandem
unbuckled the belt that held him to the chair. He
pushed himself upwards with a slight tap of his
foot. As he floated towards the ceiling, he put his
hands to his lips in an attitude of prayer and
adopted an expression that was a marvelous blend
of silliness and saintliness.

"Hey, Father John!" he called. "Look! Joseph of
Cupertino!"

There were embarrassed looks and a few
nervous laughs from the loungers. Even the
apostle of the Universal Light, though the padre's
competitor, frowned at what he thought was very
bad taste and, in a way, a slight upon his own
beliefs.

"Wrong attitude," he muttered, "definitely the
wrong attitude."

Father John blinked once before he saw that
Tandem was parodying the difficulties that a
famous medival saint had had with involuntary
levitations. Far from being offended, however, he
calmly took a notebook from his pocket and began
writing in it. No matter what the event, he tried to
profit from it. Even the devil must be thanked for
giving examples. Tandem's antics had inspired
him with an idea for an article. If he finished it in
time and got it off on a mail-ship, he might have it
published in the next issue of his order's

periodical.

It would be titled *The Free Fall of Man: Down or Up?*

Tandem had been briefly tempted to get off at the next stop, Wildenwooly. It was a virgin planet that offered much work to its settlers and very few avenues of amusement. Gambling was one. But the trouble with Wildenwooly was that it also did not have many men who had any really big money, and that all were pathologically quick to take offense. Tandem's luck might make them suspicious and, if an indicator were available, it might be used. Nor would it help him much to damp out his powers. The result would be just as extraordinary a streak of bad luck.

Everybody had some PK. The indicators were set too high to register the average energy. Tandem and men like him could not consistently key their output to the normal man's unless they kept a rigid control. And almost always they would get excited during a game, or succumb to temptation, and use an abnormal amount. The result would be their exposure. So, to avoid that, they had to suppress their talent completely. This ended in just as much suspicion. And, while the Woolies could not *prove* that he had been cheating, they might follow their habit of taking the law into their own hands.

As Tandem didn't relish beatings or being ridden out of town on a rail—an unlovely revival of an old American custom—he decided he would stick to the *Lady Luck* until she arrived at Po Chu-I. That was a planet full of Celestials whose pockets bulged with Federation credits and whose eyes were bright with the gleam of their ancient passion for Dame Fortune.

Before the liner got to Po Chu-I, it stopped off at

Weizmann and picked up another rich young man.
Tandem rubbed his hands and took the sucker for
all he could. This was the beauty of the
technological age. No matter what the scientific
advances, you could find the same old type of
human being begging to be fleeced. The rich young
man and he located several others who would play
with them until the stakes got too high. Tandem's
former partners, the captain, the professors, and
the two reverends were ignored while he piled up
the chips. Unfortunately, just after they took off
from Po Chu-I, the rich young man became sullen,
argued with him about something unconnected
with the gambling, and gave him a black eye.

Tandem did not strike back. He told the rich
young man that he would file suit against him in
an Earth court for having violated his free will. He
had not given anybody permission to strike him.
Moreover, he would submit willingly to an
injection of Telol. Questioning under the influence
of that drug would reveal that he had not been
cheating.

For some reason he did not understand, nobody
except Father John would speak to Tandem the
rest of the trip. And Tandem did not care to talk to
the padre. He swore he'd get off at the next stop
regardless of what type of world it was.

The *Lady Luck* balked him by setting down upon
a planet that was terra incognita as far as
Earthmen were concerned. No human settlements
had been made there at all. The only reason the
liner landed was the need of water to refill its fuel
tanks.

Captain Rowds announced to the crew and
passengers that they might step out upon the soil
of Kubeia and stretch their legs. But they were not
to venture beyond the other side of the lake.

"Ah—ladies and gentlemen—ah—it so happens
that the Federation Sociological Agent

has—ah—made an agreement with the aborigines whereby we may use this area. But we are not to enter into any traffic with the—ah—Kubeians themselves. These people have many peculiar institutions which we—ah—Terrans might offend through—if you will pardon that expression—ignorance. And some of their customs are—ah—if I may so express it, rather—ah—beastly. A word to the wise is—ah—sufficient."

Tandem found out that the ship would take at least four hours for refilling. Therefore, he reasoned, if he cared to do a little exploring, he would have more than enough time. He was determined to get at least a slight view of Kubeia. Their situation inside a little forest-covered valley forbade that. If he were to climb a hill and then a tree, he could see the city of the natives, whose white buildings he had glimpsed from the porthole as the ship sank towards this alien soil. He had no particular interest, really, except that the captain had forbidden it. That, to Tandem, was equal to a command. Even as a child, he had always taken a delicious delight in disobeying his father. And, as an adult, he would not bow to authority.

Head bent slightly downwards, his hand stroking his chin and mouth, he sauntered around the other side of the gigantic liner. There was no one there to order him back. He stepped up his pace. And, at the same time, he heard a voice.

"Wait for me! I'll go with you a way!"

He turned. It was Father John.

Tandem tensed. The priest was smiling, his light blue eyes beaming. And that was the trouble. Tandem did not trust this man because he was altogether too inconsistent. You couldn't predict his behavior. One minute he was smooth as a banana peel; the next, rough as a three-day beard.

The gambler dropped his hand to reveal his half-smile, half-sneer.

"If I ask you to go with me a mile, Father, you must, according to your belief, go with me at least two miles."

"Gladly, son, except that the captain has forbidden it. And, I presume, with good cause."

"Look, Father, what possible harm could come from just sneaking a glance outside? The natives think this area is tabu. They won't bother us. So, why not take a little walk?"

"There is no good reason to disregard the captain. He has complete temporal jurisdiction over the ship, which is his little world. He knows his business; I respect his orders."

"O.K., Father, wrap yourself up in your little robe of submission. You may be safe in it, but you'll never see or enjoy anything outside it. As for me, I'm going to take a chance. Not that it'll be much of one."

"I hope you're right."

"Look, Father, get that woeful expression off your face. I'm just going up the hill a little ways and climb a tree. Then I'm coming right back down. Anything wrong with that?"

"You know whether or not there is."

"Sure, I do," said Tandem, speaking through his fingers, now held over his mouth. "It all depends on your attitude, Father. Walk boldly, be unafraid, don't hide from anything or anybody, and you'll get out of life just what you put in it."

"I'll agree with you that you get out of life just what you put in it. But as to the former part of your statement, I disagree. You're not walking boldly. You're afraid. You're hiding."

Tandem had turned to stride away, but he halted and spun back.

"What do you mean?"

"I mean that you feel you must hide from someone or something all the time. Otherwise, why do you always cover your lips with your hand, or, if not with that, with a shield of playing cards? And when you are forced to expose your face, then you twist into a rictus of contempt for the world. Why?"

"Now it's psychiatry!" snarled Tandem. "You stay here, Father, stuck in your little valley. I'm going to see what the rest of Kubeia has to offer."

"Don't forget. We leave in four hours."

"I have a watch," said Tandem, and he laughed and added, "I'll let it be my conscience."

"Watches run down."

"So do consciences, Father."

Still laughing, Tandem walked off. Halfway up the hill, he paused to peer back between the trees. Father John was standing there, watching, a lone and little black figure. But he must have turned a trifle at just the right angle, for the sun flashed on the crescent of white collar and struck Tandem in the eyes. He blinked and cursed and lit a cigarette and felt much better as the blue curtain drifted up past his face. There was nothing like a good smoke to relax a man.

It might have been said of Tandem that he had been looking all his life for black sheep to fleece. Nor did he have any trouble finding them now.

From his spy-post near the top of a great tree, he could look down into the next valley. And there he could see the black sheep. Even on Kubeia.

There was no mistaking the purpose of the crowd gathered into two concentric rings at the bottom of the hill. There was the smaller circle of men inside, all on their knees and regarding intently some object in their center. And behind them stood a greater number of people, also watching intently the thing that resembled, as near as he could tell, a weathercock. Obviously, it wasn't that. He could tell from the attitudes of those around it what its purpose was. And his heart leaped. There was no mistake. He was able to smell a crap game a mile away. This might be a slightly different form than the Terran type, but its essence was the same.

Hastily, he climbed down the tree and began threading through the trunks that covered this hill. A glance at his wrist watch showed him he had three and a half hours left. Moreover, it was inconceivable that Captain Rowds would set off without his passenger. Tandem had to watch this Kubeian game of chance. He wouldn't enter it, of course, because he didn't know the rules and had no local currency with which to buy his way in. He'd just observe a while and then leave.

His heart beat fast; his palms grew moist. This was what he lived for, this tension and uncertainty and excitement. Take a chance. Win or lose. Come on, cubes, roll Daddy a natural!

He grinned to himself. What was he thinking of? He couldn't possibly get into the fun. And there was the possibility that the Kubeians would be so upset by the appearance of an Earthman that the game would break up. He doubted that, though. Gamblers were notoriously blase. Nothing but cataclysm or the police could tear them away as long as there was money yet to win.

Before he revealed himself, he examined the players. Humanoid, they had brown skins, round heads covered with short coarse auburn hairs, triangular faces innocent of whiskers except for six semi-cartilaginous bristles on their long upper lips, black noses like boxing gloves, black leathery lips, sharp meat-eater's teeth, and well developed chins. A ruff of auburn hairs grew like a boa around their necks.

All were dressed in long black coats and white knee-length breeches. Only one wore a hat. This native seemed to be a ringmaster of some sort, or, as Tandem came to think of him, the Croupier. He was taller and thinner than the others and wore a miter with a big green eyeshade. He stood on one spot, arbitrated disputes about bets, and gave the signal for each play to start. It was the Croupier, Tandem realized, who would govern the temper of the crowd towards the newcomer.

He breathed deeply, adopted the familiar rictus, and stepped out from behind the bush.

He had been right about the attitudes of the Kubeians toward strangers. Those on the outer fringe looked up, widened their somewhat slanting eyes, and pricked up their foxlike ears. But, after glances that assured them he was harmless, they returned to the game. Either they were following a cultural pattern of feigning indifference, or they actually were as adaptable as they seemed to be. Whatever their reasons, he decided to profit by them.

He gently tried to work his way through the throng of spectators and found them quite willing to step aside. Before long he was in the front row. He looked squarely at the Croupier, who gave him an enigmatic but searching glance, and then raised both hands above his head. Two of his four fingers on each hand were crossed. The crowd gave a single barking cry and imitated his gesture. Then the Croupier dropped his hands; the game went on as if the Terran had always been there. Tandem, after a moment's shrewd study, was convinced that he had found his element and that this was nothing other than a glorified version of Spin-the-Milk-Bottle.

The center of attention was a six-foot-long statue of a Kubeian. Its two arms were extended at right angles on either side, and its legs were held straight out on a line with its body. It was face downward and whirled freely upon its navel, which was stuck on a rod whose other end was cemented firmly into a large block of marble.

The figure's head was painted white. Its legs were black. One arm was red; the other, green. The body was a steel gray.

Tandem's heart accelerated. The statue, he was sure, was platinum.

He watched. A player took hold of one of the arms and crooned a liturgy to it in his exotic tongue, a chant whose tones matched exactly those used by a pleading Terran before he casts his dice. Then, after a signal from the Croupier, he gave the arm a vigorous shove. The figure spun around and around, the sun glancing off it in red and green and black and white and silver flashes. When it began to slow down, the players crouched in breathless anticipation or else held out their arms to it and pleaded invocations that were Galaxy-wide, no matter what the language.

Meanwhile, both the players and the spectators were making side bets. Each had one or more smaller duplicates of the central statue. As it whirled around, they gesticulated at each other, chattered, then tossed their figures up in the air so they revolved around and around. Tandem was sure these statuettes were of platinum, also.

The spinning figure stopped. Its green arm pointed at one of the players. A cry went up from the crowd. Many stepped forward and piled their figurines before the man. He gave the Whirligig—as Tandem now called it—another shove. Again, it spun around and around.

The Earthman had now analyzed the game. You took one of your little whirligigs and tossed it in the air. If one of its limbs or its head sunk into the soft earth, and it happened to be the same color as the big Whirligig's extension when it pointed to you, you collected the statuettes that had landed upon extensions of a different color.

If the Whirligig singled you out, but your statuette had sunk an indicator of another color into the earth, you neither lost nor won but got another try. Otherwise, the person next in line tried his luck.

Tandem rubbed his mental hands. He showed his watch to a neighbor and indicated he'd like to trade it for a whirligig. The naive native, after getting the high sign from the Croupier, readily accepted and seemed quite pleased that he was several thousand credits the loser.

Tandem made several side bets and won. Armed with the whirligigs, he boldly pushed into the inner ring. Once there he coolly exerted his PK to slow the big Whirligig down and stop it at just the right person and on just the right color. He was clever enough not to have it indicate him over a few times; most of his rapidly building fortune was made on side bets. Sometimes, he lost on purpose; sometimes, by chance. He was sure that many of the Kubeians had an unconscious PK that was bound to work for them if enough happened to concentrate on the same color. He could detect little slops of emanations here and there but could not localize them. They were lost in the general shuffle.

It did not matter. The natives would not have his trained talents.

He forgot about that and watched the temper of the crowd. He'd been alone among aliens and had seen them turn ugly when he began to win too steadily. He was ready to start losing so they would cool off, or, if that didn't work, to run. How he expected to make any speed with the weight of his winnings dragging him down, he didn't stop to think. But he was sure that, somehow, he'd come out ahead.

Nothing that he waited for came to pass. The natives lost none of their vaguely vulpine grins,

and their rusty-red eyes seemed sincerely friendly.
When he won, he was slapped on the back. Some
even helped him pile up his whirligigs. He kept an
eye on them to make sure they didn't conceal any
under their long fuzzy black coats, so much like a
Terran preacher's. But, nobody tried to steal.

The afternoon whirled by dizzily in flashing
greens and reds and whites and silvers and dull
blacks. Not too obviously, the whirligigs at his feet
began to build to a small mountain.

Outwardly cool, he was inwardly intoxicated.
He was not so far gone that he did not glance
occasionally at the watch strapped around the
hairy wrist of the Kubeian he had traded it to.
Always, he saw that he had plenty of time left to
make another killing.

Busy as he was, he noticed also that the crowd
of spectators was increasing. This game was like
any game of chance anywhere. Let somebody get
hot and, through some psychological grapevine
that could not be explained, everybody in the
neighborhood heard of it. Natives by the dozens
were loping through narrow passes into the little
valley, pushing the watchers closer to the players,
chattering loudly, whistling, applauding with
strange barking cries, and building up a mighty
stench under the hot sun with the accumulation of
sweaty, hairy bodies. Slanting rusty-red eyes
gleamed; sharp pointed ears waggled; the auburn
hairs of the neckruffs stood up; long red tongues
with green bulb-tips licked the thin black-leather
lips; everywhere, hands lifted to the skies in a
peculiar gesture, each with two of its four fingers
crossed.

Tandem did not mind. He had heard—and
smelled—crowds like this before. When he was
winning, he reveled in it.

Let the Whirligig spin! Let the statuettes soar!
And let the wealth pile up at his feet! This was

living. This was what even drink and women could not do for him!

There came a time when only four natives were left with any whirligigs before them. It was Tandem's turn to spin. He threw his figurine high up, saw it land with its black legs stuck into the soft earth, and stepped forward to give the big figure a whirl. He shot a side-glance at the Croupier and saw tears brightening the rusty eyes.

Tandem was surprised, but he did not try to guess what caused this strange emotion. All he wanted to do was to play, and he had the go-ahead from the native.

But as he laid his hands upon the hard green arm, he heard a cry that shot above the roar of the mob, stilled it, and seized him so he could make no move.

It was Father John's voice, and he was shouting, 'Stop, Tandem! For the love of God, *stop*!"

"What the hell are you doing here?" snarled Tandem. "Are you trying to queer the deal?"

"I've come the second mile, son," said Father John. "And a good thing for you, too. One more second, and you would have been lost."

Streams of sweat run down his heavy jowls into his collar, now turning gray with dirt and perspiration. A branch must have raked a three-fingered red furrow across his cheek.

His blue eyes vibrated to the tuning fork deep-buried within his rotund body, but the note was not that of mirth.

"Step back, Carmody," said Tandem. "This is the last spin. Then I'm coming back. Rich!"

"No, you won't. Listen, Tandem, we haven't much time . . . !"

"Get out of the way! These people might want to take advantage of this and stop the game!"

Father John threw a despairing look towards the sky. At the same time the Croupier left the spot on which he had stood during the game, and advanced with his hand held out towards the padre. Hope replaced despair on Father John's face. Eagerly, he began making a series of gestures directed at the Croupier.

Tandem, though exasperated, could do little else than watch and hope that the meddling officious priest would be sent packing. It irritated him almost to weeping to have complete victory so close and now see it destroyed by this long-nosed puritan.

Father John paid no attention to Tandem. Having snared the Croupier's wet and rusty-red eyes, he then pointed to himself and to Tandem and indicated a circle around them. The Croupier did not change expression. Undaunted at this, Father John then pointed his finger at the natives and described a circle around them. He repeated the maneuvers twice. Abruptly, the slanting eyes widened; the rusty-red gleamed. He rotated his head swiftly, an action which seemed to be his equivalent of nodding yes. Apparently he understood that the padre was indicating that the two humans were in a different class from the Kubeians.

Father John then stabbed his index finger at the Whirligig and followed that by pointing at the Croupier. Again the circle was drawn, this time clearly circumscribing the native and the face-downward statue. Then another circle around the two Earthmen. After which, Father John held up the crucifix hung from his neck so that all could clearly see it.

A single-throated cry rose from the mob. Somehow it held tones of disappointment, not surprise. They pressed forward, but at a bark from the Croupier, they fell back. He himself came forward and eagerly inspected the symbol. When he was done, he looked at Father John for further signs. Tears streamed from his eyes.

"What're you doing, Carmody?" said Tandem harshly. "Is it going to hurt you if I win something valuable?"

"Quiet, man, I've almost got it through their heads. We may be able to call off the game yet. I don't know, though, you're so deep in it now."

"When I get back to Earth or the nearest big port, I'll sue you for interfering with my free will!"

He knew that was an idle threat, for the law would not apply to this case. But it made him feel better to express it.

Father John had not heard him, anyway. He was now struck into the attitude of a crucifixion, arms straight out, legs together, and an agonized expression on his face. As soon as he saw the Croupier rotate his head in comprehension, the padre pointed again at Tandem. The Croupier looked startled; his black boxing-glove nose twitched with some unknown emotion. He shrugged his shoulders in a gesture that could only be interpreted in a Gallic fashion, and he lifted his hands up, palms turned upwards.

Father John smiled; his whole body seemed to hum with the invisible tuning fork inside him. This time, it was a note of relaxation.

"You were lucky, my boy," he said to Tandem, "that, shortly after you left, I remembered an article I had read in the *Interstellar Journal of Comparative Religions*. This one was written by an anthropologist who had spent some time here on Kubeia, and . . ."

The Croupier interrupted with some vigorous signs. Evidently Father John had mistaken his meaning.

The priest's lips and jowls sagged, and he

groaned. "This fellow has heard of free will, too, Tandem. He insists that you make up your own mind as to whether you care to . . ."

Tandem did not wait to hear the rest but gave a glad shout.

"Gentlemen, on with the game!"

He scarcely heard the padre's cry of protest as he seized the Whirligig's green arm and gave it a shove that sent it around and around upon its navel. Nor could he have heard any more from Father John, so rapt was he in waiting for the moment when it would slow down to the point where he could begin to exert the tiny shoves or pushes that would bring the black legs pointing straight at him.

Around and around it went, and while it spun, the statuettes of the side-betters flashed in the sun. Fortunes were made or lost among the natives. Tandem stood motionless in a half-crouch, smug in the knowledge that he was not going to lose. The four who faced him did not, individually or collectively, have what he had on the ball. See! Here the Whirligig came, slow, slow, coming around for one more turn. The green arm swept by, then the legs passed him. A little push, a little push would bring them back in their circle, then a small pull, a small pull to keep their speed, and finally, a fraction of a shove to halt them entirely.

This is the way they go. Here they come, long and black with the stylized feet stuck out in the same plane as the legs. Here they come, whoa, whoa, gently, gently . . . aah!

Hah!

The crowd, which had been holding its breath, released it in a mighty burst, a howl of surprise and disappointment.

And Tandem was still frozen in his crouch, his mind not believing what his eyes saw, and the hairs on the back of his neck prickling as he detected the sudden and irresistible power that had leapt out and swung the legs enough to miss him and make the green arm point at one of his opponents.

It was Father John who shook him and said, "Man, come on. You're wiped out."

Numbly, Tandem watched the weeping Croupier signal to natives who swarmed over his pile of figurines and crated them across the circle to the winner. Now, though he had not realized it, the rules had changed. It was winner take all.

Before they could go, the Croupier stepped up to the padre and handed him one of the statuettes. Father John hesitated, then lifted the chain from around his neck and handed the crucifix to him.

"What's that for?"

"Professional courtesy," said the padre as he steered Tandem by the elbow through the mob of wildly howling and leaping Kubeians. "He's a good man. Not the least jealous."

Tandem did not try to decipher that. His rage, sizzling beneath the crust of numbness, broke loose.

"Damn it, those natives were hiding the power of their PK! But, even so, they'd not have been able to catch me off balance if you hadn't stopped the game when you did and allowed them to gang up on me! It was only pure chance that they happened to be working together! If you hadn't been such a puritanical dog-in-the-manger, I'd have won for sure! I'd be rich! Rich!"

"I take full responsibility. Meanwhile, allow me to ex—Oops, watch it!"

Tandem stumbled and would have fallen flat on his face if Father John had not caught him. Tandem recovered and was angrier than before. He wanted to owe the padre absolutely nothing.

Silent, they made their slow way through the

heavy vegetation until they came to a break. Here, at Father John's gentle insistence of hand upon his elbow, Tandem turned. He was looking through an avenue in the trees at a full view of the valley.

"You see, Roger Tandem, I had read this article in the *Journal*. It was titled 'Attitudes,' and a good thing for you, for our previous talk about wrong attitudes brought it back to my mind. I decided then and there, to—if you will pardon the seeming egotism of the statement—to go the second mile. Or a third, if need be.

"You see, Roger, when you saw these people, you interpreted the scene in terms of the signs and symbols you are used to. You saw these natives around a device that seemed clearly to be for gambling. You saw further evidences: people on their knees, feverish betting, intent concentration upon the device, and you heard chanting, supplication to Lady Luck, grunts, exclamations, screams of triumph, moans of defeat. You saw a master in charge of ceremonies, the head gambler, the house master.

"What you did not perceive were certain similarities between the postures and sounds adopted during a gambling contest and those that mark the gatherings of certain types of frenetic religious sects in whatever area of the universe you happen to be. They are much the same. Watch the players in a hot crap game and then observe the antics of the less inhibited devout at certain primitive revival meetings. Is there so much difference?"

"What do you mean?"

Father John pointed through the break.

"You almost became a convert."

The winner was standing proudly by the great pile of statuettes at his feet. He seemed to be exulting inwardly in his victory, for he stood straight and silent, his hands by his sides. But not for long. A number of the burly players seized him from behind. His arms were straightened out and tied to a beam of wood. Another beam, at right angles to the first, was applied to his back. His legs, waist, and head were strapped to it. Crucifix-wise, he was picked up and carried forward.

At the same time, the Whirligig was taken off the post.

Even then, Tandem did not see what his fate might have been until the native was poised face down over the post and its sharp point inserted into the navel. Then a worshiper seized the extended arm and pushed.

If the living Whirligig gave any cry of pain, he could not have been heard above the howl of the assembled faithful. Until the tip of the post thrust into the wood beam on his back, he spun, and the mob chanted.

Father John prayed half-aloud.

"If I have interfered, I have done so through love for this man and because I must choose according to the dictates of my heart. I knew that one of them must die, Father, and I did not think that the man was ready. Perhaps the man of this world was not ready, either, but I had no way of knowing that. He was playing with full knowledge of what he must do if he won, and this man Tandem was not. And Tandem is a man like unto myself, Father, and I must presume that, unless I have knowledge of signs to the contrary, I must do my best to save him so that, some day, he may do his best to save himself.

"But if I have erred, I have done so through ignorance and through love."

When Father John was finished, he led Tandem, who was pale and trembling, up the hill.

"The house always wins," said Father John, who was himself a little pale. "That man that you thought was the Croupier was the head priest. The tears you first saw in his eyes were those of joy at making a convert and those you saw later were those of disappointment at losing one. He wanted you to win in this millennia-old ritual-game. If you had, you could have been the first Earthman to be the living representative of their deity, who was sacrificed in that peculiarly painful fashion. And your winnings would have been buried with you, an offering to the god whose living image you became.

"But, as I said, the house never loses. Later, the head priest would have dug them up and added them to his church's treasury."

"Do you mean that all those signals you were making at the Crou—the priest—were to convince him that I . . . ?"

"Belonged to the God of the Upright Cross, yes. Not the God of the Horizontal Cross. And I almost had him convinced until he must have thought of free will, too, and gave you the chance of joining his sect. I, as you have commented, am not so backward about interfering."

Tandem stopped to light a cigarette. His hand shook, but after a few puffs, with the smoke drifting by in blue veils, he felt better.

Squaring his shoulders and lifting his chin, he said, "Look, Father John, if you think that this is going to scare me so I'll jump in under the shadow of Mother Church's wings, you're wrong. So I made a mistake? It was only a half-error, you'll have to admit, for they *were* gambling. And anybody could have been fooled. I didn't need your help, anyway."

"Really?"

"Well, I suppose it was a good thing that you came along. . . . No, it wasn't. I lost; I couldn't have won with those four ganging up on me. So what did I have to lose? I had a good time, and I'm out nothing."

"You lost your watch."

Father John did not seem to have recovered yet from the shadow that had fallen over him since he had led Tandem away from the valley. The tuning fork inside him hummed deep and black.

"Look, Father," said Tandem, "let's drop all those morals and symbols, huh? No comparisons between my watch and my conscience, huh? You can stretch these things all out of proportion, you know."

He walked fast around the great curve of the ship so he could leave the priest behind. But as he did so, he stopped. A thought that had been roosting in the shadows suddenly hopped into light. He turned and walked back.

"Say, Father, what about those four who were left? I'd have sworn they didn't have enough . . ."

He stopped. Father John was about 25 yards away, his back turned to him. His shoulders were thrown back a little more than they had been, and there was something in the set of his whole body that showed that the humming fork was beginning to vibrate to a lighter note.

Tandem perceived that only half-consciously. It was what Father John was doing that seized him and demanded all of his attention.

The priest was whirling the statuette up into the air and watching it land upon its black legs. Four times, he repeated. Always, the legs dug into the dirt.

Even from that distance, Tandem could feel the power.

THE END

More Bestselling Science Fiction from Pinnacle/Tor